OATHBREAKER
A PRINCE
AMONG KILLERS

ALSO BY S R VAUGHT AND J B REDMOND

Oathbreaker: Assassin's Apprentice

OATHBREAKER
A PRINCE AMONG KILLERS

A continuation of Part I: *Assassin's Apprentice*

S R VAUGHT and J B REDMOND

BLOOMSBURY

NEW YORK BERLIN LONDON

For Victoria and Erin,
who believed in us

Published by Bloomsbury U.S.A. Children's Books
175 Fifth Avenue, New York, New York 10010

Library of Congress Cataloging-in-Publication Data
Vaught, Susan.
A prince among killers / by S.R. Vaught and J.B. Redmond.—1st U.S. ed.
p.   cm.   — (Oathbreaker ; pt. 2)
Summary: Assassin's guild apprentice Aron, his master, Stormbreaker, his teacher,
Dari, and his mysterious acquaintance, Nic, join their formidable talents of
mind and body as they battle the leaders who want to destroy their land.
ISBN-13: 978-1-59990-376-7 • ISBN-10: 1-59990-376-8
[1. Fantasy.] I. Redmond, J. B. II. Title.
PZ7.V4673Pri 2009   [Fic]—dc22   2009007625

First U.S. Edition December 2009
Book design by Donna Mark
Typeset by Westchester Book Composition
Printed in the U.S.A. by Quebecor World Fairfield, Pennsylvania
2 4 6 8 10 9 7 5 3 1

Choices are the hinges of destiny.

—Pythagoras

CODE OF EYRIE

I. Fael i'ha.
The Circle in all hearts. To disobey the Circle is Unforgivable.

II. Fae i'Fae.
Fae keep to Fae. Cross-mixing is Unforgivable.

III. Graal i'cheville.
Graal to the banded. An unfettered legacy is Unforgivable.

IV. Massacre i'massacres.
Murder to murderers. Unsanctioned killing is Unforgivable.

V. Chevillya i'ha.
Oaths to the heart. To break an oath is Unforgivable.

VI. Guilda i'Guild.
Guild dues to Guild. To dishonor Stone or Thorn is Unforgivable.

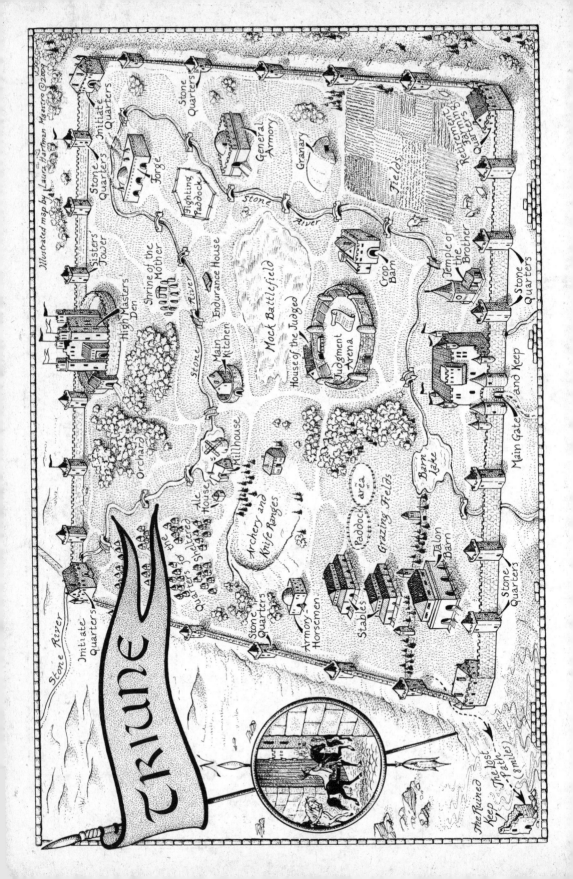

OATHBREAKER
A PRINCE
AMONG KILLERS

INTRODUCTION

In a time before written history, humans conquered Earth's magical societies. The Fae fled in defeat, taking with them a handful of loyal human servants. Using ancient understanding of the stars and universal energies, they migrated to a new world of blue-white sunlight and nights bathed in the glow of two moons—but they could not escape their fractious past. Vast dynasts rose and fell. The Fae strove for greater magic through genetic experiments until they devastated their own society. Fae bloodlines mingled with human, old magic began to fade, and for a time, the world of Eyrie knew war and darkness. Centuries later, Eyrie remains troubled, barely governed by a Circle representing the surviving dynasts, and two powerful guilds sworn to abstain from the battles between noble families. There is little hope for unity, and less hope that the old magic and glory of the Fae can be recaptured. Until now.

Aron Brailing has been Harvested by the Stone Guild and forced to become an assassin. When his family is murdered by their own dynast lord, Aron throws himself into his training, intent on learning the art of killing to avenge the deaths of his loved ones. Though his guild master is kind and supportive, Aron finds cold welcome at Stone's castle of Triune. He's tormented by fellow apprentices, dreams, and seemingly by Eyrie's old gods themselves. In punishment for a fight, he's sent on an impossible mission with an enemy, and he's about to face the full measure of horrors Eyrie can offer.

Darielle Ross, survivor of a powerful magical race thought extinct, has entangled herself in the affairs of the Fae in order to locate her unstable twin sister, Kate. Dari has been searching the countryside, but finding only a confusing array of feelings for the Stone Brothers assisting her. Time is running out for Dari. If she can't locate her sister, the king of her race will—and Kate will be killed to protect the secrets of Dari's people.

Nicandro Mab, the last remaining heir to the highest throne of Eyrie, has been thrown from a castle turret and left for dead. Mysteriously recovered from lethal injuries, he's traveling slowly toward Triune with a vicious yet intriguing Stone Sister who is more than aware of his identity. She's determined that he regain his strength and claim his birthright. Nic has no intention of surrendering his chance to live a life free of his insane mother and the madness of ruling a kingdom that seems intent on tearing itself apart.

As war devastates Eyrie's dynasts and the remnants of Fae magic, the destinies of Aron, Dari, and Nic intertwine. In their hands, minds, and hearts lies the fate of their people—and the fate of their world.

PART IV

Eltagh

FATE CHOOSES

CHAPTER THIRTY-FOUR

ARON

A blast of Stormbreaker's lightning crackled overhead, giving Aron a surge of courage as mist struck him in the face. The unnatural gray fog of the Deadfall immediately obscured his vision, and it smelled of old graves and bones left to mildew in caves. Aron decided to breathe through his mouth, at least until he grew accustomed to the odor. His eyes watered in the wet air, but he kept his gaze on the gray folds of Galvin's tunic.

Whispering met his ears, not human, not intelligible, and somewhere nearby, a rock cat howled. Something moaned, setting Aron's teeth on edge.

Then something screamed. Up ahead. Not far away at all.

A sly, grinding sound came from behind Aron, like creatures sidling and slithering across the same rocky ground he had just crunched beneath his boots.

"I'm an assassin's apprentice," he said to himself to drive down the rolling gallop of his heart. He closed one hand on the hilt of his short sword and the other on the metal grip of a dagger.

From in front of him, Galvin Herder grunted, and Aron saw the mist swirl as the older boy drew his long sword and held it at the ready.

"I'm an assassin's apprentice!" Aron yelled, taking strength from the words as he drew his own blades.

He could only hope the creatures flying, crawling, creeping, and charging *to meet them would know him for what he was, and fear him as much as he feared them.*

Aron Weylyn kept his fists tight on the hilts of his blades and Galvin Herder's faint image in view even though the older boy was using his height and longer stride to move quickly through the fog.

This journey across the worst eight miles in Eyrie was supposed to settle the dispute between Aron and Galvin, but Aron was convinced it was hopeless. The reality of impending death crackled through his muscles and bones, chilling him. Each step he took felt heavier and slower than the last. The day should have been bright, but no light fought its way through the dense mists.

"I won't save you," Galvin called from ahead of Aron. "If I live and you don't, so much the better for Stone."

Aron cursed the fog obscuring his view. Galvin seemed to float forward, then disappear into the unrelenting gray.

The silver dagger Stormbreaker had given Aron weighed in Aron's palm, and he wished he could throw it with accuracy—in the direction where Galvin had vanished. As his training masters had taught him, he checked ahead and beside him in both directions for threats, once behind, then moved forward to catch up to the older boy.

The path to the Ruined Keep revealed itself in pieces, mostly dirt and rock and bleached branches scattered like bones reaching into the mists. Aron noticed each unusual pattern of sticks and memorized it, in case he needed markers for his return journey.

Rocks crunched behind him.

His heart lurched as he whirled around, dagger and short sword raised.

A large black snake launched toward his legs, mouth open for the strike.

Aron shouted and sliced down with his short sword. The blade tore across the snake's too-broad head, leaving a bloody rent in its slick scales. The creature hissed and jerked away from the blow—and started to change.

"Mocker!" Aron yelled to warn Galvin, in case the monster got past him.

He tried to breathe and coughed at the wet-grave stench of the air. His eyes teared, but he slashed at the scaly abomination before it could assume its humanlike form. This time, he caught the creature directly across its now-childish face. Fat cheeks and lips ruptured as the thing hissed and bawled and tried to spit at him. Wings crackled outward from its shoulders as blood and liquid trickled from its damaged mouth.

Aron swallowed before he could retch and raised his sword again. The mocker moved faster.

Claws sharper than straight razors ripped toward Aron's belly. He leaped backward and dropped to his backside just in time to avoid a stream of blood-flecked spittle. The poisonous liquid spattered on the ground near his foot, sizzling holes into the rocks and dirt.

Aron rolled away from the stinking discharge and scrambled to his feet, dagger and short sword extended. A quick glance around told him that Galvin was nowhere near.

The mocker let out a screech that made Aron's breath stick in his throat. It looked like a deformed infant, human from waist up, snake from waist down, flapping oily, thick wings against the encroaching fog. It was tall, almost as tall as Aron, but with a snake's thin, twisty build.

Aron's vision narrowed as hours upon hours of sparring and battle training took hold of his habits. He flexed his knees and checked his balance, circling the mocker-snake as it turned in the air to keep pace with him. His pulse surged each time his feet struck the barren ground.

The mocker-snake gave a cry that was mingled hiss and screech.

The sound raked Aron's nerves, but he didn't react. The reality of his situation left him, along with the fog, the cries of other creatures in the distance, and most of his fear. His dagger and short sword took on a different weight, comforting instead of challenging, and he moved them fluidly, keeping the metal as a shield between himself and the monster.

Scales rattled as the mocker-snake spun to keep Aron in front of it. It pulled back its malformed lips and spit again, but Aron turned like a dancer, letting the poison scar the ground again. If only he could throw his dagger well—this battle would be ended!

The mocker-snake arced toward him, human mouth wide to show rows of dripping fangs.

Aron pivoted on his lead foot and brought his short sword down hard as he raised his dagger. He felt the jolt of contact up to his elbows, but didn't drop his blades. For a bleak, horrible second, the mocker's childlike head kept flying toward him. Aron's heart stuttered and his concentration broke.

He jerked sideways, and the mocker-snake's head crashed into the rocks at his feet.

The snake's partly human body landed a sword's length away, spilling dark red blood onto the path. It had an unnatural acrid stench, making Aron's eyes water all the more.

He stood for a few moments, breathing in and out so hard his chest ached in the center. The taste in his mouth soured like the dead mocker's venom, and he couldn't stop staring at the pieces of the creature's corpse.

Death.

Death and killing.

These were things he had to embrace. He had slaughtered hogs, dispatched manes, plotted the deaths of Lord Brailing and his Guard, even watched Stormbreaker give a boy Mercy, but—

But real death, real killing of a thing with a human baby's face—

Aron's hands shook until the tips of dagger and short sword danced across swirling bits of fog. The sight of the gory blades made his insides lurch. A coldness overtook him as he resisted surrender to grief and a bitter wave of gut-sickness, like the coldness he felt when he'd realized his family was murdered because of him. Like the coldness of the air itself, deep and without limit.

"Concentrate," he whispered to himself, sounding like a Stone training master, and gradually his awareness returned to his full control. Immediately, he knew more scavengers were lurking in the low-hanging clouds shrouding the path to the Ruined Keep. They growled softly as they tracked the scent of his fresh kill.

It was move now, or meet the bloodthirsty worst of Eyrie's Deadfall, Outlands, and Barrens.

Aron's teeth chattered as he wiped his blades on the leg of his gray pants, but by the time he set off toward the Ruined Keep, he had mastered his chill. His gray *cheville* felt icy and heavy against his ankle as he made progress, first in minutes, then in stretches of minutes, then hours.

How far was the Keep—another hour ahead? Maybe two?

There was still no sign or hint of Galvin. Aron's muscles ached, but the chilled weight of his *cheville* continued to comfort him as he covered more and more of the foggy, rocky path. At least when something killed him, the *cheville* would keep his soul safely bound to his body until it could be dispatched. He wouldn't become a carnivorous mane, sliding through the darkness searching for prey.

As if summoned by his thoughts, the unmistakable moans of the hungry and restless dead drifted toward him from the south, from the patch of Deadfall that touched the point of Triune.

Aron's skin tightened against his bones. He walked faster, then began to jog.

Some distance later, when the moans grew louder, he ran, slicing at the fog as if he could part it with his weapons. He would rather be fodder for mockers or natural predators than a meal for manes.

From ahead in the fog, Galvin shouted.

The bellowing growls of rock cats drowned the older boy's yelling.

Aron hesitated for only the briefest second, then shoved aside the flash of anger at the older boy for being cruel, for leaving him behind. No decent person would leave another to be eaten by wild animals, and Stormbreaker was counting on Aron to do what was right, to acquit himself without the use of his legacy.

Aron plowed through the mists, blind now, seeing nothing but white fog and drops of water. His heart slammed in time with his motions, and the muffled crack of a sword striking stones rattled his mind. He burst onto a clear, open patch of ground, and before he could orient himself to the parting of the fog, a rock cat barreled toward him.

The cat pounced.

Aron swept his short sword upward and caught the cat in its throat. Its claws sliced into his shoulders and arms as it fell dead, and Aron cried out from the fiery bursts of pain. Hot blood trickled onto his chilled skin as he made out Galvin still ahead of him, swinging his sword at three more attacking cats.

The nearest beast had its back to Aron. He ignored the throbbing ache in his wounded arms and leaped forward like Tek might have done in battle. Once more, he brought his short sword down in a jab-bing swipe. The blade sank into the rock cat's back between its shoul-ders, driving the animal against the rocky path. It rolled in its death throes, ripping the hilt of the sword from Aron's grasp.

"Cayn's teeth!" He lunged for the sword, but one of the cats swiped his ankle with knifelike claws.

Fresh agony staggered Aron. He couldn't get a grip on the sword hilt and swung wildly at the cat with his dagger. The beast howled as the small blade sliced across its nose, but it gave no ground.

Aron's blood thundered in his ears as the rock cat's muscles bunched to attack. He fumbled to free his sword from the dead cat, failed, then readied himself to throw his dagger. He swore again, knowing the last thing he would see would be his blade missing its target.

Galvin lopped off the cat's head before it could spring.

More blood filled Aron's vision, spattering on his tunic and face like dozens of hot, sobering slaps. He managed to rip his blade free and raise it. No target. The rock cats were all dead. But the manes—

All the blood was drawing them like a coppery beacon. Their unearthly moans grew so loud Aron couldn't manage a complete thought—and from above came a spine-slashing shriek Aron had never heard before.

Galvin's expression, which had been a mixture of surprise and relief, shifted to horror and dread. He jerked his gaze skyward and froze with both fists still on his blood-coated long sword.

"Great Roc," he said, still looking up. "It's hunting. It's hunting us."

Aron felt nothing but burning in his arms and ankles, and an equal burning that seemed to come from the center of his mind. Great Roc. One of the giant white predator birds from the Barrens. How could he and Galvin defend themselves against a bird double the size of a bull talon, and the onrushing manes, and whatever else might be in the mists?

He didn't know whether to keep his gaze on the fog and wait to fight the blood-seeking manes, or watch the shrouded sky like Galvin, waiting for death to drop on them from above.

The whumping pump of huge wings sent the mists into a swirling frenzy. Pebbles rattled on the path and struck Aron in his shins and knees.

At the same moment, the mane of a robed man came staggering through the nearby curtain of fog.

Aron snarled at the thing, then glanced upward at the swirling clouds again.

Something huge and heavy was dropping toward them like a weight in a well. Aron could sense its enormous presence even though he couldn't see it. Yet.

Then claws three times larger than a talon's tore through the thin ceiling of mist.

Aron and Galvin dodged at the same moment, going in different directions.

Giant dagger-nails clicked shut on dirt and rocks, and the thwarted bird let out a will-stealing cry. The sound reverberated through Aron's bones. His skin and shoulders burned, and his blood froze even as it oozed from the cuts around his neck.

The mane moaned as it lurched forward, dragging one foot. Its eyes burned like black fire. Already, it was reaching for Aron with one unnaturally pale hand, reaching for his warmth and life.

Aron shifted his attack stance to favor the silver dagger, doing what he could to ignore the throb of his wounds. He barely got his arms and weapons into defense position.

The mane never slowed its shambling approach.

Aron tried not to think at all as he rammed his silver blade deep, deep into the onrushing mane's belly. He sealed his mind against the rush of wet, clinging cold that claimed his wrist, fingers, and forearm. Like plunging his blade into a vat of chilled cooking oil.

The creature's features contorted as it shrieked.

Aron jerked his blade back, but the mane's essence fell away to nothing. Its freed soul burst outward, then upward, taking the shape of a tall, winged man as it fled this world for the next.

Aron shook his blade arm, as if to clear the greasy sensation.

More manes stumbled, lumbered, and dragged themselves into the space now free of mist. Aron counted two, then four, then five and too many to keep counting.

Galvin shouted again and again, bashing the Roc's legs each time the bird attempted to pluck him from the path.

Aron's panic burst through him like the mane's spirit leaving its long-dead body. He saw the area free of fog too sharply, his awareness wrapping around each movement and detail. His arm moved as if it didn't belong to him, plunging his dagger into mane after mane. He turned in circles, cutting first one, then the next, and from somewhere in the still-shrouded regions of the path, more rock cats gave wailing, starved cries. Feral, unfamiliar howls joined the lethal chorus, coating Aron's thoughts and nerves in yet more ice. The pain tearing at his shoulders grew distant, as did the mind-hammering sounds of the attack.

He had time to think that Stormbreaker might approve of Galvin and Aron dying together in such a battle. Then the Roc's snatching claws caught him on the side of his head, knocking his senses loose like so many broken teeth.

Aron pitched forward at the feet of a dozen or more manes, both blades sailing out of his hands and clattering against the rocky path. Dirt filled his mouth and nose and eyes, and he saw only rocks and mist and a pair of shining black leather boots striding through the manes as if the dead spirits didn't even exist.

CHAPTER THIRTY-FIVE

ARON

"You are strong," the woman whispered to Aron, seemingly across some far-reaching breach.

He tried to listen, though a distant aspect of his consciousness was certain a mane was draining away his blood, his spirit, his energy—everything that made him human. His body would become a dead husk, and his soul would be twisted and tortured until he wanted nothing but to feed off all the warmth and life he could find. He was dying, but he couldn't bring himself to care.

The rest of his mind seemed to hover in a blank, black place. He couldn't see anything or feel anything at all.

"Very strong," the woman murmured.

The voice drew him and terrified him at the same moment. He sensed power and curiosity behind each word. He wanted to use his *graal* to learn more about the woman, who seemed to be the strange, mystical lady he had seen at Triune, and in his dreams before.

Aron imagined himself reaching out his hand, imagined the beautiful lady and how radiant she must look in her silvery gown made of starlight.

Could he almost see her? There—that point of light in the distance! The lady, and she seemed to be surrounded by—by children?

We need you, the lady sang in his mind, still so far away, but coming closer. *Eyrie needs you. All the strong must band together, stand together, or the power of our people will be lost forever.*

The sound was so sweet Aron wanted to weep. He tried to turn his consciousness toward the lady, to extend his arms until he could embrace her. He could see hands reaching toward him now, wispy and unreal and long enough to stretch over mountains and fields and forests. The tips of his own fingers strained to touch the lady.

Almost there. Almost connected.

Brilliant colors blasted through Aron's darkness, slamming into his eyes, his thoughts like an onrushing bull talon. He cried out from the shock and force as a wall burst into existence, sealing his consciousness away from that of the lady. Aron jerked awake, gasping, head pounding, to find himself staring at a cracked stone ceiling.

What kind of *graal* had so many colors, an appearance that rich, that deep? Was that wall even made of *graal*?

Aron blinked a few times, grieving the loss of the lady in his vision and waiting for his sight to clear. The throb in his head gradually eased, and he realized he was lying on a rough blanket inside a circular stone room ringed with crumbling windows. Weapons of all varieties lay against the splintering walls, from swords to crossbows, and even staffs and shields of different sizes and hefts. Supply trunks littered the floor. Some had been scratched or chewed, and some torn open, but many were intact. Beyond the trunks, fog rushed past the decaying windows, but above it the steely light of a gray sky illuminated the room. Aron realized he was at some elevation. High up, above the ground clouds. Maybe in a tower.

The Ruined Keep?

"Galvin," he tried to shout as he pushed himself up on his elbows, but his voice had no more force than a crushed mouse.

"Your companion is wounded, but healing," a man said from Aron's left. "He is safe in the granary vault downstairs."

The words were so deep and forceful that Aron wondered if he might still be dreaming. All the hairs on his body sprang up in a tingling rush. If Cayn himself had a voice, it would sound like that.

For a moment, Aron couldn't make himself turn his head. He was terrified he'd find himself gazing at the great horned stag, come to use its sharp antlers to dispatch his soul.

"You are frightened," said the terrifying voice in an accent both familiar and unfamiliar. Aron had heard something like it before. His *graal* reinforced a feeling that lying would mean immediate death, so he nodded.

"You sense that I am dangerous to you." The voice sounded mildly amused, but far from warm or kind. Then the tone dropped so low Aron fought a new round of shivers. "Your instincts serve you well."

Aron made himself turn toward the man.

It took the full force of his will not to fall backward on his blanket.

Not Cayn, no.

But close.

It was in the man's hard ebony eyes. More death than a Stone Brother might deal in a lifetime.

Aron didn't even bother to hide his shivering. He felt like a passerine in the paws of a rock cat, and he was certain his existence was just as tenuous. Strangely, though, the wounds from his earlier battles seemed to be gone, but for a lingering soreness in his shoulders and back.

Someone—likely this man—had saved him and healed him. For what purpose, Aron was too frightened to guess.

The man was sitting on a large trunk, his limbs arranged in a way that suggested both a warrior's strength and a cat's balance. His skin was a tawny golden color, but his hair was as black as his eyes. He was dressed simply yet elegantly in leather breeches and boots and a leather tunic stitched with fine ruby thread in a shape that reminded Aron of Dyn Mab's crest—the head of a red dragon. The pattern across this man's chest was a dragon's head, but its full body also, wings outstretched, rising in flight. In a few moments, Aron realized the man had no weapon.

The man seemed to track Aron's gaze to his waist, and the corners of his mouth curled into a slight smile. "I need no iron, steel, or silver to defend myself."

Aron's *graal* confirmed this bold assertion.

The man's smile faded, and his dark eyes narrowed.

Had the man sensed Aron's use of his legacy?

But how?

Dari had taught him to conceal his thoughts and abilities so well that only she—

And Aron understood.

He stopped shivering, because what he felt now was beyond fear. He had no word for his emotions save for panic, and fear for Dari and Dari's sister. He sat up straighter on his blanket, then lowered his gaze to the man's black boots and bowed his head in the best gesture of respect he could muster.

The man snorted. "If she has told you so much that you recognize me, Aron Weylyn, she must have explained that we do not hold with empty traditions like bowing to nobles."

Aron swallowed, feeling the dry catch in his throat. Had the man read his name from his thoughts, or did he know Aron through reports made to him by spies and confidants?

"I don't know what else to do to show respect," Aron said, at a loss for any other explanation.

"Look me in the eye again." The man's voice was louder, yet somehow less threatening. "Show me courage despite fear. Show me that you would meet your fate without whining or pleading—*that* I would respect, if that concerns you."

Aron lifted his head and forced himself to hold the gaze of Dari's cousin Platt, the Stregan king. In that moment, Aron's *graal* showed him the outline of a great black dragon so massive it would blast the stones of the Ruined Keep into so much dust.

Brother have mercy.

With power like that, why did the Stregans keep themselves hidden? They could dominate the land, take back all that was lost to them. Aron could hardly get past his own surprise, and the hopeless feeling of being outmatched.

"You are doing well so far." Platt looked amused again, and also a bit surprised. "So my respect does matter to you?"

Aron kept himself still on the blanket, refusing to lower his head, and once more, he told the truth. "You're a stranger to me. Your respect doesn't make a difference in my life, should you permit it to continue, but Dari's does. I would show you deference to please her, and to protect her."

Platt went silent, and his expression froze into a glare. A minute or so later, when he spoke, his words came through his teeth. "And what is Dari to you?"

Dozens of answers occurred to Aron. Words like "friend" and "teacher" and "shining light" competed for selection, but in the end he chose, "Dari is the best person I know."

"Ah, but she is not a person, Aron Weylyn." Platt shifted on the trunk to lean toward Aron. He was no more than an arm's length away now, and Aron's body trembled at the nearness of such a predator. "Though we use the terms '*person*,' '*man*,' and '*woman*' in conversation, they are not accurate. Dari is a Stregan as surely as I am, despite the measure of Fae blood in her veins. Have you considered this in your late-night moonings?"

Aron's cheeks burned at Platt's insinuation, but he could no more deny his love for Dari than he could deny the sky or the moons or the sun. "Dari is Dari," he said, unable to mask the anger in his voice even if the man was close enough to snap his neck. "She's my teacher and my friend. I really don't care what kind of blood she has." He rushed on, before he lost his nerve. "Have you come to force her to leave with you?"

Platt's expression shifted from avid and intense back to mild surprise. He sat back on the trunk. "I considered that option, yes. But that is not our way, Aron. Dari is an adult, free to make her own choices, provided she does not compromise the safety of my people beyond what I consider to be tenable."

Aron's fists clenched against the rough surface of the blanket. "And if she did, you would kill her?"

Now Platt looked shocked. "I would not. Just because we have the strength to deal death like your storied guild doesn't mean we choose to use that strength." He frowned at Aron, as if deeply troubled by the question. "Killing and war are as distasteful to us as torturing an infant would be to your people—or at least the good-hearted amongst you."

Aron's insides recoiled from that image, and Platt seemed to sense his reaction. He inclined his head, as if to communicate approval, and continued. "We do not invest in death and ways to die, but in our future. Dari is a brilliant and powerful young Stregan. We have great need of her talents and leadership."

"But you would kill her sister." Aron's fists remained tight on the cloth, and new dread and fresh panic surged through him. "Is that why you've come? For Kate?"

"That situation is beyond your understanding." Platt's answer was sharp, clipped. Too quick.

Aron didn't need his *graal* to understand that he had struck close to the truth.

"I know Kate is soft in the mind," Aron said, fishing through his mind for options, a plan, some course of action that would spare Kate, and thus save Dari from a blow that would crush her spirit. "I know Kate isn't stable because of the Wasting. I also know how much Dari loves her. Is that beyond *your* understanding?"

Platt stood so suddenly Aron almost fell backward. He recovered himself and got to his feet so the man—the Stregan—wouldn't tower over him, glaring like he was.

"You cannot possibly—" Platt began, but Aron didn't let him finish.

"If you kill Kate, you'll kill a part of Dari. She'll never recover from it." Aron touched his chest, where he felt the steady pound of his heart. "I understand loss like that, and the damage it does. If you really need Dari's brilliance and power, then don't break her and leave her grieving and resentful for the rest of her life."

Aron heard his own words, and something shifted inside his own understanding. Something about what it meant to be a part of the Stregans, or the Stone Guild, or any other group that depended on what each member had to offer. He hesitated, feeling suddenly guilty about the anger and pain he had been nursing since the death of his family, perhaps to the detriment of everyone around him.

"No one has had word or sign of Kate since she slipped away from us." Platt moved away from Aron toward the crumbling windows, his booted feet making no sound on the dusty stone floor. "You and your friends and Dari have not found her." Mists slid by outside, competing with the bright gray sky as he propped both hands on a sill. "My warriors have not located so much as a trace of her existence. It is likely that Kate met some misfortune in the forests, or fell to her death along some forgotten path."

"Then one quiet evening, we will find her bones," Aron said. "We will send Kate's spirit to the stars and do whatever we can to help Dari through that *natural* loss."

"Do not think I want to see harm come to Kate." Platt kept his back to Aron. His tone was gentler now, almost soft. "But you must understand, she could be used for a weapon, against the Stregans—against anyone. Kate's involvement could decide your war, and not in your favor."

Aron had debated this point with Dari many times, and he found himself countering with Dari's standard argument. "If someone had a weapon so powerful, surely they would have used it to gain advantage by now."

Platt said nothing, and the silence stretched so long Aron imagined he could hear the whisper of fog against the stones of the Ruined Keep. There were no sounds of predators below, natural or unnatural.

Aron realized that nothing would hunt when the king of hunters was at hand.

"From your lips to the ears of all the gods and goddesses." Platt sounded sincere. He paused another few moments, then seemed to regain his own resolve. He turned and folded his arms, studying Aron as if Aron might be a scroll he was attempting to decipher. "I did not come here to debate morality with you, and I had no intention of allowing you to speak about Kate or Dari, or my decisions concerning either of them. Your loyalty is impressive, and I must admit, persuasive."

Aron felt a mad rush of relief, but he didn't dare let himself believe that Platt had decided to spare Kate, or to leave Dari in peace. He wasn't even completely certain that Platt would allow him to leave the Ruined Keep alive, but he felt more hopeful now, despite the Stregan king's very intense stare.

"Now, Aron," Platt said. "Let us get to the heart of what I need to know. And for your sake, I hope you are as truthful as you have been in our encounter thus far."

CHAPTER THIRTY-SIX

ARON

Aron tried to keep a relaxed posture and maintain eye contact, but his body reacted of its own accord. Preparing to run. Preparing to do anything but be subjected to more confrontation with this dangerous man. His thoughts dashed from Dari to Kate to Stormbreaker to Galvin to the purpose of their journey to the Keep, and how he would explain any of what had happened to Lord Baldric.

"How did you come by such a powerful *graal*, that it takes a Stregan to teach you?" Platt's question was casual, but his forceful stare communicated the importance of Aron's answer.

Aron lowered himself back to his blanket, folding his legs and shifting to ease the pressure on his sore back. "I think I got it from my father."

"You could have used your *graal* in that battle, but you fought with your hands." Platt shook his head and glanced toward the circular row of foggy windows. "You were fighting against odds too great for your abilities, but you did do well, and in defense of a companion who has not been kind to you. Those things are admirable, but if I had not come when I did, you would be dead, and your companion as well."

Aron couldn't string enough related thoughts together to formulate a more complicated answer than, "It was a matter of honor. A promise I made to my guild master. I needed to make this journey without using my legacy."

At this, Platt returned to his narrow-eyed and angry expression. "The Fae are fools. *Graal* is not to be feared, and neither is it to be worshipped. It is a tool, no weaker and no stronger than the soul who wields it."

"A tool." Aron felt his cheeks burning again, and he wanted to defend Stormbreaker and Lord Baldric—all of Stone, of Eyrie, if necessary. "A tool like that used by craftsmen and farmers."

Platt opened his arms. "Exactly."

"Then choosing when to wield it and when to lay it aside for the good of my canvas or clay, or for the benefit of my fields, that would be my prerogative?"

Platt's only response was an irritated shrug at Aron, and a baring of his teeth in obvious disgust for Fae prohibitions against dangerous *graal*. Since Aron couldn't understand all of that, or defend it well himself, he changed the subject with, "The manes and mockers, even the wild beasts of the Barrens and Outlands fear you."

"Of course." Platt's posture remained tense. "No beast or spirit, no matter what the form or deformity, will stand against a Stregan's wishes when we are not concealing the truth of our essence."

Aron felt a wash of surprise, even though he had suspected as much. "If you can command wild animals and mockers and manes, why do you not march into this terrible war and put an end to it? Why do Stregans hide at all?"

Platt's frown renewed Aron's fears for his own life, and he had to work not to move away from the man as Platt lowered his arms. "Involvement in Fae wars and affairs cost my people most of our population, and wiped out entire Fury races."

Aron's heart beat faster and faster, and he couldn't help a flash of guilt over what his people had done to Dari's people during the mixing disasters. The Fae had feared and turned on their more powerful though peace-loving neighbors. In a coordinated effort in every dynast save for Dyn Ross, the Fae drugged Furies at feasts and celebrations, then massacred them as they slept—much as Lord Brailing wiped out his own dynast subjects along the Watchline.

"Those betrayals were horrible." Aron said. "But they are a long time past. The perpetrators have been dead for generations. This war, it's not ancient history. It's happening now, and it's killing that could be stopped."

Platt seemed to consider his argument, maybe even how ending the war would help Dari and Kate. But after a time, he shook his head. "No, Aron Weylyn. The mixing disasters were not so long that we have forgotten the lessons. Only death comes from mingling with the Fae. Your people crave power and value ambition over life itself, and Stregans want no part of your society—or what is left of it."

Frustration struck inside Aron's belly like an angry mocker-snake, but he controlled his reaction and didn't give in to the wave of hopelessness for Eyrie, and for Dari's quest to find her sister. His thoughts moved immediately to people like Galvin Herder and Lord Brailing, and he sighed. "People in power can't imagine people who don't want it."

Platt once more inclined his head, accepting Aron's observation, and his mood shifted again. More peaceful now. Contemplative and focused. "My people will not act against our beliefs with respect to war again."

Aron held the man's gaze, staring deep into Platt's black eyes. "I understand."

"You do. I see that." Platt didn't blink, and Aron felt the touch of Platt's *graal*—though he couldn't really call it that. It was more like being seized by unimaginably powerful hands and squeezed until his knees shook and his breath came short. He had been sized up and evaluated in an instant, every aspect of his body, being, and character. Of that, he had no doubt.

Platt seemed to debate with himself a moment, then come to a decision. His formidable mind-talents released Aron, who wavered a moment before regaining a firm stance and keeping eye contact with the Stregan king.

"I came here to save you, Aron." Platt watched Aron's reaction carefully, and Aron knew he must be seeing Aron's surprise, and his disbelief.

The Stregan king's assertion didn't seem possible, or real. Why would a king—especially this king—deign to intervene in the fate of one boy, only an apprentice—and in a guild that practiced arts abhorred by the Furies?

Aron shook his head before he realized what he was doing, unable to accept what Platt was saying.

Platt gestured to Aron. "Do not measure your worth by your role in Fae society. That is of no consequence to me, or to my people. Iko came to me and asked me to see to your safety because you are important to Dari, and to Iko, because of his personal pledges to his god."

When Aron couldn't respond, Platt added, "A request from a friend to save a life. That's reason enough for me to act. Does that surprise you?"

"Yes," Aron whispered, still numb with shock. Platt was telling him the truth, but perhaps not the full truth. There was more to the king's motives, and Aron's *graal* told him it had something to do with Iko's beliefs, which were similar to Zed's. Old ways. Old beliefs.

Zed had told Aron that in desperate times, fate watches, fate circles, then dives like a hungry hawk, striking people who will be important to Eyrie. Aron had ridiculed him for such a thought. Now, though, here above the mists of the Deadlands, the sands of the Barrens, and the rocks and pits of the Outlands—here in the Ruined Keep of Triune, staring into the liquid-coal eyes of the king of the Stregans, who had journeyed from the safety of his own stronghold just to rescue one boy—Aron believed for the first time that he might have some unusual destiny.

Tears formed in the corners of his eyes, because he didn't know how to figure out what great task he needed to accomplish. How could he know that? How could he shed the anger and grief that he had only just realized held him back from his potential and made him less useful to his chosen family of Stone, and discover what task had been set for him by fate itself?

"You do not have the heart and soul of an assassin, Aron Weylyn," Platt murmured, once more studying Aron like an undecipherable scroll.

Aron didn't know whether that was a compliment or an insult, but given the beliefs Platt professed, he decided on the former.

"Do I have the heart and soul of an oathbreaker?" The question left Aron before he had a chance to consider whether or not he wanted to hear the answer.

"You do not have the heart and soul of an oathbreaker," Platt said, sounding certain. "You would follow your promises to your own peril, as you've already demonstrated."

"Then I must learn to be a killer, because I'm an assassin's apprentice." Aron heard the same heaviness in his voice, and felt it, like chains forming in his chest, tugging his heart downward, toward his toes. "I'm of Stone now, just as surely as you're a Stregan."

"What you must transform is here." Platt tapped the side of his head. "Strengthen and protect your will, your essence, your intelligence. You have one of the powerful old mind-talents of Eyrie. Through you, and through those like you, the Fae might regain some of what they destroyed."

Aron blinked at the Stregan king. "You would be happy about that?"

Platt's formidable countenance softened, and for a moment, Aron saw a glimmer of the compassion and depth of emotion that drew him to Dari. "Fae and Fury were once as close as Dari and her twin, Aron." The man's voice was softer, too, and Aron caught another echo of Dari, her vulnerability when she showed the truth of her emotions. "Without one another, we are none of us complete."

Aron stood in silence for a time, absorbing Platt's admission and the sight of the man's sorrow and hopelessness, that such healing and reunion could ever occur. Aron had no such hopelessness. In that moment, he could imagine an Eyrie once more made whole, with all its peoples and all its powers as they once were. Unbroken by disasters. Repaired from wars and senseless killings. His back itched between his shoulders, where wings might have grown, when Fae could still fly. His mind itched just as fiercely, as if eager to use its talents and powers, freely and unfettered, and without fear of doing harm. He was so absorbed by sensations and visions of potential that he barely understood that Platt was speaking, and beginning to move away from him.

"You may mention my visit to Lord Baldric, Stormbreaker, and Dari," Platt said as he once more approached the open window arches. "Otherwise, be cautious about who you take into your counsel. I will trust your discretion, but I advise you not to disappoint me."

Platt leaped onto the nearest decrepit stone sill, and the stones beneath it gave way.

Aron yelped with concern, but Platt was gone before the first rock struck the floor.

Aron heard a rush of wings, saw the stirring of the fog below the windows, and he knew the Stregan king had shifted to his winged form.

By now, Platt might be halfway to Eyrie's blue-white sun.

It took Aron many long minutes to come back to himself completely, and that heavy feeling Platt's words had given him didn't retreat. It kept him calm when he made his way to the granary and woke Galvin, who immediately demanded to know how they reached the Ruined Keep.

"It's not clear to me," Aron said, which was truthful, if incomplete. "You must have driven the Roc away, and perhaps the Roc frightened other predators."

Galvin scrubbed a hand across his face as he glanced around the chamber full of grain sacks. "*You* didn't finish that battle and carry me all this way."

"No," Aron admitted. "I don't think I did."

Galvin let out a frustrated growl and came close to Aron, standing over him.

Aron felt no fear at all, not after his encounter with the king of the Stregans. He felt only weariness as Galvin glared down at him.

"You're weak," Galvin said, clearly flustered by Aron's refusal to argue or explain any further. "If I had been the one to keep my wits in that battle, I would have killed you."

Aron met the older boy's gaze without effort, seeing fear and confusion where he once read only coldness and cruelty. "I'm an assassin's apprentice, not an oathbreaker. No matter what you say, I think the same is true for you."

Galvin's mouth hung open, then snapped closed. "I am an apprentice, an apprentice who's saddled with the likes of you," he said with his jaw clenched. "All of Stone must bear the burden of you, most of all those of us in the Den. Where's the justice in that?"

"I didn't choose to be here," Aron said, hoping that would appease Galvin so they could move on with their duties, eat, rest for the night, and return to Triune on the morning.

"I *did* choose to be at Stone," Galvin countered, his entire body going stiff with his rising anger. "And you may expect to fight me every day. You'll improve, or you'll die."

Aron considered the older boy's words, and he heard in them an odd sort of bargain. It was a deal he thought he could make, so he assented with a nod. "Agreed. I'll improve, or I'll die by your hand, and without complaint."

Once more, Galvin's mouth came open, but this time, he didn't bother to close it right away. He stared at Aron and fumed for a time, then seemed to realize that Aron would not argue with him, no matter what threat he employed. He also seemed to grasp that the mystery of the battle and the end of their trek to the Ruined Keep might reflect as poorly on him as on Aron, so he let the matter drop.

They went about checking and inventorying supplies as instructed, then made dinner of boiled corn and dried meat in the Keep's small kitchen. The night passed without incident, and at sunrise, they made the long journey back to Triune in absolute silence. The mists kept their distance, and they didn't hear so much as a whisper or growl from any predator. Galvin kept looking from left to right in wonder. Occasionally, he glanced at Aron, and Aron knew the older boy understood that their safety was somehow tied to Aron's presence.

Aron was relatively certain that Platt was somewhere nearby, or that the Stregan king had somehow instructed manes and mockers and the beasts of the land to give them wide passage. Still, he was more than relieved to see the gray stone walls of Triune looming ahead of them.

As they reached the castle's entrance, the wooden gates that had sealed them from safety swung wide to reveal Stormbreaker, Dari, Lord Baldric, Windblown, Zed, Iko, and Blath standing side by side in a straight line like a welcoming contingent. Something about their stoop-shouldered postures and ruffled appearances made Aron wonder if they had slept, or if they had kept vigil in those very positions the entire day before, the long night, and today as well. He made a point of not looking too closely at Iko, lest he react in some way that might make the others suspicious about what took place at the Ruined Keep.

Aron crossed through the archway back into Triune beside Galvin with a sense of returning home, to the place he most belonged, to the closest thing he would ever again have to a family. Dari, Blath, Zed, and Iko let their relief show on their faces. Windblown had a blank expression, and Stormbreaker seemed both miserable and elated, perhaps guilty for setting Aron such a task.

Lord Baldric looked unusually kind and jovial as he opened both arms and boomed, "Welcome. I—er—trust you checked the supplies?"

Aron quickly gave his memorized report, detailing the status of weapons, food, and water, and he noted that he and Galvin repaired two of the lower Keep doors to better deny entry to scavengers.

"Excellent," Lord Baldric said, then turned his attention to Galvin Herder. "And what report do you bring me? Should we keep this boy, or send him to judgment?"

Aron's pulse stilled as he turned his head to stare at Galvin. He hadn't considered that Galvin would have been charged with observing him, and carrying information back to the Lord Provost and likely to Stormbreaker as well. He certainly hadn't considered that Galvin would be given any voice in Lord Baldric's decisions about Aron remaining at Triune.

Galvin's expression remained angry and distant, as it had since he woke in the Ruined Keep. For the moment, he remained sullen, but when he did begin to speak, Aron fully expected some sort of indictment, perhaps even accusations that he had used his *graal* to get them safely to their destination, or return them to Triune without attack.

Aron couldn't make himself breathe. He knew panic again, hard and desperate, charging through every muscle and vein, and it was all he could do not to start shaking, or explode, or swing his fists at Lord Baldric.

This wasn't fair. After everything he had been through since Harvest, not to mention the last day, how could his status at Stone come down to the opinion of one boy who despised him?

Heat flowed through Aron's body like a red, burning wave.

Galvin's expression turned even darker, and he cleared his throat. "Aron Weylyn does not need his legacy to fight. He will be better served to work on close combat or far-distant attack. Middle-range weapons are not his strength."

Aron's thoughts crackled between his temples as Galvin's report sank into his consciousness. He heard Dari's intake of breath as Zed and Iko grumbled to themselves. Windblown and Blath offered no reactions.

"Thank you," Stormbreaker said to Galvin. "Your assessment closely matches mine. Very few can be master of all methods of fighting. With your leave, Lord Baldric, I believe both apprentices should go to the infirmary for a check from the healers."

Lord Baldric grunted his assent, and Galvin Herder walked away in the direction of the infirmary building.

Aron found he couldn't get his limbs to cooperate. He stared after the older boy, watching him stride toward Triune's main byway, but he remained paralyzed by a mixture of anger and relief and surprise, and complete confusion.

Blath, Windblown, and Zed took their leave, while Dari, Iko, and Stormbreaker remained close. Dari looked as angry as Aron felt.

"How was it right to give that boy any voice in Aron's fate?" she asked, her tone conveying the full measure of her scorn for that action.

Aron expected a rebuke from Stormbreaker or a brutal retort from Lord Baldric, but Stormbreaker remained silent. The Lord Provost spoke to Dari as a teacher would address a student. "At Stone, our fate always depends upon the cooperation and support of our fellow guild members." He gestured to the massive battlements surrounding them. "As you well know, and you'll hear often at Triune, we have no friends outside these walls. We must forge our alliances within them."

Dari looked like she wanted to debate the point, but Lord Baldric held up one hand. "If Galvin had spoken against Aron, it would not have sealed Aron's fate. It would have sealed mine."

Lord Baldric lowered his hand and turned his gaze to Aron. For once his brown eyes seemed absolutely gentle, and as his bald head gleamed in the afternoon light, Aron thought he saw the man's eyes glisten with a hint of tears. "I would have had a choice to make, a choice that would leave me wounded and Stone weaker by one strong fighter. Fortunately, it did not come to that. Both apprentices have exceeded my expectations, and earned some leeway—however small—in my esteem."

So why did Aron not feel light and carefree?

Aron lifted his hands and pressed them against his chest, as if he might actually touch the heaviness that pressed so fiercely on his insides.

"Infirmary, Aron," Stormbreaker said, patting Aron's shoulder. "Have a good meal, then return to me for training."

"Yes, Master Stormbreaker." Aron's response was automatic, but his eyes had moved to Dari.

She gave him an impatient, almost irritated frown as she often did when he was misbehaving in *graal* lessons. The expression saddened Aron and increased the weight inside him as he realized he likely had not shown her sufficient gratitude or respect.

"When you have a moment, I would speak with you," he said, hearing that strange deepening in his voice that he had noticed after surviving Platt's scrutiny in the Ruined Keep.

Dari's eyebrows pulled together, and Aron felt the touch of her *graal*.

He didn't resist her, even when the touch deepened to an outright exploration. The irritation left her face, replaced by worry, relief, and something like grudging affection.

He left for the infirmary without waiting for her response.

She would catch up to him, and he would tell her about his visit with Platt. Then he would explain the encounter to Stormbreaker and Lord Baldric, and return to his training at Stone.

"Thank you," he said to Iko, who was following behind him at a reasonable distance.

As always, the Sabor offered little in the way of response, but Aron heard the boy mutter quick thanks to Cayn.

After a moment, Aron did the same. Cayn, the Brother, the Goddess—he wasn't certain who had chosen him, but it seemed prudent to speak to all of them, just in case.

CHAPTER THIRTY-SEVEN

ARON

The news of Aron's encounter with Platt seemed to sustain Dari for a time, which gave Aron a sense of relief. She told Aron she felt like she had been granted a reprieve, that she at least had a reasonable chance of finding her twin before Platt's warriors located her, especially since they had been unsuccessful thus far.

It didn't take long, though, for disappointment to return. When night after night of searching turned up nothing, Dari seemed more unhappy than ever, and Aron would have done anything to please her, including doubling and tripling his efforts in their *graal* training sessions.

What do you see?

Dari's voice floated like sweet music through Aron's senses, heightened by the depth of perception he enjoyed on the other side of the Veil. He tried to focus on the lyrical notes of her speech, on the gauzy warmth of her spiritual presence beside him, but it was no use. He couldn't do what she was asking him to do, and he hated himself for it.

Aron slid back to full awareness and opened his eyes, taking in the stone floor and bearskin rug beneath him, the stone walls of Dari's bedchamber, the fire blazing in her hearth, and Blath sitting in a chair by the far window, staring away from them, into the gray light of the cloudy day. Aron's fingers traveled down his leg until he touched the polished gray *cheville* that marked him as a Stone apprentice. The smooth, banded agate he now wore seemed perfect to his eye, more complex than he ever imagined colorless rock could be, and he knew its contours, shades, and hues so well he might have had this very *cheville* since birth. Like the gray tunic and breeches he wore, it was part of his life now, a fact he accepted. His *cheville*, his apprentice's clothing, the never-ending ache in his muscles from training and the additional exercises he took on to improve himself, the bruises on his back from his latest round of extra "training" with Galvin Herder . . . at least those things were simple and easy.

Dari was not, and neither were her demands.

The outer surface of the rock felt cool to his touch. Dari's room was cold despite the fire, but she was so close to Aron, sitting almost knee to knee, that he wondered if her presence kept him warm.

What do you see?

The question echoed through the faint mental connection that remained even though Aron was no longer in a meditative state.

"Nothing," he said aloud. "Well, nothing but you and Blath and your bedchamber and the light coming through your window. I can't see Iko in the hallway, but I'd wager he'd yelp if I stuck a burning stick beneath the door."

Dari's eyes opened, and Aron stared into the dark, glittering depths. No matter how tired and sad she had become over the days and weeks and cycles of fruitless searching for her sister, she remained endlessly beautiful to him.

"Aron, you have been at Stone for a year and a half." Dari rubbed the sides of her head, then fidgeted with the peridot *cheville*—a fake, fastened by clasps—that she kept on her ankle during waking hours. "You have mastered the basics of regulating your body and thoughts, of healing yourself and others from minor accidents and wounds, of understanding the world around you in new and deeper ways. You've even become skilled at tasks like reading the nature of legacies and concealing your own mind-talents from any who might try to pry. What stops you from using your *graal* to look across distances on the other side of the Veil?"

Aron's cheeks warmed even as his belly tightened. He tried to use some of that regulation of body and mind she had taught him and shrugged in response, hoping his expression remained as placid as Stormbreaker's always seemed to be. "Perhaps it's a talent I don't have."

"You've done it before." Dari gazed at him, and Aron was aware she was searching for the truth. Maybe sensing it, like he was supposed to able to do so easily. "You could do it again, but you don't choose to try."

With a frown, Aron did his best to keep a dense cloak about the innermost workings of his mind. He even repeated the words to a traveling song to himself, over and over, to keep her from prying too deeply through the trace of mental connection they shared. That was, of course, futile, at least where Dari was concerned.

"You don't . . . want to view the countryside of Eyrie from the other side of the Veil. But why?" She stared at him all the harder, her black eyes bright with frustration and confusion. "Stormbreaker and Lord Baldric value war news, especially what they can learn from sources other than the endless streams of messengers and demands from Thorn and the dynast rulers."

Aron almost regretted their proximity now, as it would be easier to ignore Dari or mislead her from across the room. Perhaps from somewhere else in the vast compound of Triune. "It's almost the sixth hour past middle-night, though I can't see the sun behind the clouds. Time for weapons practice, and the High Masters' apprentices are to meet at the horseman's armory. I should go—but I'll double my efforts tomorrow."

Dari's scrutiny didn't ease. "Are you frightened? Do you think

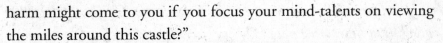

harm might come to you if you focus your mind-talents on viewing the miles around this castle?"

Aron glared directly at her. He straightened himself on the floor, speaking faster than he intended—and louder. "Of course I don't fear harm. Not harm to me."

Blath glanced at him as if to appraise his level of threat to Dari, then went back to staring out the window. The bells along Triune's battlements begin to ring. It was a simple pattern—two quick rings, then a long toll. More messengers were arriving. Likely with more tidings of how Lord Brailing and Lord Altar were succeeding in their march across Dyn Mab. Aron didn't want to hear any such news, and he didn't want to discuss with Dari his feelings about traveling above Eyrie on the other side of the Veil.

He focused on the ringing bells and tried to ignore the sense of pressure in his mind. Too many nights now, he had suffered from new and bloody nightmares—or were they fantasies?—of slaughtering the Brailing Guard. Any of them. All of them. Then being killed by Lord Baldric for his oathbreaking. And then there were his worst dreams, the darkest ones that made him wake Zed and bring Iko running into the bedchamber to make sure he wasn't being murdered. The ones that left him cold and shaking and wide-awake for nights on end. Those were about the godlike creatures he had seen in the Shrine, or about being locked in Endurance House, chained to a wall, screaming as some winged mocker bore down on him to spit poison and dissolve him into a bubbling mass of blood and melting bones.

It made no sense, really, his unreasonable fear of Endurance House. Stormbreaker had never consigned Aron to serve time there, preferring teaching, lectures, and hard physical labor for his discipline. Zed had been to the punishment building several times, as had many others, and they had all come out unmarked and unscarred, though they didn't discuss much about the experience.

It's different for everyone, Zed had told him. *There's nothing there at all. It's just a place to think, to face yourself, and evaluate your choices, that's all. For me, I don't like all the silence and stillness.*

Though at that moment in Aron's life, silence and stillness just might have been welcome.

"You fear you'll see the Brailing Guard and break your word to Stormbreaker and Lord Baldric—and me." Dari's confusion shifted into awareness and at least partial understanding. "You fear your own temper."

Aron looked away from her, toward the chamber door. His jaws locked, and he could offer no response except a rough bunch of breathing as the anger he had worked so hard to shed surged into his chest and up his throat. Even thinking about the Brailing Guard made him consider oathbreaking and vengeance, yes. He had no doubt his urge for retribution would overcome him if he caught even a glimpse of the murderers who had slaughtered his family.

Dari's fingers fluttered against his elbow, and even so long back on this side of the Veil, the contact was almost excruciating. The heat of her fingers on his skin made him twitch and drove his words farther from his own reach.

"But that's why I'm here, Aron. That's why I'm helping you, in case something like that happens. I won't allow you to lose control."

Aron clenched and unclenched his teeth, forcing his mouth to work under its own power once more. He kept his eyes on the door, on escape, and his heart beat faster. "What if you can't stop me, Dari?"

Her fingers fell away from his arm, and her soft laughter cut him as deeply as any dagger. "I don't visit the full strength of my *graal* on you, but only so I don't overwhelm you. If I chose to overtake your essence on the other side of the Veil, you would be powerless to stop me."

Aron blinked at the door, heat rising and waning on his face. He knew from his encounter with Platt that she was probably right, perhaps even understating her abilities. Yet her assertion humiliated him. Strangely, it also soothed him. He didn't know whether to offer her thanks or stalk out of the chamber.

Why did he always feel so confused and stupid in her presence?

"Please don't feel any shame with me." Dari's soft tones made him look at her again, despite his embarrassment. "I know these lessons weren't your choice—that very little has been your choice. But mastering your legacy is perhaps the most important task you have at Stone."

"Why?" Aron almost shoved himself to his feet, then decided that would be childish and kept his seat. "I'm not allowed to use it, and if Lord Baldric has his way, I never will be."

This made Dari sigh, then frown. "I know he's the Lord Provost of Stone, but Aron, your *graal* isn't like Stormbreaker's. My cousin was right. Your mind-talents could be used, I think, if properly controlled."

Aron shook his head, relieved, at least, that his cheeks weren't so hot anymore. "I don't understand."

Dari raised her arms and gestured, like she was drawing down the sky. "Stormbreaker's emotion brings weather to him, or generates aspects of weather where none should exist. Even if he could channel it and direct it against one person, or a group of people—or into some far more benign task such as stopping a dangerous storm— the consequences would be far-reaching for all of Eyrie's climate. We couldn't predict what effect it might have, either locally or across the entire land. There is no such thing as using his *graal* safely. As a rule, there is no controlling a merging of natural phenomena and *graal*. His legacy is more a curse than a useful talent."

Aron still felt hopelessly confused. "And my legacy is useful?"

"It could be." She lowered her arms and let her hands rest in her lap once more. "There are ways to employ it in limited fashion. For example, you could truth-seek when everyone being confident of the truth might facilitate peace or agreement. And you could be present for important meetings, and share with your friends and allies any insight your *graal* gives you—the kind that happen without you even seeking them."

Aron tried to imagine this, then realized in times past, that was probably how Brailings served the ruling lines—when they weren't the ruling line.

"I also believe you could use your *graal* to avoid killing, to save lives." Dari spoke more quietly, as if she might be telling a secret. "Though again, such a use would have to be very limited."

It was all Aron could do not to laugh. "Lord Baldric wouldn't agree with you. Stone never uses unfair advantage. You heard him."

"I'm not talking about hunts or combat, or even Stone business." Dari sighed again, fell silent, then focused her dark, sparkling gaze on Aron's face. "When the time comes, Lord Baldric may not be present to make your choices for you. All I can tell you is, robbing a human being of free choice, truly taking a person's will, is a violation. It could be a murder of the soul. You will never use the full measure of your *graal* without being changed by it. Yet there may come a moment when using it is the right thing, for the greater good of someone else, or even Eyrie itself."

Aron's mouth came open, and it took him several long moments to add up her words in his mind. The embarrassment came creeping back. "I'm an oathbreaker waiting to happen."

Dari narrowed her eyes. "You aren't."

Aron could have sworn he heard the rest, the *not yet* that Dari kindly kept to herself.

"It's still half an hour until weapons practice begins." She tugged at his tunic sleeve. "Try one more time to travel over distance with me. I'll help you—to prove what I say about being able to help you if your resolve weakens."

Aron intended to refuse her, but he wasn't much good at that, and he saw little point in pretending he could walk away from her wishes. So, moments later, he was seated in front of her again, breathing slowly and deeply, pushing himself back toward the Veil. He didn't think he could relax enough to comply with the task she had set for him, but he would try.

Soon enough, the world took on a louder quality, with colors flaring brighter, and the tiniest details of his surroundings growing large and obvious. He could count the legs on the tiny spider spinning its web between Blath's foot and the warmth of the hearth. If he studied the busy creature long enough, he would be able to see the fine hairs on those legs, maybe even smell its acidic, spidery scent. The stones under Blath's feet were dusty. Blath's soft leather boots were dusty, too. His mind was fully on the other side of the Veil now, yet his body remained safe in Dari's bedchamber, contained behind the thick walls of the High Master's Den, and ultimately Triune itself.

Focus, Aron, and be at ease. Dari's thoughts were controlled, muted, almost a whisper, yet commanding nonetheless. *Here. Come with me.*

Aron turned his attention to her, glancing at her only from the corner of his eye, so he wouldn't get caught up in just staring at her. The dull green energy, the disguise she kept around her legacy, blazed a sharp peridot with crimson flecks.

The essence of Aron's head snapped backward as something like red and green fire flowed across him, turning into dozens of hues and shades. It was hot and heavy, pressing in on him—yet cool at the same time. Comforting. Then relaxed and gentle, like the feel of holding Dari's hand.

He risked a full glance at her face, or the strong, sharply defined essence of it, and saw that she was smiling. He was captured by the curve of her lips, the lift of her cheeks, and the depth of her eyes, even though he knew such things weren't exactly real or accurate on the other side of the Veil. Dari seemed as much herself as ever, and he realized that it didn't trouble him as much as it should have, the fact that she had completely overpowered him, taken control of his essence, just as she said she could do.

It's not unpleasant, he thought, forgetting to keep the appropriate guards around his own mind. The words came out loud inside the shell of rainbow light covering them both.

Dari blinked from the noise.

Aron gave her an apologetic look and controlled himself better as she took them out of her bedchamber and lifted their combined awareness over Triune. She kept them below the clouds, as a bird might try to fly if forced into the air during such weather, but of course the patches of mist and rain did not touch them at all. Aron was usually a bit cold on the other side of the Veil, but not this day. Half-absorbed by the sensation of being so close to Dari, wishing he could hear her thoughts to know if she enjoyed being close to him, Aron made himself look at the Stone stronghold below him.

The cloud-choked sunlight that had seemed so gray before he came through the Veil, it was bright now, playing off damp branches and roof thatch. He felt himself squinting, even though he knew his body was well warmed inside the bedchamber, so close to Dari's hearth. To his right, in the clusters of huts that comprised the quarters for the sheltered, children wrapped in rain leathers were already at play or chores, plowing through puddles and mud. Smoke billowed from the main kitchens nearby, along with the smells of baking pies and bread. The archery and knife ranges were deserted, but a small crowd had begun to gather further to the south, toward the horseman's armory. These were the regular apprentices, boys and girls Aron had little contact with, since the apprentices to the High Masters were kept to themselves for living and training.

Aron studiously kept his attention away from the structures on his left. He wouldn't have minded seeing into the House of the Judged or the Judgment Arena to the far south, or even the courtyard of the main gate and keep. It was the structures closer to him, Endurance House and the Shrine of the Mother, that put him off. He was grateful that Dari didn't seem to notice that as she took them higher, through the billowing gray clouds, and higher still, until they broke into the bright morning sky.

The flood of blue-white brightness flowed over Aron, touching him inside and out, filling him with a wild energy and hope he so rarely felt when his awareness was bound firmly into the flesh of his body.

Now you lead, came Dari's urging. *Take us far. Anywhere. Whenever you're ready, imagine us heading toward the ground, through the clouds.*

Aron pulled his mind this way and that, soaring upward, then imagining his arms stretched outward like he might be a Great Roc in flight. Dari's laughter echoed inside their shell of light, along with his own.

I didn't remember this part, the freedom, Aron admitted, carefully modulating the force of his thought so the words would remain quiet and private, within the energy Dari had extended around them both.

It is wonderful—but it can be dangerous to some. Dari always seemed to speak so effortlessly, her voice so calm and flowing. In such moments, Aron's troubles and worries seemed so far away they didn't even feel real to him, and he had no desire to join with them again. *I have known some of my people to stay too long in this state, and never wish to return to their physical essence.*

Aron felt himself drawn to a distant spot in the clouds, a spot his instincts told him lay north and east from Triune, near the midway point of the Scry. He headed toward it. *What happens to them, the Stregans who fly too long on the other side of the Veil?*

The energy they shared surged with a tingling warmth, moving Aron faster toward the clouds below him. *Much like those who grow overly fond of mead, they gradually cease to live normal lives. They lose the people close to them and ultimately waste away until they die.*

Aron contemplated this, easily understanding how such a thing could happen, as they once more plunged into the gray fields of moisture, then emerged into the gray and sullen weather below the clouds. A vast stretch of plains seemed to reach endlessly as far as Aron could see in any direction. *Dyn Cobb*, he said, to himself and aloud as well. *The southern portion.* There were scattered villages instead of clusters of towns like he would have found in Dyn Brailing, no natural stone formations to suggest they were above Dyn Altar, not enough rock to be Dyn Ross, and too much open, treeless space to be Dyn Vagrat or Dyn Mab.

Aron searched the rainy landscape below, looking for what had snagged his instincts so thoroughly. His mind—his legacy—told him to go closer, to take a more narrow view of the ground, so he moved their awareness lower, lower, until individual clumps of trees began to take shape.

Clumps of trees and . . . there. A small village, with a few people out and milling about the streets.

In fact, Aron counted four people, two in a slow-moving wagon and two on horseback. All four were slumped forward against the rain. They were moving toward what looked like an inn.

Dari remained silent as Aron focused on the people, trying to understand why they had drawn his attention. It took some time, but eventually he saw a flash of energy playing about the edges of the wagon. Red energy. A crystalline sort of ruby from the boy in the back—and in the front, from the woman guiding the two ice-crusted oxen, an occasional flash of silver that seemed like something he had seen before. The woman felt . . . familiar, somehow, yet utterly strange to him, too.

Who are those people? Dari asked, and Aron almost shouted from the surprise.

I—I don't know, he answered when he had gathered himself enough to be certain only Dari would hear him. *But I've seen the boy in the back of that wagon before. And the woman—there's something about her I should recognize. At least I think I should.*

He didn't really want to remember, not anything from that terrible night he went after the Brailing Guard. This was important, though. Aron knew enough about legacies now to understand that his mind wouldn't have led him here for no reason.

He tried to go lower, get closer.

At the instant he drew close enough to make out the details of the people below, the silvery energy from the front of the wagon lashed upward and exploded—into the form of a huge hood snake straight from the hot, gritty sands of Dyn Altar.

The essence of Aron's heart went completely still.

The image of the impossible creature filled his awareness. He could see its black head, its huge fangs dripping terrible, stinking venom, even the emerald wickedness of its slitted eyes. Every child in Eyrie knew about hood snakes, at least enough to recognize one if they came across it—and run away as fast as they could.

The snake danced for one second, two seconds, its hood expanding like the wings of some vicious mocker.

We should leave, Dari said in that oh-so-quiet voice, not reflecting an ounce of the terror Aron felt gripping his nonexistent body. Her energy tugged at his. *We should go now, Aron.*

Aron couldn't tear his eyes from the snake's. His energy and essence seemed immobile, as if he had turned to rock on the spot. Fear drained away from him. All emotion. He was nothing now. Just a rock hanging in the sky, waiting to fall. Some part of his mind knew he had felt like this before. The confusion blossoming in his mind felt too frightening. The sense that he would die here, that he might not even care, that was familiar, too.

The snake's red tongue whipped outward as it weaved, seeming to take up the sky, the entire countryside, blocking any view of the people below.

Were there people below?

Aron thought he might have been confused about that. Maybe he had imagined the boy with the ruby legacy, since he had seen such a boy before on the other side of the Veil.

Aron! Dari pulled at him so hard the essence of his shoulder ached from the force.

The snake struck.

Fangs swept toward the essence of Aron's face.

Hundreds of colors blasted across his vision.

Black nothingness swallowed him as he tumbled backward.

A void. The huge darkness he had seen before when he fought the manes the night his family died, and again the night he tried to kill the Brailing Guard. So dark. So cold. And he was falling, shooting downward into nothingness until—

His eyes opened, and he found his awareness once more in his body, as gently as if his own mother had reached down from the heavens and set him back inside his own skin. There was no pain, no confusion, no nothing. Just . . . he was in Dari's bedchamber, and awake, and staring at her, and she was smiling.

Aron didn't know what to say, what to feel, so he just sat where he was, stunned by the warmth of the fireplace and battling a sense of numb unreality.

"Some trick, wasn't it?" Dari's eyes sparkled. "Many of my people couldn't have managed such an image on the other side of the Veil."

Aron just stared at Dari, waiting for her to make sense, hoping he would eventually grasp her meaning.

When she spoke again, she sounded not only admiring, but delighted. "Make no mistake. If I hadn't been with you, she could have killed you, and been within her rights, since she was protecting the weak in her care."

The sudden, dreamy look on Dari's face lit a taper inside Aron, that slow burn of anger he felt more days than not—though he couldn't have said why if Lord Baldric himself were standing over him with swords drawn. "Who? She—who? Dari, I don't understand."

"Couldn't you sense it?" Dari clapped her hands together and stood, letting her gray robe swirl around her ankles. "That was Stormbreaker's sister. That was Tia Snakekiller. He'll be so happy and grateful to know she's alive."

For a moment, Aron was swept up in realizing why the woman in the wagon seemed so familiar yet so strange. Stormbreaker's sister. Of course. Her legacy was somewhat like his in color and force, the sense of her—and yet Aron had never met her in person.

"Blath, get your wrap and mine." Dari gestured toward the trunk at the foot of her bed. "We'll need to hurry to reach Stormbreaker before he's swallowed up by the training day."

The joy on Dari's face stirred a nameless darkness inside Aron. His awe at understanding why Snakekiller had drawn his attention on the other side of the Veil swept out of him, replaced by the bleak bitterness of how much Dari wanted to go to Stormbreaker. It was obvious that all she could think about was being close to Stormbreaker, giving him good news, making him happy.

If she hadn't been standing right in front of him, Aron might have smacked his own head with his fists. Why did he keep letting himself forget the truth where Dari was concerned? Wasn't his stupid legacy supposed to be all about truth?

"How do you know for sure it was Snakekiller we saw?" he grumbled. "We might have been mistaken."

Dari took her wrap from Blath's outstretched hand as Aron got slowly to his feet. "Tonight I want you to meditate on musical notes played together, two notes that match, that have a resonance together. Harmony."

He glared at her, failing to grasp the connection. He wished he could turn himself into the image of a great snake and strike at her happiness over going to Stormbreaker.

"Discerning truth from illusion, prophecy from reality, instinct from the urgings of legacy—this is an advanced skill of *graal* work, one most Fae never achieve." Dari pulled on her wrap but left the hood down. "I believe with work, you could. It's like the feel of two notes harmonizing, the music of sounds blending. Do you understand?"

"Prophecy?" Aron knew he was being surly and picking at small points, knew in fact that he *had* seen a few visions of the future, but he couldn't help himself. She was speaking to him like he was a little boy again. "You know seeing the future is not my talent."

"Seeing bits of what was, what is, what will be—that afflicts everyone with any legacy, though of course those with the Mab mind-talent and the old Lek abilities much worse than others." She was getting impatient now. Aron could tell because she was pulling at the sides of her wrap. "I'll tell you again, we can all do bits and pieces of what another with a legacy can do—a legacy is the ability to perform one talent very, very well. Your legacy is about truth, and you would know for sure that we just saw Tia Snakekiller if you could learn to feel the truth, that harmony. There's a sensation, here."

She put her hand on her belly.

Aron stared at her long fingers and the way they pressed into the soft folds of her robe. "Or here." She moved her hand to her chest. "Or maybe even here." She lifted her fingers to the side of her head. "Or all of them, all at once. A resonance, like two notes played perfectly together on a lyre or lute. Like stars forming a line beside the moons. Think about it."

She smiled anew, and this time, Aron felt the smile was for him. It was enough to ease some of the burning pain forming in his depths, and he suddenly wished he could see the future, at least enough to help her find her sister this night, right now, before she suffered another moment of pain.

But if she finds Kate, she might leave.

More than once, he had considered this possibility, then worried he might unintentionally use his legacy to keep Dari from learning Kate's location. Yet if he was the one who brought Kate safely home to Dari, or led Dari to her sister's hiding place, she would have to realize he was more than some little boy she was tutoring, wouldn't she?

"You should hurry to the horsemen's armory," Dari said. "Time grows short."

And before he could move, she was out the door, Blath trailing silently behind her.

Iko stood in the open doorway, gazing in at Aron with his typical implacable expression.

It took all of Aron's strength not to pound the boy right in his blue face as he stalked out of Dari's bedchamber, just to have something to hit that might feel his punch.

CHAPTER THIRTY-EIGHT

DARI

When winter finally eased completely, Dari found herself glad for the growing warmth, even as tidings of the war worsened. Brailing and Altar soldiers now commanded almost half of Dyn Mab, with no end to the conflict in sight. Canus the Bandit and his forces raged across Dyn Cobb and Dyn Ross, attacking Brailing and Altar Dynast Guard, but also pillaging and looting seemingly at will—if reports from messengers and guardsmen could be believed. With most Cobb and Ross forces committed to defending dynast boundaries, there was little to stand in the way of outlaws, robbers, and Eyrie's most base opportunists.

Spring came and went, with its thaws and endless rains, and Dari's days felt just as endless and gray. She had been at Stone almost two years now, and she had absorbed their rhythms of life almost against her will. She rose with the sun, danced the *fael'feis* in the courtyard of the Den, worked to train Aron, then spent the remainder of her day assisting in the infirmary, the quarters for the sheltered, or the farming quarters. Guild members who could no longer serve in their full capacity transferred into the agricultural section of the compound, so many of Stone's farmers were elderly or disabled, or even dying. At least once every week or two, Dari was called upon to dispatch the spirit of a guildsman or guildswoman who had succumbed to age or illness. Three nights a week, she and Stormbreaker combed the countryside, searching for any sign of Kate. They had covered most of Dyn Brailing and Dyn Altar, and they had begun to traverse the skies of Dyn Cobb.

By the dull, gray morning after the first full moons of summer, she had fallen into a misery even Blath's gentle ministrations could not relieve.

"Get up from that bench and put on your robe." Blath finished working oil through Dari's braids and curled the loose wisps against the side of her face. "You'll be late for Judgment Day."

Dari closed her eyes and remained on the bench positioned before the modest mirror Stormbreaker had hung for her, where it caught the light of the window behind it. Despair worked deep inside her essence, surging and receding like the clouds so common late in Eyrie's rainy season. It seemed to her anguished mind that all the land must be captured in those oppressive clouds. "I don't want to go to the arena." She breathed deeply of the sweet-pepper oil Blath was using, then opened her eyes. She didn't focus on Blath, or the window and weather outside, or even the glass in front of her. Her chamber robes felt tight and uncomfortable, though they were well fitted and spun with the softest thread available inside the walls of Triune. "I don't wish to see anyone. Not today. The air—my thoughts—*something* feels wrong."

Blath made a noise of understanding, and Dari studied her companion's solemn face in the mirror. Blath's skin had tinted a darker blue, as if she, too, felt the unrest hovering above Eyrie. "We could return," she said after a telling pause. "I could take you over the borders myself, with ease."

Dari didn't even bother to refuse the offer. She looked away from the intensity of Blath's dark eyes, unreduced by reflection in the mirror.

"I know you stay for Kate," Blath continued, "but do you also stay for Stormbreaker?"

Studying every stone on the wall beside the mirror, Dari ground her teeth. The question hurt her, though it was fair enough. She spent what little spare time left to her with Stormbreaker, and he didn't send her away. Sometimes they shared a touch or an embrace, even a few more kisses, but in many ways, he remained as strange and unknown as the day she met him.

Blath cleared her throat, bringing Dari's eyes back to her reflection in the mirror. Her brown short-sleeved robes seemed to hang a bit looser, as if their stay at the Stone stronghold was taking some unnamed toll on her physical essence.

"Stormbreaker spoke his truth to you," Blath said.

Such a gentle voice, but such harsh words. Dari wished she could shut out those truths, but knew, in the end, she could not.

"You told me so yourself." Blath's look was as soft as her voice. "His heart lies elsewhere."

"Where?" Dari murmured, finally forcing herself to take stock of her own drawn, worried face. "With whom?"

Of course, Blath had no answer for those questions.

The bells along the castle battlements began to ring, shattering Dari's thoughts and what little calmness she had managed to establish as she spoke with Blath. She didn't hold back her groan. "Another bunch of messengers? Will they never understand that Stone won't take part in this conflict—in *any* fashion?"

"Not messengers." Blath turned away from her to stare out the window, as if she could see each bell along the battlement. Her posture grew more rigid, and the blue in her cheeks darkened yet another shade. "A dynast lord has come to Triune."

Dari stood, her own muscles tightening until rising felt like moving against rock.

A dynast lord. Gods.

She gripped the edges of her sleeping robe and wished she had changed already, after all.

Was this the doom she had been feeling for so many days? Was Lord Brailing mad enough to bring the fight to the gates of Stone?

She joined Blath at the window, and the two of them stared intently into the gray morning light.

"No massing of guildsmen," Blath said, as if taking stock of the threat just as Dari was doing.

Dari gestured to the nearest of the outer walls. "No Stone Sisters taking to the battlements to work their treachery. Perhaps it's no attack. Just a visit."

"We will find out soon enough, if we head to the Arena." Blath's tone of triumph was hard to miss, but Dari knew she was right. Now they would have to go to Judgment Day. Dari couldn't surrender any opportunity to gain information that might lead her to her sister, or a better understanding of the danger and doom that seemed to stalk all of Eyrie.

She was relieved, at least, that there was no visible panic inside Tri-une. Below them, apprentices, Stone Brothers, Stone Sisters, and some of the sheltered milled about, preparing for Judgment Day. Dari saw stable hands heading toward the gates, and cooks with wagons laden with breads and sweets and treats for both the Judged and spectators.

At Stone, no one met death, or even watched death, with an empty belly.

Her gaze drifted eastward, closer to the Den, and fixed on the road between Endurance House and the Shrine of the Mother. Dari narrowed her eyes, then felt them widen with surprise.

Aron was standing with Zed and Iko, directly in front of the Shrine. Beside them stood the little redheaded boy Raaf, the rescued child who often tagged behind Aron. The younger boy had recently gotten word that his father had succumbed to drink and died in the worst of the winter, and she had feared he would take vows at Stone out of sheer grief and hero-worship. This day, though, Raaf looked the calmest in the group.

Iko stood stiff as a blue plank behind Aron, and Zed was pacing.

As for Aron, he seemed unsteady on his feet, lurching forward toward the Shrine, then stumbling back again, letting Iko right him. When she checked, his *graal* was almost fully visible, a blinding halo of sapphire making him a target for any who chose to look through the Veil.

"Something's wrong," Dari murmured.

Blath moved in front of her so quickly Dari felt a sharp breeze across her cheeks. She moved to the side to keep her own view as Blath's lips drew back, revealing whiter-than-white teeth, already getting longer and sharper. A low growl rose in her throat until she saw the source of Dari's additional disquiet.

"Aron, yes," Dari confirmed, and immediately, the signs of Blath's change began to ease.

As her body returned to its normal still state, Blath frowned. "Something is always wrong with that one. His eye is still black, is it not? From another conflict with Galvin Herder?"

Dari clenched her fist at the mention of the ongoing fights between Aron and Galvin. She had asked Stormbreaker to put an end to it a dozen times, but Stormbreaker told her over and over again that Stone apprentices were left to find their own path with one another, and that Aron and Galvin seemed to have some working arrangement.

It's our way, Stormbreaker kept insisting. *They must build their own bonds now, to honor those bonds later.*

Dari seriously doubted Aron was bonding with the older boy, or that he would ever honor the likes of Galvin Herder, but that opinion was met with polite silence from Stormbreaker.

Had Galvin struck Aron again? Perhaps too hard this time?

The bells kept up their announcement, as if to underscore the magnitude of the troubling energy gripping all of Triune. Dari tried to ignore the incessant sound, but the chimes seemed to peal through her skull and chest. "Look at how Aron's moving," she said to Blath. "Zed and Iko are virtually holding him on his feet—and he's scarcely concealing the strength of his legacy."

Without waiting for a response, Dari focused her own mind-talents on Aron, and let her awareness slip through the Veil. The cloud-covered day immediately took on a silvery-white brightness that was almost too much to bear, but she ignored her enhanced vision, her heightened hearing, and the almost overwhelming smells of pies, breads, cakes, roasts, potatoes, sweat, oxen, horses, and even the stinging, acrid whiff of fear billowing up from the House of the Judged. Instead, she let her thoughts, her essence streak toward Aron, meet him, and join with him.

He didn't resist her mental touch, and in fact seemed to welcome the strength she lent him. Images flew at her, of the Shrine, the clouds, of Endurance House, then back to the Shrine again. Waves of frustration boiled off Aron like heated water. His full attention was riveted on the ring of stones, but Dari saw nothing out of the ordinary, with her own perceptions or those she shared with him.

Steady, she told him, and was relieved when he gave her his full attention and began to recover from whatever had addled him. *Go*, she instructed, shielding her words so that only he could hear them on the other side of the Veil. *Stormbreaker will be looking for you at the Arena.*

Dari felt his assent as much as heard it, and let go of her contact with him. As she slid back to normal awareness, she muttered, "Why does he keep returning to that spot? We've examined that shrine hundreds of times."

"There is nothing in that place but rocks and leftover prayers to the Goddess," Blath agreed, as below them the boys began to lope southward, into the teeth of the Judgment Day madness and—Dari realized with a jolt—into the company of a visiting dynast lord they had yet to identify.

She spun to fetch her woolen robes, and began to dress herself as quickly as she could.

Blath was still at the window. "Perhaps," she said, "Aron wants your attention and sympathy more than an understanding of reality. Maybe that's why he spends himself in pursuit of phantoms at the Shrine."

Dari pulled on the gray robe Stormbreaker had fashioned for her on their journey to the castle. "He's just a sad boy, Blath."

"He is almost a grown man," she countered, turning the force of her gaze on Dari, who waved her off.

"He won't even be sixteen until after the first of the year." Dari reached for her summer boots and snagged one with two fingers.

"Which will make him a grown man, and only a bit more than a year younger than you." Blath's stare deepened, and Dari endeavored to keep her focus on her second boot.

When she didn't respond, Blath moved a step closer and spoke even more quietly, yet forcefully. "He has the height of a man now. The thoughts of a man. He is passionate." She paused a moment, then added, "And passingly handsome, as Fae go, which you might have noticed."

Dari jammed her foot into her boot and straightened herself to face Blath. For reasons she couldn't explain, her face felt hot, and she had an urge to let her own fangs grow—at least long enough to give Blath a moment's hesitation before she continued her lecture.

"What are you saying?" Dari asked, hearing the edge in her voice.

Blath's determined expression never shifted. "I am saying that it may be time to pass Aron's training on to someone else." She reached for Dari's arm and let her fingers brush Dari's elbow. "I'm saying—again—that it may be time to leave this place."

Dari swallowed hard. The spot where Blath had touched her burned, as if Blath had imparted some absolute fact, some dire warning, and the universe had chosen to underscore her meaning.

A mix of anger, worry, and affection for Aron lurched through Dari's consciousness, surprising her and confusing her at the same moment. Tears jumbled into her eyes, and more emotion rose to the surface—Kate, and the war, and her long absence from home. How utterly out of place she still felt in the lands of the Fae, and how hopeless she had become about finding her sister.

In that moment, she was closer to agreeing with Blath than ever before.

And in that moment, a knock sounded at her chamber door.

Dari's senses and feelings were so raw and exposed that she knew immediately her callers were Stormbreaker and Windblown. She was struck by a mental image of both men standing outside the wooden door, Stormbreaker with his fist already raised, ready to knock again.

Blath kept up her searching stare, as if willing Dari to tell the men to go away, as if praying Dari might finally agree to depart. To flee Eyrie, and go back to the relative safety of her own people.

Stormbreaker knocked a second time.

The melancholy flood inside Dari slowed to a trickle faster than she imagined possible, and she looked away from Blath, to the smooth gray stone of the chamber wall. "Let them in," she whispered, and tried not to let her tears fall when Blath's face fell into the very picture of disappointment.

Without further comment, Blath complied, moving quickly to the chamber door and admitting Stormbreaker and Windblown. Both men wore their ceremonial robes, a richer, silkier gray than day-to-day garments, and both seemed barely able to contain their agitation.

"Lord Altar has come for an audience, and to witness Judgment Day, as is the right of any dynast lord."

Stormbreaker held himself back for a moment, and Dari knew he was giving her time to absorb his words.

Lord Altar.

Lord Altar, here.

Why?

"Lord Baldric would like you to attend the meeting in his chambers," Windblown finished, tugging at the chain around his neck. "He wants Aron present, too."

Dari's mouth came open. "That's far too dangerous! What if Lord Altar grasps his identity and informs Lord Brailing of Aron's whereabouts?"

Stormbreaker seemed ready for her objections and held up both hands. "That's unlikely. Aron's more Stone than Brailing now, and you'll be present to make sure he keeps his *graal* concealed. Lord Altar has no reason to be searching for Aron, least of all in the heart of Lord Baldric's study, under his very nose. The need outweighs the risk."

There was truth in that assertion that Dari couldn't deny, even though she wished to find some reasonable objection. If Lord Altar had made the journey to Triune, the Stone Guild needed all the assistance they could recruit to determine his true purpose, and the level of danger his interest posed.

"We'll keep you safe," Stormbreaker said. "Windblown and I will serve as your protectors in Blath's absence. Lord Altar will think nothing of two High Masters being present for this meeting."

Dari's jaw clenched, then set, and she knew she was starting to glare. Not this again. Not Stormbreaker treating her like some fragile bit of flower in need of a pair of swordsmen to defend her.

Did he not see her for what she was—for all she was?

The tears that had been gathering behind her eyes all morning finally spilled over, but she swept past Stormbreaker before he could see her emotion, out of her chamber, and into the hallway.

"See to finding Aron, and ensuring his safety," she called over her shoulder as she stormed toward the steps that led down to the Den entrance. "I can take care of myself."

CHAPTER THIRTY-NINE

DARI

Dari seated herself on the hearth of a dormant fireplace and assumed the posture of a dedicated servant, a Ross pigeon in attendance simply to be certain no souls needed dispatching from Lord Baldric's chamber this day. His rooms were cool but well lit, with the shutters open, and the air still smelled of the cedar logs he had burned for warmth in the winter. Dari breathed deeply of the comforting smell as she fingered the knitted sock in her palm, grateful that some seamstress had already finished the project. Lord Baldric, who was pacing in front of her, had given her some needles and yarn to toy with—as if she had any idea how to make a proper stitch. Sewing had been Kate's province, not hers. She preferred daggers to needles.

"Lift it here," Lord Baldric grumbled as he stopped his frenetic walking, gesturing to a spot midway on his own chest, as if he might have knitted the sock in Dari's hands himself. The image made her smile, but Lord Baldric didn't return her expression. The depth of his frown was matched only by the rusty red flush outlining his cheeks. He stalked to his formidable desk and took a seat in his wood and leather chair. He made for quite an imposing figure, bedecked in his own ceremonial gray robes, but Dari thought at any moment the many *benedets* marking his face would crawl right off his skin. The two of them were alone, awaiting the arrival of Stormbreaker, Windblown, and Aron. Once everyone had arrived, Lord Baldric would summon Lord Altar.

"I'm weary with so many visits." Lord Baldric leaned against his chair so hard the wood creaked. "So many requests. Every messenger purports to carry tidings of Stone's best interests, but it's the interests of the writers that will be most truly served if I comply with any of them."

Dari knew better than to make a comment. Lord Baldric had vowed many times, with increasing volume and vitriol, that Stone would in no way be drawn into the war.

"This bastard, he'll be wanting some assurance or promise or the other, mark my words." Lord Baldric's voice grew louder with each word. One of his big fists rested atop the desk, and Dari thought he might have been more comfortable if he could have held a throwing knife in his tight grip.

The door to the chamber opened, and Stormbreaker hurried in, leading Windblown, Aron, and Zed. Dari glanced at Stormbreaker's worried expression, but it was Aron's appearance that gave her a jolt.

It wasn't so much his pallor or the circles beneath his earnest sapphire eyes, but other changes that drew her attention. Changes Blath had alluded to, but that Dari had somehow failed to notice. As her heart skipped from the shock of her realizations, she had to acknowledge that Aron had indeed grown as tall as Stormbreaker and Zed now, though he kept a lean, lanky awkwardness. His face, though—it was no child's face. Not anymore. There was a sharpness to the powerful line of his jaw, and his nose had developed the slight curve often associated with Fae nobility. His right eye was still green-blue from his last battle with Galvin Herder, and Dari had little doubt he had other bruises and scrapes too serious for simple healing by *graal*. Still, he gave no hint of discomfort or soreness.

No hint of weakness. Seeing the totality of him, of his aging and changes, made her chest ache for the wide-eyed and gentle boy he had been. *Stone is making him hard.*

The thought rested painfully inside her for a moment; then she chastised herself for once more forgetting where she resided. At Triune. With a guild full of assassins. Of course their training was toughening Aron. It had to be so, or he'd be killed in his trial, or by his Judged when he drew his first stone.

He came to her quickly with Zed behind him, keeping his gaze fixed on her face, and once more, Dari saw something that she must have been missing all this time. A slight blaze of affection, and of something like hope, too. Dari shifted on the hearth as Aron sat on her right, and Zed on her left. Zed's nod was pleasant, but he regarded her as nothing more than a friend, just a companion at Stone. Aron, on the other hand, kept up an almost painful scrutiny of every move she made.

"What did you see at the Shrine?" she asked Aron, more to defuse her own tension than to discover information.

As Windblown left to summon Lord Altar, Stormbreaker and Lord Baldric conversed in low tones. Aron kept his gaze on them as he said, "Nothing distinct. It was like always. I saw images of . . . something, but what, it's hard to say."

Aron closed his bright eyes for a moment, and when he opened them, Dari knew he was holding something back. Perhaps he had grown weary of not being believed, or at the very least, of having no proof with which to support his claims of visions at the Shrine. A vague guilt seized Dari, and she found herself staring too deeply into Aron's face, as if she might absorb the truth of what he had seen—if it was anything beyond the physical manifestation of his own fears.

Why would he see it, and no one else? His legacy is powerful, but no greater than my own graal.

As Dari finished the thought, she found herself wondering for the first time if she might be mistaken about the extent of Aron's abilities.

Was it possible that any Fae could have mind-talents as powerful as a Fury's skills?

And if that were true, what kind of disaster might she foment in continuing his training?

He was staring at her now, and the sparkle in his eyes reached her awareness. She looked away, feeling heat in her face. It took several breaths to center herself from the series of shocks over all the realities she had failed to comprehend.

She glanced at Zed on her other side, but he was combing his blond forelock with his fingers, acting as if he heard not a word they had exchanged.

Kate's been the only important thing. Kate . . . and Stormbreaker. And all this time, Aron's been here, getting older and stronger, and perhaps more dependent on me than I ever should have allowed.

She had barely regained her emotional footing when the chamber door sprang open. In strode Windblown, who quickly stepped aside to admit a tall, heavily muscled man with weathered skin, white-blond hair, and eyes the color of a deep, crystalline lake. He wore copper-colored robes trimmed with steel gray, and he bore matching tattoos on either side of his neck—the image of a Great Roc with wings spread, a sword in one set of talons and arrows in the other. His essence shimmered about his head and shoulders like brilliant copper waves, and his presence was so commanding that Dari had to force herself to remain still.

Hunter, her instincts screamed, and the more primitive part of her nature wanted to flee or fight him, here and now. In days of old, Fae with the Altar *graal* of tracking prey were the closest thing her people had to natural enemies.

"Lord Bolthor, Altar of Altar." Lord Baldric stood and offered a polite bow first, though he was not obligated to do so in his own stronghold. Stormbreaker bowed as well, as did Windblown.

Lord Altar did not bow in return. Bleak anger seemed to emanate from his scarred face and clenched fists, as powerful as his *graal*. Dari sensed distrust, determination—and something else.

Something like . . . defensiveness? Shame?

Lord Altar turned toward Dari before she could look away from him. Even as she dropped her eyes to the sock and yarn clutched in her hands, she felt him appraise her, give Aron and Zed passing attention, then return the force of his focus to her.

His attention felt like clawed nails scraping down her senses.

Hunter. Hunter!

She had no doubt if she raised her eyes, she would see a manic, barely controlled expression on Lord Altar's face. It would be the look of those with the Altar legacy when they were on the hunt and had caught scent of their quarry.

"By the Brother's grace, Baldric—a Ross pigeon?" Lord Altar's voice issued in the powerful, gravelly bass Dari expected from such a man. "Do you plan to do killing in these chambers today?"

"She is pledged to Stone and stays near me most of the time." Lord Baldric lied with a grace and fluidity Dari had to admire. He came around his desk to stand beside his guest, keeping Stormbreaker and Windblown on his far side. "Pay her no more heed than the apprentices."

Lord Altar grumbled something unintelligible to himself, then turned his back on Dari, Aron, and Zed.

Dari's mind reeled off the nickname *Rockiller*, which she knew Lord Altar had earned in his Guard service, fighting the many lawless, rebellious tribes that populated the deserts of his dynast. *Warbirds*, his people were called, with good reason. It was said if Altars ran out of bandits and enemies, they'd turn on one another just to have someone to fight.

After seeing this dynast lord in the flesh, Dari could believe that. She dared a quick glance at the fearsome man.

How easy it must have been for Lord Brailing to draw this man into his treachery. Lord Altar seemed to be a war waiting for a battlefield.

Aron, on the other hand, had gone so still Dari actually looked at his chest to be certain he was breathing. She checked the color of his legacy to visible eyes—dull, with barely a dollop of sapphire. He was doing so well with this disguise, it seemed almost second nature to him now. The lines of his face remained smooth, and his expression was one of polite disinterest. Another disguise, because his eyes . . .

The white-blue blaze in his slightly narrowed eyes . . .

Dear gods and goddesses. Dari's muscles tightened, as if readying for battle against her will. *There may be murder today, after all.*

Lord Altar's deep voice rose over the racket of her mind as he announced, "I've come to watch Judgment Day, to see the killing of the rapist who sullied my niece."

Lord Baldric straightened a little at this announcement. "Laird Reese. Yes."

"I have his stone." Stormbreaker rested his hand against a leather bag tied to his waist.

For the briefest of moments, Lord Altar gave his attention to Stormbreaker. "Very well. See that you don't waste it."

Once more, Dari checked Aron's essence. She saw no flickers of energy or other indications that he might be losing emotional control, despite the fact he had just learned the Stone Guild would be doing something to aid a man he considered complicit in the murder of his family. His body remained equally placid. As before, the only indication Dari had of his true feelings was the furious gleam in his eyes.

"Why is Canus the Bandit not up for trial this day?" Lord Altar demanded, keeping his back to the hearth.

Both Aron and Zed seemed to take interest in this question. They shifted forward and seemed to be listening more intently.

Lord Baldric's color deepened, and Dari saw him dig his fingers against his palm. "We have received no judgment on him from any dynast. As far as Stone knows, his deeds are as much rumor as reality. We cannot hunt an unconvicted phantom."

Lord Altar swore, then reached into his robes and withdrew a folded bit of parchment. "A decree from the Court of Altar at Can Olaf, convicting the outlaw of his crimes in my lands. *Now* you have a judgment against the outlaw, and shortly one will follow from Lord Brailing, and perhaps Lord Cobb as well."

Dari's teeth ground together at the thought that Lord Cobb might be cooperating with Lord Brailing and Lord Altar in any fashion, even in a matter where they shared common concern.

Lord Altar put the parchment on Lord Baldric's desk and thumped it with two fingers. "This bandit is no better than a desert sand-rat, murdering soldiers and raiding villages. And he has followers. Growing numbers. I want him stopped."

Lord Baldric picked up the parchment, studied it, then placed it back on his desk. "And so he will be. If he can't be brought in, his charges will be read In Absence."

"That takes time!" Lord Altar's shout thundered through the rock chamber, but no one in the room flinched.

"It does," Lord Baldric said in a calm, overly quiet voice, and Dari couldn't help noticing that the Lord Provost wasn't using the honorific of *Chi* to append any of his statements. "Unless he can be captured, we have no alternative but to make a reading every cycle, until at least six readings have been completed. Then and only then can we draw stones for him and begin the hunt."

"That is unacceptable," Lord Altar growled. "Canus the Bandit is dangerous. He's a monster!"

Stormbreaker and Windblown coughed at the same moment and lowered their gazes. Lord Baldric seemed to have to gather his wits before responding, as if taken aback by hearing Lord Altar call anyone else *outlaw* or *monster*. Dari could hardly blame him for that. Aron remained in his oddly calm state, but that light in his eyes was brighter than ever.

When Lord Baldric at last decided on his words, he said, "Canus the Bandit may indeed be dangerous, but he is also a man, a citizen of Eyrie, with the right to fair reading, and a chance to present himself for Judgment Day."

Lord Altar grabbed the edges of his robes, making a show of controlling his temper. "Stone shouldn't tarry in this process. I wouldn't be surprised if he turned out to be responsible for that unpleasantness along the Watchline."

Dari moved before her mind completely processed the words, grabbing Aron's wrist with one hand even as she forced her consciousness through the Veil. She gave herself less than a second to adjust to the brightness, the enhanced sounds and images of her increased perception; then she let her strength blend with his, lending him soothing and self-control and deliberately muting the color of both of their legacies.

He accepted her intervention with no resistance or resentment, but moments later, his eerie-calm mental voice echoed across her awareness. *Thank you, Dari, but I'm fine.*

She immediately realized Aron had carefully contained that thought-message, so that only she could hear it. She didn't believe him, though. Not even for the second it took her to return to normal levels of awareness.

Stormbreaker's face was as passive as Aron's, and Windblown seemed to be pretending he hadn't heard the dynast lord correctly.

Lord Baldric, on the other hand, was glaring at Lord Altar with no further pretense of politeness. "Unpleasantness?" The question was so tight and pointed that Dari felt the stab in her own belly. She wondered if Lord Baldric might end up as one of the Judged for slicing a dynast lord's throat.

Lord Altar's face colored an even deeper, uglier red than Lord Baldric's. "I know what you think. You and every bastard behind these walls—but it's not true. I had no part in that madness."

"You had no part in stopping it, either," Lord Baldric snarled, leaning toward Lord Altar until Windblown caught the Lord Provost's robes from behind.

Lord Altar's fist drew back so quickly Dari couldn't believe Stormbreaker managed to lunge forward and catch the man's elbow before he swung. The dynast lord wheeled to face Stormbreaker and cursed him even as Stormbreaker let him go and bowed his apology for laying hands on a noble without permission. Stormbreaker made no attempt to challenge the furious man again, and Windblown kept his gaze respectfully averted.

Lord Baldric did not, and when Lord Altar once more looked the Lord Provost of Stone in the face, Dari caught a wave of the shame she had sensed earlier.

"I joined forces with Helmet Brailing to do what must be done for Eyrie—not to murder fools and simpletons." Lord Altar's tense face relaxed a little, lending the barest of credence to his assertion.

Aron moved on the hearth, making Dari jump so badly she dropped her false knitting project and had to snatch it back off the floor. She almost leaped through the Veil again, but Aron's outward calmness remained intact. It was almost as if he had forged a full metal fighting shield out of thin air and the force of his will, and now had it firmly between his heart and anything Lord Altar might say. For that, at least, she was greatly relieved.

"If Stone had true mettle," Lord Altar added, raising both hands, palm upward, as if he were pleading with the furious Lord Provost, "every guildsman who could bear arms would march out of Triune with me and help us finish this war for the good of Eyrie."

Lord Baldric didn't struggle against Windblown's grasp, but he swore before declaring, "Stone will not be a party to war. Not now, and not ever. We're a guild, not an army."

"Thorn is taking a broader view." Lord Altar wisely moved a few steps toward the chamber door, away from the Lord Provost. He brushed Stormbreaker out of his path with a single sweep of one arm. "My cousin Pravda has ordered Thorn to offer aid to Altar and Brailing soldiers, should we choose to send them into Dyn Vagrat. It's either that or deal with the armies of Mab and Ross."

"Your *cousin* may do as her conscience allows, I suppose, even when her guild charters demand otherwise." Now Lord Baldric's words were condescending, and something beyond angry and disgusted. He jerked himself free of Windblown's grasp, and Dari didn't know whether to keep herself seated or leap to her feet and prepare to draw weapons. "Family ties are supposed to be severed and forgotten when guild vows are taken, but perhaps Thorn has let go that tradition as well."

Lord Altar seemed to hesitate. When he continued he sounded even more like he might be pleading—or as close to pleading as a man like him ever came. "Gemelle Mab has been fragile since her childhood. You know this, Baldric. Everyone does. She cannot bear the burdens that have been laid upon her." He gestured toward the chamber's north window, as if to point all the way to Can Rowan. "If she would listen to reason and allow the Circle to truly assist her with the rule of Eyrie, I would stop this campaign now."

Lord Baldric didn't grace those comments with a retort, but Dari couldn't help staring at Lord Altar, relieved that he couldn't see her in return. She could scarcely believe anything she was hearing. The oddly gentle tone, not the words he spoke, came near to stunning her senseless.

Did Lord Altar actually care about Lady Mab, in some personal sense?

A memory nudged at her, far in her mind's distance. Something she had heard in childhood a few times.

Yes. I remember now. A tale of how Lord Altar in his youth had tried to woo Lady Mab, but failed. She wasn't interested in a man so much her senior, and her attention had already been captured by the man who would become her husband.

Could that old story possibly have some truth to it?

And all these years hence, was Lord Altar still obsessed with a woman who had spurned him?

She had no time to ponder the possibility or its implications, because Lord Altar had decided his audience was at an end. To Lord Baldric, he said, "Remember my words. If you ever have a chance to persuade Lady Mab to listen to reason, take it." Then he nodded to Stormbreaker, as if suddenly remembering the Stone Brother existed. "And you—fight well. I want blood for my niece's pain and insult."

Stormbreaker gave the dynast lord a polite bow as Lord Altar proceeded past him, to the chamber door, and out into the hallway, letting the heavy wood slam into place behind him.

No one spoke.

No one so much as moved, except Aron.

Dari watched him stand and bring himself to his full height.

Stormbreaker was watching Aron, too, his handsome face taut with concern. Windblown had his hand on his sword hilt, as if he might have to draw his blade to keep Aron in check. Lord Baldric and Zed didn't seem as concerned, but both remained silent and alert.

"He was truthful in all he said, except the bit about Canus the Bandit being responsible for the Watchline massacre." Aron's essence remained calm, at least on the surface, and his disguise of dull colors, perfect in every respect. "He well knows who ordered those killings, though he may not have been directly involved—and I don't believe he approves of what Lord Brailing did."

The conciseness of Aron's report surprised Dari as much as its contents. She had been so distracted by worry over Aron's reactions that she sensed little from Lord Altar other than anger and aggression, and that last bit of weird affection for Lady Mab. As she stood and took her place beside him, she was captured by a moment of admiration and pride, that Aron had used his legacy so efficiently, and concealed it so very well.

"I have nothing to add," she admitted to Lord Baldric. "Aron read Lord Altar better than I did."

Lord Baldric clenched his jaw, then released it and spoke more to Stormbreaker than anyone else. "Altar's displeasure with Brailing's crime wasn't sufficient to sway him from allying with the old bastard to start a war. If I'm not here when this is all over and the recriminations begin, remember that."

"Lord Altar believes the war is necessary," Aron said, keeping his gaze on the door. "He believes he's right, and that we're all fools or cowards here at Triune."

"Cayn take him and his Thorn cousin, too," Lord Baldric snapped, waving a hand to dismiss them all.

As Aron waited for Stormbreaker and Windblown to exit ahead of him, he seemed absolutely in control of himself, except for the way he stared out the now-open wooden chamber door—as if he could see through halls and walls and track Lord Altar's every move. His fingers, long fingers, a man's fingers, twitched as if his entire essence itched to take an action he knew he had to avoid.

Blath was more right about Aron than I imagined. Perhaps than even she imagined. Dari studied Aron with a new and anxious wariness.

Aron was almost grown. Soon enough, Lord Altar and Lord Brailing might make his acquaintance more directly, and discover that for themselves.

CHAPTER FORTY

DARI

The six stone pillars marking the Judgment Arena loomed like gray arms reaching toward the morning sun. Dari eyed them as she approached. Her heart pounded louder with each step, drowning out the happy chatter of sheltered boys who liked to help out on Judgment Day.

Triune's lower grounds overflowed with apprentices and Stone Brothers making preparations. By now, the Stone Sisters in residence would have withdrawn to guard the living quarters of the sheltered, as many who sought refuge at Stone would not feel safe out on the grounds when the public was permitted inside, even only as far as the arena. Abused women, children who had fled their homes in terror—Stone determinedly fended off any lingering threat to those they accepted for protection.

Dari wanted to stop at the House of the Judged, a large building on the north side of the arena. She usually remained there with a handful of older Stone Brothers to dispatch the spirits of the dead, as need arose, because she had no interest in watching combat. Worse yet, if Stormbreaker was involved in one of the fights, she would have to live through each blow and strike, and feel it nearly as if it were her own.

Today, though, she had no option about attending, thanks to Lord

Altar's visit. She had to go into the arena and keep an eye on Aron, since Iko couldn't very well show himself to the multitudes without creating a total political disaster for Lord Baldric.

Dari kept her feet firmly on Triune's main byway, and moved with the increasing swell of castle occupants heading southward toward the arena's entrance. The younger children beside her were all laughter and bluster, but the older sheltered and the few Stone Brothers had grim expressions to match her own. This was no festival, despite the busy, noisy atmosphere. Men would die today—women, too, though women amongst the Judged were few. Dari had noted that for a woman to be given over to Stone for judgment, her crimes had to be heinous indeed, and Stone Sisters usually took the draw for such cases. Even behind the walls of Triune, where some of the fiercest female warriors in the land resided, the unspoken code of men that prohibited them from harming women remained a powerful force. It was difficult to persuade a Stone Brother to pick up weapons to strike down a woman, no matter how many people that woman might have murdered.

The arena's gates stood open, and the sight of the barrier made Dari's chest that much tighter. She slipped inside with the other spectators, then sought a view of the roof of the House of the Judged, barely visible over the north wall, to get her bearings. The Judged, who had been carried to Triune in barred wagons across the cycle, would enter from a small gate in that wall. Beside the smaller gate, there was a set of rooms where the Stone Brothers and Stone Sisters readied themselves to perform their duties. Apprentices sat on benches outside the rooms, prepared to assist their masters as needed.

This is barbaric and foolish, insisted the part of Dari's mind still rooted in her own culture, where crime was rare and murder almost nonexistent. Stregans dispatched murderers immediately, or rather her cousin Platt did, as was his duty as king. This business of reading charges, of giving the accused an opportunity for a second judgment from the gods and goddesses—that was laughable to Platt, to all of her people. A sign of Fae weakness. Dari herself had believed this without question, until she came to Triune.

Now she saw that the process had a certain elegance. A fairness to it. The Judged were at a disadvantage, in that they were pitted against trained assassins who would fight them to the death, or hunt them to the same ends. To Dari, this was as it should be. Those who murdered or raped or pillaged at weapon point deserved no level battlefield. Yet the Judged *did* have a chance. If fate chose to shield them, or give them good fortune, if somehow they deserved some second opportunity at right living, granted by whatever deity they claimed as their own, they might receive it.

But today Stormbreaker faces combat with a vicious rapist, a desert rat who's probably killed more people than any Stone Brother. If that rat receives his second chance at Stormbreaker's expense, how then will I feel about these customs?

Dari rubbed her palm against her chest as she edged through the crowd inside the arena gates, slipping behind the small fence separating the arena's dirt surface from the stone and wood benches built in tiers into the arena walls. She moved closer to the small gate and ready rooms, until she spotted Aron taking his position on the bench right next to Zed, as she expected. She checked the color of his essence, pleased to find it was still a dull, disinteresting shade of blue. By Aron's posture, he was still calm, but focused on his day's duties, which gave her some measure of relief. Galvin Herder sat on the far end of Aron's bench, but to Dari's relief, his attention appeared to be completely diverted by the day's demands.

Perhaps he'll stay too interested or too busy to make more trouble today. Dari picked at her thumbnail with her teeth. Not far away on her right, Lord Altar and his traveling party took their seats in one of the six partially enclosed areas reserved for dynast nobles. The walls encasing them on either side bore the steel and copper colors of Altar, and the back panel had been decorated with sword crossed with arrow, clutched in the talons of a great white Roc—just like the tattoos on Lord Altar's neck.

Dari couldn't help noticing how out of place Lord Altar seemed, despite his fierce, angry countenance and the way he glared at the gate where the Judged would enter. From what Lord Baldric had told her, it wasn't unusual for members of a noble line to attend Judgment Day, but exceedingly rare in these days for a dynast lord to be present himself. The arena crowd, comprised of the sheltered and people from nearby towns who found this process amusing, milled in slow groups, staring up at Lord Altar and his retinue.

Meanwhile, handfuls of goodfolk in travelers' clothing filed into the seats nearest the arena floor, and Dari knew these were the family and friends of the murdered, raped, or grievously injured, come to see justice done. Many of these would have ridden for days or even weeks to arrive, and there were no smiles amongst this sad, tired group.

Dari's heart went out to those poor souls who had been so wronged. She settled herself on a strip of wood where she had an easy view of both Aron and Lord Altar, but her attention kept returning to the travelers.

"What's he doing here, y'think?"

The voice startled Dari so badly she almost bit the tip of her thumb clean off.

When she looked at the seat beside her to see who spoke, she realized it was Raaf Thunderheart. Like Aron, Raaf had gotten older, seemingly when she wasn't looking. He had fewer freckles, more pounds and muscles, and his red hair was shoulder length now. She tried to make herself smile at the boy, but the gleam in his eyes, obviously from anticipation of the day's events, made her want to sigh. Every day, Raaf grew more caught up in the life of Triune, in being

Aron's little tagalong, and no doubt he drew closer to taking vows at Stone.

And why did that bother her? Stone offered many an honorable profession, she had decided. Necessary in the structure of Fae life and society. But Raaf knew nothing of other options, and that ignorance of choices bothered Dari.

"Today brings justice for Lord Altar's niece," she said, hoping that would appease the boy's curiosity.

Raaf looked at Lord Altar again. "Seems to me the likes of him, he'd have other reasons to be here. Now, I mean. Instead of out on the battlefield."

Dari gave Raaf a longer, more discerning look, even checking once more to be certain he had no significant amount of legacy. "Very few lords actually fight with their armies," she countered, relieved and disappointed to find nothing special in the color of Raaf's essence.

Raaf seemed oblivious to the close brush of her mind-talents. "Lord Brailing fights with his army. Aron says it's madness and meanness that drives him."

Dari coughed and glanced around to be certain no townspeople were close enough to hear the boy's disrespect. "Lord Cobb and Lord Ross often fight alongside their Dynast Guard," she said, lowering her voice in an attempt to lead Raaf to do the same.

"Courage, Aron says, drives those two." Raaf spoke just as loudly, still staring openly at the steel-and-copper-colored viewing box where Lord Altar waited. "So what does that make him up there? A coward, a cautious man—or up to something?"

Aron shouldn't have spoken so freely in front of this boy—in front of anyone outside the Den. "Perhaps today, Raaf, Lord Altar is only an uncle who wants to see his niece's rapist put to death."

Raaf looked as though he was getting ready to debate with her, but Triune's bells began to ring. Three long, dolorous notes. A pause. Three more sad notes, another pause, then three more after that.

The Call to Judgment.

No other bell sequence sounded so formal, or so final to Dari's ear.

The ringing of the bells crushed the crowd's talk. Bits of words and phrases just spoken lingered in Dari's mind, echoes of the liveliness that had seconds ago surrounded her—now every bit of it had been converted to unnatural silence. Almost as one, onlookers found seats, and all eyes turned toward the gate where the Judged would enter.

On his bench, Aron sat straight and still, also staring at the door.

When it swung open, Lord Baldric stepped into the fiery blue-white sunlight, carrying a long parchment. He let the wooden gate slam firmly closed behind him, the sound like the crash of a mallet against a tree trunk.

He's walking on the blood of hundreds, even thousands, of men and women. Dari sucked down a thick breath of early-summer air, and waited for him to reach the center point in the oval. *How many Stone Brothers or Sisters have died across the centuries, right where his boots now tread? How many criminals have perished on the same spots?*

Odd, that connection between Stone and its many Judged. They bled the same. They died the same. Did anyone at Triune ever pause to give that reality some serious consideration?

Aron's firm, placid expression gave her the answer.

Of course not.

As far as Stone was concerned, this was inevitable, and decreed by both courts and fate, and absolutely right.

The doorway to the ready rooms opened as well, and Stone Brothers and one Stone Sister Dari recognized as the tall, willowy, blonde called Marilia Deadeye filed out to stand behind the apprentice bench. Each wore their traditional gray robes and scabbards crisscrossed over their backs. Sword hilts rose like horns from behind their shoulders, and Dari knew each guild member also carried at least one dagger. They, like their potential prey, were allowed to bring up to four weapons of their choice into combat.

"There's Stormbreaker in the front," Raaf said, disrupting Dari's firm attempt not to look directly at the Stone Brother's face.

When she did, she immediately wished she hadn't.

His squared stance and folded arms made him seem otherworldly, and his emotionless expression made him that much more enigmatic and handsome.

Dari tried to breathe, but found her chest too tight. Her fingers worked into a tangle with one another, jumping in her lap like some child's captured frogs.

Raaf put his hand atop hers and patted her once. "He'll come out the winner," the boy murmured so quietly his words seemed like nothing but a bit of breeze. "He always does."

Dari glared at the boy, then immediately felt ashamed of herself when his cheeks colored and he snatched his hand back before adding, "I've come to every Judgment Day since we got here, that's all. I've seen Master Stormbreaker with his blades. Nobody can beat him."

"Good," she whispered.

"Most sword battles are over in just a few seconds," Raaf went on. "The first blow landed—it's usually the last."

Enough, Dari wanted to shout, but she somehow held her peace. Her chest squeezed tighter and tighter, and it was all she could do not to make some sign against ill fortune, like a superstitious Fae.

Lord Baldric came to a halt in the center of the arena, pushed up the sleeves of his spotless gray robe, and unfurled his parchment. In his gruff, booming bass, he gave the traditional statement that marked the true beginning of Judgment Day.

"Be it known that we have gathered here on the morning after full moons, in the fourth cycle, in the year one thousand forty-eight from the founding of Eyrie, to seek justice and pass sentence on the Judged."

As Dari forced herself to study Aron or Lord Altar or Raaf,

anyone but Stormbreaker, Lord Baldric read seventeen names, all male, and listed crimes that ranged from repeated robbery to rape to murder or murders. He added dates to each crime, then announced the date of conviction, and the dynast court that issued the writ against each Judged.

The entire time he spoke, no one in the crowd uttered so much as a whisper. Raaf remained motionless beside Dari, and she was overly aware of how loud her own breathing seemed in the freakish quiet.

When he completed his list, the apprentice nearest the gate— Aron—stood, walked quickly to the closed barrier, and pounded his fist against the wood three times. Before he got back to his seat on the bench, the gate once more swung wide to admit seventeen Judged. They filed in one after the other, walking without chains or shackles, and they wore the clothing they came with, varied in design and tradition, but all clean and in good repair. Three had swords from Stone's own armory, and bulges in their tunics and breeches suggested concealed weapons. Dari knew that these, at least, would fight. The other fourteen men seemed twitchy and overly focused on the gates, and Dari figured these would elect to flee and take their chances.

Indeed, Lord Baldric then read fourteen of the seventeen names, and those men stepped forward. "These are the Judged who have chosen flight. In the order that I spoke your name, do you have anything to say on your behalf?"

Each man denied the accusations against him. Dari couldn't listen to their explanations or speeches. She didn't care what they had to say, only that Laird Reese, the name of Stormbreaker's Judged, hadn't been included with that list. So he must be one of the three men remaining.

One of the three very seasoned-looking opponents who planned to fight their way out of condemnation.

Dari wished Raaf would take her hand again, but she didn't want to appear weak or stupid, seeking comfort from a child.

Stormbreaker is a Stone Brother. He knows how to handle himself.

She tried to make her muscles relax.

But it's not impossible.

Dari squeezed her eyes closed.

For the sake of all the gods, stop this chatter in your own head!

She made herself look at the Judged again, and chastised herself a few more times for her worry as Lord Baldric read two more names and sets of charges, and noted that these were men charged In Absence—convicted, but hiding from Judgment Day, not yet captured. Even this strategy couldn't delay Stone forever.

"This is their third reading, and this day, they join those who flee." Lord Baldric's statement was simple enough. The men In Absence, having been given ample chance over the past year to present themselves at Triune, or surrender to a Stone guildhouse, were now to be hunted, whether or not they knew their doom was coming.

"Upon the next ringing of the bells, the gates of this Arena and the gates of Triune will be opened. Leave as you will. You will not be watched or followed. At this same time tomorrow, the bells will ring again, and you will be hunted by all fair means. May fate favor the truly innocent."

A few of the Judged who planned to run looked smug, even excited, but most already had the wide eyes of prey too close to fangs and claws. Every Fae in Eyrie knew that combat offered a chance of survival, however small, but flight almost always resulted in death on some random and lonely night in the future. Still, more often than not, criminals fled, as if each hour they remained free and alive gave them power and bettered their odds of victory.

Moments later, the bells along Triune's battlements gave another trilogy of jangling rings. Dari's gaze returned to Stormbreaker, and her heart seemed to jump with each beat of clapper to sound bow.

At that moment, she would have traded her own breath for Stormbreaker's Judged to be leaving with the rest. Aron, on the other hand, his lanky frame and tousled hair almost glowing in the day-bright sun, looked eager for combat to begin. So did little Raaf, hanging at the edge of his seat beside her.

Dari wanted to slap them both.

Each time she took a breath, she smelled dirt and sweat and fear and excitement. She smelled soaps and perfumes from nearby onlookers, and even a hint of the roasts Triune's kitchens must be preparing for lunch.

The thought of a normal meal on Judgment Day seemed awry to Dari, and she couldn't reconcile what her senses told her with what her mind knew was about to happen.

The gates opened.

Most of the criminals ran from the arena, while three sauntered out at their own pace. Dari watched their slow egress, and realized they must have some plan or plot. They must believe they had their battle won, or not care about the outcome. She had no other explanation for why they would waste a single precious second in getting clear of Triune.

The moment the last of the men walked through the arena's big gates, the wooden barrier swung shut, sealing off the field of battle.

Dari's breath deserted her once more, until her throat threatened to crush itself along with her chest.

Don't let him be first.

Or last.

Gods, resolve this some other way and don't make him fight at all.

Once more, she wove her fingers together and squeezed her own hands.

Not first. Not first.

She didn't want to see this. She didn't want to watch.

But there was Aron, little farther from Lord Altar than most apprentices could toss a rock. He was still peaceful and focused, still doing well concealing his legacy, but she kept herself ready to act, should his composure falter.

CHAPTER FORTY-ONE

DARI

"Zane Morgan," Lord Baldric read from his parchment. "Laird Reese. Coryn Kull. These are the Judged who have chosen combat. In the order that I spoke your name, do you have anything to say on your behalf?"

Dari stared at the second man, the tallest and most muscular of the bunch, with his thick black hair and scarred face, barely hearing Zane Morgan proclaim his innocence. Laird Reese said nothing. Coryn Kull only bowed toward a front row of spectators and said, "I ask your pardon, and hope my death brings you comfort."

The peal of Stone's bells almost made Dari cry out, though she knew by now to expect them.

Zane Morgan strode to the center of the arena as Lord Baldric walked to the bench where the apprentices waited and took up a position behind it.

Marilia Deadeye's eldest apprentice rose, checked the soundness of her scabbards, then sat as his mistress glided out to meet her Judged. Her movements were more liquid than solid, and Dari remembered how graceful she was each morning, dancing the *fael'feis* in the Den courtyard. Stormbreaker's sister would be proud of her former apprentice when she returned.

Dari felt the barest measure of pity for the man Marilia would face, Zane Morgan from Dyn Cobb, convicted of murdering a man in a tavern brawl. She gave him a moment's attention, from his average height and build to his brown hair and beard that he kept long in typical Cobb fashion.

He didn't really look like a killer or even a criminal, nothing at all like the glowering moving mountain Stormbreaker would have to fight. To Dari's eye, Zane Morgan appeared to be carrying nothing but a single sword from the Stone armory, and a dagger strapped to the outside of his thigh. He might have the other two weapons he was allowed concealed somewhere on his person, but she couldn't detect them.

His expression was grim as he faced Marilia Deadeye, who was easily a hand shorter than her opponent. Marilia's countenance held no emotion at all, much like the blank looks Stormbreaker seemed to achieve so easily. After a quick mutual bow, the two combatants crossed swords in greeting, as was traditional in any civilized fight between two Fae.

Dari kept trying to breathe correctly and failing. This was all happening too quickly. Why had she thought it would take longer? It needed to take longer. All day, even. She didn't want to watch Marilia fight any more than she wanted to watch Stormbreaker's battle.

Ignoring Dari's wishes completely, the clang of metal on metal tore open the arena's stillness, and a roar rolled through the crowd.

Moving exactly with the noise, Marilia leaped backward and swung her sword in a tight arc, barely missing Morgan's chest as he dropped to his knees to avoid her blade.

Cat-fast, the man sprang to his feet and drove straight at Marilia, smashing his sword against hers with such force Dari thought her own teeth might rattle. How Marilia kept her footing against such an assault, Dari couldn't begin to guess. Her fingers ached, she was clenching them together so hard.

The Stone Sister seemed to flow backward, spinning and pivoting, keeping her blade high and her arm flexible. Morgan couldn't get any closer to her than the edge of her sword—or swords, once she drew her second blade.

"Get him," Raaf murmured beside Dari, moving his fists in rhythm with Marilia's footsteps.

Fighting two-handed, Marilia parried and moved again and again, deflecting Morgan's powerful lunges and even his brutal overhead swings. She regained balance, and her blades seemed to twirl like spinning lightning as she drove Morgan back toward the fence separating the apprentice bench from the arena.

None of the gray-clad apprentices moved, except to lean forward and gain a better view of the fight.

"Power and determination against skill and speed," Raaf allowed as Marilia caused Morgan to stumble. When the crowd's roar died, the redhead said, "An even match."

Dari glanced down at Raaf because the boy had sounded worried. He looked worried, too, as if he could see something in this fight that she might be missing.

She quickly turned her attention back to the battle, sizing up both combatants as they disengaged and paced around each other like a pair of prowling rock cats. Both were breathing heavily already, from the exertion of their first engagement, but they both seemed oddly relaxed. Feet apart. Shoulders wide. Bodies balanced.

That's it, Dari thought. *Raaf sees that Morgan knows to keep his muscles loose and ready.*

So the man must be experienced at battle, from the Dynast Guard or some other training. And calm, even though he knew this fight would end with Marilia's death or his own. Morgan matched Marilia motion for motion, sliding his feet along the dirt to be certain his balance never suffered. Sweat beaded across his forehead, and his grip on the hilt of his single sword seemed to tighten.

Morgan's next charge was slower. Much more deliberate—and

even stronger than his first assaults. He had the measure of his adversary now. After a few parries, Marilia spun in an outward circle and disengaged.

The crowd muttered in nervous waves, and most spectators were watching even more closely.

Before the noise died away, Marilia took the lead and sprang at Morgan, once more driving him hard toward the wall protecting the apprentices. The man gave ground easily and quickly, keeping his balance, blocking each strike. Between blows, his elbows remained bent, and his sword pointed directly at Marilia's throat. To compensate for height, Marilia moved even closer, her two swords flashing so fast in the sunlight Dari had to blink from the glare.

As Marilia danced closer, Morgan raised his blade out of battle position, as if he might be frightened or overwhelmed, or even overmatched.

Marilia took her opportunity and lunged forward, blades extended.

"No!" Raaf jumped to his feet at the same moment Aron did, and two other apprentices Dari knew to be proficient with bladework.

Before Marilia's tips plunged into Morgan's chest, he made use of his advantage in arm length and drove his blade crosswise across Marilia's throat and chest.

Her eyes flew wide, her arms jerked backward. She let go of one sword, then the other. Both blades clattered into the dirt.

"I'm sorry," Morgan said, loud enough to be heard in the row where Dari stood with the now-trembling Raaf. Morgan stepped aside and lowered his sword as a ribbon of blood flowed from Marilia's throat, slow for a moment, then horribly fast and thick. "I told you I was innocent."

The crowd went silent and still again, this time in shock. Many had mouths open, or hands to their faces. Disbelief permeated the atmosphere of the arena, but Dari gripped Raaf's shoulder to hold him still. Below them, the apprentices all stood motionless, too, faces struck with misery and grief.

There was no denying this outcome.

Marilia Deadeye had lost her combat.

The Stone Sister remained on her feet for another few seconds, then toppled forward, falling like a tree hacked in a forest. She struck the arena floor as hard as lifeless wood, no spark of existence left in her.

Dari felt absolutely numb. Her senses switched off completely, except for her vision, but she couldn't quite believe what she was seeing.

A Stone Sister defeated in combat. Had such a thing ever happened in recent history? Dari was almost certain it had not. If Stone Brothers were deadly, then Stone Sisters were a moving apocalypse. Yet Marilia Deadeye lay before the crowd in the Judgment Arena, already gone from this world and waiting for the next.

Dari was too stunned to cry, and too frozen to look at Stormbreaker. Her eyes turned to Aron, who stood as if the backs of his legs had been iced to the apprentice bench in the deepest freeze of winter.

Lord Baldric moved from behind that bench and walked slowly into the arena. When he reached Zane Morgan, he touched the man's shoulder with his left hand and raised his right hand toward the clear summer sky.

Triune's bells gave three booming rings, unlike any Dari had ever heard before in her tenure at the castle. She flinched from the noise each time. None of the Stone Brothers or apprentices had any physical response, but to Dari's horror, Aron's essence gave off a brilliant sapphire flash, like a shooting star rising from the very top of his head. Even as she drove herself through the Veil and used the bulk of her energy to shield Aron's legacy from view, her gaze whipped toward Lord Altar.

His head turned in Aron's direction.

By the time the dynast lord fully focused on Aron, Aron's essence had gone back to the same dull blue he usually maintained, and Dari's control reinforced the perception.

Cayn's teeth! She barely managed to cloak her thoughts to keep them silent. *Did he see?*

She felt half-battered from the emotion of Marilia's defeat and the fear that her distraction might have just cost Aron his safety. If Lord Altar had noticed—what then?

Dari cursed herself a hundred times for not keeping her awareness on the other side of the Veil, and keeping a forced contact with Aron. Lord Altar might have sensed something amiss, but he wouldn't have been able to discover what it was, not in the limited time afforded by Judgment Day.

Lord Baldric had his back to the bench as he stood with Zane Morgan, and Dari knew he hadn't seen what happened with Aron. Stormbreaker must have noticed, though, because Dari heard thunder far in the distance. If she could have made thunder, she would have brought an entire storm. As it was, she divided her awareness as best she could, and kept a bit of her essence very close to Aron's.

I'm sorry, came his quiet, anguished whisper through the Veil. *It won't happen again.*

Through their mental connection, Dari could almost taste his sadness at Marilia's death, and the anger of another loss dredged out of his depths. Images flashed through her awareness—Lord Brailing's face, a group of people that could only be Aron's dead family, the Brailing Guard contingent Aron had almost killed. A wave of rage battered against Dari's control, but she knew Aron wasn't fighting her on purpose. In fact, he was battling with all of his will to stop his own emotional reactions. Shame and humiliation mingled with his anger, and Dari did her best to withdraw her essence as far as she dared, to give him his privacy.

On this side of the Veil, Aron looked at the ground.

Bit by bit, his awareness receded from Dari, until his thoughts were once more completely his own.

"Zane Morgan, by the will of fate, you are deemed innocent." Lord Baldric's voice was as forceful as ever, though his features seemed pulled down, toward the bloody dirt at his feet. "As is my right and duty, I restore to you your full rights as a citizen of Eyrie. You are free to depart from Triune."

In the preternatural calm of the arena, Morgan's voice sounded as loud as Stone's bells. "With your leave, I would stay until the lady's essence is dispatched." His voice faltered, and for a moment, his head drooped. When he gathered himself, he added, "I would like to be in her honor escort."

Lord Baldric granted the man's wish with a nod.

This seemed to rattle the apprentices into action. Aron once more knocked on the small gate, while Marilia's apprentices moved onto the arena floor. Two older Stone Brothers entered, and together with Morgan and the apprentices, they lifted Marilia's body. In a quick, steady procession, Marilia was removed from the grounds to the House of the Judged, to await the dispatching of her essence after all combat had been completed.

The small gate swung closed.

The arena audience waited another breath or two before taking their seats.

Once she settled herself beside Raaf, it took Dari one long, awful moment to realize the bells were ringing again, sending Stormbreaker and the rapist Laird Reese to the arena floor.

The bit of her awareness on the other side of the Veil almost tumbled back to her, leaving Aron exposed. She had to breathe, and breathe again, and draw up images of her home and her sister and anything that might calm her to maintain her own control. It would be a sad thing if Aron ended up shielding *her* during the fight.

Dari's teeth dug into her lip, and she realized she had spent too much time training Aron and searching for Kate, and not enough time practicing skills with her own mind-talents. The time might come when she would have to use them at levels that would demand precision and complete readiness. After today, she would do better, even if she had to sleep less.

Heartbeat by heartbeat, she caught hold of herself, and kept that all-important shield around Aron, just in case. All the while, she was far too aware that Laird Reese had a broadsword, long and heavy, befitting his muscled arms and massive frame. Stormbreaker had both of his jagged blades drawn, and after the ritual bow, he crossed them to cradle Reese's bigger weapon.

The crowd remained mostly silent in the wake of Marilia's death, and Dari felt her own essence whisper into near nothingness as the two new combatants stared each other down.

Dari had never seen Stormbreaker so focused. His loose stance belied the storm in his essence, and she knew he was having to spend some energy, at least, holding back the weather that wanted to burst from his mind.

Laird Reese gave the ear-crushing battle roar of a desert bandit, leaning forward into Stormbreaker's face even as Dari and most of the audience leaned back to escape the noise.

Stormbreaker remained as still as an ancient mountain.

Courtesies were over. The battle had begun.

Reese moved back from his opponent faster than Dari would have thought possible. He raised his huge blade two-fisted, high above his head.

Dari's blood seemed to stop flowing in her veins.

Kill-stroke. First blow landed—usually the last.

She almost jumped up and screamed, but Raaf chose that moment to whisper, "Stupid."

Before the boy finished pronouncing the word, Stormbreaker had

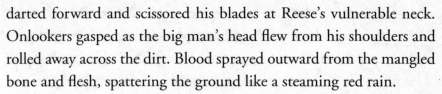

darted forward and scissored his blades at Reese's vulnerable neck. Onlookers gasped as the big man's head flew from his shoulders and rolled away across the dirt. Blood sprayed outward from the mangled bone and flesh, spattering the ground like a steaming red rain.

This time, Dari couldn't keep any of herself on the other side of the Veil. Her awareness rejoined completely just in time for her to turn her head and try to wipe the visual image of Reese's decapitated corpse from her mind. The sound of body striking earth did little to help with that, but the relieved shouts of the crowd helped shore her strength.

"Not even a minute this time," Raaf observed as shouts became cheers, and Stone's bells rang out for Stormbreaker's victory. "That's worthy of recording, even for Stormbreaker."

Apprentices swept forward to remove Reese's body. Aron was on his feet, essence the exact color it was supposed to be, going to meet his master and take Stormbreaker's blades for cleaning once the third combat ended.

Which, mercifully, didn't take long.

Coryn Kull, the third criminal who elected combat, apologized to his victim's family again. Then, instead of bowing and crossing swords, he knelt before his Stone Brother and bared his neck for a quick, painless death.

Raaf shrugged this off as he stood to leave. "A lot of them do that. Remorse or terror—who can say."

He actually sounded disappointed.

As soon as the last corpse had been removed, Lord Baldric marched to the center of the arena and raised his hands once more. "This Judgment Day has ended," he boomed, barely completing his sentence before the castle bells gave a long set of peals to underscore its finality.

Dari got to her feet, ears ringing with the bells, irritated to feel her legs tremble as she made her way out of the seating area and onto the arena floor, heading for the entrance to the House of the Judged to dispatch the souls of the dead. Stormbreaker and Aron were already waiting to follow Lord Baldric and the rest of the Stone Brothers and apprentices through the small gate, no doubt on their way to pay respects to Marilia and witness the release of her essence.

Thank all of fate's tricks that this is finished.

Dari glanced to her right, into the stands, expecting to see Lord Altar and his party leaving the steel and copper-colored box and heading back to the day like everyone else.

Instead, Lord Altar was standing before his bench, arms folded, staring directly at Dari.

She startled from the shock of it, but then cool dread uncoiled in her midsection. She traced the dynast lord's gaze more directly to the small gate, and confirmed her suspicion.

Lord Altar wasn't looking at her after all.

He was staring directly at Aron.

CHAPTER FORTY-TWO

ARON

Aron followed the small, bush-crowded byway out of the northern Cobb village, keeping his footfalls silent and gliding, as he had learned from many hours of training with the trackers at Triune. His gaze remained focused on Dari's gray cloak, which was barely visible in the scant moonslight, and both hands remained close to scabbards holding swords he was strong enough to wield. Even now his shoulders ached from hours of carrying water buckets, bushels of grain, and pig iron for the forge—but such extra training was well worth its benefit. When he had proven his mettle to Stormbreaker with his journey to the Ruined Keep, and many more times on the mock battlefield, Stormbreaker had at last agreed to allow him to take his turns at assisting Dari in her systematic, village-by-village hunt for Kate.

It was already cold, even this far north, and the remnants of Dari's breath flowed behind her like silver fog. Tonight, in her Stone apprentice disguise, she smelled like apples—but when she was upset, Aron always caught a hint of fire and something like talon oil, especially when his senses were still raw from going through the Veil.

Somehow, the fire scent seemed stronger than usual. And the oil smelled a little different. He struggled to keep up with her, then draw even with her, and he barely dared to glance at the taut line of her jaw. Sadness and fury seemed to flow just as silvery-real as her breath,

making Aron ache to soothe her. He wanted to say something, desperately needed to find the right words.

"We'll go to the next villages on our route," he whispered as they
covered the dark ground between the village and the woods where
Blath waited in her gryphon form, prepared to bear them back to
Triune.

Dari said nothing.

Aron's head drooped. What a pathetic effort. Couldn't he come
up with something better? Of course they would go on to the next
villages. Of course she knew that. There were hundreds of villages in
Cobb alone, much less the aspects of Mab and Vagrat and Ross they
hadn't begun to search. Communications to outlying Stone guild-
houses had proven fruitless, but for several rumors of dark-skinned
foundlings, each of which they carefully traced—with no results.

The woods were still just black streaks on the horizon, a long way
ahead. Dari walked that much faster. Part of Aron's awareness realized she was hurrying because of dawn's nearness, but it felt so much
like she was running away from him, from his efforts to make her feel
better.

She had been so concerned for him after the Judgment Day when
Marilia died, worried almost half out of her own mind that Lord
Altar would bring an army back to Triune and demand his head to
end the siege. Nothing had come of that.

"If there's some legacy skill that would help, I'll learn it," he called
to her as she brushed past bushes on her way toward the distant shadows of trees. His clenched his fists against the knot in his belly. "I
don't care if it's dangerous. I'll do whatever it takes to find her, Dari."

A fresh silver cloud flowed around Dari's features as she finally
slowed, then stopped and turned to face him. Even in the moons-
kissed darkness, he could see each line and curve of her face, her neck,
her shoulders. Just being this close to her when they were alone made
his thoughts muddle.

"I know you'd never let me down, Aron." Her voice sounded tight and thin, so tired, like it always did after a failed night of hunting. "I probably don't tell you often enough that I appreciate your willingness to help me."

"You're my oath-sister." He risked brushing his hand against the sleeve of her robe, and felt a charge when she didn't pull away. "I'll always help you."

Dari's expression softened to one of grief, mixed with a touch of shame. "There is no legacy skill I know of that could find Kate if I, her twin, can't sense her. If there were, I fear I would have already asked you to try to learn it, or worked to practice it myself, no matter the risk."

Aron stood a bit straighter and looked directly into Dari's eyes. Even in the low lighting, they sparked with life and power, drawing him in yet again.

"My sister is Stregan and unstable, and somehow—somehow shielded. Either she's keeping her own mind sealed away from mine, or someone else is doing that job for her." Dari shook her head, and Aron once more brushed the sleeve of her robe.

Her tremulous smile felt like a treasure chest of reward, but a breath later, she was walking again, toward the trees and away from him. Once more, Aron found himself running to catch her.

I'm always trying to keep pace with this one. The thought came without effort, because he had it often these days. His sixteenth birthday was creeping closer, but what hope did he have that Dari would finally begin to notice him as something other than the boy she helped rescue from the Watchline massacre?

The scent of oil grew stronger, and mingled with something metallic now, rasping against Aron's senses. He forced himself forward, demanded that his mind stay focused on Dari, on seeing to her safety, but his *graal* grabbed at his awareness until he stumbled.

Unease slithered across the back of his neck as he slowed and righted himself, looking to his left and right. Cycles of training at Stone gathered inside him, and his muscles bunched. Both hands moved to the hilts of his swords. Instead of drawing them right away, he dashed forward, overtaking Dari at the same moment he whispered, "Wait!"

Dari stopped walking immediately, and her palm dropped toward the hilt of her single dagger. Her glance darted toward the trees, where Blath had sheltered herself. Too far away to call out, or make a run for it.

"Something feels wrong," Aron said, low enough to keep their conversation private from any ears that might be listening. He had learned not to fear manes, mockers, or beasts, even rock cats, when Dari was present and allowing a bit of her true essence to be known, but far more dangerous creatures with two legs and sharp swords crept about Eyrie at night.

"Come," Dari said, gripping her dagger. "If we dash for the woods—"

Nine robed men, faces wrapped like desert bandits, stepped out of the brush pushing against the sides of the byway, surrounding them as neatly as a net drawn upward with a sharp tug. They had blades drawn, and two had bows with arrows at the ready.

Aron and Dari drew their own weapons in silence, and the nine men ringing them walked slowly in a circle, keeping their shoulders squared and their weapons pointed forward. Aron tasted the copper tang of his own fear and once more smelled the strange oil he had detected earlier. Some sort of polish or conditioning for the swords or bows, no doubt.

The men wore no dynast colors, and by their stance and behavior, Aron guessed these were rogue soldiers.

"Can you summon her?" Aron whispered, meaning Blath, hoping Dari understood, but she paid him no heed.

One of the men, the tallest in the bunch, spoke. "Apprentices?

What business does Stone have in Dyn Cobb, in the middle of the night?"

"*Stone* business," Dari responded in her coolest, sharpest voice. This was preplanned, her handling any verbal confrontation, since most people feared Stone Sisters even more than crazed mockers or rabid rock cats. "Do you mean to interfere?"

One of the men snorted. "Would you be intending to steal our children, then? Many enough have disappeared, all across this dynast and others, too. It would make sense for Stone to be involved in the likes of that."

Aron had no idea what the man was talking about, so he made no response. Neither did Dari.

For a time, the men said nothing else. They kept up their stalking movements, around and around, drawing the circle tighter with each pass. Dari and Aron moved closer to each other until they stood back-to-back, and Aron passed her one of his swords to hold in addition to her dagger. She could fight two-fisted as well as he could, and he wanted her to be the one holding two weapons. A better chance for her to escape. Perhaps more safety, if there was anything such as safety with odds as bad as nine seasoned fighters against two apprentices—with one of those being a pretender, on top of everything.

Each breath Aron took grew deeper, until his head spun even as his pulse thumped in his ears and neck.

Just get yourself and Dari home.

Those were his only instructions from Stormbreaker, who believed he was ready for whatever fate might pitch in his path.

But nine men against the two of us?

"We'll be interfering with Stone business, then," the tall man said with a cold calm that matched Dari's, icicle for icicle. "If you'll come with us peacefully, there'll be no need to fight."

Aron desperately worked to sort out if he should use his *graal* in this situation. They were threatened. Their lives were in danger. Was this an incidence of serving the higher good?

Dari might think so, but Lord Baldric had told him never, no matter the circumstances, and Stormbreaker never resorted to using his mind-talents, even to save his own hide, or the lives of those in his care.

Platt said it was a tool—my *tool. And Stormbreaker's* graal *is different from mine. His is harder to control.*

"Come with you where?" Aron asked, not intending to let Dari die or be captured, no matter the personal price.

"Our camp. To meet our . . . guild master, if you will. Canus has special interest in all Stone apprentices." The tall man nodded toward Aron as clouds of breath laced his shrouded face. "Especially boys."

A fresh, righteous anger kindled in Aron's depths. Canus the Bandit was at the root of this attack. Canus was the real foe in this situation; these were just his foe's outstretched hands.

"He likes boys," another of the robed outlaws agreed. "Takes most stray lads in and raises them for his own. You'd be a nice addition to the collection."

Aron clenched his jaw so firmly it ached.

Even if they fought well, they had no prayer against so many. But he could use his mind-talents and get them safely home. Lord Baldric would likely send him to Judgment, but Dari would be free and breathing. That's what mattered.

"Don't," she said, as if she knew what he was thinking. "Not now. Not to save me."

"I will," he countered, fighting to regulate his mental focus. "If it's the only way."

Dari's answering snarl sounded more animal than human, and Aron's heart stuttered. His concentration wavered, and the tip of his sword dipped, sending moonslight fracturing through each level of his thoughts.

"He's trying to go through the Veil," one of the men shouted. "So is she."

Before Aron had time to be surprised at their awareness, the tall man bellowed, "Take them now!"

All nine bandits lunged toward them at the same moment, blades raised.

Reflex forced Aron to sweep his sword in a low arc, but the man nearest to him blocked the blow so completely it nearly jarred the weapon out of Aron's grip. His hand clenched on the hilt, then burned from the impact. Before he could recover, fingers dug at him. The men pawed and grabbed, snatching at his legs, his shoulders, his elbows. Aron slashed and struck with his sword and fist, but the men wrestled him to the byway dirt and tore the hilt of his blade from his desperate grasp.

Dari screeched, sounding more angry than afraid. Fury blasted through Aron and he fought his captors even harder, until he thought his muscles might burst. He had to get free. He had to help her!

With what little focus he could grasp, he tried to throw his essence through the Veil, and caught bits of what the outlaws were saying to each other, mind-to-mind.

Don't allow it. . . .

Hurt him if you have to. . . .

Kill her; she's not the one we're hunting. . . .

The bandits' legacy conversation shifted to echoes.

"No!" Aron roared with all the force left in his lungs. "Leave her alone!"

He could see nothing but blurs and dashes of moonslight. Feel nothing but the crushing weight of bandits covering his body. One of the men stuffed his sleeve into Aron's open mouth, choking him on salty, oily cloth even as he reached the edges of enhanced perception.

Dari's mental strength surged around him, touched him, but

didn't rest in his awareness or restrain him. Her energy felt different. Larger, somehow.

Buried beneath a pile of growling outlaws, Aron kicked against his attackers. He tried to spit the cloth out of his mouth, but the man nearest his face shoved his burly arm harder into Aron's lips and teeth. Aron ignored the agony. Reached with his mind. Reached harder.

Even as his five senses exploded with furious awareness on the other side of the Veil, Dari's *graal* crushed against his in a splendor of colors, more brutal than any bandit's fist. Aron's head slammed backward into the dirt as his essence hurtled back through the Veil to normal space and time. The bandit's arm seemed to sink completely into his mouth, separating his jaws as he let out a shout of pain and surprise.

More shouts rose.

These were terrified.

The arm crushing Aron's mouth withdrew, and almost as fast, the bandits let go of him. He heard them stumble and struggle, falling backward, falling away as popping and groaning and new, terrible shrieking rose into the night. Blood flowed across Aron's teeth as he managed to close his lips and roll to his side, then stand and snatch his sword from the dirt.

The nine bandits slammed into one another as they ran, screaming, and flung themselves into the brush.

"Blath," Aron mumbled through his swelling, bleeding lips, assuming Dari had sent a mental call to the Sabor hiding herself in the trees. He knew people feared Sabor in fighting form, but these men had to be pure cowards. When he heard the telltale whump of big wings, he turned to see Blath soaring across the tableaux of black sky, white stars, and glowing twinned moons—and dropped his sword.

Aron's knees went soft on him, and he wavered on his feet, coughing up a bloody, hacking gasp of surprise.

Blath sailed downward toward where he was standing, directly in front of a scaled, long-necked beast the size of a castle tower.

The creature was white with dark markings about its clawed forelegs, a barbed tail that seemed as long and pointed as a *dantha* tree, and massive, outstretched leathery wings. It had luminous eyes like black, liquid pearls, and its mouth was open to reveal rows of teeth like white, curved blades. A thin reed of smoke stretched upward from the beast's nostrils.

Dari, he thought weakly before his stunned mind began to urge him to move before the beast belched a flesh-eating cloud of fire.

Dari was nowhere to be seen.

You are *seeing her,* his mind jabbered. *You've always known she was Stregan. That her other form was dragon, not human.*

A sensation like rope unraveling at the fibers overtook him as he tried to keep hold of reality, to accept it, and failed.

"Dari," he said aloud, hardly able to pronounce the syllables with his damaged mouth.

There was no hint of recognition in the creature's hungry, enraged gaze. Fire licked around its deadly teeth. Aron's *graal* calmly informed him that if he moved, she would cook him and eat him before the smoke died away.

If he didn't move, the same fate awaited him.

"Dari," he said again, hearing the loss of hope in his own voice.

In her Stregan form, this magnificent dragon had no inkling of who he was, past an easy meal offering itself to her on this remote Cobb byway.

Blath had landed, and Aron saw that she had shifted back to human form. She was running toward him, full speed, arms outstretched, as if she meant to fling herself at him before he could mount any type of defense.

Fire ripped from the dragon's throat.

Blath reached Aron, and the flames struck her from behind as she wrapped him in her arms. Heat melted over both of them, singeing his hair, reducing him to a gasping, wheezing child squeezed in Blath's powerful embrace.

The Sabor had to be dissolving where she stood, but Aron couldn't smell anything burning beyond cloth and some nearby leaves and branches.

He managed to look up into Blath's face, and her golden eyes bored directly into his consciousness. "My skin protects me," she said in a harsh, pained voice. "But not for long. Please. We have no choice."

Aron understood what he needed to do.

He didn't think Blath was instructing him, mentally or any other way. No. It was more like he was remembering a moment many cycles ago, when Lord Cobb's riding party had overtaken the Stone travelers and rescued them from the Brailing Guard.

He had commanded Dari with his mind-talents that day, and stopped her from changing. It had been an accident born of fear and worry—but if he had done it once, perhaps he could do it again. He had to take some sort of action, or both he and Blath would pay with their lives, and who knew what would become of Dari.

Aron closed his own eyes, took a deep breath of hot air and Sabor sweat and ash, and forced himself through the Veil. Almost as fast, he separated his awareness from the body Blath protected with her own, and let his essence drift upward, slowly, controlled, until he guessed he was at the same level as the dragon's open mouth. The pound of his heart sounded like wild drums to his enhanced awareness, and the stench of smoke and the most acrid scale-oil he had ever experienced nearly overwhelmed him.

He forced his eyes open, and found himself face-to-face with an enormous white dragon that seemed even more fearsome on the other side of the Veil.

Now he could see that the dark patterns on its legs and neck were deep green swirls almost identical to the *benedets* of a Stone High Master. Aron could sense the fire inside the beast, feel it like a crackling pain flowing across his essence, and he understood that Stone must have modeled the marks given to its most deadly members after the appearance of these unbelievably powerful creatures.

The intelligence in the dragon's eyes was animalistic and heartless. Aron could tell it cared nothing for anything outside itself and its own kind. It could strike at him in the real world, or on this side of the Veil. Somehow, it lived in both places.

Stregan, Aron thought, not bothering to shield the word and keep it private.

The force and loudness of his own mental voice surprised him, and he was suddenly concerned that anyone in Eyrie possessed of any legacy might have heard him.

The creature paused in its fire-roaring attack and gazed at him with something like menace mixed with respect, because it *had* heard him. And on some fundamental level, it understood that he was brash enough to address it as an equal.

He centered himself as quickly as he could, focused his mental energy, and projected the full weight of his own *graal* into his next word.

"Dari."

As he spoke the syllables aloud and in his mind, as he heard his call reverberate around them, he focused on an image of Dari as he knew her, and willed that image to be reality.

The Stregan didn't change, except to pull its fearsome mouth wider. Hooked teeth flashed, and more smoke and flames tumbled forth. On this side of the Veil, the flames seemed to crackle in slow motion, with a sound like dozens of trees being bashed in half at the trunks.

Aron shoved back his own fears, lest he make them as real as the dragon he faced. "Dari."

This time, he spoke with even more force.

The Stregan still didn't react to his command, and when the flames struck him, he felt a wicked, terrifying heat that didn't kill him only because Blath had hold of his physical body. On some level, Aron could sense that the color in the Sabor's skin was more than just pigment, but something like a repelling force or charge, dissipating the effects of Stregan fire.

For now. The shield was definitely waning.

Panic competed with determination as Aron once more gathered his essence for counterattack. He let instinct guide him and threw his awareness forward, much as Tia Snakekiller had struck at him with her dangerous hood snake illusion. A harsh, hot jolt told Aron his energy had made contact with that of the Stregan before him—an instant before a crushing pressure on his essence nearly exploded his mind like an egg beneath a massive, falling stone.

He hurled his will against the multicolored pressure with the entire force of his being, and his whole mind insisted, *"Dari!"*

At the same instant, he imagined himself reaching inside the great dragon, finding the soul of the girl he wanted, the girl he knew, seizing hold of her shoulders, and hauling her straight out of the scales and teeth and wings and flames threatening to consume him.

He touched something—what, he couldn't say—

And his mind blasted outward in fragments of light and bright color and terrible, hissing fire—

And there was nothing now, nothing but flying, so high Aron knew he would never touch the ground again.

CHAPTER FORTY-THREE

ARON

Cool water trickled through his thick lips, and Aron woke feeling like every bone in his body had been rendered to liquid, then re-formed at strange angles. This troubled him, but only marginally, as he was grateful to wake at all. For a moment, he imagined he was back at the Ruined Keep, but then he realized there were no walls around him, and he was still outside.

His skin and mind tingled with the warmth of foreign energy, and he realized Blath had been ministering to him with some powerful and deep healing *graal*. The Sabor woman was bending over him, covered by nothing but the burned tatters of the brown robe she typically wore on their outings from Triune. Moments later, he felt almost whole again, save for some slight swelling and cracking in his bottom lip.

Cool blue light broke the gray clouds above Blath's head, signaling dawn breaking across the northern reaches of Eyrie. "He's awake." She stood and walked away from him, not bothering to clutch the tatters of her robes. She was already shifting, with streaks of yellow-golden fur forming along her limbs as she moved. "We should leave now."

Aron's mind turned sluggishly toward the person next to him.

Dari.

With no scales, no fangs, and no gouts of fire spilling from her pale, pressed lips.

She was only Dari again, oddly small in her scorched, smudged gray robes. She was hugging herself and shivering, her skin a sickly ash color, and her dark hair hung in disarray about her face and shoulders.

When she looked at Aron, she seemed both ashamed and angry. "Never take a chance like that again. I cannot understand how you're still alive."

"I had to do it." He straightened himself on the ground and tried to look as certain as he sounded. "You're the one who told me there would be times when it served the greater good to use my legacy. It was either die in one fashion, or risk death in the other. Besides, you might have regretted roasting me and Blath, too, and making a meal of us both."

Dari frowned at him. "I wouldn't have harmed you."

Aron heard the worry and doubt in her tone, or his *graal* perceived it, but he didn't challenge her. "The bandits?"

"Gone." She closed her eyes and rested her head atop her drawn knees. "No sign of them, according to Blath. It's as if they vanished into the dirt, rocks, and trees."

Aron said nothing, but wondered what Blath might have done with the bandits, if she had found them. Perhaps it was better not to ask that question.

"No one will believe a handful of rogues," Dari said as if she hoped to convince herself. Her lips pursed as a few yards away, Blath finished her transition. "No Fae has ever been able to command a Stregan, Aron."

"That we know of," he countered, wondering if his care and concern for Dari gave him some sort of advantage she didn't expect. "In the old times, such things might have occurred. We did live in peace once, Fae and Fury."

He remembered what Platt had told him, about how the two races needed each other, about neither being whole without the other, and felt like he understood this even more.

Dari got to her feet, still seeming drained to half of her usual presence. As she walked toward Blath, her gait was stiff. Aron forced himself to get up and follow her, feeling just as awkward and sore as she looked.

When he reached her, he felt compelled to tell her the one lingering truth still troubling him. "I thought I understood, about you and Kate and what you are, especially after meeting with Platt—but I didn't."

Dari reached Blath and placed her palm against one furry shoulder. She didn't look at him. "I know. You didn't, and Stormbreaker doesn't. That's something I should remember."

The sadness and resignation in her words made Aron want to reach out and take hold of her, but he couldn't seem to move. He hadn't meant that her Stregan form put him off, only that he better grasped how important it was to locate Kate, before someone did manage to employ her powers for their own ends.

Dari leaped upward and took her position behind Blath's neck before Aron could form the right words, and a few moments later, he gave up trying. Dari had almost killed him, but she had no less effect on him now than before.

With now-practiced ease, Aron used Blath's bent back knee to climb to her broad back. It was the next part that gave him trouble, the sliding forward and easing into position behind Dari, then gripping her waist as Blath raised her huge wings to fly them out of Dyn Cobb.

As wind blasted against his face, his senses, his very essence, he forced himself to keep his hands perfectly still, lest she take offense to any of his movements.

Why do I torture myself?
And yet how would I even begin to change what I feel for her?

• • •

The sun was bright in the morning sky by the time Blath landed in the Den courtyard. It was so late that the *fael'feis* was finished as well, and most of Stone was already about the day's business. Blath had flown low and wide the last length they had traveled, to avoid villages and passersby and entered Stone with the High Master's towers for cover, but her muscles had grown tighter with each moment they were so exposed. When they rejoined each other in the courtyard after changing into fresh clothing, Blath's first words to Dari were, "Our trips need to stretch overnight, and we should shelter during the next day. We cannot take such chances so frequently."

All the aches in Aron's muscles intensified when he saw Dari's wordless, pained surrender to this pronouncement. He wished Blath would head inside to the Den and leave him to talk with her, to see if he might finally find the comforts that would matter to Dari— but he had no fortune in that respect. Blath seemed opposed to leaving them alone for long stretches, except on hunts for Kate, and even then, she was overly attentive the moment they returned to her sight. He sought to catch the Sabor woman's eye to try to signal her to give them some privacy, but she seemed opposed to that, too.

Aron considered asking Blath about why she didn't like him, especially after she had saved his life and he had saved hers the night before, but the bells along the battlement began to ring. It was a quick pattern, and he couldn't help gazing up at the nearest bell cove. "Stone Guild, coming home from a journey."

Dari's brow furrowed, as did Blath's. "There are no traveling parties due to return today," Blath said as Iko came out of the Den door to shadow Aron. Raaf wasn't with him, but only because the boy was likely be waiting near the stables with Tek already saddled for Aron's mid-morning talon-back weapons training. Windblown had taken Zed on a hunt, but they weren't due back for many days.

"Where's Stormbreaker?" Aron asked Iko, fighting the sudden lurch of unease that threatened what little store of energy he yet possessed for the day. "We bring news of Canus the Bandit."

Dari's expression and even Blath's mirrored Aron's distress as Iko responded. "The High Master went to the main gate over an hour ago. He has been waiting there, watching over the horizon."

As if they were possessed of one mind, Dari and Blath started for the main gate and keep at the same moment Aron did, and Iko followed only a step behind. After the night of poking about darkened village doorways, checking barns and stables, questioning Stone informants, and standing down dragons, the walk seemed overly long to Aron. His breath came shorter with each step, but his curiosity and concern didn't wane with his body.

"Perhaps someone happened upon Canus the Bandit or his nine terrified outlaws," he murmured, doing what he could to ignore a fierce stab of disappointment at that thought. Other than Dari's presence, the thought of capturing the outlaw raider was the only thing that stirred Aron's emotions to the point where he felt completely real and fully human.

"I doubt that," Dari said. "I can't believe Canus would get himself captured so easily—and those nine are probably still running, and may run all the way to the shore and sea in Dyn Mab. When Stone goes after that dark-hearted monster, they'll have to send the best at Triune."

"It will be whoever draws a stone on the bandit," Blath reminded her. "Fate rules such decisions, not Lord Baldric or any of his guildsmen."

They reached the main keep and walked quickly through the rock passageway marking the keep's center. In moments, they reached the courtyard, just as the main gate began to open. Aron spotted

Stormbreaker coming down from the battlements, with Raaf hurrying along in his wake. Energy sparked around Stormbreaker like a thick yellow-black cloud, and thunder sounded somewhere above the castle. Raaf's eyes went wide, but he didn't flee or even shrink back from his pursuit.

As Aron studied Stormbreaker's grim expression, a new dread bloomed in his chest.

What if these guild members had been ambushed on the road? Canus the Bandit, the Brailing Guard trying to set stores for another winter at war, or even panicked villagers thinking they were about to be attacked, not trusting Stone's neutrality—anything was possible.

What if it's Zed, maimed or killed?

Fatigue fell away from him, and Aron quickened his own pace, drawing ahead of Dari, Blath, and Iko. He reached Stormbreaker as the gate opened enough to admit a very tall brown-haired Stone Brother and his equally tall apprentice. The two rode bay geldings with leathers that looked to come from Dyn Cobb, and Aron couldn't help noticing their appearance was so similar they might be father and son. Both of the new arrivals glanced past Aron toward Blath and Iko, and shared almost identical looks of surprise that gave way to deliberate masks of nonexpression.

The weather brewing in Stormbreaker's essence increased, and thunder cracked twice, then three times, seeming closer to the castle with each rumble. From the corner of his eye, Aron saw Raaf cower against Triune's curtain wall, as if to hide from the bits of lightning lashing out from Stormbreaker's shoulders. Aron no longer shared the boy's fear of Stormbreaker's displays, as he had learned that even distressed, Stormbreaker had remarkable control of his unusual mind-talent. He was only venting emotion, not preparing to strike out. Stormbreaker would never harm another living creature with his talent.

Because he has a good heart, Aron thought as he kept his eyes on the man and boy approaching on horseback. *And because Lord Baldric would put him down like a mad talon.*

As if summoned by Aron's thoughts, Lord Baldric emerged from the keep's archway, barreled past Stormbreaker and Aron, and shouted a greeting to the returned guildsmen. "Hasty! Terrick! Thank the Brother. We've had no word from the lot of you in over a year."

The names struck a chord in Aron's memory, and he suddenly grasped the nature of Stormbreaker's unrest. These were Tia Snakekiller's traveling companions, the two who were supposed to be with Stormbreaker's sister. Instinctively, he glanced over his shoulder at Dari, who was standing post-still between Blath and Iko, worry etched across her features.

"We're bringing word, Lord Baldric." Hasty's bass voice seemed as loud as Stormbreaker's thunder as the big gray-robed man dismounted and handed his reins to Raaf, who had finally dashed past Stormbreaker to help with the horses. "Tia Snakekiller sent us to you with her fondest regards."

All the lightning and thunder faded away from Triune. Aron felt Stormbreaker's relief like the rush of a warm breeze as Lord Baldric grunted. "That's a blatant lie, and you know it. She'd sooner send me a poison dart with my own name etched on the shaft."

Hasty shrugged as Terrick gave his mount over to Raaf. "She's a Stone Sister. What do you expect, kisses and roses?"

Lord Baldric looked faintly ill as he gestured to summon Terrick, Hasty, Stormbreaker, Aron, and Dari into the main keep. No doubt Blath and Iko would follow, but Aron knew Lord Baldric preferred they remain outside his chambers. He couldn't stop the rumors about impropriety and side-taking generated by the presence of Sabor at Triune, but he at least made a point to minimize perceptions that they were influencing Guild decisions.

Once they reached Lord Baldric's rooms, he seated them around his table and poured tall, frosty glasses of raspberry water.

Hasty took only one drink before he asked, "Sabor? Here?"

Lord Baldric gave the Stone Brother a quick, hot glare. "Not my idea." Somehow, he managed not to look at Dari, but he said, "They're bound by birth-promise to Dari, here. She's one of our sheltered, and she's been helping us train some apprentices who have particularly strong legacies."

Before Hasty could even ask why in the name of the gods Lord Baldric was sheltering someone bound to Sabor protectors, Lord Baldric cut him off with a shake of the head. "I'm sorry, but that subject's closed."

"Tell me about my sister," Stormbreaker said in a soft voice that nevertheless seemed as powerful as any storm he might conjure. He sat forward in his chair, resting his arms—and his clenched fists—on the table before him.

"She's in the village of Finmont in Dyn Cobb," Hasty explained, leaning away from Stormbreaker. "She's caring for a rescue, a boy we found in Dyn Mab so grievously injured we all doubted he would survive. We intended to spend only one winter there, but Nic remained too ill to travel, and we weren't comfortable leaving Snakekiller behind to tend him on her own. She's strong and powerful, but hefting the weight of a grown man—an invalid—it's quite a chore. Even after much healing and time, Nic's better, but still unable to travel long distances."

Nic . . .

The name echoed through Aron's awareness, and for a moment, he completely forgot himself. Only the sudden mental grip of Dari's mind-talents stopped his free fall in remembering the boy from his visions. He had a sensation of her shaking him, and quickly checked his own essence, concealing the colors as quickly and efficiently as he could with such a shock.

After a moment, Aron realized that both Stormbreaker and Lord

Baldric were looking at him, but Hasty and Terrick didn't seem to notice.

"Nic Vespa. At least he says that's his name." Terrick had a grin that reminded Aron of Zed, friendly and relaxed. "I've had my doubts about his story, but he was in such a bad way when we came across him in the streets. Can't blame him for not wanting to risk his people ever finding out where he's gone."

"There are a fair number of Vespas in Dyn Mab." Stormbreaker sounded almost casual, but his steady gaze at Aron carried the force of a rebuke. "Most are upstanding goodfolk, but I suppose any orchard can grow bitter fruit."

Aron shivered under Stormbreaker's scrutiny, and forced his attention to cooperate enough to control the color of his legacy. The name Nic Vespa scrawled through his mind like words carved in bright colors, shades of red—yet it didn't seem right. Terrick might have a point, that the rescued boy had lied about his name to keep himself safe from his attackers.

Nic. He told me his name was Nic, on the other side of the Veil.

Yet Aron knew it was possible to shade the truth, if Nic had a strong enough *graal*.

Hasty made a snapping motion with both hands. "Poor Nic's back was twisted near to broken, and he took what looked like a hammer blow to his head. Broken legs, broken arms—I've never seen anything like it. Whoever attacked the lad meant for him to die, and die horribly. We thought he was gone from us more than once."

No! Lie down! Aron twitched at the shout of his own memory, at the image of a broken boy whose spirit was trying to leave until Aron shouted at it the night the manes attacked. He had told Nic . . . what? To heal himself. Aron had ordered Nic to heal himself.

Cayn's teeth.

Had Nic lived because Aron had used his *graal* to command it?

Was that even possible?

Aron almost lost his own control again, but caught himself at the last minute. He was beginning to shiver in earnest, and he wished he could go back to the High Master's Den to sort out his confusion.

Surely it wasn't possible to use his legacy to keep someone alive. Dari would have told him if that was the case.

But then Dari hadn't realized it was possible for him to use his *graal* to command her in her Stregan form. Perhaps there were other uses of the Brailing mind-talent that she didn't know, or perhaps, even, that the Fae had withheld from the Furies during the years of peace.

Aron stole a quick glance at Dari, but all her attention was focused on Hasty and Terrick.

If she knew anything like that, she would have told him.

Of course she would have.

If it is possible, and if I could have been there when the Guard attacked my family . . .

No. That was too awful to contemplate. To think he might have had the power to keep his parents and brothers and sisters alive, with just words. Aron's teeth chattered, and he had to press his lips together to stop the reaction.

Stormbreaker's eyes narrowed, and he seemed on the verge of standing and sweeping Aron out of the room when the bells started ringing again.

Lord Baldric cursed. "Messengers. Brother preserve me, but I'd rather kill the lot of them than hear one more plea or demand to do with this infernal war." He grumbled to himself another moment, then seemed to gather his temper but for the glowing flush in both cheeks. "No matter. The Brothers manning the keep will see to them. I've told them I don't want to be bothered. Go on, Hasty."

Hasty was grinning at Lord Baldric, and looking both tired and happy, as if he were glad to find that some things, at least, had not changed in his long absence. For some reason, the man's expression eased Aron's nerves, and helped him to put aside his thoughts about his family in the interest of learning more about Nic.

"Nic healed across the winter, in body, at least," Hasty said. "He's taken to fits now, though, and they leave him drowsy and weak for a day or more each time. We wintered with them in Finmont, then stayed with Snakekiller long enough to help her make a large store of nightshade wine, bruise poultices, and some elixir to reduce the fits—then we rode ahead to bring word to Triune. Snakekiller refused to employ a messenger. Said we were vulnerable enough without broadcasting our whereabouts. She's far behind us on the road, because Nic can make only a few miles each day, even in the wagon."

"We're going back to meet her," Terrick added. "Just as soon as we've rested and packed milk thistle, skullcap, and valerian to make more elixir."

"I'll go," Stormbreaker said immediately, but Lord Baldric shook his head.

"You will not. I'm sorry, Dun." Lord Baldric's frown conveyed genuine regret. "You're the only High Master in the castle right now, and I need you here."

Dari looked relieved at this announcement, but Stormbreaker looked more rebellious than Aron had even thought possible.

"We know her route," Hasty told Stormbreaker. "We'll go straight to her—and you know she's worth a Guard regiment all by herself."

Stormbreaker's arms pressed against the table so firmly his elbows trembled. "Not with a wounded, helpless boy to look after."

Nic's not helpless, Aron thought, but didn't speak the words aloud. Instinct or *graal,* he had no idea, but he knew that was true. Nic Vespa's *graal* had a strength that reminded Aron of Dari's mind-talents, though he had no idea if Nic knew how to use his legacy.

"Terrick and I won't let harm come to your sister," Hasty said, and Aron heard the truth in Hasty's voice.

Stormbreaker didn't seem convinced, but a loud round of knocking on Lord Baldric's chamber door ended the discussion.

"I'm sorry, sir," came a shout from the hallway, "but this messenger will speak only to you."

"Who sent him?" Lord Baldric snarled, rising from his chair.

"Thorn," the Stone Brother in the hall answered, a little more quietly, as if fearful of the Lord Provost's reaction. "It's the First High Master of Thorn, Eldin Falconer."

If Lord Baldric had possessed a talon's battle ring, it would have flared open like a deadly circle of poisoned daggers.

Aron found himself standing, along with everyone else, pulse beginning to thrum in his ears. "The bells," he stammered. "They didn't ring right. Shouldn't the bells have told us that someone of rank was approaching?"

"Yes," Stormbreaker said, his single utterance like the strike of hammer to anvil. Lightning leaked from all over his body, striking the chamber's rock floor with little cracks and pops. Aron felt the press of Dari's *graal* like a cloak over his own senses, but he didn't fight her presence. She was only trying to protect him, he knew, and this once, he didn't mind the protection. He had never before seen Stormbreaker look so angry—or so worried.

"Manage yourself," Lord Baldric ordered Stormbreaker, who didn't seem to heed him at all. "Falconer was likely traveling under cover of disguise. There's a war, Dun, or did you forget?"

Stormbreaker didn't answer, and Aron's anxiety doubled.

He had gotten a few glimpses of Stormbreaker's neutral to negative feelings about Thorn in the past, but nothing—*nothing*—like this. Whoever this Eldin Falconer was, Stormbreaker had some unpleasant history with him.

Lord Baldric glanced at Dari, and Aron was surprised to feel some of her energy flow away from him. He could almost see the tendril of her essence wrap around Stormbreaker, holding back the fearsome power he could wield.

Stormbreaker startled, then turned to Dari. His voice was sharp when he spoke. "I don't need your assistance."

"I say you do," Lord Baldric countered, and that seemed to bring Stormbreaker to heel. The muscles in his shoulders bunched and flexed, but he once more turned toward the door. The weather lining his shoulders and head faded slowly away to faint black shimmers of energy.

The damage, however, was done, as far as Aron could see. Dari looked as though she'd been slapped, or had her heart crushed by Stormbreaker's reaction to her mental touch. Aron could feel her pain through his connection with her, and he had an urge to pound Stormbreaker into so many pieces of rain and wind. How could he hurt Dari like that?

A roiling wave of emotion rose through Aron like one of Stormbreaker's lightning bursts, but he made himself contain it so he wouldn't tax Dari further. *Later*, he told himself, glaring at Stormbreaker. Guild master or no, they would discuss how Stormbreaker treated Dari.

Lord Baldric shifted his focus to Aron. "Your mind-talents would be extremely useful to Stone in this situation, but if you can't contain your *graal*, leave now, through my side door."

"I can control myself, sir," Aron said quietly, folding away his nervousness and discomfort like one of his apprentice tunics. He imagined himself tucking every bit of his emotion into a trunk like the one near his bed, and turning the lock and key. "I'm fine."

Lord Baldric looked next to Dari, who nodded and seemed very focused on her duties to Aron and even to Stormbreaker.

"Well, then." Lord Baldric seated them all at the table, then stalked toward the chamber door. "Let's see what these bastards are up to *now*."

CHAPTER FORTY-FOUR

ARON

Aron tried to work out whether or not he should stand to greet the First High Master of Thorn. It would have been proper, yet no one at the table so much as stirred in their chair, so Aron kept his seat.

Lord Baldric jerked open his chamber door, grumbled a greeting, and admitted a tall man with Mab-blond hair turning ash at his temples. The man wore brown breeches, a brown tunic, and a brown traveler's cloak with the hood pushed back. If it weren't for his king-like bearing, his dark blue eyes, and his *benedets*—crystalline tattoos of thorny rings in the same spots where Stormbreaker's face boasted dark spirals—he might have succeeded in appearing nondescript and unimportant. As it was, Aron could well imagine him in cardinal robes, flashing the traditional winding silver arm bracelets associated with the Thorn Guild. He was a bit disappointed not to actually see those robes and bracelets, as he had been told the color of the cloth and the shine of the jewelry's silver were vibrant enough to attract all the attention Stone's gray robes sought to repel. Aron noted the deep lines at the corners of Falconer's eyes and mouth, and realized that he might be much older than his appearance suggested.

Aron chanced a quick look at Stormbreaker, who seemed to have turned to a statue, back straight against his chair, arms pressed firmly into the table, palms down.

For a moment, Aron wondered if Falconer would like to grow any older. In the next moment, Stormbreaker's discomfort seemed to wash over Aron.

What in all of Eyrie could make a man like Stormbreaker so rigid, so angry and fearful? Aron felt his guild master's unrest like hot bursts of lightning stabbing into his throat and chest. It was enough to make his eyelids flutter, and he had to put his hands on the table, almost mimicking Stormbreaker's posture.

Meanwhile, the Thorn Brother's eyes moved from Dari to Aron to Terrick, and it took Aron a moment to realize Falconer seemed to have no interest in Lord Baldric, Stormbreaker, or Hasty.

Aron allowed his awareness to slide toward the edges of the Veil, hoping to heighten his understanding of Falconer's motives and purpose, but he knew better than to risk slipping into that vulnerable state.

"Lord Baldric," Falconer said, keeping his attention fully on the youngest people in the room. His voice was quiet, yet eerily resonant and powerful, and he pressed his hands together as he spoke, fingertip to wrist. Aron immediately thought of the few times he had seen rectors in their temples, and the deep timbre of their lectures and cautions. "The Lady Provost of Thorn sends her greetings through my presence."

Falconer gave a quick bow, then rose and managed to look at the man he had supposedly come to see.

The harsh glint in Lord Baldric's eyes suggested he was thinking of many responses other than the one he offered, which was an answering bow with a grudging, "Please give Lady Pravda my greetings upon your return."

Stormbreaker's fingers curled against the wood of the table, drawing Falconer's attention. At first his appraisal of Stormbreaker was quick and cursory, but Aron saw the Thorn Brother pause as he at last registered Stormbreaker's unusual hair and eyes.

Falconer's brow furrowed. "Have we met, High Master? You have the look of a child of Dyn Vagrat."

Moments passed. Then more moments.

Only after a glare from Lord Baldric did Stormbreaker give his answer.

"We might have crossed paths in the past." Stormbreaker's voice was barely louder than a whisper, but Aron could almost feel the bellows he seemed to be holding back with the straining muscles in his neck.

Falconer studied him longer, but ultimately shrugged off whatever curiosity had possessed him. Aron was aware of Dari forcibly mediating the appearance of his legacy, making it even duller at the same time her worry for Stormbreaker escalated. Hasty and Terrick seemed uncomfortable yet intrigued, and Lord Baldric not-so-politely annoyed as Falconer got to his point.

"Lady Pravda sent me to gather all unclaimed orphans. It's my wish to rest, then leave with the children in the morning."

Aron sucked in a breath as Dari's soft mental touch abruptly withdrew. He blinked rapidly, trying to understand what Falconer had just announced. In the man's essence, Aron detected only truth and the desire to see to his assigned task—but that was mingled with an odd, almost calloused weariness. As if Falconer would rather be anywhere but here, doing almost anything but this.

Lord Baldric's mouth had come open, as had Terrick's, Hasty's, and Dari's. The bunch of them looked like siblings, mimicking one another in some deranged game.

It was Stormbreaker who finally broke the silence, and this time, he spoke with more force. "You cannot truly intend to herd a band of helpless children across Dyn Brailing and Dyn Cobb in the midst of a war."

"It would take cycles to make such a journey." Dari sounded horrified. "They would be fodder for guardsmen and bandits."

Falconer gave Dari an indulgent look. "Others of our ranks have visited villages and guild houses all across Eyrie, and accomplished just such a feat. Thorn is as capable of defending its charges as Stone."

Aron saw the lie in that assertion, and his legacy picked out the last of the statement as the source of the untruth. Falconer well knew that Thorn would be leading children into extreme peril, but he intended to proceed, nonetheless.

"I cannot allow that," Lord Baldric said. "Those who have sought shelter in our stronghold have been guaranteed Stone's full protection. Releasing them for a death march would be unconscionable."

Falconer stood straighter, conveying his affront with a subdued frown. "The Guard in all six dynasts have guaranteed our safe passage. They have agreed to escort us when necessary, or we would not have undertaken this journey."

"Guardsmen protecting you?" Hasty's deep voice carried none of its initial jocularity, and Aron saw the flash of disbelief in the Stone Brother's wide brown eyes. "That would be like wolves tending to the sheep. The roads are not safe, least of all in the presence of any Dynast Guard save perchance Cobb, and Ross if you're fortunate enough to have their support."

"Stone may have its issues with dynast armies, but Thorn does not—and seeing to the welfare of orphans is Thorn's duty." Falconer's composure never faltered, and he kept right on sounding like a rector plying his trade. "I know Lady Pravda has sent many communications to you since the start of this conflict. The children's need for safety has never been greater than it is now, so we must act."

"Now." Lord Baldric's laugh sounded as sharp as a polished battle blade. "So it's now, right now—after all these years of dereliction?"

Falconer's calm expression wavered. "We have received no messengers from Stone asking us to retrieve orphans." His voice shook on the last few words. "It is your responsibility to tender them to us after you take them in."

"Since when does Stone have to send messengers to encourage Thorn to follow its own code?" Stormbreaker stood, his nails still digging into Lord Baldric's table. "Since when does Thorn show interest in children who bear no wealth or importance to increase Thorn's status?"

The tension radiating from Stormbreaker was so palpable Aron stood himself, more to withstand it than in a show of unity. He was dimly aware of Dari rising to join him. Hasty and Terrick remained seated, but they looked as angry as Stormbreaker.

"Dun." Lord Baldric's whispered caution made gooseflesh rise across Aron's neck and shoulders. There was new energy in the room now, energy Aron had never felt before. He perceived it as a humming white cloud, a quiet, but deliberate force, and it made his bones ache when it passed over him.

Lord Baldric? His eyes moved from person to person, desperate to understand the sensation. *Falconer? Could Hasty or Terrick have abilities like this?*

Be still, came Dari's private, urgent mental communication. *You know nothing. You feel nothing.*

Aron did his best to comply with her wishes, but had no idea if he was achieving his goals. Falconer didn't seem to be aware of him now at all. The entirety of his attention was riveted on Stormbreaker.

"You *are* a child of Vagrat," Falconer murmured, his expression shifting to wariness, or even worry. "And you would have been Harvested . . . when?"

"That is none of your concern," Stormbreaker said through his teeth.

Lord Baldric moved to stand between the two men, using his considerable bulk like a wide gray buffer wall. "Enough of this. Master Falconer, I'll have quarters prepared for you. Hasty, Terrick—see our guest to the kitchens while his chambers are made ready. "

Falconer didn't at all look like he wished to leave, but at the same time, his eyes darted from Stormbreaker to the chamber door.

At last he realizes his peril. Aron almost wished Stormbreaker would let loose a volley of lightning and rain, just to see how Falconer responded, but he also realized it was important to Lord Baldric to keep the peace.

Falconer seemed to weigh his situation and options, and to grow more distressed with each passing moment. He regarded Stormbreaker with much higher interest now, or perhaps it was terror, though of what, Aron couldn't say.

Terrick and Hasty stood and formed an escort, and Falconer allowed himself to be ushered to the door. He stopped long enough to turn and address Lord Baldric once more. "I sincerely regret any misunderstanding that may have grown between Stone and Thorn over the handling of orphans these past years." His words sounded more sincere as he continued, but his gaze continued to shift to Stormbreaker every few seconds. "Rock and leaf, stone and thorn— we are both as essential to the life and growth of Eyrie as we always have been. Please allow me to begin to heal any breach that might have formed. I'm certain Lady Pravda would wish me to make reparations on her behalf."

He bowed, and waited for Lord Baldric's response.

Stunned by the man's shift from arrogant demands and pro-nouncements to humble supplication, Aron stared at Falconer. Then he watched Lord Baldric breathe slowly at least three times before he growled, "Yes, I'm *sure* Pravda would want just that. We'll meet on the morning to make plans, if that will satisfy you."

Aron needed no touch of the Brailing legacy to read the sarcasm and mistrust in Lord Baldric's tone. It was laced with something like despair as well.

Falconer raised his head. Despite Lord Baldric's attitude, the Thorn

Brother seemed genuinely relieved. "Thank you. I'll look forward to our talk tomorrow, and I appreciate this opportunity to rest and restore myself."

The door had barely closed behind him when Dari dropped into her chair and released her mental touch on Aron and, Aron presumed, on Stormbreaker.

Lord Baldric faced off with Stormbreaker and pointed a thick finger right in his face. "Grudge or no grudge, you *will* respect visitors when we receive them." Then, softer, and with less force, "Don't make me regret naming you our First High Master."

Stormbreaker offered no apologies, but he did seem more subdued following the reprimand. Aron found himself holding his breath, as if waiting for a new storm to burst from the depths of Stormbreaker's essence.

For her part, Dari remained silent and withdrawn. Her eyes were closed. Exhaustion seemed to roll out of her, along with distress and pain she didn't bother to conceal. Aron was caught between going to her to offer comfort and remaining absolutely still to avoid interrupting the Lord Provost.

Lord Baldric lowered his hand and folded his arms across his broad chest. His expression shifted to that of a father, and his next question to Stormbreaker was gentler still. "Can you forgive them, Dun?"

The rest of Stormbreaker's tension left him like a breeze blowing through open shutters. His shoulders drooped forward, and he leaned on the table in front of him with his head down. "I don't know."

"Not the people." Lord Baldric's tone remained softer than Aron was used to hearing from him. "I would never ask that of you or your sister—but can you grant that as an institution, Thorn may have some good left in it, some righteous honor that one day may be salvaged?"

Stormbreaker snorted. "With that one taking over for Pravda Altar if she ever has the decency to die?"

"Falconer was little more than an apprentice back then," Lord

Baldric said. "He did what was asked of him in Dyn Vagrat. Were I you, I'd reserve the force of your inner storms for those who commanded him."

"And now?" Stormbreaker asked. "When he intends to lead dozens of children into hardship and death?"

Lord Baldric's tone shifted again. "I'll do what I can, Dun. What's within my power—our power, as the Stone Guild. *We* are not oathbreakers here, in the literal sense or the figurative sense, either."

Dari stirred from her stupor and sat up straighter. "Can you refuse Falconer? Can Thorn's demands be turned down?"

"Were you listening?" Stormbreaker snapped as he gestured to Lord Baldric. "He's telling us what options we have available to us as keepers of our own oaths. None!"

Aron saw each sharp word fall like a blow on Dari, and once more, he didn't know what to do when Stormbreaker growled, "Come, boy. If you have no insights from your *graal*, I should return you to your training."

Stormbreaker stalked toward the chamber doors, and Aron went after him, as much out of confusion and frustration as anything else. He glanced once over his shoulder as the door closed behind him, and was relieved to see Lord Baldric approaching Dari with a kind look on his face and an outstretched handkerchief.

As they clambered down the steps of the main keep, dozens of rebukes rose to Aron's mind, but he voiced none of them. The edgy rumbles of thunder overhead kept putting him off, until he hated himself for his own cowardice, and hated Stormbreaker almost as much for bringing his weakness to the surface so easily.

Iko fell into step behind them as they swept onto Triune's main byway, but Aron ignored the Sabor as thoroughly as he usually did. He could not, however, ignore Iko's companion. Raaf tagged along at Iko's elbow like a redheaded shadow, and the sight of him filled Aron with an entirely new dread.

Worry drove him to speak to Stormbreaker, despite the weather stirring above their heads. "Is Raaf considered an orphan, since you severed his ties with his family when you claimed him from his abusive father?"

Thunder rattled the clear sky as they passed the Judgment Arena.

Stormbreaker stopped and rubbed his hands across his face. More thunder exploded above them.

"Yes, Aron." Stormbreaker sounded miserable and furious all at once. "Raaf is an orphan. Come the morning, if Lord Baldric finds us no path out of this madness, he'll be taken to Thorn with all the rest."

CHAPTER FORTY-FIVE

ARON

Aron almost grabbed Stormbreaker's arm and would have, if respect hadn't held him back. "This can't be allowed! How will Stone stop this madness?"

Stormbreaker said nothing, but the thunder answered for him. The lines of his face remained tight as he started walking again, and his skin was as pale as the dust swirling above the mock battlefield. Aron could see groups sparring, wooden blades smashing against wooden shields and other blunted weapons, but for once, he had no wish to ask to join in and gain extra training time. Worry for Dari's broken heart and Raaf's safety claimed him for a few moments, followed by confusion over Stone's stance against Thorn's demands.

Stormbreaker even seemed angry with him, though Aron had no idea what he might have done to set off his training master.

Unless . . .

He almost stumbled with the force of his next thought.

"This is my fault." He caught Stormbreaker's gray sleeve and stopped him halfway between the archery and knife range and the main kitchen. "It's because of me Thorn came here, isn't it?"

Stormbreaker first glared at him, then seemed to wake to himself and finally regard Aron in a more familiar fashion. "We have no proof of that. You should not make such assumptions."

"Stop." Aron knew Stormbreaker's partial denial was proof that he was correct. "Tell me why. No, don't. Don't say anything to me."

Aron turned away from Stormbreaker, careful not to look in Raaf's direction, or toward the Shrine of the Mother. He rested his eyes on the dirt of the byway and tried to stop grinding his teeth. Everything inside him hurt anew. When he did open his mouth, emotions burst out of him as violently as any of Stormbreaker's lightning. "Why did you treat Dari so horribly? Don't you understand she cares about you? Doesn't it matter to you that she *needs* you?"

Stormbreaker glanced at Iko and Raaf, who remained a respectable distance away. Then his gaze shifted toward the main keep, as if he might be searching for Dari. A look of regret claimed his pale face, and color slowly seeped back into his cheeks.

"The heart is its own master, Aron. You above all others should understand me in this. I can no more force myself to love Dari because she cares for me than you can force yourself to cease loving her when she does not return your feelings."

Aron flinched at the tender brutality of Stormbreaker's words. Embarrassment boiled inside him, bitter and hot, but at the same time, he felt his fury leak out of his essence.

Stormbreaker let out a slow, measured breath. "It is time we laid this bare between us, so it divides us no further. I will apologize to Dari for my insensitivity, but I don't wish to encourage her affections more than I have, since I cannot return them."

Aron knew he should feel overjoyed at this declaration, but he felt nothing but sorrow, and worry for Dari. "Why not? How could you possibly find Dari lacking?"

"That's a deeply private matter, Aron, and something I cannot share because the tale isn't all my own to tell." Stormbreaker broke eye contact and stared off into the distance, and his throat worked furiously as he swallowed more than once.

Aron recognized the gesture, from the many times he had done it himself, trying to contain his feelings for Dari.

"You love someone else." Aron spoke while staring at his own knuckles, somehow too ashamed to keep staring at Stormbreaker.

"Yes." Stormbreaker still sounded distant, and Aron still couldn't look at him.

When Aron finally managed to lift his head, he murmured, "And you cannot see your way clear to putting this person aside for Dari's sake?"

Stormbreaker grimaced, then brought his attention back to Aron. "You care for Dari very deeply. Perhaps more than I realized."

Heat flushed across Aron's skin, but before he could return his gaze to his knuckles, Stormbreaker caught his chin and held his head in place.

"Don't feel shamed, Aron. I'm your guild master, and responsible for all aspects of your growth—including helping you to learn your own heart. Perhaps this situation with Dari has made me remiss in this duty, and for that, I apologize. There is nothing off-limits between us."

"Nothing?" Aron asked as Stormbreaker let him go.

Relaxing into his more typical stance of arms relaxed by his sides, Stormbreaker said, "Nothing that I am not prohibited from sharing by edict of Lord Baldric or guild tradition."

Aron tried to mimic Stormbreaker's posture, despite being nervous about his next question. "Then why do you hate Falconer?"

Stormbreaker remained casual in his stance, but he looked so pained Aron almost regretted his rash prying into the man's private history. When Stormbreaker did speak, his words were quiet and even, as if he had imagined telling his tale, but never practiced it. "The First High Master of Thorn was correct. I'm a child of Vagrat—as most suspect, given my appearance."

Aron reminded himself to nod, so Stormbreaker would keep

talking. Overhead, the sun seemed to blaze like a bright blue eye, staring down at them, warm despite the ever-cooling air of the season.

"Perhaps I should have told you this story long ago, Aron, but I did not know how you'd take it." Stormbreaker's smile was apologetic. A bit sad. "When I was a child, life in Dyn Vagrat was very different than life in other dynasts. Lady Vagrat—Vagrat's seat passes through the female bloodline, you'll remember from your lessons—she did not stay in a castle. Like her mother and grandmother and great-grandmother before her, she lived in the marshes and villages, moving from place to place among us, as one with us."

Aron's eyebrows lifted in surprise. He had never heard such a thing about Vagrat, or come across it in his studying of history and protocols. In fact, he had discovered next to nothing about Dyn Vagrat, save for brief mentions—which was fine by him, as it was Brailing and Altar he studied most fiercely.

"There were no nobles and goodfolk. Lady Vagrat decided disputes, but she shared her wealth with us, and bore her daughter and heir in the tradition of Vagrat—without naming a father, or forging allegiances based on the child." Stormbreaker smiled, as if remembering a private joke, but just as fast, the expression faded, and his stance grew more tense. "When Pravda Altar took her seat with the Thorn Guild, she began to protest Lady Vagrat's 'Brotherless conduct,' and the fact she kept no proper seat of government, no 'nest' of her own."

Aron could imagine his mother saying such a thing, after one of her visits to the nearest village. *Brotherless conduct.* He had heard that phrase more than once, before his parents died. He had never liked it then, and he liked it less now.

Stormbreaker closed his eyes, and now he seemed to be laboring to speak instead of relating an enjoyable yarn about his past. "At first the Lady Provost's protests came in the form of entreaties and letters.

Then she began enforcing obscure agreements Thorn made with Dyn Vagrat upon the formation of their stronghold on the island of Eidolon. When her efforts to corral and control Lady Vagrat failed, the Lady Provost declared Lady Vagrat of infirmed mind, and asserted her right to act in Lady Vagrat's stead."

Silence fell between Stormbreaker and Aron for a moment, and Aron found himself looking back at Iko and Raaf. Part of him wanted to run away from Stormbreaker rather than hear the rest of his story, the story Aron himself had as much as demanded—because he had a dread sense of where the tale was headed.

"They were in our village at the time," Stormbreaker said, and he stopped again when his voice broke.

"You don't have to—" Aron began, but Stormbreaker plowed forward, now staring intently into Aron's eyes.

"We hid her, of course. Lady Vagrat and her daughter." His voice broke again, and he folded his arms across his chest as if to hold himself upright. "Thorn let it be known that Lady Vagrat must have been taken hostage. Since Vagrat had no army, the Lady Provost sent an armed contingent of Altar Dynast Guard to track and retrieve Lady Vagrat."

Aron's heart squeezed, and his own throat closed a little tighter.

"My village had no weapons. That wasn't how we lived, or how we thought."

Stormbreaker opened his hands and stared at his palms.

"No one made it out of the village," Stormbreaker whispered a few moments later, his gaze so distant Aron feared he might be losing touch with here, with now, that his essence might sweep back to that terrible past and remain there, grieving for eternity. "Not even Lady Vagrat. Later, Thorn claimed it was a terrible accident, that her madness drove her to hurl herself against the blade of one of her rescuers."

"How did you survive?" Aron asked, his question barely audible.

Stormbreaker gazed into the sky, into the brightness of the sun, and blinked over and over again. "My sister and I were at play with Rakel Seadaughter, Lady Vagrat's heir, in the marsh leeway. Falconer, two other Thorn apprentices, and three Altar guardsmen took Rakel from us, but Tia and I escaped their vengeance by swimming away under the marsh surface. Then we walked to Dyn Cobb, and we were eventually discovered and dispatched to Lord Cobb at Can Lanyard."

So that's how he came to know Lord Cobb, and well enough to return to visit him later. And of course he would have wanted to see Rakel Seadaughter again, when he had the chance.

Aron could well imagine the surprise of Cobb villagers at finding fair-haired, fair-skinned children of Vagrat trying to hide amongst them.

"Lord Cobb took no position on the tale we told him, but it was clear he feared for our safety. He arranged for some visiting Brailing guardsmen to escort us to Triune to be sheltered." Stormbreaker held out his arm and ran a finger across one of his *dav'ha* marks. A sun linked with Eyrie's two moons. "The Brailing guardsman who personally saw to my safety on that journey gave me this to remind me that time passes, that the sun and moons rise no matter how deeply my heart may ache."

Aron stared at the mark, his memory of his own father's *dav'ha* runes flickering like a dim flame at the center of his essence.

"He helped me, your father." Stormbreaker withdrew his arm, then met Aron's shocked gaze. "I tried to help him in return, tried to save not just your life, but his and your family's as well, but I failed. For that, Aron, I am sorry, and I'll be sorry forever."

Aron completely lost the ability to respond for a time. He stood on the byway with Stormbreaker, staring everywhere but at the man, until he was certain he could do so without losing what little control of his emotions he yet possessed. Through his teeth, he asked, "Why did Thorn never pay for their crimes?"

"Some did. Eldin Falconer's guild master, for example, and a number of the Altar Guard. But in the end, the Lady Provost insisted the action had been necessary to rescue Lady Vagrat and her heir." Stormbreaker frowned, and Aron recognized how hard his guild master was working to manage his own anger. "After all, there were none to speak against her, save for two Brotherless orphans locked away at Triune."

Stormbreaker and Snakekiller.

Suddenly, Aron wanted Snakekiller to return to Triune alive and well.

"Thorn has always been powerful," Stormbreaker continued, once more resuming his relaxed stance. "Most of the dynast lords and ladies were educated there, and ties and loyalties run deep. I think Pravda Altar imagines an Eyrie under Thorn's rule, or at least its control. I think she's seeking to surround herself with those who possess powerful legacies, beginning with Rakel Seadaughter, to bring that vision to fruition."

"About the orphans," Aron whispered. "Will we just . . . surrender?"

"This is not a battle, Aron." Stormbreaker crushed one fist into his palm. "Would that it were. In the end, going against our own charter, becoming oathbreakers, that would be as destructive to Eyrie as this damnable war. If Thorn wishes to resume its rightful and proper duties to orphans, Stone has no legal cause to stand in its way."

Aron gulped back a shout of frustration, then once more glanced at their audience down the byway. His mind whirled through the possibilities of finding some way to use his *graal* to affect this situation. He could confuse Falconer and send him back to Thorn emptyhanded. Or instruct any beast of burden Falconer employed to return to Triune at sunset. The possibilities were limitless.

Would he be within bounds to do something to stop this travesty?

No, his mind told him.

"What about Raaf?" he asked.

Stormbreaker's eyes flashed in an entirely new way, and when he spoke, the thunder came back, only this time in his voice. "Raaf can take vows to Stone, if he wishes to stay."

Aron's jaw loosened from surprise. "I thought you wouldn't allow a rescue to pledge himself to Stone until he reached at least twelve cycles of age."

"That was before Thorn chose to assert itself in such a fashion." Stormbreaker sounded both grim and triumphant. "If Raaf and any of the other rescues don't choose to submit themselves to Thorn, they may remain here as apprentices. Thorn has no claim on Stone apprentices."

"So it is a battle, of words and rules and wits—and wills." Aron realized he was speaking out loud, then decided not to censor himself despite an approaching group of Den apprentices. "One Thorn may find difficult to win."

The Den apprentices passed by, Galvin Herder in the lead, and as always, the older boy—*the perpetual apprentice*, Zed now called him—reserved a special, threatening glare for Aron.

Stormbreaker made as if not to notice.

"I will probably need punishment by morning," Aron muttered to release his own tension. "Galvin and I fought again last evening. If you need to send me to Endurance House for smashing his teeth with my fist, I'll understand."

"Herder again." Stormbreaker shook his head and glanced at the apprentices as they made their way past Iko and Raaf on the byway. "Did he wound your lip?"

Aron raised his fingers to the swollen, cut tissue, and suddenly the story of the previous night's events seemed too great to tell, especially the part about him almost using his Brailing *graal* against the bandits who attacked them. "No," he said. "Blath can explain better than me."

And perhaps she'll omit the more troubling aspects of the night.

Stormbreaker didn't seem to believe him about the lip and gestured toward Galvin. "Leave it be, Aron. Leave him be."

"I can't, because he won't." Aron sighed. "Am I to be his punch-dummy forever?"

"I don't care what Herder does or doesn't do." Stormbreaker adopted a firmer tone. "I expect you to take the next right action—and fighting with your Brothers and Sisters is never the next right action, especially in such a difficult time, when we are being pressured from outside these walls. Find another way."

Aron didn't answer, but he did lower his gaze, then offered Stormbreaker a bow of capitulation.

He would try to stay away from Galvin. He always tried. He just never managed to be successful.

CHAPTER FORTY-SIX

ARON

You should use your graal *on the girl again. Convince her of your affections, and the truth of her own feelings for you.*

The Goddess spoke to Aron as she always did, in a kind voice edged with blood and murder. She wore the same radiant silver robes, and she looked even more beautiful than usual with her blond hair piled atop her head in flows of ringlets. Aron had grown used to the soft blue of her eyes, to the silver energy and strands of copper essence that seemed to highlight every perfect feature of her face and body.

She does care for you. More deeply than she understands.

He knew he was dreaming, so he didn't bother to answer, to tell the Lady—for that was how he thought of this being now, as the Lady, the Mother of Mystery herself—that he would never do something so awful to Dari.

You know she is lonely. With a few moments of effort, you could comfort her—and bind her to you for all time.

Aron felt himself smiling at the thought of easing the pain in Dari's heart, but he held his silence. He couldn't even consider what it would be like to have Dari bound to him. That seemed impossible, and wrong, though also beautiful and desirable in its own way.

The Lady's answering smile warmed him and chilled him at the same moment. *No? Not yet? Then finally, finally allow me to give you this gift.*

Aron tried to rouse himself, but waking deliberately from these dreams was never easy. He pinched himself, but felt nothing. He bit his own lip, but remained where he was, drifting in what felt like a soft blanket of nothingness, next to the Lady.

She stretched out a graceful hand, and a vista opened beneath him. He knew what he would see, knew he shouldn't look, but he couldn't help himself.

Below him, hundreds of soldiers wearing the sun blue and yellows of the Brailing Guard were gathered on an open field next to soldiers bearing banners with the steel and copper colors of Dyn Altar. They were facing soldiers bearing banners of Dyn Mab's crimson and white.

Night after night, I offer you your due, for all you have suffered. The Lady gave him a loving glance. *Will you still refuse my generosity?*

Energy flowed through Aron, from his mind to his hands to his fingers, and he had a sense that if he stretched out his own arm like the Lady had done, some of the Brailing Guard would fall dead. Maybe the very guardsmen he wanted to find and hold accountable for the deaths of his family.

As if in response, a few of the guardsmen glowed more brightly than the rest.

If you practice, you could become proficient. First one, then several. We can't begin to know your limits, or lack thereof. Try it now, with these, the ones you seek.

The faces of the guardsmen etched themselves into Aron's mind. Beards and moles, scars and marks, the color and length of their hair, their height, even how they wore their uniforms or carried their weapons. He thought he might recognize them now, anywhere, anytime.

The skin on his fingers hummed and buzzed, then began to burn with the need to touch these men, to command each of their hearts to stop beating. He could do it. He knew he could, and no one but the Lady would ever know. She was the Goddess, and she was as much as telling him to do it.

The Lady waited, more patiently than she usually did. Her voice grew even lower and more inviting. *Stone does not understand you, Aron. If you had killed the outlaws who tried to claim you, I would have come to your defense against these barbarians. Use of your* graal *to protect your life, and the life of someone else, would have been a blessing.*

Aron stared at his fingers, which now glowed a brilliant sapphire. He felt a dizzying need, a flash of inner power and will, then a spark of guilt over never telling Stormbreaker about how he almost used his legacy to strike down Canus the Bandit's men in Dyn Cobb.

The Lady stroked his shoulder with long, warm fingers. *Go to High Master Falconer and petition him to return to Eidolon. I will bless his efforts, Aron. It* will *happen, if I command it.*

Aron turned his hands palm upward, and the sapphire energy arced between his wrists and fingers.

So after all this time, he had a choice about his future, at least in his dreams.

Stone or Thorn.

Service to one guild master, or service to another.

If he had been given the choice the day he was Harvested, Aron had little doubt which path he would have chosen. He never would have known Dari, never come to understand a man as complex as Stormbreaker. There would have been no Raaf, no Zed, no Iko in his life. But also no Lord Baldric looming to menace him each time he became angry, and no Galvin Herder to hit him or kick him or try to get his talon killed.

Perhaps Thorn didn't have so many restrictions on the use of legacies.

Aron kept staring into the sapphire energy of his own hands. In the glittering light, he saw an image of Eldin Falconer in his cardinal robes, delayed these many days at Stone while Lord Baldric found excuses not to release the children Thorn wished to absorb into their folds. Falconer stood side by side with an image of Stormbreaker in his Stone Guild gray. The two men merged and separated, merged and separated, as if each was forming the other—or destroying him.

"Stormbreaker," Aron whispered, and the word was louder than the crack of rock breaking in a deep canyon. He slammed his hands together, and a hot blast of blue fire shattered his muscles, his bones, his skin and teeth—

He woke without shouting, and without startling Raaf, who was sleeping in a third bed that had been placed between Aron's and Zed's after Raaf took his vows. Sweat bathed Aron's neck and shoulders, and when he swallowed, his throat felt raw and abused.

That dream had been worse than most, and he sighed as he assessed the reasons.

His worry for Dari, who had been distant since he saw her shift into her Stregan form.

His self-recrimination for not telling Stormbreaker about his confusion over using his legacy in the battle with the bandits.

His concern for Raaf, who had become Stormbreaker's junior apprentice to avoid being forced to leave Triune. There were many new junior apprentices these past few weeks. More than should have been, had Thorn not attempted to insinuate itself into lives better left without their influence.

Some of those things, Aron was powerless to change, but others, he knew he needed to make more effort to correct.

These were only dreams. He had discussed them with Stormbreaker and Dari enough times to know that. They were expressions of hidden desires, or even his deepest fears. Nothing but wishes, made into pictures.

Still, Aron wondered what might happen if he took the Lady up on her dark offers, if he ever surrendered to that type of temptation even in his dreams.

That, he didn't want to imagine.

"Up," Aron said as he climbed out of his bed to rattle Raaf awake as Zed had roused him so many times his first few days at Triune. "Come on. We'll be late for *fael'feis*."

• • •

At the end of his morning training with Dari, Aron mastered his own anxiety enough to tackle one of the main causes of his heightened dreams. It took a great deal of determination, but he caught her attention by placing his hand on her wrist. When she met his gaze, he swallowed hard, then got the essential words out without major disaster. "What happened two cycles ago, it didn't bother me." He swallowed again. "Seeing you as you are in your Stregan form, I mean."

Dari's smile was gentle, and heartrending. "I wish I could believe you." She stood slowly, smoothing her gray robes, and gestured for Aron to rise as well. "I'm not ashamed of my Stregan essence, Aron. Please understand that. I just know how . . . alien it must seem to you."

And to Stormbreaker.

She didn't say that aloud, or even through their lingering mental connection, but Aron knew that was what she believed. That Stormbreaker could muster no interest in her because she was, at base, Fury and not Fae.

She had to know that wasn't true, and she had to know he didn't feel that way either—didn't she?

"I've never discussed what happened that night with Stormbreaker," he said, hoping to spare her feelings as he joined her by the chamber window, paying little heed to Blath, who sat quietly nearby.

"Blath spoke to him after we returned." Dari nodded in Blath's direction. "Stone had to be informed about Canus the Bandit's activities in Dyn Cobb, and Stormbreaker had to know that rumors of Stregans in Eyrie might begin to appear."

Aron wanted to take hold of Dari and turn her to face him, but he thought that might be too forward. Somehow, he had to reach her, break through that wall she seemed to have constructed between them since that fateful bandit attack. "Stormbreaker hasn't asked me any questions about you. What you were like when you changed."

Dari's expression shifted to sadness, then anger. "I suppose I should be grateful for his disinterest."

Now Aron wanted to groan. Was there ever a right thing to say to this girl? He was beginning to believe there wasn't. Dari felt farther away than ever, and he knew he was the cause of it, though how to mend the situation eluded him completely. If Zed didn't come back soon, Aron realized he might start talking to Iko, or even Raaf, just to maintain his sanity.

Aron had been counting days as Lord Baldric stalled Eldin Falconer in his desire to leave with Stone's orphans, fifty-seven so far, and Zed had been gone two weeks longer than that. As if summoned by his thoughts, Thorn's High Master stalked past Dari's window, heading toward the Shrine of the Mother.

The sight of him made Aron think too much about this morning's dream, and he shivered.

"Making a list of candidates was a plausible reason for delay," Dari said, following Falconer with her eyes as he passed. "This latest bunch of excuses from Lord Baldric—the late-season chill, and the whole bit about waiting for messengers to return with release letters from village elders and possible long-lost relatives—it's a stretch."

Aron nodded. He had watched as the Thorn Brother observed training sessions, and he had seen the man attempting to interview any unattached child he passed. Everyone seemed kind and tolerant in their dealings with Falconer, but he rarely gained more than a few minutes of polite interchange with anyone.

At best, he had gained permission to leave with four children, and three of those were incorrigibles who would likely steal his purse and robes and be back at Triune by dawn the day following his departure.

"Galvin Herder has petitioned Lord Baldric to allow him to go to his final trial. Again. Did you know?"

Aron tried to hold back his frown, but could not. He did know, but only because he had overheard the argument while hiding around a corner, waiting to ambush Galvin in the Den and get a head start on the night's inevitable battles. The sight of Galvin so desperately making his demands to Lord Baldric had averted the confrontation, and added to Aron's troubled thoughts and no doubt his more active dreams.

"Perhaps the Lord Provost will allow him satisfaction," Aron murmured, trying to be gracious even though he knew Dari held Galvin in no greater esteem than he did.

Dari relaxed a fraction. "You have the box today, do you not?"

Aron averted his gaze from Falconer before he had to look fully at the Shrine of the Mother. More often than not, especially after such an active night of dreaming, the sight of those stone pillars made him dizzy and weak. "Yes. I have the box."

"I don't know how you stand that, Aron." Dari faced him, and Aron was pleased by the concern radiating from her beautiful face. "I don't know how any of you bear some of what Stone puts you through."

"It's all necessary." Aron gave the answer quickly and easily, because he believed it as deeply as he could believe anything. "Who knows when I might have to wait in cramped quarters, maybe for hours, or even days, to stop some rapist or child-killer?"

For a few seconds, at least, Dari seemed totally her old self, accessible to him in most ways, and not so burdened with her own worries. "Do you think you'll always be so committed to Stone's aims?"

"Yes." That answer came easily too, yet Aron fidgeted as he gave it, sensing another potential girl-problem in the making. "But—but I do have room in my heart for other commitments. Few men and women are willing to share lives like ours, but we're allowed to have relationships. With Guild permission, we can take promise-mates."

Blath coughed, and Dari's eyes widened before she turned back to her study of the castle byway visible outside her window.

Was she smiling or frowning?

Had he stepped correctly, or made some grievous error?

Aron wondered if he should present himself at the infirmary near the farming quarters and petition to have his tongue removed, but he decided to take one more risk before excusing himself. "I would be happy to escort you to the main kitchens tonight, or tomorrow night if I don't get out of the box in time. If, I mean, you, if that is, you would like to have dinner with me."

Blath gave another cough, but Dari laughed. This time when she looked at him, her eyes seemed a little brighter, and her gaze was more direct. "You're persistent, Aron Weylyn."

Aron almost thanked her, then wondered if he should be offended. In the end, he opted for, "I hope you value persistence."

"It can be annoying." Dari patted his hand. "And at times, endearing."

Later, in the cool heat of the fall sunlight at midday, as the forge master fastened Aron into the body-sized box where he would stand and observe the world through a tiny slit in the metal door until the master released him, he wondered which one he might be to Dari—annoying or endearing.

Then he wondered if he truly wanted to know the answer.

CHAPTER FORTY-SEVEN

ARON

Annoying.

Endearing.

Was one better than the other?

Aron did his best to focus on what he was supposed to observe, but his thoughts wouldn't leave him alone.

"What do you see, boy?" The forge master's voice rasped through the box's metal opening, pushing the scent of chewed roast and cream ale into the stuffy space. Aron couldn't see the man, but he could imagine the tall, brown-bearded giant. The forge master usually wore nothing but gray breeches during the workday, donning his robes only for meals and after-daylight activities.

How long had Aron been in the box? Three hours? Four? He had lost track, and in truth it didn't matter, for he would be there until the forge master set him loose. His longest stretch so far had been six hours, and Stormbreaker had brought him two dinner portions to help him recover.

Aron's stomach rumbled, and his knees and ankles felt numb, but he stared through the opening and gave a full report. "The byway, three pine trunks, the eastern stream three hands below normal, and the eastern tip of the mock battlefield with no combatants visible."

"Anything unusual?" the forge master's question was casual, but Aron knew the force of the cuffing his ears might take if he answered incorrectly.

"No, forge master."

The man sniffed, which he usually did if Aron was correct. "Are you certain?"

Aron relaxed against the warm metal sides of the box for a moment. "Yes, forge master."

"Your life may depend on certainty. Stay alert."

Aron closed his eyes and held his breath, bracing for what came next.

The box swung in a tight circle, around and around and around, propelled on its wheel by the heavy-armed forge master until Aron thought his entire brain must be spinning. It was hot in the box this time of day, even so late into the fall, and the combination of hours and fatigue and heat and the smells of the forge master's lunch made Aron's stomach lurch as the box stopped.

Facing Endurance House, and beyond that, the Shrine of the Mother.

Aron turned his head, feeling his pulse surge in his ears.

By the Brother's grace, he would not be left in this position terribly long.

The forge master's boots ground against the rock of the forge yard as he strode away.

And time began to pass and stand still, and stretch and pull in ways Aron couldn't begin to explain.

Now and again, he glanced in the direction he was supposed to study, but almost immediately, a silvery light would flare from the Shrine, a light Aron could imagine his dangerous Goddess striding through and reaching beyond to grab hold of him and finally force him to accept one of her terrible "gifts" or "blessings."

I am no oathbreaker. I will not become an oathbreaker.

Even with the blessings of a Goddess, he would not surrender that bit of himself, of his true identity, given to him by his father and now fostered by Stormbreaker and Stone itself.

Minutes later—though it might have been much less or much longer—the voices of apprentices rattled through the training yard. Newer voices. Perhaps of the newer apprentices not consigned to the High Master's Den.

"I'm the Bandit," one boy said.

"No, it's me today. I'm Canus, and I'm going to kill your soldiers and take your winter stores!"

Eyes closed, Aron frowned at the admiration in the boy's voice, and he wished he could wheel the box around and confront the two upstarts about holding a criminal in reverence.

You're Stone apprentices now, he wanted to tell them. *Canus the Bandit is your prey, not your hero.*

The sound of practice swords clattering against each other blotted out his next thoughts, and he dared a quick glance at his target area. More eerie light from the Shrine. Some odd darkness rising off Endurance House. Nothing else that he could see in his cursory appraisal. Aron closed his eyes again as the bells on the battlement rang, announcing the return of members of the Stone Guild who had been away. So many were out hunting, it was impossible to say who might be coming back, but of course Aron hoped Zed was amongst the group, even it meant having Windblown back as well.

He tried to will away the cramping in his calves. There was precious little room to move in the box, but occasionally, he managed to pull himself into a *fael'feis* pose to stretch out his back or give his knees some relief.

Aron . . .

The voice was so sweet. So kind and soothing.

What pains you, Aron?

The Goddess was calling to him. Reaching for him after all, intent on capturing him while he was helpless in the box.

I'll save you. Fear not. I'm coming.

Aron wasn't really aware of when he fell asleep and started dreaming, but he was more than aware when the forge master smashed his fist against the side of the box and nearly rattled Aron's heart straight out of his chest. He startled and slammed his head against the warm metal, and a blaze of light from the Shrine of the Mother stabbed deep into his consciousness. The bells along Triune's battlements began to ring, and the light from the Shrine blazed all the brighter. Dust rose on the byway between Endurance House and the forge yard, as if the Goddess might be striding forth at last to claim him.

Aron babbled out a quick report, including the bells and dust.

What was the pattern of the bells?

He couldn't read it, couldn't keep his mind on the stops and starts, on the clans and peals.

A dynast lord? But no, slightly different. Something he'd never heard before.

When the forge master didn't respond to his report, Aron feared he was about to be hauled from the box to receive his punishment for surrendering his awareness.

Instead, the forge master said nothing, and Aron couldn't help noticing who was emerging from the dust cloud on the byway. Eldin Falconer's cardinal robes were unmistakable. Behind him, the light in the Shrine died away as the bells once more gave a set of unusual rings. Aron became aware of Stone Brothers crossing in front of Thorn's First High Master, Stormbreaker leading the charge, rushing toward Triune's main gate and keep to greet whoever was arriving. They weren't drawing weapons, which was a good sign, but Aron's insides vibrated with curiosity and frustration that he was confined and couldn't join the procession.

When Falconer reached the forge, he strode straight to the box, swept out of Aron's view, and apparently came to a stop directly before the forge master. "Who do you have contained within that beastly contraption?"

The forge master took his time in answering. Aron couldn't see either man, but he imagined the big forge master folding his heavy arms over his bulging, scarred chest. When the forge master spoke, his voice was polite and calm—yet also hard and definite. "I can't see that being any of your concern, High Master Falconer, but it's one of our apprentices. A good boy. A strong boy. One of our best."

The compliment made Aron straighten despite his aching muscles, even as Falconer snorted his disapproval and growled, "What infraction did the poor child commit to earn such a punishment?"

Aron's eyebrows lifted. For a moment, he thought to protest the misconception himself, but the forge master spoke before he could figure out what to say. "He isn't being punished, sir. He's working at his observation skills, his awareness under duress, and his tolerance of small spaces for long stretches—all skills needed by the Stone Guild when we're about Stone business."

He emphasized those last two words, as if to make a point that though this was training, it was still Stone business, and Falconer shouldn't be interfering.

Falconer's next command was louder and more strident. "I want you to release the boy this minute. This is inhumane, and I won't stand by and see it done."

"I don't need releasing, sir, thank you," Aron called, then winced as the forge master smacked the side of the box.

"You, get back to your assignment," the forge master instructed. Then, to Falconer, the forge master said, "That you may take up with Lord Baldric, amongst your other demands. I'm certain he would be receptive to meeting with you, after he receives his guest."

"What guest?" Falconer sounded confused, then more annoyed

than ever. "Thorn doesn't have these damnable bells breaking the peace every quiet moment."

The forge master chuckled. "There. You see now? If you had spent time in the box like Aron here, you might have studied Stone's bells, and then you'd know for yourself that Lady Vagrat has come to Triune."

Aron actually stood straight in the box and opened his eyes wide. Behind High Master Falconer, the Shrine of the Mother seemed dull and peaceful, and Endurance House was nothing but a building beside the byway.

"Lady—are you—Lady Vagrat?" Falconer's voice climbed an entire octave. "Rakel Seadaughter has come *here*?"

"Yes, sir," the forge master said, but he need not have bothered.

Aron heard no more from the First High Master of Thorn, and was aware only of the man's cardinal robes as he swept back past the box, heading toward the main gate and keep.

"You." The forge master's dark black eyes peered through the slit in the box. "You've got quite a bit of energy. Let's see if we can put it to good use."

Aron scarcely had time to brace himself before the box gave its mightiest spin yet.

• • •

When the door to the box opened the next morning, Aron fell straight out on the ground, but managed to wheeze out his report of what he had seen and heard in the night, including the slow, sad tolling of the battlement bells as dawn broke. Once more, it was a pattern Aron had never heard before, so he could do little save for describing it.

The forge master pulled him to his feet, pounded him on the back twice, hard enough to make him wheeze all over again, and said, "Well done," as he pushed Aron toward a boy standing off to Aron's right. "You there. Feed him, and see that he gets more water."

It was Zed who caught Aron and held him upright, and Raaf who helped Zed steady Aron as he tried to shake the stiffness out of his legs and arms. He grinned at Zed, then felt a rush of concern when Zed didn't return his joy. The blond boy was more tan than Aron remembered, and taller still, with a man's bulky muscles now. And he looked beyond grim as he nodded his greeting, turned Aron loose, and handed him some hardtack and a wineskin.

Aron drank half the skin, then crammed the bits of dried meat into his mouth. He glanced at Raaf as he chewed, and noted that the younger boy, too, looked unhappy.

"What?" Aron asked after he swallowed, his aching body growing stiff all over again. "Is Windblown—"

"Herder didn't make it," Zed said, avoiding Aron's gaze.

When Aron could only stand mute and gape at him, Zed added, "His trial. When we returned yesterday, Master Windblown granted Herder permission to go to the Ruined Keep for his trial. He didn't survive."

Aron rubbed his wrists, trying to understand what Zed was telling him. "Galvin Herder . . . trial? Last night? He went last night?"

Aron couldn't believe it. If he had known, he would have—

What? Gone to the battlements to cheer on the manes and mockers? Of course not.

Zed pointed to the battlements. "The bells rang for him this morning, when they found him. Dari dispatched his essence—though there was scarcely enough left of him to hold to his *cheville*."

Aron realized he had only heard joyous bells after trials since his arrival, never the dolorous tolling he had marked this morning, after his night in the box. He had seen apprentices bruised and bloodied, even scarred—but he had not known a death at trial since he came to Triune. And now Galvin Herder . . .

Galvin Herder was dead.

The news simply wouldn't sink from his mind to his heart, and when it did, Aron fought to understand his own sudden grief and horror. Galvin had always been a trial in his own fashion, a daily struggle for Aron. Aron had always figured that defeating Galvin more regularly, or finding some way to make a true peace with him, would be part of what let Aron know that he, himself, might be ready for his own trial—and now Herder was . . . gone.

Just gone.

It was a strange sensation, as if a bit of his own identity had been stripped completely away, leaving him less than he had been only moments before.

Aron shook his head again, trying to deny his own confusion.

This was his enemy Zed was talking about, a boy who had had pounded on him and worked to humiliate him since the very night he arrived at the stronghold—but Aron couldn't help remembering the report Galvin gave to Lord Baldric upon their return from the Ruined Keep.

A shadow fell across Aron's path, but he didn't react, recognizing the presence of Iko, which had become as familiar as the companionship of a brother. The Sabor came to a stop beside him, crossed his arms over his chest, and kept a wary eye on the Shrine of the Mother in the distance.

"How did it happen?" Aron asked, hearing the catch in his voice.

Zed frowned and gazed off to the west, as if he could see through Triune's thick stone curtain, all the way to the Ruined Keep where Galvin died. "Might have been rock cats or Rocs on a night hunt. Or mockers. It wasn't manes. There was too much blood, according to Dari. Manes would have taken the blood for themselves."

That image disturbed Aron. He tried not to allow his mind to see it, but he couldn't help imagining Galvin's bloody remains scattered across the cracked stone floor of the Ruined Keep.

"He died fighting." Raaf caught Aron's hand in his much smaller fingers. "That's something, at least? That's something, right?"

Aron gazed down at the boy and had an urge to rip off the gray tunic and breeches that marked Raaf as a Stone apprentice. He would have, if it would have made a difference in whether or not Raaf ever subjected himself to such a lethal test of his abilities. His next urge was to stride down to the main gate and keep, find High Master Falconer, and punch the man right in the face for forcing Raaf to choose between Thorn and Stone long before the boy should have been pushed into any such decision. Maybe he would strike Lord Baldric, too, for not being more forceful with Thorn, and for allowing these idiotic trials to begin with.

"What kind of foolish tradition is this?" Aron pulled free of Raaf, then rubbed his own back with both hands. "Why should anyone who makes it through Stone training have to go through something like that?"

"To bind us together." Zed was still staring in the direction of the Ruined Keep. Above them, the sky grew evermore blue and bright on the cloudless fall morning, perfect in all ways but for the fact they were discussing the death of a Stone apprentice. "That's what Windblown told me. Surviving the trial is a shared experience, and proof that we're ready to be part of the guild."

Even though he knew it was one of the few forbidden questions at Stone, Aron asked, "But what really happens? Does Stone just set a person adrift in that broken-down tower and put out a call to all the monsters in the Barrens, the Outlands, and the Deadfall?"

Zed shrugged, but the gesture was anything but casual or relaxed. Raaf stared at his feet, and Iko remained on guard, gazing at the Shrine of the Mother.

For a moment, Aron did the same.

Once more, he experienced no strange unease, and saw no odd collections of lighting over either Endurance House or the Shrine.

Had he been truly *afraid* of those places? They seemed so peaceful now, in the face of such a tragedy. Why had he maintained such senseless fears instead of confronting them more directly?

Aron became aware of his own clenched fists, but he couldn't make himself relax. Galvin was dead now. He was dead like Aron's family, and so many others, and for what? For some ideal of what makes a guild, or true companions?

Aron wanted to demand answers from Windblown, and Lord Baldric, too. Maybe even Stormbreaker—and *because it's always been that way* simply would not be a good enough reason.

"Where is Stormbreaker?" he asked Zed, his wrists and fingers beginning to throb along with the rest of his muscles.

"Last I saw him, he was near the main keep." Zed pointed south, and a little to the east. "He was walking with Lady Vagrat and her heir."

Aron nodded to Zed and Raaf. "I would have a word with him, then. Alone. I'll find the two of you later, in time for riding practice. Raaf, if you would saddle Tek for me, it would be a great help."

CHAPTER FORTY-EIGHT

ARON

As Zed and Raaf peeled away from him, heading toward the Den, Aron set out for the crop barn and fields, walking as fast as his exhausted, weak legs would allow, with Iko following quietly behind. He almost wished he still had buckets of rocks to carry, but he had abandoned that habit once he began to get his man's bulk. His stomach ached miserably from hunger, but he overrode the pain, just as he had most of the night, as he battled to increase his stamina and maintain his attention.

He intended to find Stormbreaker and get his answers about the trial, and what now felt like a completely senseless waste of life.

Galvin might have been a perfect mocker-ass, but he was a man in his own right, and did not deserve being torn apart by vicious monsters and beasts while his entire guild stood by, wishing him well but doing nothing to come to his aid. Soon it would be Aron suffering that fate. Or Zed. And one day, Raaf, if Aron didn't put a stop to this.

He passed by the mock battlefield, scarcely taking note of the apprentices hard at work in the crisp morning air. The Judgment Arena also passed by in a blur, as did the groups of Stone Brothers and apprentices along the main byway. When he came to the back of the main keep, he turned east toward the fields, and headed toward the footbridge that would take him toward the farming quarters. He expected to find Stormbreaker in one of the towers near the fields, seeing to the needs of Stone's latest guest.

What he found instead was Dari, standing on the footbridge near the Temple of the Brother, with Blath at her side. Dari's hands gripped the bridge railing, and it was obvious to Aron that she was weeping as she stared into the newly harvested fields.

A new rush of emotions flooded through Aron, these more focused and much less confusing. All of his other aims evaporated as he hurried toward her, intending to gather her to him and offer whatever comfort she might need. He would determine what had wounded her, and put a stop to *that*, too. Whatever it was.

As he reached the bridge, Blath stepped forward to block his path, shook her head with an expression that let him know she would prevent any intrusion in this vulnerable moment. Aron glared at the Sabor woman, then looked past her to Dari. He followed her gaze, until he came to what she was staring at, until he absorbed the obvious source of her pain.

It was Stormbreaker, standing beside a tall, ethereal woman with silvery hair and skin even fairer than his. Though he was at some distance, Aron could make out the woman's bright, silvery eyes as well. She seemed wispy, almost insubstantial, and if he had seen her stepping from some mist or fog, he might have mistaken her for a spirit or apparition.

His first thought was that he might be seeing Tia Snakekiller at last, Stormbreaker's sister, but this was not the woman Aron remembered from his brief legacy-guided view of her. And Stormbreaker's manner was not that of a man holding conversation with his sibling. The deferential dip of his head, the gentle fashion in which he gestured, or extended his hand to brush the woman's arm—no. This was certainly not his sister.

This had to be Lady Vagrat, Rakel Seadaughter, descendant of Eyrie's most mysterious and reclusive dynast line.

Lady Vagrat and Stormbreaker were standing at the edge of a har-vested cornfield, seemingly enveloped in sadness, but watching a lit-tle girl of perhaps five or six years of age frolicking through the remnants of broken stalks. The child had her mother's fair skin, but her hair was white and not silver, and her build seemed more mus-cled and solid than her mother's.

This would be Rakel Seadaughter's heir. A girl who would never marry, but one day would bear heirs of her own, by a male of her own choosing, who would never be named.

Brotherless . . .

The word floated through Aron's mind, spoken in his mother's voice, but he rejected it. It wasn't for him or anyone else to judge. Vagrat's ways and beliefs were Vagrat's ways and beliefs.

As were Stone's.

Aron narrowed his eyes as he thought about Galvin Herder and the dangerous trial in the Ruined Keep. Should he simply accept such a thing, because he was Stone now, and Stone had rights to their own traditions and beliefs?

And should he simply accept that once more, Stormbreaker was hurting Dari, and there was nothing Aron could do to stop it?

The air felt heavy with sadness and change, and that heaviness seemed to spread from Aron, Iko, and Blath forward to coat Dari, and farther still, to where Stormbreaker stood with a woman Aron had no doubt must be the one who had claimed Stormbreaker's heart.

He remembered Lord Cobb's greeting to Stormbreaker when they met on Aron's journey to Triune. *It's good to see you again, too. What has it been since you last visited Cobb? Three years? . . . Four . . . During Lady Vagrat's last visit.*

Aron eyed the happy little girl, who looked more like her father than her mother. It was easy enough to count out the cycles and years. His gaze then moved back to Stormbreaker and Lady Vagrat, and a flicker of his *graal* told him that he wasn't watching the reunion of two lovers who pined for each other, but rather two friends who remembered their history fondly.

Dari didn't seem to realize that the emotion between Stormbreaker and Rakel Seadaughter was something from the past, not the present. Her tears flowed, but after another few moments, she straightened herself and turned toward Aron, Blath, and Iko. The misery in the depths of her black eyes couldn't be missed, nor could the burden of dispatching Galvin Herder's essence, or the sudden concern for Aron after his night in the box.

He gave her a quick bow, to relieve her of any worry over his well-being, and as she approached, he said, "You should rest. Will you allow Blath to escort you back to the Den?" Blath gave Aron a strange look, as if she might have been expecting him to exploit Dari at this troubled moment instead of doing what he could to ease her discomfort.

Aron frowned back at Blath without planning the expression, or considering it.

Did she not understand?

If Dari ever came to him with affection, Aron wanted it to be of her free choice, something that would make her happy, lighter of heart—never more weighted, sadder, or more at a loss.

Dari stopped in front of him. "She's come, I think, to force Stone's hand about the orphans and make some peaceful solution to the demand."

Aron wondered at that, at why Lady Vagrat, who had been ill treated by at least one of Eyrie's greater guilds, would involve herself in such a pursuit, but he didn't think Dari was up to that conversation. She seemed like she wanted to ask something of him, and he waited, hopeful she might give him some concrete task he could complete on her behalf. Instead, she gazed at him, seeming to view him differently, and when she spoke, it was a simple question, friend to friend, not student to teacher, or anything else reflective of their previous difference in status.

"Did you know who it was?" Dari's voice was soft, and so terribly pained.

Aron couldn't help glancing toward Stormbreaker. "No. I knew only that he cared for someone in his past. He never told me the who of it, or the how."

Dari looked away, toward the sky, then back at Aron again, and this time her gaze was deeper and more searching. "You've never reminded me of that, even as I tried to forget it. Even when it might have worked to your benefit."

It was all Aron could do not to touch her in some way, even just his fingers to her elbow, to connect with her somehow, and let her feel the truth of his conviction in this matter. "Of course not."

She kept up her steady scrutiny, but Aron withstood it, wondering if for the first time ever, he was finally doing something correct where Dari was concerned.

"It would have been painful," she said, fresh tears gathering in the dark centers of her eyes.

Aron could think of nothing else to say beyond, "I'm sorry."

"Yes," Dari whispered, retreating inward and pulling her arms across her chest, crossed at the wrists. Aron couldn't help realizing that something inside Dari was shifting, or perhaps breaking. That the tie of her heart to Stormbreaker had loosened, and maybe even snapped.

Why, then, could he find no joy in that fact?

"Don't lose hope," he told her, desperate to ease her misery. "I believe this marks an end for them, not a new beginning."

"It doesn't matter," she said, not relieved at all, from what he could see. "At least not to me."

She walked past him, headed in the general direction of the Den with Blath at her side, and Aron knew better than to follow her.

"Giving Stormbreaker a beating would be only a momentary satisfaction, and likely more trouble than it's worth."

Iko's comment startled Aron so badly he spun toward the Sabor, then stared at Iko's face to see if Iko was somehow making fun of him. He saw nothing but stolid regard in Iko's countenance. The way Iko's fists were clenched, he, too, might have been considering defending Dari's heart in the literal sense.

The wild fury in Aron reached the tipping point, and he started walking, brushing past Iko without further comment. For so long, Lord Baldric's threats had held Aron's impulses in check, but this day, those threats meant no more to him than words lost in a loud, strong wind. He wanted to regulate his temper for himself, maybe for Dari, too. And he would do it his own way, without too much guidance or discussion, because he felt too tired, too sore, inside and out, to even be part of the living world.

Some minutes later, Aron arrived at his destination, the only place he could think to go to spend the wealth of anger and ill feelings without doing real damage, save for the Ruined Keep.

Endurance House was just as it always had been, a small building near the byway that ran past the forge, a barrier between the Shrine of the Mother and the rest of Triune. The dark cloud he had so often seen—*imagined?*—no longer hovered above it. No one was nearby, save for a squat, bald Stone Brother named Markam, sitting on the porch of the building, enjoying a slow sip of almond mead.

When Markam saw Aron coming, he put aside his metal cup and stood, his brown eyes alight with curiosity. "Aron Weylyn. I never thought to see you sent to receive my particular brand of correction. What offense has boy-perfect finally deigned to commit?"

"No offense," Aron growled, unable to lighten his tone. "No one sent me."

"Then—"

Aron cut Markam off with a sharp shake of his head. "What is this place? What is it really? Tell me, and don't play games. I have no capacity for games this day."

"Yes. I can see that." Markam's friendly expression turned serious as he gestured to the building behind them. "I know apprentices tell one another all manner of tales, but Endurance House is only a place of contemplation. A quiet space to contend with your own demons, and find peace with them. Nothing more."

Aron took that in, weighed it, and made his decision. "Admit me."

Markam shifted to worry, and pulled at his robe with both hands. "Are you certain? Some don't react well to isolation—that's where the stories began to grow, Aron."

The waves cresting inside Aron seemed to smash through his whole being. He grabbed the front of the shorter man's robes, absolutely unable to hold himself back. "Admit me! And the Sabor comes as well. If he wants."

Markam regarded Aron like he just might be completely mad, but he freed himself from Aron's grip and stepped aside to let him pass. Aron was dimly aware that Iko was following him, but he didn't care. He strode straight into Endurance House, one of the two locations at Triune he had feared above all others, and walked all the way down the first hall, to the most distant room.

When he went inside, he found nothing but a chamber pot, a pitcher of water and a cup, a single pallet, and a single blanket.

"It's only a room," he said aloud, not certain what he had expected—torture devices?

That was more the rumor and myth of Stone than Stone's reality.

Aron knew that. He *knew* it.

What had he been thinking?

Why had he built so much dread of this simple, barren building?

It was as if someone else's perceptions had been written atop his own, but now he had stripped them away.

He closed the door, leaving Iko outside in the hallway.

And for the first time in a very, very long time, Aron felt completely safe.

This was nothing but a blank, dark room, as solidly built as a forge oven, with the windows shuttered to allow no light, and the walls padded with wool, straw, and cloth to admit no sound, either.

As darkness and silence settled like a cloak around all of Aron's senses, he knew there would be no disruptions at all, save for what his own mind might provide.

That, he decided, would be plenty.

CHAPTER FORTY-NINE

NIC

Nic rose to awareness shivering and knowing something was horribly wrong.

So cold.

His breath rose in a fog as he twitched against the blankets confining him, at first thinking he was still strapped to the boards that Snakekiller had used to keep him immobile while his bones healed, almost two years ago.

But no.

These weren't the same boards.

It was the wagon's rough-hewn bottom beneath him. He was in the back of the wagon.

Nic strained for a sound, a smell, a clue to the unrest rising in his gut as he tried to push himself to a sitting position and failed. His muscles were too weak, and his left arm barely worked in the best of circumstances.

Nothing came to him, not so much as a twitch or a creak, though he could smell something burning—a cook fire, perhaps. With a hint of meat being charred.

The wagon was absolutely still. So, it seemed, were the lands of Dyn Cobb outside the wagon, though he couldn't yet lift his head high enough to see over the sideboards. He must have taken another fit, where he thrashed and twitched and lost his place in the world. Sometimes the spells lasted for minutes. Sometimes hours or days— with more days coming back to himself while sipping Snakekiller's bitter brew of milk thistle, skullcap, and valerian.

A quick glance at the sky told Nic it was early morning, and his last remembering was of sitting beside the fire for a dinner of rabbit stew and dried leeks.

A night, then. Maybe longer. He clenched his teeth against the knowledge that he was a burden, slowing the progress of his traveling party to little more than a turtle's crawl. Without him, Snakekiller, Hasty, and Hasty's good-humored apprentice, Terrick, would have long been back about their lives at Triune. No endless winter in a strange village. No begging and bartering for supplies to get them home.

Once more in Dyn Cobb, farther west than Nic thought he had ever been, fall was moving back toward winter. Since they had left the shelter of their first winter home, they had barely managed to skirt seven different bloody skirmishes between the Cobb Dynast Guard and the combined armies of Dyn Altar and Dyn Brailing. From what Nic understood, the lesser dynasts to the west were massing an ever-greater force on the southern reaches of Dyn Mab, but still raiding across Cobb borders for supplies and conscriptions. So far, Cobb was holding its own and maintaining its neutrality, but Nic had enough education and sense to know that sooner or later, Lord Cobb would have to declare on one side of the war or the other.

And when he did, Lord Ross and Lady Vagrat might follow his lead.

If that happened, the conflict would be decided swiftly enough, in favor of whatever cause the greater dynasts chose to support.

Nic wasn't sure what he hoped in that respect. He had no use for the likes of Lord Brailing or the bellicose Lord Altar—but if the men could defeat his mother, stop her from attacking Dyn Ross, bring an end to her madness, perhaps that would be best for Eyrie.

The stillness around Nic began to bother him once more.

He finally managed to pull himself up using the nearest sideboard—and grunted in surprise when he saw no oxen tethered to the wagon. Fly-covered mounds in the nearby grass caught his attention, and he realized with a sick certainty that those were the missing beasts.

The oxen were dead.

And—*no, no, no!*

Nearby, the mules lay dead as well!

Nic couldn't see well enough at this distance to be sure, but one of the mules seemed to have a shaft protruding from its ribs.

A battle arrow? A hunter's mistake?

But *all* of the beasts?

Where is Snakekiller?

The thought shot through his mind as forcefully as another deadly arrow. There was nothing but endless stretches of grass on three sides of the wagon, and the dead animals. Nic's neck ached as he turned his head. A small clump of trees stood ahead of the wagons, a quarter-league or more away. A thick plume of gray smoke floated like a shroud above the leaves.

Nic realized he hadn't been smelling a cook fire.

More likely, it was a funeral pyre.

Or many pyres.

His heart began a frantic pounding as he struggled to use his good arm to lever himself out of the wagon.

"Snakekiller!"

His voice sounded like a whisper in the vast space, and his teeth began to chatter. His fingers and toes felt so cold he might be part-dead himself.

Where is Hasty? Why can't I hear Terrick laughing or swearing or singing?

Nic rolled himself over the side of the wagon, fell like a rock wrapped in gray cloth, and struck the ground with a jaw-snapping thud. Pain fractured his body, his awareness, and Nic feared he would sink in to another round of fits and die where he lay, in the cool grass beside the wagon's wheel, on some deserted field of Dyn Cobb. He held out his arms and tried to grip the wheel's spokes to hold himself still, to stave off the shaking of the fits—as if that would do any good.

His consciousness wavered, and his next sensation was a powerful, hurtful grip under both of his arms as someone hoisted him to his feet.

Nic smacked at the arms supporting him, but he might as well have been beating the thick branches of the largest heartwoods in Dyn Mab.

"I won't harm you unless you try to harm me," said a man's voice as Nic felt himself propped against the wagon, shoulders against the rough boards for support. Fear flooded through him, but he didn't have the strength or coordination to resist or flee. Standing was hard enough.

"I haven't come here to kill children," the man said, "though it looks as if someone already had a fair go at you."

The man let him go.

Nic struggled to keep his feet and his wits. The man who had lifted him off the chilled ground was tall and dressed in dark robes, with what looked like a standard military sword belted at his waist, but the metal scabbard was scorched almost black and seemed to be rusting in places. That was strange enough, but the man's face and head were wrapped in the fashion of those who lived near the Barrens in Dyn Altar. Nic could see nothing of the man's features but an outline. Even his eyes were obscured by a thin piece of gauzy cloth. His hands, though, those were bare, and huge, and scarred and calloused, like the hands of men who worked hard at some physical labor the entirety of their lives. Some of the flesh seemed red and angry, as if he might have thrust his fingers and palms into boiling water.

Trembling and hating himself for his physical weakness and his fear, Nic took in the air of menace about the man. Threat and despair seemed to hang above his robed shoulders like the smoke over the trees in the distance, tainting every aspect of his being. The rawness of that danger made Nic's breath come in short pants. He wanted to run, but he didn't know where to go, and he knew he'd likely collapse after a few steps anyway.

The man pointed to Nic's limp arm. "Did the Stone Guild do this to you?"

"No. Of course not." The absurdity of the question cleared Nic's senses completely, and shifted some of his panic to anger. "Who are you? Where is Snakekiller?"

The man cocked his head as if considering the question. "I don't know any Snakekiller, but I'm called Canus these days. Some extend that to Canus the Bandit. And you are?"

Nic let go of the wagon, intending to get himself far away from this Canus and his well-hidden face. Immediately, he swayed and had to grab the wagon's sideboards to steady himself.

Canus held up both hands as if to show he hadn't drawn any weapons, that he meant Nic no harm, as he had claimed. "I don't think you're ready to light out on your own, boy. Be sensible."

"Where is she?" Nic snarled as he gripped the sideboard with his good hand and wished he had a sword to pull, then wished harder that he had the strength to wield it. Morning sunlight made him blink too fast, and the cold air he kept gulping made his chest hurt. "What have you done with Snakekiller?"

"Your guild master is female?" Canus lowered his hands, obviously surprised. "Snakekiller is a woman?"

Nic's body tightened at the subtle insult, and he stood up straighter, without propping on the wagon. "She's a Stone Sister. She could kill you before you finish your next breath."

"A pleasing thought," said a hypnotic voice from the other side of the wagon.

Before Nic could react, Tia Snakekiller leaped into the wagon, then out of it, reaching Canus in a single jump. Her jagged blade was drawn as she landed, and the tip of her sword gleamed in the sunlight as she drew back into ready stance, close enough to take the man's head if he twitched in a manner that displeased her.

Relief almost made Nic fall back to the ground. He didn't care that she had come to protect him, only that she had come back to him. Her face, arms, and gray robes were bloodied and soot-streaked, and he noticed she was breathing heavier than usual—but she was alive.

The man once more raised his hands in a gesture of weaponless peace, though this time much more slowly. Nic knew the man was likely surprised by the combination of her brown skin and white-blond hair, that he couldn't determine her bloodline or allegiances from her appearance, save for the gray robes and *cheville* announcing her attachment to the Stone Guild.

"I'm no enemy to you," Canus said, though he sounded uncertain.

Snakekiller snorted and moved the tip of her blade forward as if to hook the cloth obscuring Canus's features. "Then uncover yourself and let me see your face."

The man leaned back to prevent her from exposing him, but he made no move to draw his own sword.

"I'm no enemy to you," he repeated. "I'm not looking for you, or for this boy."

"Neither were the Brailing guardsmen who killed my companion and his apprentice, and our oxen and mules." Snakekiller kept her sword at the ready, unwilling to surrender her advantage.

Nic took in her words slowly, understanding but not wanting to believe that Hasty and Terrick were dead.

"H-how?" he stammered, but Snakekiller didn't answer him.

Canus once more lowered his hands, curling his fingers to fists. "Which way did the murderers go? Tell me and I'll see to it that your companions are avenged."

Snakekiller laughed, though the sound was harsh. "There are none left. I burned all nine of them with Hasty and Terrick, in the copse of trees yonder, should you wish to count the bones."

"Nine." Canus sounded impressed, though his fists remained clenched like he wished he could beat the dead guardsmen himself, just to be certain of their demise. "You've almost doubled my best count. I managed only five on my last outing."

At this, Snakekiller finally stepped back, though her sword remained raised. "Canus. Canus the Bandit. We've heard tell of you on our journey."

Canus laughed, making the cloth over his face shiver in the cool morning air. "I suppose those murdering Brailing bastards consider me a greater criminal than themselves. If you've heard of me, then you know I'm more friend to you than foe, even if you do hail from Triune. Have most of this year's Harvest parties returned to the stronghold?"

Snakekiller tensed, as if getting ready to spring, and her next words came out with enough menace to rival the threatening aura Nic kept sensing from the cloth-wrapped man. "I wouldn't know—and why would you need to?"

Canus moved his right hand closer to his sword, but kept his tone light. "I have my reasons."

Snakekiller remained silent, waiting him out, and Nic once more wished he was capable of drawing a weapon and standing beside her. He felt foolish and useless, trapped by his own infirmity, too afraid to move more than a step from the wagon lest dizziness knock him to his knees again.

"I'm searching for a boy," Canus said, apparently deciding to trust Snakekiller with that much information. "A boy with loud blue eyes. He's a Harvest prize, but not a new one, and he would be traveling with a High Master of Stone, a man with rank-marks on both cheeks and his forehead, like your own."

Canus pointed to his own face, to indicate the position of the *benedets* he described.

At this, Nic once more had to grab the wagon's sideboard for balance. His mind filled with rapid-moving images of a boy, a boy ringed with a legacy so blue and bright that it blinded him.

He's talking about the boy I keep seeing on the other side of the Veil.

Did Snakekiller realize that?

Nic almost called out to her, but thought better of it before he spoke.

"Our conversation is finished." Snakekiller was obviously furious or frightened. Nic had trouble telling those emotions apart, where she was concerned. "Take yourself away from here, or I'll add you to the pyres in the trees."

"You won't get far with him on foot." Canus pointed to Nic, who was still clinging to the wagon. "Cobb's grasslands are full of raiding Guard. They're desperate, with another winter coming on and supplies already so low. Let me help you to the next village, at least."

Snakekiller gave a single shake of her head. "We'll take our chances, Bandit. Go now, before I regret my decision to let you live."

Canus hesitated a few moments, then gave a quick bow. "As you wish."

With that, he turned and strode away, across the vast, empty plains, toward nothing, as far as Nic could see.

For a long time, Snakekiller remained between Nic and the retreating man, until he became nothing but a dark, moving speck on the horizon.

"Where is he going?" Nic asked as she finally lowered her sword.

"Likely to the farming village we passed last night, while you were sleeping." Snakekiller sheathed her blade, and her shoulders drooped almost immediately. When she turned to face Nic, he saw how pale she was. With her left hand, she gripped her side, and Nic realized that some of the blood on her robes was brighter red.

Fresh.

"Are you wounded?" he asked, but his voice came out nothing but a whisper.

She shrugged as if to make little of her pain, but the motion made her gasp. "It's not lethal, but I need rest and nourishment, as do you. Are you well enough to help me carry what little food and water we have left to the trees? I know the pyres will make for poor scenery, but we'll have cover, and we can spend the night there if we must."

Brother help us. She can't travel. Nic bit his lip. *How can I keep her safe when I can't predict or control my fits? What should I do?*

He stumbled toward the other wagon to collect supplies, worrying with every step that Snakekiller would collapse while he wasn't looking.

When they reached the edge of the trees, she fell.

Nic saw her hit the ground in front of him and cried out. He threw down the dry rations he was carrying and lurched to her, the lingering pyre smoke stinging his wet eyes. When he got to his knees beside her, he could barely breathe. Her color—so pale. Listless. When he lifted her wrist, it was limp in his grip.

Mumbling prayers to the Brother, he pulled aside her robes enough to see the sword slash in her side, a raw, gaping mouth of a wound, seeping blood with each beat of her heart.

The sight of it made him weep outright.

This was . . . it was hopeless.

He had no skill with healing, no understanding of herbs or wounds. His hands were too misshapen to stitch up the rent in her flesh, even if he knew where to find needle and thread strong enough to complete the task.

"Please don't die," he said, lifting her hand to his lips and kissing the cool skin. His body felt just as weak and useless as hers seemed to be, and for a moment, he was nothing but a soft, round boy again, trapped in the stifling heat of his poisoned sister's bedchamber.

He hadn't been able to save his father, his brothers, or Kestrel. He couldn't save Snakekiller either. He knew that, yet his mind refused to allow that fact to gain footing in his essence. Heat pumped through Nic as he thought about what might happen to Snakekiller out in the open, helpless against soldiers and predators, and after sunset—

Manes. Maybe mockers, too.

Nic ground his teeth and forced his arms to move, demanded that his hands work enough to tear off his tunic. He thrust it against the wound, then used Snakekiller's belt to cinch it tight against her. At least he could slow the bleeding. And if he worked hard, he could pull her fully under cover of the trees and maybe use the supplies in the wagon to fashion a sling to lift her out of harm's way before sunset. A fire for warmth. Yes. And he could help her drink, if he could rouse her enough to swallow. If she regained consciousness, she could tell him which of her goatskins or herb pouches to use and mix. He already knew which skin held the nightshade wine mix she used to relieve his pain—

And which pouch to use if she needed Mercy.

No. She wouldn't need Mercy. He could do this. He could save her.

It took him the better part of the morning just to get her to the edge of the trees, and by the time he propped her against the firm, wide base of a *dantha*, he was so cold the skin on his bare chest had gone numb. His gnarled hands shook, and his weak legs shook harder. He could scarcely work the flints to start a fire, and when he got it going, it quickly went out before he could pull enough sticks into the flames to build the blaze.

He knew he had to get her warm, and he had to get her to drink.

Nic pushed himself off the ground and left the trees once more, this time to retrieve the food and water he had dropped earlier, when Snakekiller collapsed.

His entire body ached and trembled as he staggered onto the open grasslands, and his thoughts kept going fuzzy. His perceptions wavered as he scanned the horizon, and at first the glint of light off steel seemed like another false dream.

Helmets.

Scabbards and bridles.

Someone was coming.

The Guard was riding toward them. A plentiful lot of them, bearing banners and leading what looked like a royal procession as gaudy and huge as any Nic had ever seen in Dyn Mab.

Emotion flowed out of Nic until his insides felt as cold as his outsides. He let himself fall, intending to crawl to the food and water and try to drag it back under tree-cover without attracting attention.

Brother save me, what if this is my mother, come to reclaim me after all?

He would almost submit to such a horror, if it would save Snakekiller's life.

Maybe he could cover the provisions and Snakekiller and himself with leaves and branches, and hope the procession passed by without noticing them—but the fit seized him before he ever reached his goal.

Nic's last thought was of Kestrel and Snakekiller, wound together like one person, but crying out to him in two pitiful, fading voices.

I'm coming, he thought as the edges of his thoughts frayed into nothing. *I'm almost there.*

CHAPTER FIFTY

ARON

Aron had no idea how long he had been alone in the dark when Iko came into the silent space and brought him a loaf of bread, a pear, some cheese, and some water. Aron blinked at the sun-ringed outline of the Sabor standing in the doorway, and accepted the food. "Thank you."

Iko closed the door, but remained in the room with Aron.

A rustling of leather told Aron that Iko had seated himself on the floor, so he did the same. Then he consumed the gifts Iko had presented with greedy precision, even though he couldn't see them. As he washed the last bites down with the fresh, cool water, Iko spoke.

"I believe gods are real, but I do not believe gods make mistakes, or do anything by accident—or that they do evil. That's why you've put yourself here, is it not? To better understand the nature of fate, and what fate might require of you?"

"I'm . . . not sure. About any of that." Aron dusted crumbs off his mouth and chest, then leaned his head against the wall behind him, grateful for the absolute darkness. The black curtain of nothingness surrounding him felt like a shield between him and Iko, or between him and the world.

Though for some reason, he didn't mind Iko's presence. He even welcomed it, and was intrigued by the fact Iko seemed in the mood for conversation.

"Do you believe the gods show themselves to people?" Aron asked, hopeful that the Sabor might answer him.

"Yes," Iko said without a hint of annoyance. "But so do evil things who would have you believe they are gods."

Aron licked a remaining crumb off his bottom lip, staring wide-eyed into the darkness. "Evil things like . . ."

"Tricksters and misbegots." The air rustled, and Aron imagined the shrug of Iko's shoulder. "Liars who would use you for their own purposes."

Aron pondered this for a few seconds, then found it unusually easy to take the next risk. "I see the Goddess in my dreams."

"I know."

The response startled Aron.

He didn't want to begin to guess how Iko knew what happened in his sleep, but he was struck by the memory of Dari in her Stregan form, and how she seemed to be complete and whole on both sides of the Veil at the same time. Who knew what Sabor could really do with their mind-talents?

"Have you seen the Goddess, Iko?"

"No," the Sabor said. "My allegiance lies with Cayn, who guides me and shepherds all of my people."

Aron couldn't help touching his cheek against ill fortune—and against ever having an outright vision of Cayn. "If the creature I'm seeing in my dreams isn't a Goddess, if the light I see from the Shrine sometimes isn't a holy light, what do you think it might be?"

There was no hesitation before Iko said, "I do not know."

The simple admission made Aron like Iko more, rather like the day Iko told him he would protect Tek even if he let Aron take a beating. "Do you think—do you think if I seek out the Goddess when I'm awake, I could find out?"

"Perhaps."

"Stormbreaker and Dari don't see what I see," Aron said. "They're not certain anything is there, in the Shrine."

"Are *you* certain?"

Aron gave this some contemplation, and realized he was certain. Absolutely sure, and his *graal* lent more force to his conviction. He knew Stormbreaker and Dari allowed for the possibility that he was, indeed, seeing something in the Shrine, but they put little stock in his nightmares, no matter how consistent and disturbing they might be.

Would Dari approve of him going through the Veil alone today?

She was in no shape to help him—and he would be completing the exercise with no intention to cause harm or take action, only to seek information. Ultimately, he wanted to decrease his own anxiety, and improve his own temper, too. Those were reasonable aims.

Aron called a halt to his inner debate and relaxed into the darkness, letting his body grow still, allowing his breathing to assume a rhythm and pattern conducive to going through the Veil. When he next opened his eyes, the darkness seemed just as dark. Blacker than before, and deeper, as if the air itself were made of some deep velvety fabric. He reached out with the essence of his hand, stroked the space before his eyes, but felt nothing.

It really was relaxing, being here in this dark place. He wished he hadn't avoided it for so long, and sacrificed such an effective method of calming his own mind.

Iko's breathing and heartbeat sounded like rocks rumbling through a cave, and Aron felt grateful to leave them behind as he let his awareness drift upward, out of Endurance House, and into the white-blue light of day.

The sudden increase in stimulation momentarily stunned him, but he breathed through it, using skills taught to him by Dari, and rehearsed twice a day, almost every day since he first met her. The Shrine of the Mother lay below him, just ahead—

Nothing but monoliths and grass, an absolutely peaceful scene, rendered as perfectly as a painting.

Stormbreaker and Dari had been right all along, hadn't they? There was nothing in the Shrine. Nothing he should fear, and nothing attempting to harm him.

That meant his dreams were likely phantoms of his own mind as well.

Aron didn't know if he felt relief or shame for his childish worries, or perhaps a little of both. He stretched his mental muscles, letting himself drift higher.

Stormbreaker, Lady Vagrat, and Vagrat's heir were no longer in the cornfield, and in fact, Aron sensed Lady Vagrat's shimmering silver energy in the main keep. She was probably meeting with Lord Baldric, and likely Stormbreaker and Falconer as well. He knew better than to eavesdrop, though a small part of him was tempted. Likewise, he didn't allow his essence to shift toward Dari's quarters, and intrude upon her privacy.

He moved higher, letting his perspective expand, like a bird flying into the clouds. A slight flicker of movement caught his attention to the east, something happening on this side of the Veil, and that intrigued him.

He had no idea how to call to the Goddess in his dreams, if she even existed, which he now doubted very deeply, so it seemed the best idea to simply investigate what presented itself to him.

No fear or dread dissuaded him as he moved himself outward, toward the increasing motion and light he could see rising above what was likely the nearer reaches of Dyn Cobb.

At least, not until he got closer and got a better look at a familiar red glow, like flames in a ruby. Red blazes flared across the horizon, blinding in intensity as they rose, then exploded and fell into fading sparks.

Tension rose within the essence of Aron's body. He was aware of his heart rate increasing, and his breathing growing more rapid.

Nic.

The boy Aron had made contact with, the boy who was being sheltered by Tiamat Snakekiller, Stormbreaker's sister.

Aron moved faster, hurling his awareness toward the display. He wondered if Blath felt this way when she lowered her head and flew, really flew, with air rushing hard against her face and shoulders. It was perception, he knew. Nothing but how he imagined flying so fast might feel—yet it seemed more real than the reality of the dark room in Endurance House, where his body waited for this spiritual part of him to return.

The ruby-crimson lights intensified, and Aron willed himself to reach the spot now, right now, exactly now.

He pitched and tumbled ahead, the essence of his stomach lurching with the speed of his forward movement, then the force of his halt above the spot above the fountain-shots of color. When he forced his eyes open, the first thing he saw was a great horned stag, dark and spectral, standing with the majesty of a mountain and the fierce solemnity of a storm about to rain its fury on the lands below.

Beside the creature stood a man larger and more perfect than any statue of the Brother, and near to them, a lady, but not the Goddess Aron thought he knew. This woman's splendor defied all description and understanding, and she was infinitely more beautiful than he had ever before dreamed.

They took no more notice of his presence than Dyn Altar's Great Rocs would acknowledge a gnat. These beings were so magnificent, so huge that Aron could scarcely perceive them, so vast that he knew he wasn't really seeing them, but only the bits of their essence his faculties could comprehend.

He opened his mouth to cry out from the flaming pain of their existence, but that fast, they were gone—and in their place stood copies of the beings, smaller and meaner, more realistic, and infinitely more . . . human. Even the stag now had the presence of a person clinging to its fur and horns, a person almost familiar to Aron, no matter how hard he worked to project the image of hooves and discerning, feral eyes.

Aron's mind spun as the lady of the group drifted toward him, revealing herself as the Goddess of his dreams.

Yet everything about this was wrong—and real—and he knew this with every fiber of his *graal* and being.

My boy, the shimmering lady said, her words echoing and enhanced, as if she might be borrowing power from many other voices. *You've come. Welcome.*

Aron's essence flowed away from her, countering her progress measure for measure. He didn't want her any closer. The man and stag followed her lead, each approaching Aron, and he knew he was in serious trouble.

He should make a break for his earthbound body—but what of Nic, still sending up desperate flares of crimson to light the other side of the Veil?

Nic was in trouble, and likely Snakekiller with him.

The lady reached out a long-fingered hand. Once more she spoke in that awful, enhanced voice. *Don't think to defy me, Aron. We've come too far together, you and I.*

Aron intended just that, absolute defiance and disregard, but the first vision hit him like a boulder to the side of his head.

Harvest. The last time he saw his father, his mother, his family, as they disinherited him and allowed him to be taken by Stone. His heart almost broke at how close they seemed, how tangible. If he took a deep breath, he was certain he'd smell his mother's spiced bread, or the oil of the leather straps in the family barn.

Something like tears formed in his real eyes, and the essence of his eyes as well. Was he still breathing? He wasn't certain. Couldn't feel the air flowing through him anymore. He wasn't even sure he cared.

Next he saw the pile of bodies and bones, all that was left of the people he loved, languishing into decay on a forest floor.

Don't make more mistakes, Aron, the lady he had taken for a goddess chided. Through her strange voice, Aron thought he could hear whimpering and crying, as if her presence might be hiding dozens of miserable children or wounded animals—or both. *You have caused enough death, enough disaster for one lifetime.*

Aron stopped moving away from the woman, overcome with the force of his own grief and recriminations. If he faced her now, took her on and put a stop to her, or whatever game she was playing, would that somehow begin to make up for all the lives lost in his name?

The mane of his brother Seth wavered beside him now, whispering just at it had done the night Aron saw him.

"Where are you, brother?" Seth—or what was left of him—asked, his inquiry eerily silent when it should have been so loud. His eyes were empty, and his mane's fangs were already beginning to extend as the lady moved ever closer. "We have to find you. We can't leave you behind."

"Please," Aron said aloud, aware of the boom of his voice. "Don't leave me."

The words came unbidden, an echo of what he told the carnivorous ghost of his brother after Seth died—but this couldn't be Seth's mane. Stormbreaker and Dari had dispatched his family's essence that terrible night.

The lady was almost upon him now, arm still outstretched, cornflower eyes blazing with a new and hateful light. Her companions, the false stag and the man Aron supposed was designed to represent the Brother, marked her step for step, each staring at him with increasingly malign intent.

Aron's essence sank to his knees beside the horrible image of his brother, his heart aching so badly he was certain he was dying, on this side of the Veil and back at Endurance House, too.

Red flares, *graal* energy, exploded through the clouds, as if to divide Aron from his attackers, but Aron knew Nic couldn't help him, wherever Nic might be. No one could help him now. He couldn't even muster the will to help himself.

The hand of the lady inched closer.

Aron lowered his head, knowing he should do something, but unable to understand what that something might be.

"Leave me alone," he whispered. "I want nothing to do with you and the death you deal. Leave me be!"

The lady's laugh was the worst thing he had ever heard. The sound seem to tear his ears from his head and crush what little hope he had left in his squeezing, struggling heart.

You're mine, she said privately, to no one but him. *Now at least you understand that, and we can dispense with these foolish pretenses.*

Aron turned his cheek before she could touch him—and something burst through the sky, letting out a soul-chilling hiss as it came, swaying and knocking the would-be goddess onto her backside. Through his fading awareness, Aron managed to perceive the huge black head, the venomous fangs, and the blazing emerald eyes he had seen once before.

Hood snake. Snakekiller's essence on this side of the Veil. This time, the snake was twice as furious, and twice as large as he remembered, with its coils wrapped firmly around a glowing ruby egg. Power seemed to flow from that egg, joining with the snake and imbuing it with even more force and form than Aron thought was possible.

The lady scrambled to her feet, eyes wide.

The snake's hood spread wide as it warned the lady off her egg, and seemingly off Aron, too.

The lady and her companions staggered back from the image, but they didn't flee.

Not until the snake was joined by a new image.

A Sabor appeared, easily as big as the snake and much more real, carrying long silver daggers in both blue fists. Iko strode past the snake, walking on the clouds like they were made of the firmest dirt and rock.

The lady swore at him, then ran, vanishing as she passed the man and the stag.

Iko reached the fake god of death first, raised one of his daggers, and brought it down with a swiftness that startled Aron.

Before the blade struck home, the stag and the man burst into sparkles and disappeared.

When Iko turned to regard Aron, the snake and egg vanished as well, as if they had never appeared.

"Return with me now," Iko commanded, and Aron lifted the essence of his wrist for Iko to grab. He felt the electric jolt of contact, then a sweeping rush of speed as the Sabor once more set off across the clouds, heading straight back for Triune.

• • •

Aron came back to himself in Endurance House, shaking and coughing and feeling a beyond-painful cold, like someone had dipped his skin in ice water.

Iko was seated beside him, and was indeed pouring water on Aron's face. Two silver daggers lay beside his leather-clad blue legs, and the Sabor had opened the room's door and window to admit as much light as the space and design would allow.

"That boy," Iko whispered, clearly distressed. "His body. You—I didn't imagine—I never thought to see anyone who survived injuries like that."

"We have to go back." Aron's teeth chattered. "We have to get to Nic and Snakekiller before they do. Those false gods."

Iko responded by standing, sheathing his daggers, then pulling Aron to his feet. Determination fueled and powered Aron, though he felt near to physical collapse. Blood beat against his ears, hot in his throat and chest, and his breath came shorter with each ragged gasp. He caught the salty scent of his own sweat, but the smell of woods and grass clung to his mind, a remnant of where Nic and Snakekiller had been when he left them.

Like two parts of the same body, Aron and Iko hurried out of Endurance House, past Markam, who made no attempt to stop them, or even to speak.

Aron realized that was probably because Iko was in the process of shifting, his blue skin sprouting fur and claws and feathers with each step they took. By the time they reached the byway separating Endurance House from the forge and the mock battlefield, Iko walked on four wickedly clawed paws. His lion's tail trailed in the dirt, and his eagle wings lifted toward the clear blue sky, white feathers gleaming. He had a leather band spanning his girth, and Aron could see the hilt of the silver dagger nearest him, at the ready if it was needed. Iko knelt, and Aron grabbed the Sabor-now-gryphon's mane and hoisted himself up behind Iko's neck. He knew they were being watched, that dozens of reports would fly back to Stormbreaker, Dari, and Lord Baldric, too.

Good. Let them come. Let them follow.

"They can find our bodies, at least," he shouted into the wind as Iko charged down the byway in the direction of the forge. Then Aron clung for his life as his huge wings flapped, lifting them over the eastern wall of Triune and up into the vast skies of Eyrie.

CHAPTER FIFTY-ONE

ARON

Aron's teeth clenched against the frigid wind as Iko flew high and fast.

How long since he had awakened in Endurance House? Fifteen minutes? Half an hour—or more? Time was slipping away just like his balance.

Iko's wings seemed much larger than Blath's, as did his entire gryphon body, and Aron lurched and slid with each powerful flap. His tunic and breeches whipped and stung his legs and face. It was almost impossible to breathe, and when he could gulp air, he had to fight to close his mouth again. Aron was convinced that any second, his skin would strip off his bones, leaving Iko to land with a frozen skeleton as his only passenger.

When Iko did dip beneath the clouds, Aron battled to turn his head left, then right, eyes watering even as he tried to take in the rapidly approaching landscape below. Grasslands stretched across his view like a woven green rug, but he saw no nearby villages. As Iko took them lower, Aron squinted and made out copses of trees and even small wooded stretches. Smoke rose from one of those patches. Their destination.

Aron's heart beat even faster when he realized a group of guardsmen were bearing down on that same location.

He had two swords and three daggers, but only two hands, and no great years of experience. How could he take on a contingent of fifteen men—no, twenty, maybe more. Some sort of procession. Brother save them all.

The lead horsemen had spotted them, and Aron saw them rein their mounts. When the roar of the wind lessened against his ears, he could hear them shouting along their column, passing word of a winged creature ahead.

Iko's wings swept upward and held, and the force of their descent nearly jarred Aron free all over again. He had to throw himself forward and wrap both arms in Iko's mane to keep from tumbling to his death.

Heedless of Aron's distress, Iko struck the ground so hard Aron's bones rattled with the thump, then each slowing step. He half slid, half fell to his feet as popping and cracking sounds reverberated from Iko. In moments, the Sabor was back to human form, running beside Aron toward the clearing, daggers already drawn.

Aron's senses swam from the harsh flight, and his body buzzed from the wind's abuse. The pain kept him alert, and he quickly counted seventeen horsemen leading a procession of four wagons and a finely wrought yet hardy-looking covered travel carriage. The horsemen remained where they had been. They pointed to Iko and Aron, and more shouting ensued.

Aron didn't bother trying to discern their words or meaning. "They're in the trees," he called to Iko. "Nic and Snakekiller. Can you get them to safety?"

Iko slowed his pace, putting himself between Aron and the woods. "Them, and you as well, unless that Guard contingent has bowmen. Any bird, even gryphons, can be felled by holes in the wings."

Aron pumped his arms as he sprinted forward with absolutely no idea what he would do when he drew even with the Guard. He hadn't even figured out if they were friend or foe, since they weren't wearing colors or bearing any standards. No matter. Instinct—no, *graal*—told him they shouldn't be allowed to reach Nic or Snakekiller.

"I'll stand them off, Iko. Take Nic and Snakekiller to Triune, then come back for me."

Iko stopped running, forcing Aron to slow, then stop to listen to him as he assumed cranelike battle stance. "You are overly optimistic, and I'm not here to serve you—or leave you to be Guard fodder."

Three guardsmen had broken away from the rest, and they were slowly edging their mounts toward Iko and Aron's position. The men wore standard battle armor, leather, copper, and silver, with some iron at the chest and neck, but without rank marks or insignia. Even more confusing, the color of the clothing beneath their battle gear and the blankets beneath their saddles was a mixed confusion of black, red, brown, and even some greens and yellows.

Who were they?

On whose behalf did they ride?

Brother help me, they could be messengers, for all I know.

Aron grimaced as Iko raised his daggers. His stance was slightly off balance, weight on his forward foot, left hand extended. Aron recognized the posture from watching the Stone Brothers who best understood knife throwing, and knew that Iko could shift his balance and hurl his first blade overhand with a force and accuracy he would never want to challenge. Aron decided he would do better with his swords in closer quarters, so he gave Iko room and drew his own blades.

Messengers or no, Aron wanted the mounted men to give ground, at least enough to allow him time to retrieve Nic and Snakekiller, and figure some method of fastening them to Iko for the brutal ride back to Triune.

The soldiers kept coming.

Aron tensed.

They were still many lengths away, but each nervous, sideways step of their horses brought them closer.

Aron knew that even if he and Iko managed to avoid being trampled and dispatch these three, there were the other fourteen to deal
with, not to mention wagon drivers and whoever—or whatever—
might be in the traveling carriage.

"Use your *graal*," Iko whispered. "Send them away."

Aron almost dropped one of his swords in shock. He glanced
toward Iko. "If I harm them with my mind-talents, Lord Baldric will
kill me with his own hands."

Iko's response was resolute. "I didn't say harm them. I said send
them away."

"No!" Aron whispered.

Then, desperate to find some other solution, he reached for some
plausible way to persuade the soldiers to leave.

"You there," Aron shouted at the soldier in the lead, doing his
best to sound older and confident, and refusing to let his sword
waver. "Stand down and return to your traveling party. There are ill
and wounded here, having need of Stone's Mercy. Some may be con-
tagious."

"A Stone apprentice and a Sabor, loose in Dyn Cobb?" the man
called back, his voice low and challenging. Judging by the rasp and timbre, Aron judged him to be in his middle years, though his nondescript
clothing and brown hair gave no hint of what dynast he might serve.

Despite the man's doubting tone, he and the other two soldiers
reined their horses, at least for the moment.

Aron gripped his swords tighter. "Even Stone faces hardship in
times of war. We send who we can to do the task—and I would advise
you not to interfere with our business."

"We have business here as well," the lead soldier called back. "As
much as you, I think. Illness and wounds, you say. Well, we have two
rectors among us. Stand down, and we'll send them forward."

From the clearing came a long, pained moan. Male or female,

Aron couldn't tell. He cursed his own stupidity, and wished he had told the soldiers they were battling plague or Wasting, or something that might have terrified them.

"This is no task for rectors," he said, hoping that would suffice.

A surge of energy made him tremble and raise his eyes to the distant carriage.

Had someone in the covered, reinforced wagon just used *graal* to communicate? He threw a bit of his awareness toward the Veil and strained to detect a color, a hint, a sign—anything—but found nothing.

As if responding to words Aron had not been able to hear, the three mysterious guardsmen drew their swords,

Aron's chest tightened, and his insides heaved. His arms felt strong, and his swords felt balanced against his palms as he raised them in answer—but this was no mock battlefield. He would likely die here this day, and fail Nic and Snakekiller in the bargain.

The three men spurred their mounts forward, and Iko let fly with his first dagger.

The lead soldier pitched sideways off his mount, and the horse ran free—straight at Aron.

He shifted out of the animal's path at the same moment his mind yelped, *Move!*

The horse veered crazily at his command and shot off toward the open grasslands instead of waiting for its rider's command, like most trained military mounts.

Iko's second dagger found its mark even as bits of an idea gathered themselves in Aron's mind. He quickly focused his mental energy on the third horse and allowed his mind to form a picture of the horse carrying its rider far away. No throwing or biting, no running until the animal collapsed, just inexorable progress away from this spot. North would be good.

Holding tight to that image, he forced his awareness into something like an arrow and imagined his wishes firing straight into the remaining horse's essence. *Now*, Aron commanded. *Away now!*

The horse slowed despite the protests and urgings of its rider. Stamping its feet, it sidestepped, then pivoted and backed up no matter how its rider tried to regain control. The soldier tore his feet from his stirrups, leaped off the horse, and came storming back toward Aron.

Hours and days, weeks and cycles of training kicked Aron's senses into a state not unlike going through the Veil. He judged the man's distance, the force with which he would strike as he approached, and held his ground.

Iko was running toward him from behind. Aron judged his distance as well, but knew he wouldn't arrive in time to break the soldier's first assault.

And the first blow would likely be the last, just like on Judgment Days.

The soldier's face loomed in Aron's vision, and he heard the man's battle-bellow as he pummeled the grass with his big, booted feet.

I'm a stone of Stone. Aron blocked the whump and pound of his own pulse from his awareness. He forced himself to breathe, to stand still. No faltering. No flinching.

The soldier drew back his blade.

Aron darted forward under the strike and scissored both of his swords, striking the soldier in the belly.

The man's momentum drove Aron's blades up and back, almost into his own shoulders and neck, but Aron let himself be driven off his feet, into the ground. Hot blood and the stink of bowels sprayed over his face and chest as he used his legs to fling the soldier off him.

The man's sword flew from his grip and slapped into the grass.

The man himself fell heavily with no attempt to use his own arms or legs, as if he were no more than a sack of feed.

Even as Aron staggered to his feet and dropped his swords, he sent mental commands to all the other horses and even the pack mules. *Away. Go, but do no harm.*

Could beasts understand instructions? Nuances?

Aron hoped they grasped the images he was sharing.

He stumbled toward Iko, who was using his toe to flip the soldier Aron had killed onto his back.

Would the horses be put down because of him?

How many of the soldiers would fight their way out of the saddle and come back?

And how fast?

As Aron's mind brushed past the reinforced carriage, his vision of what he wanted the animals to do faltered. He had to shake his head to clear his senses from a sudden, bitter dulling, like taking a huge gulp of nightshade wine. Whatever was contained behind those strong wooden walls, it wasn't something he wanted to encounter again.

Iko grabbed his arm and held him upright beside the soldier.

Aron looked down, then sagged into Iko's grip.

The soldier's wide, empty eyes stared up at him. Blood smeared the man's mouth and covered his battle clothes. He was still twitching, and the stink rising from his exposed bowels was fetid and choking.

Aron shook his head slowly, trying to comprehend that he could have given the man some mental command and sent him away from here, but he had used his blades instead. It had been a fair fight, Stone apprentice against soldier, in defense of innocents, as his guild charter demanded.

He coughed at the stench and tried to stop staring at the fresh corpse.

This—this *death*—it was preferable to a moment's loss of free will, being subjected to Aron's *graal*?

Iko was shouting at him, calling his name, then shaking him.

When Aron focused on the Sabor's face, Iko said, "I'll shift to my gryphon form—but you have to get them on my back if I'm to fly them to Triune. Unconscious, they would slip through my talons."

Aron could do nothing but stare at Iko now, frozen, his muscles and mind refusing to cooperate with what was left of his will. Iko spun him toward the woods and propelled him forward. "Fate has chosen you. What you choose will shape fate."

Aron tried to pull himself free, but the Sabor held his arms with fingers that seemed to be made of forge iron as he forced Aron ahead. "You with the *graal* of ultimate truth, you must begin to find your own truths, not just those dictated to you by those who do not bear your burdens. There are lives to save—and one of those lives you altered long ago, when you used your legacy to order that boy not to die. "

This confirmation that Aron had indeed accidentally used his *graal* to interfere in Nic's fate on Harvest rattled Aron so deeply he couldn't begin to understand the rest of that admonishment. He stared straight ahead, openmouthed, as Iko let him go. When he glanced back, Iko was already beginning to shift from blue to golden and furry as the Sabor began to expand in width and height, reassuming the formidable countenance of a gryphon.

In the distance, the creaking of carts and wagons and the shouts of guardsmen receded, but soon enough, the shouting began to grow loud again. The guardsmen were coming back, no doubt on foot, and no doubt running.

On wobbly legs, hardly able to get a full breath or think through the endless rushing of his own thoughts, Aron approached the trees. Almost immediately, he saw a woman in bloody gray robes propped against a *dantha*, her head drooping to one side.

Snakekiller.

Though Aron had seen her only once in a vision, he knew her, recognized the feel of her energy, as familiar to him as that of Stormbreaker. Her chest rose and fell, shallow yet even, but her color was that of days-old milk, off-white and fading.

A few paces from where she rested lay a thin blond boy with clawlike hands. From the odd angle of his body, Aron could see that the boy's spine was misshapen, curved in several places, and one of his legs seemed to turn inward. His breathing was deeper than Snakekiller's, but his essence seemed somehow more distant.

The sounds of approaching soldiers grew louder.

Aron rushed to Nic and tried to lift him, but found him much heavier than he expected. He would never be able to carry them both at the same time. With a creeping, crushing sense of dread, Aron realized he wouldn't be able to get Nic and Snakekiller back to Iko and secure them to the Sabor's back before the soldiers returned.

And his swords—he had left them lying on the grass of Dyn Cobb's field. When the soldiers returned, he wouldn't be able to fight them.

Panic flared like fire in his chest, and it took him only moments to make his next choice, though he knew at every level of his being it was the most fateful decision of all. Forcing his own breathing into a steady pattern, he moved his awareness through the Veil with a bleak determination he had never felt before in his life. It took no time for him to locate the red energy streaming off Nic, and the more muted greens and reds of Snakekiller's mingled legacy. Working part on intuition and distant memory and part on the training he had received from Dari, Aron let his own *graal* mix with theirs, lending them some of his physical and mental strength.

He sucked in a breath.

The truth of Nic, the reality of him, what he was and who he was, hit Aron in the gut. The rightful heir to the throne of all of Eyrie, and the key to finishing this terrible war.

Aron caught his breath by sheer force of determination, for now there could be no doubt what he must do.

This was it.

This was the moment he had been chosen for—or one of them.

I'm sorry, he said to Nic and Snakekiller, fairly certain they would never remember his apology. What they would remember and respond to, against their wills and against even the demands of their own bodies, was the command he challenged the rest of his energy and awareness into forming.

Wake.

As he spoke the word in his mind, Aron let go of any attempt to control the color and force of his *graal.* He had no doubt that people as far away as Triune and even Eidolon heard his command if they were on the other side of the Veil, but he hoped it would not touch anyone he didn't intend.

The effects on Nic and Snakekiller were immediate—and terrible.

As Aron came back through the Veil, Tiamat Snakekiller's eyes flew open. She let out a scream of agony that threatened to curdle Aron's essence. Nic moaned and thrashed as Aron made himself stride forward, tears flowing.

To Snakekiller, he said, "Soldiers are coming."

She stared at him, uncomprehending.

Nearby, Nic was wide-eyed, sweating and panting, and Aron almost folded in on himself as he remembered his long-ago oath.

I'll meet you, he had promised, at Nic's insistence.

He had given his vow to meet Nic, to be the one who found him when Nic needed to be found—but Aron had never imagined he would fulfill his obligation in such a dark fashion. Not like this. No, Brother save them all, it shouldn't have been like this.

Snakekiller screamed again, and Aron wanted to fall down dead and never hear that sound ever, ever again, but half measures would do no good here. Shaking like a *dantha* leaf in a powerful wind, he opened his mind and moved through the Veil again, and this time, he commanded, *Get up.*

Moaning, huffing like beasts in labor, Snakekiller and Nic lurched to their feet. Their limbs moved like wood attached to rope.

Through waves of nausea and guilt, Aron stepped them through each motion.

Walk.

Watching them stagger, hearing them shriek in absolute anguish— Aron knew he would never rid himself of these images, of the nightmares that would come from them.

Then, with his assistance, *Mount.*

Wrap your hands in the gryphon's mane.

He put Snakekiller nearest Iko's neck, and ordered Nic to hold on to her as well as Iko's mane.

With each movement, they roared with misery. Spittle flecked Nic's mouth, and Snakekiller bled from her parted lips.

As Aron climbed on behind them, he felt the awful tension in Iko's muscles and understood it, but he proceeded, because stopping now was as unthinkable as starting down this path in the first place.

As the soldiers thundered toward the clearing on foot, blades flashing in the blue-white afternoon light, Aron sent every one of the men a single command.

Sleep.

He paired it with the mental image of a few minutes passing in the movement of the sun across the sky. He knew that when they dropped their weapons and collapsed in slumber in Dyn Cobb's meadow, they would be vulnerable to predators, but he hoped the risk would be small. They were, after all, trying to attack him, and maybe even kill the helpless quarry Aron was torturing in his attempts to return them to Triune for true aid.

"Go!" he shouted to Iko, careful to keep the force of command from his tone, holding back his *graal* as firmly as he gripped the groaning Nic to steady him.

Iko needed no urging to rumble forward and leap into the air, flapping powerfully once, twice, and again, then spreading his wings to soar, as if the wrenching cries of his unwilling passengers were forcing him to go more slowly, fly more steadily despite the need for haste.

Minutes passed, interminable, in the wind with the blood and screaming.

Aron's muscles throbbed like they might tear apart, so tightly did he hold Nic, who at his command was working just as hard to steady Snakekiller. His mind seemed to unfurl behind him, scattering itself into the merciless, cloudless sky. Whatever he had been when he woke in Endurance House, that version of himself was gone forever.

What remained, he couldn't say.

By the time Iko set them down in Triune, directly in front of the infirmary in the farming and retirement quarters, the better part of Aron hoped Lord Baldric would kill him on sight. He was only marginally aware of Stormbreaker, Windblown, Zed, Raaf, Blath, Dari, and seemingly the entire Stone Guild rushing to help as he released Nic and Snakekiller from his mental commands.

Only the wild flurry of hands reaching to bear them to the ground kept both of them from tumbling to their deaths off Iko's tall gryphon back. Stormbreaker scooped up his sister, while Zed collected Nic, and the two of them led Raaf and the sea of gray away from Iko and Aron, leaving only Blath, Dari, and Lord Baldric in its wake.

Aron slid to the ground on his knees.

He threw up until there was nothing left inside him but emotion, nameless and endless and as terrible as Snakekiller's screams. If he could have thrown up his very heart, he would have done it, just to be free of sensation, of memory, of responsibility, of his own dangerous, unforgivable essence.

Iko shifted quickly back to his Sabor form and walked away without a single glance in Aron's direction. Blath followed him, silent, concern etched across her normally stern and blank blue face.

Aron couldn't make himself get up. He couldn't do anything but hug himself and stare at the ground in front of him.

"Aron." Dari's whisper was so painfully gentle it made him want to break down the center. The softness of her touch was even more unbearable. Seemingly since the day he met her, he had been waiting to hear that kind of feeling in her voice, that level of regard when she spoke his name. He had dreamed of the day she would touch him out of love—the love of woman to man, not teacher to student, or caregiver to orphaned boy.

Now here it was, and he wanted nothing more than to push her away and assure her he had nothing to offer, nothing to give, not now, and likely not ever.

When he lifted his head, he forced himself to look past her to Lord Baldric.

The Lord Provost's large face was sad beyond measure, and he clutched his chest as if to hold back some indefinable darkness of his own. The man's eyes had been stripped of all merriment and mischief, and even the anger and authority Aron had, if he admitted it, found comforting.

Aron rose from his knees, trembling, fists clenched. His breath came in short, rib-aching bursts, but he found his voice nonetheless.

"I used my *graal*, and I will use it again, any time that I might save innocent lives, or avoid needless slaughter." He offered the Lord Provost a bow, but couldn't make himself even look at Dari. "From you, I ask only this: trial or Judgment. I will await your decision."

Then, before either of them could say anything to break his mind further, Aron limped away, headed for the House of the Judged, for that was the only place in Eyrie he truly thought he should be.

PART V

Eldruidh

FATE STRIKES

CHAPTER FIFTY-TWO

NIC

Hands on shoulders . . .
  Shoving, pushing . . .
  Air. Falling. I'm falling!

Nic sat up in his bed so fast that pain blinded him. He groaned as his twisted spine burned as if it might blister just below his shoulders. Sometimes it seemed his bones were trying to shove through his skin, and he thought he might die from the agony. Instead, he usually suffered through a round of fits, the kind that left him flattened for a day, or even many days, afterward.

Gentle hands steadied him, gripping his shoulders, then rubbing the tops of his arms. His vision was too blurred to see who comforted him, but Nic assumed it was Snakekiller. The thick, sweet taste of nightshade wine lingered in his mouth, mingled with the bitter elixir she used to manage his fits.

He reached through his mind to remember what he had been doing before the latest fit struck him, but came up with nothing. All he could recall was traveling toward Triune, then . . . a man . . . a man wrapped like a desert traveler . . . and Snakekiller, and—

"Snakekiller!" He tried to push himself out of the bed, but the hands on his shoulders held him in place.

"Be easy, Nic," said a female voice Nic didn't recognize. He still couldn't see the speaker, other than as a blur of bright colors. "Snakekiller is well. She's already back at the High Master's Den, and she'll be here soon to see you."

Nic blinked, trying to clear the water and crust from his eyes. The woman who was comforting him turned him loose, and he shifted his aching body until his legs hung from the side of his bed. He faced his nurse and mumbled, "Where am I now? What is this place?"

"You've reached Triune. You're in the infirmary, in the men's ward—our only occupant right now, which is unusual."

Triune. The Stone Guild stronghold. Relief washed through Nic like a slow, healing wave, easing the pain in his muscles and helping to focus his thoughts. The rest of his recent memory realigned itself, and he remembered waking after the Guard attack, Canus the Bandit, Snakekiller's terrible wounds, the approach of the strange caravan with more Guard and the unmarked carriage, and—

And Aron.

Finally meeting the boy in his visions—and how Aron saved them.

Nic's stomach rolled over, and he shivered from the memory of having his mind, his essence, touched against his will. Just the thought of it made him want to vomit, and yet he knew he was alive because of what Aron chose to do. Even better, Snakekiller was alive. As far as Nic was concerned, the outcome justified the methods. He wanted to meet Aron again and thank him properly.

"Is it more clear to you now, everything that happened?" asked the woman beside Nic's bed.

He nodded and rubbed the sleeve of his sleeping robe across his eyes. As he moved the cloth from his face, the world came into sharper view. The stone chamber where he lay was huge and full of beds, with several big, roaring fires to keep the rock walls warm. Pots and cauldrons bubbled on hearths beside folded cloths. Flasks, wineskins, and bowls were abundant on many small tables beside the beds, and herbs hung drying down the walls like green and brown tapestries.

When his gaze shifted to the woman, he squinted because he still saw nothing but a brilliant array of colors. A strange dizziness overtook him, and the colors arranged themselves into the image of a lovely woman holding a baby. Then a standing corpse. Then a giant dragon too large to be contained in the room.

Nic's heart flooded with surprise. He caught his breath, closed his eyes, and opened them again. This time he tried to come to awareness more slowly, letting the light from the chamber's many windows blend with the orange flames of the fires until he could see the woman who was sitting next to him. Tall. Dark-skinned. Sleek, glistening hair pulled into thin braids and gathered at both sides of her head. She seemed about his age, close to eighteen, certainly no more than twenty. She wore a green robe, long-sleeved, with gold braiding at the neck and wrists. Her thin, graceful hands were folded in her lap, and her expression conveyed concern along with a sadness he sensed more than saw.

Such a powerful, deep unhappiness.

Her pain hurt Nic as if it were his own, and he wanted nothing more than to relieve her of it. "It's all right," he murmured, unable to stop himself from staring into her wide, dark eyes. "I'll—I'll help you."

The woman started at his words, tried to smile, then shook her head. "Excuse me?"

"You're unhappy. I can feel it." Nic remained overwhelmed by the force of the woman's emotions, now stronger than ever after his offer of assistance. He lifted his stiff arms and forced his misshapen hands forward until he covered her fingers with his own. She felt warm and soft, and also infinitely strong, and he knew immediately that the colors he had seen were part of some unusual *graal* he had never encountered before.

It wasn't proper, touching her like he was. He didn't even know her, but he couldn't do anything else. He had to try to soothe her, as she had no doubt soothed him during his most recent illness.

"This place has so many medicines," he said. "Have they nothing to ease your pain?"

The woman didn't move her hands. She seemed both surprised by and grateful for the contact, and when she spoke, she didn't disguise the sadness anymore. "There's no elixir or poultice for the likes of me, I'm afraid. I'm very worried about someone." She glanced toward the door of the chamber, as if wishing that someone would come striding in to meet her. "And I'm confused about so many things."

Her lips trembled, and moments later, tears rolled down her cheeks.

Nic said nothing. He kept his hands on hers, wishing he knew anything about healing hearts, about offering real comfort aside from just sitting next to someone.

"I'm sorry." The woman gathered herself enough to stop the flow of her tears. "I don't know why I told you any of that, Nic."

Nic did his best to give her hands a squeeze. "Would you tell me your name, since you know mine?"

"Darielle Ross," she said, moving her hands away from his to dry her tears. "Dari, to those I know."

Nic felt the loss of contact with her like a physical pain, but he rested his palms on his legs. "Dari," he said, enjoying the sound of it.

He couldn't tell from Dari's reaction to him if she knew the truth of his identity, but he didn't think she did. He hoped she didn't. In truth, despite Snakekiller's ceaseless tutoring and encouraging, Nic thought less and less about who he used to be, and more about who he had become, and what he wanted for his own future. "What can you tell me, Dari, about this place, about Stone—and about Aron? I would very much like to speak with him."

Dari's reaction was immediate and unmistakable. Her flinch made Nic grip his knees in frustration and curse himself for not guessing the source of some of her misery. "I see. Aron is part of what's worrying you. Was he injured in our rescue?"

"No." Dari glanced at the door again, then sighed and met Nic's gaze. "When Aron returned from your rescue three weeks ago, he demanded that the Lord Provost send him to his guild trial, or send him to Judgment. Lord Baldric will do neither, until he comes of age just after the first of the year." Now she stared down, seemingly at her fingernails, and Nic struggled with an urge to tip her chin back up so he could look into her face again. "Aron's been choosing to stay in the House of the Judged because of what happened with you and with Snakekiller."

Nic pulled his arms to his belly and folded them in a position that eased the ache in his bones. "That's foolish. Aron did nothing wrong. He saved our lives."

Dari returned her attention to Nic, her expression more troubled than ever. "It's more complicated than that."

"Why?" Nic asked. When Dari didn't respond, he added, "Perhaps I've traveled with Snakekiller too long, but I've started to believe as she does, that the world is often simpler than we allow it to be. Aron has a powerful and dangerous legacy, but he put it to good use."

Dari's mouth came open, as if she was pondering his opinion. Then she seemed to accept it, and for the briefest moment, she showed a hint of relief. It lasted only seconds before her worry seemed to double. "Would that the Lord Provost saw it your way." She frowned. "I wish Aron could see it your way, as well."

Nic studied Dari's face, her posture, and the truth showed itself clearly enough. "You care very much for Aron."

"Yes," Dari said, then lifted her hand to her mouth, her eyes wide. She quickly lowered her fingers, coughed, almost raised them again, then gripped a fistful of her robe. "I mean, as a friend. A student. I mean—oh, I don't know."

Nic knew.

Snakekiller was right, about how people convey so much of their truths and feelings with their actions. Dari might as well have been shouting that she had deep feelings for Aron, which bothered him, though he had no idea why.

"Aron was very brave when he rescued us," Nic said, hoping that would give Dari a moment of pride for Aron, and some ease. "I will always owe him a debt for that, and his Sabor companion, too."

She nodded, and did seem slightly more relaxed. "I have no status at Stone, but I do have permission to share information with you, Nic." She rubbed the sides of her temples, as if she might be fending off a headache. "Much of it you may already know because of your connection with Aron, but some facts may need to be clarified. Events seen through the Veil can be confusing at best."

Nic readily agreed to that point, and over the next half hour or so, Dari recounted how she came to be at Stone, as well as Aron's tragic history. Nic sensed there was much she was omitting about herself and about her missing twin, but he didn't press. From his time with Snakekiller, he understood how secretive Stone could be, and he appreciated learning whatever Dari was willing to share. In return, he told her about his own journey to Triune, leaving out only the truth of how he came to be injured, and thus, where he lived and who he was before he traveled with Snakekiller's party. For all he knew, Snakekiller had shared this information, but if she had, Dari didn't seem to be showing him any deference because of it. He was very glad.

"Iko is staying with Aron at the House of the Judged," Dari told Nic after they had shared their accounts. "He's trying to be certain Aron eats, but mostly, Aron reads and trains in solitude. He won't see me, even for *graal* lessons, and he won't see Stormbreaker." Dari glanced again at the chamber door, and her body took on a new tension, even worse than before.

Nic couldn't imagine Dari being put off so easily, by anyone, and he told her so—but when she reacted with a shy embarrassment, he quickly shifted the subject.

"Snakekiller spoke much about her brother when she related the tale of her life." Nic watched the door she kept looking at, wondering if it was time for Stormbreaker to relieve Dari, as she had explained how they had been taking turns with Snakekiller, sitting with him. He hoped not. When he shifted his attention back to her, he found her staring at him.

"Snakekiller told you about herself?" She sounded impressed and also wistful. "About her whole life?"

Nic shifted under Dari's scrutiny, feeling her gaze like a tangible force on his mind. "We spent many hours in inns and shelters, and even more on the road. She shared her history, and worked to teach me skills she thought I might need."

"I see." Dari once more lowered her eyes. "Her brother has been less . . . forthcoming. At least with me."

Nic remained quiet as he watched her nervous movements, then said, "You care for Stormbreaker, too."

Dari's mouth came open again, this time faster. She closed it so forcefully Nic heard her teeth click together. "You're beginning to distress me with your insights."

"Forgive me." Nic gripped his knees harder, feeling a rush of heat in both cheeks. "As I said, I've traveled with Snakekiller for many cycles now. Her bluntness and habits of observation have become my own."

"I suspect you have your own talents in that respect." Dari leaned toward him, close enough to make his face flush even more. Nic found himself too aware of every detail of her appearance, right down to her scent of spice mixed with vanilla and lavender. "Have you always made people so comfortable around you so quickly, Nic?"

Nic laughed. "No. Rather the opposite."

Dari's smile warmed Nic deep within his essence, and he realized he didn't want to tell this woman the truth of his past, that he had been invisible to the people who knew him. That he had been a joke and object of ridicule to those who didn't know him. That he was so inconsequential he could be pitched off a tower, and some other body passed off as his without his own mother even noticing the difference.

Looking into the eyes of this intriguing woman, Nic wanted more than ever to leave that other life, that other Nic, however healthy and able-bodied, far in his past.

Sounds in the doorway made Dari draw back, and when Nic looked up to see who had entered, surprise jolted through him.

It was Snakekiller, but as a man, with lighter skin and more *benedets.* The forehead, the set of the jaw and eyes—Nic saw now, for certain, all that Snakekiller had sought to teach him about recognizing blood relations by the markers of the body. This would be her brother, then. This was Stormbreaker.

As if to confirm Nic's observations, a curtain seemed to descend around Dari's energy, muting her essence. Her expression and posture became more neutral, and by the time Stormbreaker reached her side, Dari had become unreadable, almost aloof.

When Stormbreaker saw Nic looking at him, he smiled, then offered a quick bow. "I'm pleased to see you're awake. My sister has been most concerned, as have we all. I'll send a runner to the Den to summon her."

"I'll go to her," Nic said, pushing himself to his feet only to collapse back to the bed. If Stormbreaker and Dari hadn't leaped forward to steady him, he would have toppled sideways to the stone floor in a twisted heap.

Dari's nearness made Nic's heart beat faster, despite the bitter sting of embarrassment over his weakness.

"We've kept your muscles loose by moving your limbs." Stormbreaker turned Nic loose. "But you'll need to regain your strength."

"I see," Nic said as Dari withdrew and sat in her chair once more, and Stormbreaker stood beside her. Nic couldn't look at Dari as he admitted the full truth of his situation. "The way my body works, or I should say fails to work, I'm not certain how much progress I'll make."

Stormbreaker gave Nic a look that wasn't pity, but close enough to curdle in Nic's heart. "Our healers can work wonders, even with old damage, Nic. They cannot repair your bones and joints from your initial injuries, but with some medicines and training, they can restore much function to you."

Nic averted his gaze and chose to study the big square stones comprising the wall behind his bed. "Will I be allowed to take my vows with the guild before this treatment, or must I wait until it's completed?"

Stormbreaker and Dari responded with silence, and when Nic looked at them, they both seemed so shocked that he felt his heart sink.

Perhaps they did know the truth of who he was, after all.

"Surely Snakekiller told you this was my intention, and that it has been for some time." Nic swallowed, though his throat was dry and a slow, aching pain was beginning to claim him from skull to heels. "Are the infirmed not allowed to pledge themselves to Stone?"

"That is not the issue," Stormbreaker said quietly, as Dari went back to studying her fingernails.

Nic's misery increased, though he didn't know if it was coming from his flesh or his spirit. He tried to breathe through the tension, lest he bring on another fit. "You know who I am. Who I used to be." He gazed directly at Dari, wishing she would give him some hint now of her emotions. "And do not wish to be again."

Dari didn't look up, and Nic detected nothing at all from her mind or heart. It was as if she went Quiet the moment Stormbreaker came near her.

"It is not common knowledge," Stormbreaker said. "But in rescuing you, Aron revealed his own identity and mind-talents to anyone in Eyrie who might have been listening. Many now know that one of the old legacies has resurfaced. We do not yet know what will happen as a result, but we suspect envoys if not contingents of Brailing and Altar forces are on their way, and possibly envoys or soldiers from Mab as well. We do not know how long Stone will be able to keep its many secrets." He gave Dari a meaningful look, but she kept her face turned from him. "Any of them."

Nic wanted to grab Dari and shake her so she would look at him, but she seemed oblivious to his needs now.

"Aron and Snakekiller shared the information about you with Dari." Stormbreaker placed his hand on Dari's shoulder, showing an obvious familiarity that made Nic envious. "They also told me, and they told Lord Baldric. We have, in turn, summoned Lord Cobb and Lord Ross to assist Stone in preparing for what might come of Aron's revelation of his abilities—and to assist you. They are discreet men, both of them, so I wouldn't worry they will expose you until we are all certain how to proceed."

Stormbreaker checked the nearest window, possibly estimating the time of day, or taking the exact measure of the waning winter. "It will take them many weeks to arrive, however, and I cannot guarantee trouble will not reach our gates before they do."

"Why Cobb and Ross?" Nic asked, bereft, but somehow keeping himself upright. "Won't calling on them incite the other dynasts against you?"

Stormbreaker nodded, his expression grim. "Perhaps. Lord Brailing, Lord Altar, and Lady Mab—your mother—are attempting to force Stone to pronounce loyalty and join in this conflict. This we cannot do, but we can select who will advise us and support us if we are attacked. Only Cobb and Ross possess the strength and proximity to assist in the defense of Triune—and in your protection." Stormbreaker squeezed Dari's shoulder. "And Lord Ross has his own to protect within these walls."

He let Dari go just as she shrugged off his touch and at last let Nic see her eyes again. Now he thought he understood more of the depth of her distress. She had mentioned a relationship to the dynast lord, and clearly Lord Ross's journey to Triune was not something she welcomed. Would he insist that she return with him? Would she be forced to abandon her twin to whatever fate had claimed Kate?

"I don't wish to be protected." Nic crushed his fist into the blanket beneath his trembling legs. "I wish to be useful."

Dari finally spoke. "You're the heir to Eyrie's throne, Nic. Your very existence could end this war. How could you serve this land any better than that?"

Nic turned his face until he could see nothing but the row of beds next to his and the flames dancing in the nearest fireplace. "I do not have the disposition to rule. You must know that. You must remember what was said about me before I—before I died."

"The changes from your trauma and your journey—" Stormbreaker began, but Dari cut him off.

"Hush," she said, and Stormbreaker fell silent as if she had slapped him.

Nic heard the rustle of her robes as she moved. Moments later, her spicy scent overtook Nic's mind, and he felt her warmth as she sat beside him on the bed. Her hand covered his when she reached out, much the same as he had reached out to her earlier, when her heart had been so heavy.

He felt her touch like a balm on his pain and confusion and shame.

"I know little of your history, Nic," she said, and her voice drew his gaze like nectar attracted birds and butterflies in the trees of Can Rowan. He studied her face and eyes, seeking any insincerity, but found nothing but kindness. "I have heard the cruel jibes and nicknames, but none of those match the truth of the man beside me."

Nic wanted to argue that he wasn't a man, that he couldn't

possibly return to being a Mab of Mab, much less a king-in-waiting, but Dari's presence took his words from him.

"All of Eyrie is in chaos. Goodfolk are starving. Bandits and soldiers are raiding villages, thieving stores and supplies, even stealing women and children for their own uses." Her fingers seemed like feathers against his knuckles. "The suffering must end before society collapses and we revert to living as animals in the wild."

Snakekiller had made these arguments to Nic repeatedly, but he had always debated with her until they both surrendered and returned to other topics. He didn't think that strategy would work with Dari. He couldn't imagine attempting to change her opinions, so he remained silent. Soon enough, she would see the truth of him and be disappointed, he had no doubt.

"Your experiences have changed you, like mine have changed me, like Aron's have changed him." Her smile was so kind Nic felt wounded by the sweetness of it. "Perhaps you can't see that as yet, and I can't tell you what form those changes have taken or will take. I can, however, assure you of this much—you are no longer Eyrie's hob-prince."

"Then who am I?" Nic whispered, thinking of the armies marching toward Triune, of the darkness expanding to absorb all that was left of the land his mother had failed so completely—that he, too, would fail if he was forced to assume the crown he did not feel worthy to accept.

Dari seemed to consider her response for some time. She placed her other hand on Nic's arm, deepening their contact, and the shield she seemed to have thrown up at Stormbreaker's presence melted away. Once more Nic felt the fullness of her emotion, the complexity of her mind, her essence—and that immensely powerful *graal* lurking below the surface of her consciousness. It filled his mind. *She* filled his mind.

"Who am I?" he murmured again, certain that she could tell him, and knowing that he would believe whatever she said with his all his heart, and strive to make it reality. "What am I?"

She touched her forehead to his, and he closed his eyes.

"Hope, Nic," she said, and her words poured into him like a fresh elixir. "You're our hope."

CHAPTER FIFTY-THREE

ARON

"Go away," Aron told Eldin Falconer, trying not to stare at his crimson robes and glittering silver bracelets. The bright colors stood in contrast to the Thorn Brother's dark blue eyes and his dark countenance. The crystalline, thorny spirals on his face seemed to accent the lines at the corners of Falconer's frown as he tried to move past Iko and enter the small cell Aron now called home.

The Sabor had not drawn his blades, but each time Falconer attempted to approach the door, Iko shifted to block his progress. The House of the Judged, more like a great stone barn with three tiers full of barred stalls, seemed to ring with silence broken only by the shuffle of Falconer's feet, and his snorts of disgust.

Aron shifted to a sitting position on the cot that served as his only furniture in the cell, which contained little else save for a small table with a basin and below that, in the farthest corner, a bucket to receive waste. Books littered what little space was available on the floor, along with a few dirty cups and dishes still piled with food Aron had found tasteless and unappealing. His eyes felt crusty from reading the tomes on Eyrie's history and on arcane practices associated with older *graal* talents.

When Falconer continued to try to enter and began to curse Iko for his interference, Aron folded his arms across his gray tunic and swore back at the man. At Aron's outburst, Falconer grew still long enough for Aron to say, "You should have departed weeks ago. You have all the children Stone couldn't keep from you. Why do you wait?" To Iko, Aron said, "Let him pass. Let him say his piece. Perhaps then he will go and cease to trouble me."

Iko moved aside as gracefully as a folk dancer, his leather boots making no sound against the dusty stone floor.

Falconer entered Aron's cell and glanced around the tiny space as if its size and clutter offended him deeply. As if conditioned by force of habit, he began to straighten, piling up books as he said, "My escort was diverted. The risk of leaving would be too great, until I'm certain they're in position to meet me."

A few moments later, Falconer had scraped the plates into the slop bucket and piled the dirty dishes outside Aron's cell, right next to Iko's foot. The Sabor hadn't deigned to look at Falconer again, and probably wouldn't, unless Aron asked Iko to intervene.

"My boy," Falconer said as he stepped back in the cell, his flaming red robes seeming to take up all the space he had cleared with his tidying. "When I do leave, I want desperately to take you with me. I'm certain I could convince Stone to release you to my care."

Aron laughed, hearing the sarcastic, bitter sound as if he weren't quite attached to it, as if it weren't his laugh at all, but someone else's. Someone desperate and tired and far beyond any salvation. "And would I be less dangerous in Thorn's care than in Stone's?"

Before Falconer could respond, Aron waved him off. "I have no use for you or any of Thorn's plots and aims. I have my differences with Stone, but I've cast my lot with them, and I'll meet my fate within the walls of Triune."

Falconer let out a breath. He leaned his tall frame against the wall opposite Aron's bed, and Aron thought he might have been trying to look casual, or perhaps friendly and convincing. An effective ruse, or at least it would have been, for someone who couldn't sense the truth like a bright glow off someone's skin, who couldn't smell it like a spice, or taste it like a flavor, or touch it like a texture in the air. The more Aron used his *graal,* even its simpler aspects, the stronger it seemed to become. Even though he had been blessedly free from nightmares and visions since he returned to Triune, he feared his legacy might possess him at some point, take control of his mind, or at least his sanity.

"Thorn has only one aim," Falconer said, keeping his relaxed posture. "Thorn seeks the survival and unity of Eyrie."

Aron glared at him. "You're lying."

When Falconer stood straight again, his cheeks flushing and his mouth already open to protest, Aron shook a finger at him. "Don't forget, High Master, I have the Brailing mind-talent. I can tell truth from lies without even trying, whether I wish to or not. You came here for orphans, but you seek far more than motherless children."

This gave Falconer pause, and Aron watched the color slowly recede from the man's face. "Very well," Falconer said at last, speaking as if the concession pained him. "Thorn does hope to find children with legacies of your magnitude. We wish to shelter you and offer you the proper training and protections so that such blessings are never lost to our society again. Stone has no interest in this. You've seen that. Stone wishes to suppress powerful mind-talents."

"Stone seeks peace amongst its members, and fairness for the Judged," Aron said, growing tense despite his sense that he had the upper hand with this man. "Mind-talents are nothing more to Stone but an indication of intelligence and potential."

"It's a waste," Falconer said, as if he thought Aron was agreeing with him. "It's a shame not to use such abilities, not to develop legacies to their fullest."

Aron stared at Falconer, beginning to understand that the man believed this deeply, that he might have convinced himself in part if not in full, of the rightness of Thorn's pursuits—and their methods.

"And how would you ensure the survival of my *graal*, High Master? Would you breed me like a bull talon or some prized stallion, to make sure the traits were passed on to a new generation?"

"Of course not!" Falconer's shock was genuine. "And you are young to be so cynical."

Aron gestured to the books Falconer had stacked when he was straightening the cell. "It's all there. The theories and practices that led to the mixing disasters. The guilds—both Stone and Thorn—were no less innocent than the dynast lords. First you contained the strongest amongst the Fae and Fury races. Then you 'studied' them. Then you selected pairs to intermix the traits you hoped to claim for the Fae."

Falconer's sigh had a dramatic, false quality Aron didn't appreciate. "*I* did no such thing, and neither did any living person at Thorn or Stone, or in any dynast. That's ancient history."

"Is it?" Aron didn't bother to hide his contempt. "Are you certain you want my *graal* in your presence, High Master Falconer? Because once again, you aren't telling me the truth." He was sorely tempted to use his legacy to force the man to share what he knew, but he resisted the urge.

"Thorn is protecting children with powerful *graal*, nurturing them, as we have always done." Falconer drew himself up straight again, and for a moment he reminded Aron of statues he had seen of the Brother, with one of the god's more angry and disapproving expressions. "When we became aware that certain traits were reasserting themselves, we contacted all the dynast lords and encouraged them to search their goodfolk more carefully, for treasures that might otherwise be missed." He stretched out his arms, as if to encompass Aron's cell. "We provide education and care for these children, not containment. Not imprisonment and threats about using the talents nature saw fit to grant them."

Aron pushed himself from his cot, gratified that he was tall enough to stand toe-to-toe and eye-to-eye with Falconer, even if he didn't share the older man's muscle and bulk. "Then it was thanks to your meddling that Lord Brailing grew worried about the security of his position in his own dynast and in Eyrie—since neither he nor his heirs possess strong *graal*. Is that why he sent unsanctioned assassins after the Mab heirs, too? Was it common knowledge that some of them were showing stronger traces of the old Mab mind-talents?"

"Thorn is not responsible for the Mab murders!" Falconer's face turned almost as red as his robes. He stepped back from Aron, but the cell's wall blocked a better retreat. "Nor are we responsible for the Watchline massacre. That was Lord Brailing and Lord Brailing alone, though I understand he might have had assistance from Canus the Bandit and his Brotherless followers. The same base creatures who are even now snatching children from their beds in villages all over Eyrie."

"Before you can steal them from the same beds?" Aron didn't move back, crowding Falconer on purpose. "That's what's making you angry, not that the children are being taken, but that someone is reaching them before *you* get there."

"I won't listen to such outrage." Aron noted that Falconer's condescending tone had deteriorated to anger and defensiveness. Falconer had ceased seeing him as a child and potential quarry, and was now treating him as an adversary with the power to threaten his beliefs.

"What do you know of the carriage and the Guard contingent I encountered when I made my rescue of Nic?" Aron asked, gratified to see Falconer grown even more furious. "Was that the escort that got—what did you say—diverted?"

Falconer didn't answer, but Aron gathered the truth in all five senses. Falconer well knew about that sinister caravan and the soldiers who had attacked Aron and Iko on their journey into Dyn Cobb.

Once more, the man took on a countenance that reminded Aron

of statues of the Brother, and Aron felt himself teeter on the brink of understanding something. Of grasping something of monumental import—but he couldn't quite reach it. Instinct drove him to reach toward Falconer's mind with his own, but at the same moment, Aron detected a brilliant flare of red as Falconer made full use of his own *graal*, closing Aron away from his incidental thoughts and emotions.

"You are a menace and an ingrate," Falconer growled, and Aron didn't disagree. At least Falconer was speaking the truth now, as he saw it. Whether or not it was reality, Aron couldn't say, but Falconer believed it absolutely. He also believed his next statement, which was more persuasive and devastating than any of the rest.

"Your presence here is a liability to Stone. By now Guard forces from Brailing and Altar and likely Mab as well are marching on Triune, intent on taking you for their own use, or killing you so that no one else gains the benefit of your talents."

Aron stepped back from the man. His legs struck the edge of his cot, and he sat down hard.

"I have no wish to have you in my presence, if you must know— but come with me." Falconer swooped toward Aron like a bird of prey, his arms wide again, his red robes billowing out like crimson wings. "Come with me and spare the lives of your friends. Relieve Stone of its impossible commitment to you."

Aron glared up into the man's face, knowing that his own cheeks must be as red as the man's clothing. "Leave me alone," he said, but his voice had lost its sarcasm, its anger, and all its force. "Just leave."

Falconer bent down, until his face was inches from Aron's once more. "What was so important about the people you rescued, that you would place yourself and your guild at such risk?"

Aron snatched at his blankets instead of snatching at Falconer's scant hair. "Leave now, before I lose control of myself and send you waddling out of Triune like a duck—or maybe I should have you hop like a rabbit, all the way back to Eidolon."

Falconer stood to his full height again, but he made no effort to leave the cell. Aron was breathing hard, trying to control the pound of his heart and the rush of blood to his head as Falconer struck too close to truths he didn't need to understand.

"I haven't been able to stop wondering," Falconer said, once more taking on the tone of an adult speaking to a much younger child. "Was it only the fact of your guild master's sister being at risk, or was there more? Who was the boy she was protecting, the one with mind-talents almost as powerful as your own?"

"Go!" Aron shouted, aware that he was giving away too much, but also aware that he was perilously close to striking at Falconer with his mind. "I won't ask you again."

Falconer smiled at him, and Aron's insides twisted. "Perhaps that question is worth more exploration before I leave this place. What do you think, Aron?"

"I think Aron asked you to go," Dari said from the cell door.

Her voice startled both Aron and Falconer, as neither of them had heard or sensed her approach. Aron noted that she had her *graal* completely masked, all of it. Not even a hint of color escaped her dark skin, but he thought he saw a trace of Stormbreaker's lightning in her eyes.

"Did Lord Baldric give you permission to intrude on Aron's solitude?" Dari asked Falconer, her tone calm and icy. "You have some jurisdiction to question orphans and the sheltered, but you have no business bothering apprentices of Stone—least of all those only weeks from their final trial."

Falconer spun toward her and took a quick step in her direction.

Dari stepped aside to let him pass.

For a moment, Aron was certain the man was about to grab her, perhaps even by the neck, but a pair of low, menacing growls reverberated through the House of the Judged. Aron recognized the traditional Sabor warning gesture. He hadn't seen Blath behind Dari, but he assumed she was standing with Iko, just out of his sight, but well within view of Falconer.

The man's anger seemed to flare, then vanish, as if he had crammed his emotions into some deep cavern in his heart, inaccessible even to him. Falconer's breathing slowed, and he looked less the frenzied, cruel lunatic he had been in Aron's cell. Aron watched, amazed and disgusted, as the man shrugged on the persona of High Master of Thorn as quickly and easily as normal men donned a robe or tunic.

"You, my dear, are as much a puzzle as Aron here," he said. "Aron and the boy he rescued when he retrieved Tiamat Snakekiller from the plains of Dyn Cobb."

"I suggest you concern yourself with the puzzle of leaving Triune, and getting your new charges safely back to Eidolon." Dari's voice was tense and quiet, yet it carried the force of thunder, so much so that Aron expected to hear the distant rumble. "Aron won't be amongst that number, and neither will I, nor any recent rescues."

Falconer glanced over his shoulder at Aron, his eyes blazing with new fury. "Think on what I said. If you're so good at reading truth, then you know I spoke it. You know the sanest option is to leave this place with me."

Aron looked away from Falconer, and heard the man's footfalls as he finally departed the cell, and ultimately the building.

"What an ass," Dari murmured as the outer doors slammed closed behind the Thorn Brother.

When Aron looked up at her, he had a moment of wondering if Dari was speaking about Falconer, or about him. He had resisted her visits since his return, but as he gazed at her standing at his cell's entrance, splendid in the dusty sunlight filling the House of the Judged, he couldn't quite remember why.

Reality crept back, despite her beauty.

He was dangerous. Possibly doomed by his trial, or by Judgment. He had done horrible things to Nic and Snakekiller, and should he survive the fate waiting for him when Lord Baldric decreed it, he might do equally horrible things in the future. He loved Dari, and he didn't want her to be stained or injured by her association with him.

He stood from his cot and faced her, heart beating so hard he winced from the discomfort.

"You should leave," he told her.

"You should be quiet," she shot back.

Then she stepped forward, slipped her arms around his neck, and kissed him.

CHAPTER FIFTY-FOUR

ARON

The next weeks of Aron's life passed in a blur, much like his first days at Triune. He emerged from the House of the Judged at Dari's insistence, unable to stand against her powerful will, or even the simplest of her wishes. When she so much as glanced in his direction, he felt like an eager talon, ready to strain and pull and tear up the earth to do her bidding.

At her urging, he petitioned Lord Baldric to allow him to go to his trial on his birthday, and to allow him to return to his normal training and duties in the meantime. Lord Baldric agreed that this timing was right for Aron's trial, as if compelled by an unstoppable force. A force, Aron figured, named Dari Ross.

Aron didn't need Dari's encouragement to apologize to Stormbreaker for his withdrawal to the House of the Judged, and for separating himself from the guild that needed him. He repeated that apology to Zed and to Raaf, to the other apprentices in the Den, and even to Windblown, and felt mild but happy surprise when they accepted his contrition and simply returned to life as usual, despite the pall of uncertainty hanging over Triune—a danger that Aron knew was of his own making. Lord Baldric and Stormbreaker impressed upon Aron that remaining at Stone was the best course of action, as he and Nic and Dari would be little more than Guard fodder on the byways, even with a contingent of Stone Brothers and Sisters assigned to protect them. Besides, those intent on attacking Stone would do so whether or not their quarry had fled, and Stone would be better served with extra hands in the fight than to have their might divided between Triune and a traveling party.

As for traveling parties, Thorn's First High Master Falconer didn't make his departure for Dyn Vagrat and the island of Eidolon, but he kept well clear of Aron and Dari, and Nic as well. In fact, Falconer avoided them so thoroughly that Aron wondered if the Thorn Brother had been threatened by Lord Baldric or Stormbreaker, or perhaps both of them. Not that Aron had much time to think about it. All of his free hours were spent either with Dari, or helping with Nic's recovery—and without burdening Nic with the weight of accepting or rejecting the many apologies Aron felt he owed but could never make with enough amends and reparations. Aron had even come to accept his new schedule without complaint, spending time with Dari and helping her with her search early in the week, then watching her turn her attention to Stormbreaker later in the week.

Now that Stormbreaker seemed to have made his break with Rakel Seadaughter, he had professed interest in Dari, and she had made it clear to him and to Aron that she wished to see both of them. Aron and Stormbreaker made a gentleman's agreement between them not to fight over Dari, or pressure her to make decisions she did not appear ready to make. That hadn't been easy, but it had been necessary. Aron figured that if he or Stormbreaker tried to impose their will on Dari, they would lose her immediately.

All of this occupied Aron's mind as he helped Nic to his feet, intent on meeting Dari for *graal* lessons in time.

"You're lost in thought," Nic said as he turned Aron loose and steadied himself for the trek from infirmary to the Den, which was part of the strengthening program Snakekiller worked with the healers to devise.

"That's probably dangerous." Aron rubbed the small of his own back, which was still sore from a long set of rides on Tek during weapons training. "I'll try to stay out of my own head, for the good of all of Eyrie."

They left the infirmary with Iko following a few lengths behind them. For a time, they walked in silence, and Aron enjoyed the break from the cold, and the hints of greens and yellows beginning to peek through the dead browns of winter. He also enjoyed Nic's easy companionship, as comfortable to him already as Zed's and Raaf's—perhaps even more brotherly.

Nic cleared his throat, and Aron's *graal* gave a twinge that made him lurch forward instead of taking a normal step. At the same moment, he noticed a flash of red robes, and he saw Falconer crossing the byway ahead of them, heading in the general direction of Endurance House and the Shrine of the Mother. The Thorn Brother didn't glance in their direction, but Aron had a sense that he was aware of them, that Falconer might even be snooping in his own fashion, keeping abreast of their activity—for what purpose, Aron couldn't begin to say.

Nic didn't seem to notice Falconer, or the fact Aron was having difficulty navigating a straight course down the byway. "You joke about staying out of your own head," Nic said. "You make jests about your legacy, but it's a serious thing, as is my own—though I admit I don't yet understand the extent of my mind-talents."

Aron tried to keep walking normally, though his anxiety was mounting, wondering where Nic was heading with this conversation. Perhaps it wasn't Falconer at all who had set off the warning in Aron's mind. Perhaps it was Nic's intention to bring up difficult subjects, and at last lay them open for discussion.

"I hope for your sake that your legacy isn't as dark as mine," Aron said, wishing that could be enough of an apology.

"Your *graal* isn't dark, and neither are you." Nic's response seemed effortless. Aron had noticed that though Nic didn't seem to speak as much as other people, his words usually carried some weight, as if each utterance was well considered. "*Graal* isn't inherently wrong or bad, in my opinion, so long as you choose to try to do the right things with your abilities."

"But how can I know what the right things are, with a power like this?" Aron asked the question too loudly, because it had been bound inside him for so long, at least since Platt first brought up the possibility that he could use his legacy for the proper pursuits. "In the moment, things can seem one way, then turn out to be another. Or I can command things without realizing I've done it."

Brother help him. He hadn't meant to turn the topic in that direction, but there it was. There it had always been and always would be, the issue between Nic and Aron.

"Like when we first made contact on the other side of the Veil," Nic said, confirming Aron's thoughts, and making the barrier between them all the more real. "When you forced me to live."

Aron stopped walking. He wrapped his arms around his belly and almost doubled over as air left him. Hearing it aloud, from the person he had wounded in such a fashion, felt like a blow from a fighting staff.

"There was no way I could have survived injuries like that," Nic went on from behind him, as if oblivious to Aron's reaction. "Much less the repeated bouts of Wasting that I've endured. Your *graal* is so powerful that one single word, one single command to live—and I've lived."

"When I did it, I had no idea." Aron pressed on his belly to force out the words. "I didn't know. I didn't understand."

Nic limped up beside him, then came to stand in front of him. When Aron straightened and looked into Nic's eyes, he found only bright blue interest and kindness, and a strange sort of peaceful acceptance. "It has been difficult, to approach death so many times, to need death, yet find it out of my reach. I'm certain if my wounds were grievous enough that my mind and will couldn't override my body, I would cross over to the next life—but so far, my mind wins the battle."

Nic paused, and Aron waited for the rest, hoping it wouldn't be too awful, but at the same time wishing it would be. Nic should curse him. Maybe hit him, or beat him, or even kill him for what he did. Aron wouldn't fight him. Whatever Nic said or did, Aron knew he deserved it, and worse.

"I'm not sure I would have retained my wits and thoughts if Snakekiller hadn't helped me learn to cope with the pain." Nic crossed his arms as if to fend off the thought of such agony. "But I don't regret it, Aron. Neither do I hold any anger for you forcing your will on me in Dyn Cobb, to save my life yet again."

Aron's mouth came open, and he felt punched all over again. He grabbed Nic by the arms. "Don't forgive me. Please."

Nic pulled his elbows free of Aron's grip, giving him a strange look. "Why? Do you enjoy torturing yourself with guilt?"

"It's not that." Aron almost grabbed Nic again. He wanted to shake Nic, make him take back his pardon. "It's—without the guilt, I—"

Aron closed his mouth because he didn't have words for the rest, but Nic seemed to pick up the thread. "You see the guilt as a restraint. An assurance you won't take the wrong action, or make more mistakes like the one you made with me when you demanded that I live."

To this, Aron had no response, because it was exactly correct. Heat crept up his neck, threatening to overtake his face, and he felt helpless against Nic's ability to read his meaning, and against his own reaching for the truth. The more he used his *graal*, it seemed, the less comfortable he became with lies, even the sort of fibs people told themselves and one another to ease life's daily wounds.

"I think you should trust yourself more than that." Nic took

Aron's wrist and pulled him forward, toward the Den. "I think you'll sail through your trial, and become one of the strongest Stone Brothers ever known. You'll probably draw the stone on Canus the Bandit, and I'll applaud you when you choke the life from that child-stealing, thieving sack of waste."

Aron kept pace with Nic, unable to completely shake the lingering dread and misery that had gripped him when Nic finally broached the subject of Aron's brutal intervention in Nic's life. His swirl of emotions prevented him from exercising restraint, and he immediately brought up the other subject he had so wanted to explore with Nic. "You've seen him. Canus the Bandit. You've spoken to him, face-to-face."

"Yes." Nic's legs ratcheted forward, keeping him ahead of Aron, as if the memory stole his ability to fully attend to his body's movements. "I thought at first that it might have been his men who attacked us. Snakekiller says it wasn't, but who knows if that outlaw has managed to corrupt Guardsmen to his wishes."

Aron eyed the entrance to the Den courtyard, just ahead of them. "Lord Baldric says he's stealing back supplies confiscated by Guard troops and feeding villages—and snatching children to 'protect' them from disappearing. That's why Lord Ross won't issue a writ against him. Lord Ross says he's the only man in Dyn Brailing still defending the common people." Aron glanced at the sky, judging time by the skies. "Canus the Bandit is gaining so many followers, he's becoming a guild unto himself—almost a rogue dynast lord."

Nic turned his head and spat on the ground to express his disgust. When he looked back at Aron, Aron saw anger—a rare thing, he knew, where Nic was concerned.

Nic's voice shook as he said, "It's a sad thing, that goodfolk have to turn to the likes of Canus the Bandit for protection from their own soldiers and nobles."

A halo of red formed around Nic's body, and Aron found himself easing to the side to give Nic more space as they walked. In that moment, Aron could imagine Nic's body straight and whole. He could see Nic standing fierce and tall, wielding a sword against any who sought to do harm in Eyrie.

"You told me I should trust myself," Aron murmured, increasing the distance between himself and Nic. "Maybe it's you who should trust yourself."

They crossed through the archway, Aron so far to Nic's left that his fingers brushed the stone supports. The courtyard was empty, and Aron knew very few people would be in the keep itself, since it was during training hours.

As they approached the Den's big wooden doors, Nic said, "You think I could be king."

"I do." Aron glanced at Nic again, still wary of the red fog of *graal* power ringing Nic. "In fact, I have no doubt."

• • •

Later, when Dari opened her chamber door to admit them, Aron lost himself in her smile, in each brief touch as he and Nic seated themselves beside her in preparation for the lesson. He was looking forward to the close contact with her, even if his lessons were more disturbing now, as she taught him how to focus the full essence of his *graal* and actually use it deliberately. They had touched on truth-sensing, truth-seeking, and being open to truths in the environment. They had even practiced compelling small animals to do his will, which he found distasteful, but also intriguing. Aron then remained present during Nic's lessons as a safety measure, with instructions to break in and take control of Nic or Dari if either seemed out of control, trapped, or endangered on the other side of the Veil.

"You two seem more relaxed with each other," Dari said as she surveyed Nic and Aron. "But also more tense. Did you talk about important things—finally?"

Aron sighed and nodded. After all, Dari had been encouraging him almost daily to make his apologies and amends to Nic, and have done with it. To his surprise, Nic flushed and nodded as well, and Aron realized Dari must have been chiding him, too.

By the Brother. Did she control all the men at Stone, or just most of them?

Aron could only stare at her. Jealousy stabbed at him, and he glanced from Dari to Nic and back to Dari again.

They hadn't discussed Nic as a person Dari might show interest in courting. Aron had no agreement with Nic like he had with Stormbreaker. And why should he? Stormbreaker and Aron had known Dari for many cycles now. Nic was a newcomer. What did he know, really, of Dari's strength, of the depth of her true beauty?

"Aron?" Dari's voice nudged into the whirlwind of emotion consuming Aron. "Is something wrong?"

When he made eye contact with her, he felt suddenly foolish. Her gaze was both warm and concerned, as well as guileless. Nic had a similar expression—polite concern. Nothing more. There was no undercurrent running between the two of them, as Aron had so often observed between Dari and Stormbreaker. As people no doubt noted between Dari and himself.

Yet as he gazed at the two of them sitting beside each other, staring at him, there was . . . something. Some sensation apart from the two of them, yet related to them.

Aron felt his brow furrow even as he said, "Nothing's wrong. I'm sorry. Let's move along with the lesson."

Dari hesitated, and for a moment, Aron thought that she didn't believe him, that he wasn't really upset about anything. Then he realized she was uncomfortable about what she planned to have them do today.

He heard the concern in his own voice when he asked, "What?"

Dari placed her hand on his knee, at the point where their legs made contact. "I think it's time, Aron. I want you to try compelling a person to do something. A simple action, limited, with no potential for harm."

Aron's entire essence rebelled against the idea, so much so that a tremor ran through him and he wanted to get up and flee the chamber. Gods, but weapons practice and riding Tek were so much simpler than this, so much more a part of who and what he wanted to be.

"No," he said, his voice growing more hoarse by the second. "I don't want to. Not unless I have to."

Nic's frown communicated sympathy, but Dari's face reflected determination and conviction, which made Aron groan.

"Lord Cobb and Lord Ross are only a short time from arrival." She gave Aron's knee a forceful squeeze. "Stone scouts have sent word that Brailing and Altar contingents are approaching through Cobb's grasslands, with Mab forces not too far behind. We even have word of more Thorn envoys on the road. Shortly after your trial at the Ruined Keep, we'll be beset."

Aron closed his eyes, though he knew he couldn't shut Dari out, least of all if she really wanted something from him.

"If you don't begin to master this skill now, it will be too late, Aron. The need for the full measure of your *graal* might present itself, and you wouldn't be certain and confident in using it."

Aron opened his eyes to find her studying him with that stubborn expression he knew only too well. He would either do this, or she would invent ways to torture him until he agreed. And he knew he needed to try, to have a grasp on using his legacy to achieve an end other than saving his life or someone else's in a desperate situation. His grasp on the skill was too tenuous, and he needed practice—but at the expense of some hapless, random stranger?

As if reading Aron's thoughts word for word, Nic said, "There's no need to seek a stranger. I volunteer."

Aron's eyes went wide, as did Dari's.

"I can't. No. Not you." The refusal spilled out of Aron even as Dari choked out a similar rejection, but Nic only smiled at them.

His blue eyes were calm and earnest. "My consent removes most of the ethical dilemma of using your *graal*. Just don't make me suck my toes, or do anything embarrassing in front of a lady."

Aron laughed in spite of his mounting dread. "I could make you bray like a mule."

"Or strut about like a deranged rooster." Nic's laugh sounded bright and relaxing. "But I know you won't."

"I'm thinking the mule idea has much merit," Aron said as he eased his attention and focus into the patterns necessary to slide through the Veil. He then had to spend another few minutes gaining control of his senses in such proximity to Dari. Her multicolored brilliance on the other side of the Veil was nearly overwhelming, even though he had seen the totality of it several times now. She used the force of her *graal* to pull a curtain of essence around the three of them, so their thoughts and words and deeds would remain private, even from those who sought to pry, and Aron welcomed the pleasant hum of her energy as it joined with his.

He gazed at Nic, who like Aron, looked very much like himself in this enhanced plane of senses and existence, except for the outline of ruby coloring that never quite left him.

Go ahead, he said to Aron, and closed his eyes. *Do your worst. But remember what I said about the toes—and no chickens. And no mules.*

Aron felt the essence of his chest expanding as his body drew a deep breath. He sent his best imitation of a rooster's crow in Nic's general direction.

Nic brayed at him like a blond-headed mule.

When Aron reached his thoughts toward Nic's, he encountered no resistance.

But in the first moment of contact, Aron felt a rush of confusion and uncertainty. He was as overwhelmed by the totality of Nic as he was by the nearness of Dari's powerful essence, and he didn't know which of Nic's deliberate or random ideas to seize upon, and which to ignore.

Ignore them all, came Dari's instructions. *What's in his consciousness is of no concern to you beyond what you wish for him to do. Don't let your attention linger on the complexity of his mind, or you'll risk losing yourself to it forever.*

Aron withdrew from his close contact with Nic, confused and embarrassed, but he managed to stay on the other side of the Veil.

All minds are this complex if you truly gaze into them. Dari sounded patient and unsurprised, as if she had expected this. *Even a rock cat has some rudimentary thoughts and sensations, Aron. You are full of your own ideas and energy, so you can't absorb the wholeness of another being—and you don't need to.*

Aron's embarrassment faded, but not his uncertainty. *I don't understand what to do. It's not as easy like this, when there are so many options.*

Sharpen your focus, Dari told him. *Just as you've done when necessity demanded it. Make your own thoughts a wedge, or a blade, or an arrow. Find an opening, insert your will into Nic's mind, and give him an instruction with the force of your* graal *behind it.*

Aron had a sense of queasiness, but he once more let his thoughts flow forward until he found the web of ideas and images and sensations that were so distinctly and uniquely Nic. As before, Nic offered no reaction or resistance, allowing Aron access to whatever Aron chose to hear or observe.

Aron closed the essence of his eyes to avoid becoming too distracted and overrun by the activity in Nic's mind. He wished he could shut out the sounds, the smells, the multitude of tactile memories that rushed through his awareness and threatened to topple his self-control. He saw the image of a dark-haired woman, wild-eyed and obviously insane, and knew her for Nic's mother, Lady Mab, the mad queen of Eyrie. He saw a dying girl, and felt awash in Nic's grief for his dead sister. A father. Brothers. All gone. All dead. And his body, huge and stiff and useless—no, wait, it was Nic's body, before he fell—

Ignore it all, Dari cautioned. *You are not Nic, and he is not you. You may share energy, or draw energy from each other, but don't assume his thoughts and memories. That's not your purpose. You're a blade. You're an arrow. You have a target. Now strike it.*

Aron was aware of his physical body taking another breath, and he allowed the essence of his eyes to open again. He shifted his perspective until he could see both Nic and Dari, in their relative splendor. They were right in front of him, and it was all Aron could do to resist the lure of Dari, of touching her and experiencing her thoughts at such a depth, with or without invitation.

He quickly shifted his perspective again, terrified he'd commit such a transgression, and this time when he gazed at the two people before him, Dari and Nic seemed to blend together like matching aspects of some beautiful and mysterious creation. Like a tree, with a powerful trunk, but also leaves and branches—only Aron couldn't tell which of them was which aspect of the tree. The image had such a solid, total feeling of truth that it guided his next action, almost as if it were he, Aron, being compelled.

He focused on Nic's right hand, which on this side of the Veil had no bent fingers curling inward to impair its motion or grip.

Move, he instructed, imagining what he wanted Nic to do.

Nic's hand twitched, but remained still.

Aron refocused his thoughts and tried to summon some of the *graal* energy he remembered throwing behind commands he had used in desperation. His awareness sharpened even more, until he imagined he could see the blood flowing through the veins in Nic's wrist, pulsing across the back of his hand.

Move, Aron commanded again, once more imagining the action he had envisioned.

Nic's right hand lifted until it hovered above Dari's. Moments later, his fingers settled over hers, as Aron had commanded.

Colors sparked and flowed between the two of them, and Aron again saw them blend into a tree—this time a huge, impressive heartwood, the likes of which could only be found in legend, or perhaps in the forgotten depths of the Adamantine, never before observed by human eyes.

This image was something outside anything Aron had experienced before, even more real than Snakekiller's hood snake phantasm, or the images of the goddess and gods he had encountered. It possessed a veracity that went beyond his understanding, beyond this world.

Fate.

The word echoed through his awareness, and for a moment, Aron sensed the eyes of those dangerous gods and the wicked goddess focusing on him from somewhere on the other side of the Veil.

He didn't want them to see the tree, but he couldn't stop admiring it.

Was the tree a creation of his own mind, or had he accidentally shared a piece of Nic's *graal,* and seen the future—not just his own, but in some strange way, the future of Eyrie?

Not the future, no. That didn't feel correct. Aron searched his mind, his legacy, and came to a better understanding. He was seeing the truth, and truth knew no boundaries of time or place, or even decency.

With a start, Aron lost his grip on his concentration. He slipped back through the Veil, and sat breathing as if he had run to the Den all the way from the main gate and keep. He slumped forward from the bone-melting exhaustion he had experienced only from longer Veil sessions, and stared at Nic and Dari in their human forms.

They sat motionless, still lost on the other side of heightened awareness.

Nic's hand rested on Dari's, and as Aron watched, Dari's hand moved until her fingers laced through Nic's.

A lump rose in Aron's throat, and a host of emotions exploded in his belly and chest. He couldn't name any of them, and neither could he stand them.

He knew Dari and Nic were at no risk, that Dari would guide herself and Nic back to this side of the Veil. Aron didn't want to be there when they came back to full awareness. He didn't want to have to explain himself when they opened their eyes, so he departed Dari's chamber so swiftly and quietly that Iko at first didn't rouse from his guard's stance outside the door.

Aron was halfway down the Den steps when he sensed Iko catching up to him. As Aron fled the Den, he passed Stormbreaker, and Aron turned his face away. He had an awful sense that he had just cost them both something precious and irreplaceable, but he had no way of explaining it in a way that might be believed.

Perhaps not now, not today or even next week—but soon, Dari would be lost to them. Some part of her heart was already gone. Aron saw the mythic heartwood in his mind, and the way Dari's fingers had intertwined with Nic's, and he sensed the loss like a new hole in his soul. He had no idea what to do with this fresh pain, save for saddle Tek and ride her and practice with his blades until exhaustion drove him straight into the ground.

CHAPTER FIFTY-FIVE

ARON

It was difficult, staying away from Dari and from Nic as well, but Aron managed it by riding Tek for hours each day, and by throwing himself even more completely into Stone's weapons and combat training. He worked from sunrise to moonsrise, then collapsed into his bed, hoping to avoid any dreams or visions. Many nights, he was blessed with peaceful, dark sleep, but on some nights, he had nightmares of the massive heartwood made of Nic and Dari. The tree was dying, cleaved down the center and bleeding a pool of sap at the feet of the angry goddess who always seemed to hover at the edge of Aron's awareness. Aron took this for an ill omen, a warning that the goddess would kill one or both of his friends, if given the opportunity, but he couldn't understand why—or how that opportunity might present itself.

The day before Aron's trial, High Master Falconer finally made his departure from Stone, leading with him a contingent of thirty-four children he had wrangled, argued, and bargained for with Lord Baldric. They departed with a scant escort of Stone Sisters, who had instructions to see them to the edge of the valley that contained Triune, where Falconer insisted his Thorn escort was to meet him.

Aron stood on the battlements with Raaf and Zed and Stormbreaker, watching them leave. Most of the children seemed happy and eager, but a few walked slowly and stopped often, as if they wanted to bolt and run back to the only home many of them had ever known. For those children, Aron's heart ached.

"Falconer made a fevered argument for you to accompany them," Stormbreaker said to Aron. "Had you expressed any desire to go, Lord Baldric might have agreed to allow you the freedom to choose."

Stormbreaker's assertion gave Aron pause, and he felt more pain in his chest. "Why? Haven't I earned my place at Stone?"

"No one is certain if Stone's traditions and laws should apply to you," Stormbreaker said, keeping his eyes on the retreating caravan below.

"You're different," Raaf said as Triune's main gates closed behind those who were departing.

"Not so different." Zed snorted and punched Aron in the shoulder hard enough to make him stumble against the rock abutment in front of him. "If I pitch him off this wall, he'll break and bleed like anybody else."

Raaf looked offended and Stormbreaker gave Zed a worried glance, but Aron laughed. "And if I spit in the wind, I'll get wet for my troubles."

"Exactly," said Zed. "Now come with me. We're going to the main kitchens, and you're going to eat enough to sustain you through your trial. It'll be a new tradition, one we'll follow when I'm ready for my own trial."

Aron smiled and nodded, then followed Zed off the battlements, feeling vaguely odd about facing his test before Zed, though Zed had come to Triune before he did. As Stormbreaker had told him upon his arrival, though, the time of trial was different for everyone. Zed hadn't asked for the privilege as yet. In fact, he told Aron he didn't feel ready.

I'm quick with weapons, but slow in my thinking, he had told Aron a few days ago. *Until I get that sorted out, I better keep my tunic and breeches.*

As always, Zed's shameless honesty served as a model for Aron, and he wondered if Zed knew how much his manner influenced everyone around him.

"I can eat, too," Raaf called out from behind Aron as he ran to catch up with them. "I can always eat."

Zed snickered and slowed his pace, and Aron and Raaf fell into step beside him.

"I'm glad to see the back of that Thorn Brother," Zed said as they reached the bottom of the battlement steps. "I hope he doesn't come back."

"Thorns fester," Raaf observed. "But stones can crush them."

"Except thorns grow high above stones." Aron thrust his nose into the air so high he would drown if a sudden rain exploded from the sky. "Didn't you know?" he asked with the best accent he could muster, and Raaf and Zed laughed with him.

Still, as they left the battlements behind, Aron couldn't help but glance over his shoulder, squinting to see through the passageway of the main keep, to where the massive wooden doors stood still and firm between him and the departed Thorn Brother.

Thorns fester. Aron repeated Raaf's flippant observation in his mind, feeling a deeper truth associated with that statement, though he couldn't explain the sensation, even to himself.

• • •

The morning of Aron's birthday dawned bright and warmer than usual. He finished the *fael'feis* beside Zed, as always overly aware of Dari, who had danced across the courtyard beside Nic. She spent the greater part of her time with Nic now—though seemingly only as Nic's friend and companion. Aron often saw them together, deep in discussion of some point or other, even loudly debating Fae politics, or whether or not the Stregans should remain in hiding. Yet they didn't touch or gaze at each other, or behave as though they had deeper feelings.

"I don't know enough to advise others on matters of the heart." Zed inclined his head toward Dari as he buckled on his weapons belt. "But do you think it's wise, not talking to her before you go to your trial?"

Aron said nothing, but kept his gaze on Dari, who noticed, turned her back on him, and walked away toward the wall of the Den courtyard.

Zed tracked Aron's gaze, and elbowed him in the ribs to make sure Aron was listening. "She didn't do anything to you," he said as Aron coughed and wondered if Zed had broken a bone. "You said so yourself. I don't understand why you've chosen to isolate yourself from Dari and Nic, but you've hurt them both. It's unwise to face the Ruined Keep with so much unsettled between you and those you love."

"All right, all right." Aron held up both hands. "You're right. And I'm an ass."

"So do something about it." Zed lowered his head for a moment, then raised it and met Aron's gaze without a hint of his usual mirth. "I'll be at the forge today. I'll probably be there when you return."

Aron understood Zed's meaning, and watched him go without comment. He pitied the sparring partners Zed would face today, and wondered if any of the training dummies would live until morning. If his position and Zed's were reversed, Aron would behead every last one of the straw men and barrel dummies they fought when no partners were available. It would be a reasonable way to burn through the anxiety and worry he would feel for his friend.

As soon as Zed was out of sight, Aron turned his attention to Nic, who was standing near the Den steps with Snakekiller. When

Snakekiller saw Aron approaching, she withdrew with the quicksilver grace Aron associated with Stone Sisters, leaving Nic to speak with Aron alone.

"Hello," Aron managed as he stopped in front of the friend he had avoided for days upon days.

Nic's face seemed to shadow with frustration and unhappiness. "Did I offend you that last day we worked at *graal* training together?" He spoke in a rush, as if he feared Aron would walk away before he asked his question. "Did you see something in my mind when you possessed my will—something that caused you revulsion?"

Aron felt more an ass than ever, and he found it hard to force out what he needed to say. "No, Nic. The issue wasn't yours. It's mine alone."

The shadows on Nic's face deepened. "I don't understand."

"You're my friend, Nic, and I love you." Aron was surprised at the ease with which he admitted that to Nic. He had never expressed such emotion to Zed or Stormbreaker or even to Dari, though he had felt such warmth for all of them. "I can't help loving you, and neither can anyone else."

Nic obviously didn't understand Aron's many meanings, nor did he grasp the full nature of the task Aron faced. "I'll come with you to the Ruined Keep," Nic said. "I know I'll be slow on the trail, but—"

"Thank you, more than you know, but I have to do this alone." Aron extended his hand, and was gratified when Nic shook it. "When I come back, I promise I'll be a better companion, if you'll allow it."

"I will," said Nic, "though she might be a different story."

He nodded toward an alcove in the Den wall, where Aron saw Dari standing behind a slight cover of newly budding ivy and morning roses.

"Please, Aron." Nic's tone dropped to a pained whisper. "Don't leave her confused and uncertain. I can't—it's hard to see her so wounded."

Nic's words burrowed into Aron's mind, and he well remembered how he used to hate Stormbreaker for hurting Dari's feelings. Now he had done the same thing, though his reasons, at least in his own mind, were noble enough.

"I'll see you tomorrow, Nic," he said, keeping his gaze on Dari lest she slip away before he could speak to her. "At least I hope I will."

"You will," Nic called as Aron made his way to the alcove. "I have faith in you, as always."

When Aron reached Dari, she looked as furious as he'd ever seen her. He didn't raise his arms to defend himself when she drew back her hand to slap him, and after a moment, she lowered her palm with a squeak of frustration.

Aron waited for a moment, until he was certain she wouldn't change her mind about hitting him, then pulled her to him, saying only, "I'm sorry."

It was the only explanation he could offer, and the complete truth, which she seemed to sense. When she pulled back to gaze at Aron, he kissed her, briefly, just enough to remember the sweetness of the weeks they had spent together. The days that she had, at least in part, been his. He wouldn't trade that time for anything, but neither could he continue to enjoy her, or keep falling more and more deeply in love with her, when the rational part of his mind understood that her fate lay elsewhere, with someone else.

"Aron," she whispered against his ear, her voice thick with emotion. "What did I do?"

"You've been perfect," he said as he held her in a tighter embrace. "You are perfect. But I'm not. I hope you'll forgive me for that."

For long, beautiful moments, they stood together without speaking, until Aron could almost—almost—pretend that nothing had changed between them. He wanted to tell her more, maybe everything. Words flew through his mind, forming and rising, then fading to nothing. Dari's fingers trailed across the back of his neck, and Aron ached to deny everything he knew, or work to overturn it.

Surely his knowledge gave him an advantage.

He could fight the vision, make sure that tree never grew—

But what would that mean for Dari?

That she would be forever halved, separate from her true self, her true love, her true fate?

Dari's voice seemed like a sweet, fragrant breeze through his soul, as she tempted him with, "Tell me what you saw on the other side of the Veil, Aron."

Aron closed his eyes and pressed his face into Dari's fragrant hair. He kissed the side of her head, fought with his better and worst natures another few seconds, then gave the only right answer he could imagine.

"I saw a tree, Dari."

She banged her fists against his shoulders. "You're not making sense, and you're making me angry."

Aron turned her loose and managed to smile at her. "Then I should go. I don't want you any more furious with me, today of all days."

Dari stared at him, and for a moment he feared she would cry, and break down his resolve to let her go, to let fate take its natural course in her life. He had to walk away from her before that happened, so he did, figuring that he was likely increasing her confusion and rage—at least for now. Aron knew better than to try to explain what he had seen on the other side of the Veil, since neither Dari nor Nic had shared his vision, and both would deny it. Besides, Aron couldn't say if he had seen what was destiny, or simply what *should* be, for the good of everyone involved, and of Eyrie.

All he knew for certain as he left Dari behind was that no matter how much he wanted Dari for himself, she did not—and would never—belong to him. Yet he couldn't be angry with her or with

Nic, or even with Stormbreaker for continuing to enjoy her company, unaware of what the future would likely bring. Aron couldn't form that shield of hate and anger he had used so long to survive. This time, he could only hurt, and nurse his inner wounds to the best of his ability, and try to take each day as it came.

First the trial, then, if he survived, the drawing of his first stone.

And after that, Stone's visitors—supporters and attackers alike—would begin to arrive, and fate would strike as it would, leaving the future as uncertain as the day Aron had faced Harvest.

Aron's next stop was in front of Iko, who stood between him and the courtyard's gate. "You haven't intervened this time, and you won't."

"I haven't, and I won't." Iko touched his chest with his fist to make his assurance a vow. "This is your trial, Aron. You must meet it or fail it on your own."

"And if I don't survive—"

"I will take careful care of Tek, and see that she lives a long and healthy life." Again, Iko touched his chest, and Aron gave him a bow of thanks. He didn't need to belabor any points with Iko, who was as much a brother to him now as his brothers of the blood had been. He didn't always understand the Sabor, but he had come to appreciate and honor Iko, and Iko seemed to feel the same way about him.

Aron's final and most unexpected supporter met him just on the other side of the Den gates. Lord Baldric looked as he usually did, large and powerful and slightly unkempt, though his expression was more troubled than Aron was accustomed to seeing. Lord Baldric scrubbed his hand across the top of his bald head, and seemed even more uncomfortable as Aron approached him.

Aron thought he might know why the big man had come to see him off, so he said, "I give you my word I won't use my *graal*. I'll face this test like all the Stone Brothers and Sisters before me, and rise or fall on the strength and speed of my blades and my wits."

Lord Baldric shook his head, the look of distress on his face deepening to outright upset. "Don't promise me that. Perhaps I've been wrong all along, Aron. It's your legacy, after all."

Aron managed the shock of hearing those words as well as he thought he could, remaining silent until he thought he could make an intelligible response. After a time, he put his hand on the Lord Provost's elbow, as a nephew might touch a fractious uncle whom he nonetheless loved and respected. "Thank you. But I believe you've been right, Lord Baldric, at least when it comes to my carrying out the duties of the guild. If I use unfair advantage, I won't have the respect or loyalty of my Brothers and Sisters."

Lord Baldric's grunt of assent was almost comforting. He withdrew from Aron's touch and began to walk away, but as he went, he grumbled, "Stay alive, boy. I'm preparing a host of fresh stones to be drawn tomorrow, and we'll need your strength and skill to hunt these monsters."

Along the battlements, Triune's bells rang to announce Aron's trial. He let the chimes set a pace for his steps as he made the journey along Triune's western wall, winding from the Den courtyard to the entrance to the Lost Path alone, as was custom. Every few minutes, he checked and rechecked his weapons, long after the bells fell silent and Triune returned to its normal rhythms, but for Aron being absent from them.

When he reached the side gates, he found Stormbreaker waiting for him, as Aron had known he would be. The last person any apprentice faced before his trial was his guild master, so Aron faced Stormbreaker, who said nothing, and didn't need to say anything.

"I'm ready," Aron said after his guild master hugged him.

Stormbreaker nodded once. "I know you are. Fight well, Aron."

Stormbreaker held himself in check for a moment, then placed his hands on Aron's head and whispered what sounded like a quick prayer. Aron took it for a blessing, though he hoped Stormbreaker's words hadn't summoned any of the frightening gods or the terrify-ing goddess he had dealt with so often in his nightmares and visions.

He separated himself from Stormbreaker, and gave his guild master one last look. When he saw this man again—if he saw him again—their relationship would change, though Aron couldn't really say how. The thought made Aron sad, but also excited. He wanted to make Stormbreaker proud of him one more time, this most impor-tant of times, and that wish propelled him out of the safety of the castle's massive walls.

When the gates of Triune slammed shut behind Aron, leaving him alone in the cold mists of the Lost Path, he felt fear just as he had not so long ago, when he and Galvin had made this journey together. Yet he felt different, too. Less nervous. More determined.

He set out at a rapid pace, covering ground quickly, intending to get as close to the Ruined Keep as he could before night descended. His only chance was to reach the fortification of those walls before the worst of Eyrie's predators filled the land between Triune and the tumbledown stone fortress that held a measure of food, water, and extra weapons. He couldn't see the path beneath his feet, but he felt sure of its direction, and his memory soothed him by marking clumps of rocks and rotten branches he had memorized on his previ-ous journey. There were small dips and hills, but for the most part, the land was flat and straight, though rocky and shrouded by ever-present clouds from the Deadfall.

If he could keep his speed, he knew he should make it to the Ruined Keep far ahead of moonsrise.

Aron had been running less than an hour when he heard the first moans of manes, no doubt moving toward the heat and blood they sensed. He let his surge of panic renew his speed, but he maintained his focus on the bit of path he could see through the fog. His heart was already pounding, but he refused to allow his breath to become too shallow, or to slow his progress by drawing his weapons too soon.

Though he had sworn to himself he wouldn't do it, Aron couldn't stop himself from remembering the impossible odds he and Galvin Herder had faced—and the fact that Herder hadn't survived his own trial.

Aron forcefully returned his thoughts to his running, and to the fact that he thought he understood now some of the reasons for Stone's trial. Yes, it was antiquated and dangerous beyond reason, but Aron realized that the peril had forced him to do what he could to repair damaged relationships before he left. And he would feel pride in himself for weathering this test of his skill and intelligence. Also, his first combat and first hunt would seem easy compared to this.

The moaning of the manes rose again, this time closer.

Aron told himself to stay steady, but when the howling of rock cats joined the eerie keen of the dead, the mists began to feel colder and thicker.

"I can do this," he said to himself, gasping as much as speaking as he forced himself to run even faster. He estimated he was over halfway to the Ruined Keep, and likely much closer. Another fifteen minutes, maybe twenty, and he would reach it and be able to set up his defenses for the night.

The prowling manes moaned again, joined by the feral screech of rock cats from behind Aron.

He clenched his jaw.

The predators were herding him. If he ran forward, he would find the manes, but if he retreated, he'd have to battle the rock cats.

Even as he realized this, the sound of the cats ceased in mid-warble. Aron thought he heard the cry of one of the beasts dying, then the choking hack of another. Like something had sliced open the cat's throat and left it to bleed its life onto the rocky ground.

He stopped running so fast that pebbles and branches sprayed outward from his feet, striking nearby rocks with too-loud clatters and thumps. Aron stood still, breathing so loudly he could hear little else until he managed to get control of his body.

The Lost Path went unnaturally still, and instinct loosed his *graal* even though he struggled not to use it.

Something was off.

Aron's mind hummed from the wrongness, and the sensation was so strong he had to believe he would have noticed it, legacy or no. Even the air and mists felt unnatural, if anything could, in fact, be natural along the worst miles in all of Eyrie. His first thought was that some lethal type of mocker had attacked the cats and frightened away the manes, but that didn't feel correct to his instincts.

From somewhere behind Aron, he heard a rustling and crunching along the path, almost at the same time as his *graal* absorbed and deflected a hot wave of menace. The sensation crested and broke across his face like a hot curtain of flame.

Not real fire. No.

It was legacy energy.

Aron gripped the hilt of his blades, then thought better of it. He started running toward the Ruined Keep again, this time pushing himself beyond all reasonable limits. His pulse roared in his ears, blocking out all other sounds except the inexorable crunch of gravel behind him.

Aron pumped his arms hard, driving himself harder with each stride. He leaned forward, digging his toes into the rocky ground with each long stride. His focus narrowed to the thought of getting to the fortress, because that part of his plan was the only aspect of his survival strategy that was still viable. The rest of his ideas about how to survive the night had just been shattered, and he needed time to regroup, time to think.

He knew it was time he wouldn't get.

Aron had been prepared for any number of beasts, birds, and even the blood-hungry dead attacking him in force. What he hadn't thought to prepare for—what he hadn't imagined he would need to contend with—was what tracked him with increasing speed.

Human predators.

Aron sensed skilled and seasoned minds bent on murder. These were hunters with no heart and no conscience, and they shared only one unified thought that pounded down the path toward Aron as steadily as their boots.

His name.

Aron Weylyn, once Aron Brailing of Brailing.

Aron was their quarry, their prey. He knew that as certainly as he knew the rest of the brutal truth—that he had very little hope of escaping them.

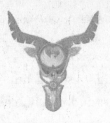

CHAPTER FIFTY-SIX

ARON

Fog distorted the landscape of the Ruined Keep until Aron could see nothing but twisted, dark shapes looming like giant beasts all around him. The pounding of his heart competed with the crush of his boots against the path's rocks and branches.

His pursuers could hear him, just as he could hear them.

Would that he were a Sabor, with the talent to walk the earth without making a sound. Aron's jaw ached from grinding his teeth.

The running footfalls behind him grew louder.

Another few strides . . .

He had only seconds to live.

He didn't even have time to concentrate enough to use his *graal*. Gods, but he should have practiced more!

Aron reached the door of the Ruined Keep and smacked his hands against the rough wood to slow himself. His arms felt stiff and jerky as he shoved the outer bolt aside and charged into the Keep's entry room, which was about the same size as his bedchamber. Dim, gray sunlight illuminated the square, foggy space as the door banged shut behind him. He slid the inner bolt into place, then turned and clambered up a stack of ale barrels and crates of dried meat. Dust clogged his nose and made his eyes run, but he reached the darkness at the top of the stack just as his pursuers threw their weight into the door.

The ancient wood splintered and cracked, letting in more light and fog.

Aron snatched up one of the smaller barrels and held it to his chest as he closed his eyes and hurled his awareness through the Veil. The abruptness of the transition between states of awareness rattled his senses and sapped him like a day-long hike. His breathing took on the sound of thunder, and the next smash against the door of the Ruined Keep blasted against his ears like a mountain exploding at its core. The sound hurt Aron so badly he staggered backward, teetered on the stack of crates, and let out a grunt of pain as his shoulders and back smacked against the jagged rock wall behind him. He strained every muscle to regain enough balance to raise the small barrel over his head.

The door below him broke open, and at the same moment, he hurled the barrel as far as his strength would allow. With much of his remaining vigor, he threw up a thick mental shield around his essence and his *graal*.

The barrel crashed against the far wall and shattered into a wash of ale and splinters as four blond, muscled men in hunter's leathers tore through the archway and rushed past Aron, targeting the noise made by the wrecked barrel.

Two had bows. Two had broadswords.

All four bore tattoos on their corded necks—a Great Roc clenching arrows in its talons.

Aron cursed to himself.

These were warbirds. Altar hunters, with great copper waves of tracking *graal* spilling from their shoulders as they used their mind-talent to locate their prey. When they found him, he'd be dead before he had a chance to speak. It was kill or die—and he had to kill them all, as fast as possible.

His heart seemed to crush into pieces as he whipped out his throwing knives and sent them spiraling toward the backs of the hunters.

One knife bounced wild and wide. The other struck its target, and a bowman collapsed.

Aron leaped down from his hiding place and swung his short sword.

He struck the second bowman in his belly, ripping the man open. As blood sprayed across his face, Aron shouted with all the force he could muster. The sound expanded in the Ruined Keep and on the other side of the Veil before Aron jerked his full awareness back to his body. He pulled his blade wide, then jabbed it forward and upward, catching a third hunter in the throat and killing him instantly.

First blow—last blow.

Aron's thoughts rattled against his skull as he yanked his sword free of the dead man.

The fourth hunter growled and thrust his blade toward Aron.

Aron stumbled over one of the bodies on the blood-slicked floor and howled as the broadsword's tip tore into his left side. Agony sizzled along his hips and back, clawing his senses. Hot liquid belched from the wound, streaming down his leg. He steadied his short sword in one hand and gripped his wound with the other, staunching the flow as best he could. The room lurched and spun, and Aron's awareness flickered as the hunter lifted his broadsword for a killing blow.

Time seemed to contract as Aron focused on every nuance of the man's stance and action. The broadsword swung toward him. Aron met the man's arm with his blade even as he pivoted away from the larger weapon.

His short sword struck bone, and the impact ripped the weapon from his grasp.

The hunter howled as he dropped his own blade, his arm collapsing useless to his side. His blood spurted out to mingle with Aron's on the stone floor, and they both drew daggers, stepping over the dead as they moved.

"Who sent you?" Aron shouted, trying to ignore the spots flashing in his vision. His hand shook as he pointed his dagger at his foe. "Lord Altar? Lord Brailing? Canus the Bandit—who?"

The hunter only snarled at him, as feral as any desert predator.

The man's green eyes blazed as he used the full measure of his mind-talents to weigh and measure Aron, but Aron deflected this effort with his own *graal*.

The hunter flinched backward and shook his head, obviously surprised by the force of Aron's mental push-back.

Aron lunged forward and shoved his dagger into the man's chest and pulled it free for another strike.

The hunter brought his dagger up just as fast, cutting Aron's shoulder.

They both lost their weapons and fell back, slipping on the wet, gory floor.

Aron hit the ground on his backside, but managed to keep his grip on the wound in his side. Pain flared along his ribs, sharp enough to force bile up his throat, but he got to his feet quickly. With numb, stiff fingers, he freed his last dagger from his belt.

The Altar hunter flailed and tried to rise, but he slid in the blood and slammed into the stone floor again, his head sounding like a melon as it struck. Aron staggered to him and dropped to his knees, straddling the man's chest and forcing the tip of his dagger under the man's chin until more blood flowed across his fingers.

"Who sent you?" Aron yelled again, this time, putting the force of his *graal* behind the demand.

The hunter's unfocused eyes blinked, and his lips moved, but he didn't make a sound.

Aron shoved aside the man's failing mental defenses and reached into his mind for the information he needed. The man's thoughts and fears and emotions seemed like no more than nattering birds in the distance as Aron grabbed for the right images, the right sounds and smells.

What he found were images of the Brother, and of Cayn, bright and vibrant and horrifying. Gods. False gods, and—

And—

Aron rejected the image he saw, certain that the hunter had managed to form a lie for him to perceive.

The hunter grabbed for Aron, then bucked as Aron released his hold on the man's mind and drove his dagger through flesh and bone, all the way to the stones beneath. The hunter gurgled and twitched once, then lay still as Aron rolled off him and lay panting on the sticky floor. He heard his own pulse, felt his blood pumping through his fingers even as he tried to get his awareness back through the Veil to do what he could to save himself.

Outside the Ruined Keep, moans filled the mists.

The manes were coming.

So much blood.

There would be an army of them.

And Aron couldn't get up. He couldn't get himself to the upper floors, or even back to the top of the crates and barrels.

Silver dagger.

Where was it?

Still in his right hand . . .

He coughed, and knew he was coughing blood.

The sick-sweet smell of death and injury overwhelmed him as he managed to get through the Veil. The energy drained by the transition nearly sent him into darkness, but he held on enough to shut out the wails of the advancing dead, take the measure of his heartbeat, slow the flow of fluids in his body, and explore the wound in his side.

It was deep.

Tears in his skin. Tears in his vessels.

His mind worked at fever-pace to patch what he could, until he was bleeding in trickles instead of spurts. Even though he was somewhat separate from his body in this state of awareness, he knew he was getting cold, and colder, too cold.

Dying.

Still bleeding.

The manes were coming.

A shuffling, slithering noise nearby caught Aron's attention, and he knew it would be a snake. Probably a mocker-snake, coming to get its meal before the dead arrived.

His vision flickered, and the darkened Keep faded away from him.

Hands gripped his shoulders and pulled him upward, and Aron tried to will himself into unconsciousness before the teeth and claws of the manes sank into his chilling flesh.

Moments later, he realized his heels were bumping on stones and someone pulled him along the floor, then lifted him. Up. They were moving up. Higher. Away from the manes.

When next Aron floated back to awareness, he found himself propped against a wall. Fingers prodded the wound in his side, and Aron groaned as bolts of pain fired with each press and touch. He tried to raise his dagger and stab this new attacker, but the blade was no longer in his hand.

Heat poured into his side, making him scream instead.

He was burning. His skin was on fire.

Then he was choking—someone was making him drink. Bittersweet, thick liquid filled his mouth, then flowed down his throat, numbing him yet waking him. The pain—a little more bearable.

Aron's senses buzzed. He realized his eyes were pinched shut, and he opened them to find himself staring at the image he had rejected from the Altar hunter's mind.

It was a god. It was the Brother, come to life, glowing with silver-white brilliance.

Only—it wasn't really a god, was it?

It was just a man wearing the mantle of a god, projecting a false image, as Snakekiller had done when she frightened Aron with her hood snake illusion. He knew this was one of his nightmare images, not come to life, but in the flesh. Aron had seen the essence of this man in his dreams and visions. This man had shielded his identity by taking refuge in the image of the Brother, which few in Eyrie would challenge.

Aron wished he had realized that before, during the weeks this oathbreaker wandered about Stone, seeking unclaimed children. As the truth settled through Aron's mind, his *graal* let him see through the illusion as if it were nothing but mist and shadows, and he wondered if anyone would be able to trick him in that fashion again.

Eldin Falconer, First High Master of Thorn, knelt before him, his dark blue eyes, cropped hair, and thorny *benedets* illuminated by candlelight. He had covered Aron with rough blankets from the Keep's supplies.

"I've worked on the wound in your side," the man said, his voice both harsh and concerned. "But you'll need time and tending to regain your strength." He pushed his wineskin against Aron's lips. "Go on, take another drink. It won't poison you. At Thorn, our medicines heal."

Thorns fester, Aron wanted to say, but perhaps his eyes spoke for him.

Falconer frowned at him. "You've made my task difficult at every turn, but I'm through negotiating with Stone. You'll come back with me now to Eidolon, where you belong."

Aron kept his mouth closed, swallowed what was left of the nightshade wine mixture in his mouth, then wondered if the medicine might be drugged to make him more compliant—or even unconscious. Instantly, he felt thick in the mind. Confused. And the pain in his side seemed to be pushing against the medicine, stabbing at him as if the broadsword were poking his wound again and again.

Was Falconer armed?

Aron's mind dully assessed his new foe, seeing nothing but the cardinal robes and silver bracelets.

Falconer tended the wound in his side again, this time with *graal* energy and a paste he produced from a small pouch he took from his belt. Aron didn't object to this assistance, but he couldn't understand why Falconer would have sent hunters to kill him, then be attempting to save his life.

"You can't be permitted to stay at Stone." Falconer spoke in a matter-of-fact tone, as if Aron would have to be infirmed in the head if he didn't agree with this assertion. "Baldric doesn't have the resources to train you, to see to it that your abilities are properly controlled. Triune has always been backward in that respect."

"I've been trained," Aron choked out, his voice dry and whispery despite the drinks from Falconer's wineskin. His throat seemed to be failing him. "I've shirked some lessons, or I'd know even more."

Falconer's disgusted snort communicated his opinion. "From what teacher? That Ross pigeon?" He fastened his wineskin back to his belt. "She might be a good bed-warmer, boy, but she's beneath you."

Aron's hand twitched. If he'd had any strength, he would have punched Falconer.

Falconer sat back and studied Aron. "Your friend Dari needs evaluation and training, but you—you could lead a dynast. In the future, Eyrie may have need of you, and the children you'll father with a proper and well-appointed band-mate. Right now, Thorn has need of your strength, and in return, we'll give you education and skills befitting a boy with noble blood and such a powerful legacy."

Aron tried again to move, and understood that Falconer's wine had eased his agony, but left him paralyzed.

Falconer smiled at him, but Aron found no kindness in the expression. "Have no fear. The effects will wear off, but not before we're many miles from this hellish place. And I'm sorry about the hunters. I didn't want to do that." Falconer's eyes briefly became distant, and Aron sensed the truth of his words. "After she came to understand the full strength of your mind-talent when you rescued your friends, the Lady Provost was clear in her last instructions. Either you leave with me, or you meet your end, for the good of Eyrie."

For the good of Eyrie? Aron wanted to argue with Falconer, to tell him that he and his Lady Provost might be as mad as Nic's mother, but his mouth and lips and throat were as unnaturally relaxed as the rest of him. He couldn't so much as make a full swallow.

"Fate decreed you should survive, so we leave at sunrise, after the manes withdraw." Falconer set about binding Aron's ankles with strips of cloth. "The sooner we return to Eidolon, the better. I've been away too long—almost three years now, doing the Lady's work. I'll dispose of the hunters but leave the blood. Your friends at Stone will assume the worst, and Triune likely won't withstand the assault that's coming. The forces of Brailing and Altar—and Mab as well—will tear down the walls of Stone forever. With good fortune, the Cobb and Ross Guard will come to their senses and assist."

Disbelief rolled through Aron, and he managed to twitch against Falconer's hands as the man bound Aron's wrists.

Falconer didn't notice. As soon as the Thorn Brother moved away from him, Aron began working to focus his mind, to go through the Veil and call out to Dari for assistance. He closed his eyes and relaxed his muscles, but the thickness slowing his thoughts wouldn't remit. He bit his bottom lip and doubled his efforts, but he felt like he was trying to think through several layers of blankets, or find his way down a blind, foggy path.

Falconer was pulling a bedroll out of a large pack he must have brought to the Ruined Keep with him. "Don't bother trying to use your legacy. I couldn't risk you sending word to your little pigeon, so I added some bullroot to the wine."

Aron forced his eyes open, though it took effort to move the lids. Falconer's image was blurry now, and the candlelight seemed dimmer.

Bullroot.

What did bullroot have to do with anything?

"If you had been properly trained, you'd know that bullroot prevents the use of *graal*." Falconer unfurled his bedroll. "The damage is not permanent unless you use it too often—and I admit, it's less reliable in cases of bastard legacies like the storm skills of your guild master. On traditional legacies, it's quite effective."

Falconer shifted his attention to nightly toiletries and devotions then, leaving Aron to his panic and private thoughts. For a time, the Thorn Brother meditated; then he stretched himself on his bedroll and soon fell into a seemingly untroubled sleep.

Aron fought the wine and bullroot, and whenever he could command a muscle, the bindings on his wrists and ankles. Time and again, he hurled his mind toward the Veil, only to fall short and crash back into his physical body.

With each passing minute, then each passing hour, he grew more desperate and angry, and more exhausted. It was like being in Stone's training box, exactly like being in the box, except he couldn't think well enough to focus his awareness on any one point.

Falconer slept on, oblivious to Aron's battle.

Aron's mind kept flashing back to the day he was Harvested, to Dari unconscious in the wagons, and how Stormbreaker and Windblown had underestimated the amount of elixir needed to keep her subdued. Was that because she was Stregan—or did those with powerful legacies require larger or more frequent dosing?

The bullroot might keep him from using his *graal*, but maybe attempting to use it would give him freedom sooner than Falconer expected.

Aron mustered his inner resolve and strength, and hurled his awareness toward the Veil.

Moments later, he collapsed back into himself, unsuccessful, but more determined.

His lids felt so heavy he could barely keep his eyes open, but he glared at Falconer nonetheless, letting his anger grow until it felt like a stoked fire in his chest.

Rage.

Desperation.

Aron welcomed any emotion. All emotion. Maybe it would help him shed the mental and physical paralysis.

He launched his mind toward the Veil again. Again. Again.

Each attempt weakened him, made him more drowsy. If he could have banged his head against the stone wall behind him, he would have done it, just to stay awake.

If he broke through the Veil, would he kill Falconer with a thought?

Could he do such a thing?

It would be simple enough to locate the man's life functions, if he could only fight off the effects of the bullroot.

Aron tried for the Veil again, but his awareness slid back into his body.

He let himself remember Falconer's insult to Dari, and what the man said about Dari needing evaluation and training. Did that mean Falconer and his friends would begin masquerading as gods and the Goddess in her dreams? Would they torture her with false images of her sister?

Aron wouldn't let that happen.

He could kill Falconer.

Aron's head drooped against his chest, and his mouth opened despite his efforts to keep his lips closed.

He *would* kill Falconer.

If he could just stay awake.

CHAPTER FIFTY-SEVEN

DARI

Dari stood at her window, gazing into the endless darkness of Triune. Her attention was riveted southward, toward the Ruined Keep, despite Stormbreaker's presence in her chamber.

"He will survive," Stormbreaker said, placing his hand on the small of Dari's back. Behind them, a fire crackled in the hearth, and the sweet smell of bubbling herbal tea wafted through the chamber.

"Herder didn't survive," Dari said, unable to stop frowning. "Why does Stone insist on this ridiculous initiation? Aron doesn't agree with it. I don't agree with it. It's archaic and foolish, and—and it's wasteful."

Stormbreaker's calm tones were almost maddening. "It's traditional. In a guild, tradition is of great importance. Shared experiences—"

"I know. I know. They bind you together." She smacked her hands against the windowsill, wishing Stormbreaker would rail against the trial, or complain about her opinion. She would have preferred anything to that frustrating, emotionless tone. It was his strength, and most times quite attractive, but this night, Dari also found it to be a weakness. His placid serenity made her feel foolish and out of control.

Where was Nic?

He, at least, had the emotions of a normal man.

And the sense never to participate in something like Stone's trial.

Stormbreaker pressed his fingers against her robe, massaging the spot on her spine where she always held her tension. "Should we call Blath back from the kitchens and journey to search for Kate?"

It was a reasonable suggestion, one that reflected how well Stormbreaker knew Dari, and anticipated her need to stay busy in the face of distress.

Tonight, though, action didn't appeal to her. It seemed wrong. Risky, and somehow disrespectful to Aron. She shook her head. "I can't focus. I'd be a danger."

Stormbreaker moved his hand away from her, and for a time, he gazed out the window with her. Then he cleared his throat and offered, "A walk, perhaps? The moonslight is bright, and the exertion might be relaxing."

Dari thought he was offering more than a walk. His attention. His strong embrace. It was a kindness, but she didn't want that, at least not tonight. For a moment, she worried that Stormbreaker would be jealous or peevish because of her concern for Aron, then dismissed the worry. He was concerned, too. And, Dari realized with a start, she really didn't care if Stormbreaker became upset with her.

What did that mean?

Once more, she wondered if Nic was awake in his bedchamber in the infirmary. If she went to see him, would Snakekiller let her pass?

Her skin chilled, and she dug her nails into the wood of the windowsill. "Something feels wrong to me this night."

Stormbreaker let out a breath. "Trials test the nerves of all who care for the apprentice."

"It's not that." Cayn's teeth, but Dari wanted to slap the man. "I mean, yes, it feels wrong to hurl Aron into mortal peril for no reason save guild tradition. But aside from that—there's strange energy about. Unrest."

"Perhaps you're sensing the forces gathering to attack Triune." Stormbreaker placed his own hands on the sill, and his tone softened—which was as much feeling as Dari could usually mark, when it came to him. "Such a thing has never happened in Eyrie's history."

"Stone can defend itself." Dari spoke the words even as she thought, *Like Aron.* But she didn't feel convinced.

Stormbreaker nodded. "Triune is more of a fortress than our foes suspect. And help will come to us, if nothing stops Lord Cobb or Lord Ross."

When Dari didn't respond, Stormbreaker lingered a few more moments, then excused himself, stating he would be in the Den library if Dari changed her mind about a late-night hunt, or a late-night walk.

His absence came as a relief to Dari, which surprised her. Yet she couldn't stand the stillness and silence that descended on her chamber once he departed. After a few unbearably quiet minutes, she wrapped her cloak around her shoulders and headed for the infirmary.

Triune's grounds seemed unnaturally quiet to her, or perhaps it was the absence of Blath and Iko, who had gone to the main kitchens for mead and bread. It was traditional for Sabor to eat and drink when they prayed, and they would be keeping vigil for Aron until morning. As would she—though in her own fashion.

Soon she came to the crossroads that led to the Shrine of the Mother, that spot that had so bedeviled Aron since her arrival at Triune. She glanced toward the spot out of habit—and stopped walking.

A silvery glow rose from the direction of the Shrine, faint, barely detectable. Almost like a wisp of smoke. It vanished before she could take a step in that direction.

"I've seen that a few times," said a voice from beside her, and Dari startled so badly she swung her fist as she turned.

Her blow connected with Nic's jaw, sending him staggering to one side. He collapsed on the byway as she grabbed her smarting knuckles and let out a shout of surprise.

"Nic. Oh. I'm—I'm so sorry." She ran to him, her heart squeezing from shock and regret. Had she damaged him? What if he went into a fit?

But he was already pushing himself to his knees as she reached him, and he was laughing. The bright, happy sound put her at ease immediately, and she appreciated him for his ability to relax her so easily.

"I think it's me who owes you an apology," he said as she helped him to stand. He rubbed the spot on his jaw where she had connected, and even in the moonslight, Dari could see his skin darkening. "I should know better than to startle a lady."

"That wasn't very ladylike, was it?" She brushed dirt off his tunic, grateful that she hadn't made him bleed all over his clothing. "I don't think playing the role of a proper noble female suits me well. What are you doing on the road in the middle of the night?"

Nic's grin flashed in the moonslight. "I could ask you the same question, but I'd like to hope you were on your way to visit me."

Dari felt her face grow warm. "I was. I couldn't sleep."

"I couldn't either, so I told Snakekiller I was heading for the Den." Nic's grin faded. "All I can do is worry." He glanced over his shoulder, in the direction of the Ruined Keep. "I would have gone with him, though I might have been a liability."

"Aron would have been fortunate to have your company." Dari wished she could go to the Keep herself, just to see that Aron was intact and fighting his way through the night. She looked away from Triune's far wall, and her attention returned to the byway she had been about to take when Nic startled her. "Did you say you saw something at the Shrine?"

"A few times. A light, or maybe some stray energy. It's never very strong, and it's always gone when I arrive." He gestured to his mis-shapen legs and limped a step. "I'm not very fast, you know."

Dari did know, but she had never felt pity for Nic. He didn't seem to seek it either, but brought up his disabilities only to explain himself or illustrate a point. He was an absolute contrast to Storm-breaker, vulnerable and open, and different from Aron, as well, with-out that ever-present menace of anger and well of misery. How had Nic been through so much, and emerged so affable? Dari thought she should take lessons from him, in both disposition and resilience.

"Aron's had trouble with the Shrine," Dari said, allowing her-self to begin to enjoy the steadiness of Nic's presence. "He's had visions there, but none of us has ever found anything out of the ordinary."

"Perhaps Aron has the stronger sight, at least where the Shrine is concerned." Nic rubbed his jaw, sending Dari into a small frenzy of guilt.

"I can't believe I hit you." She put her hand on his arm. "I was distracted."

"No worries. I can take a punch." He caught her hand with his own. "Let's pay the Shrine of the Mother a visit, for Aron's sake."

Dari found herself smiling despite her worry, and would have kept smiling if Triune's bells hadn't started to ring.

She and Nic stopped at the same moment, gripping each other's arms.

Dari's breath stopped, and she was certain she would hear the pattern announcing Aron's death. Tears rose to her eyes so fast she couldn't form even a meager defense. Sobs followed, fast and hard, and then Nic was holding her, soothing her, rubbing her shoulders as he said, "No, no, it's not that. It's visitors. Nobles. I haven't learned all the patterns yet—but it's not Aron, Dari. Look at me. That's it. Look at me."

Nic's features seemed fuzzy through tears and moonlight. He

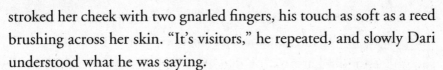

stroked her cheek with two gnarled fingers, his touch as soft as a reed brushing across her skin. "It's visitors," he repeated, and slowly Dari understood what he was saying.

"Nobles," she murmured. Then, "Nobles? Nic." She gripped his shoulders. "You have to get back to the infirmary." She was already shifting some of her awareness through the Veil, wrapping it around Nic's essence and choking out the ruby hue that clung to him, announcing the strength of his Mab legacy.

Soft, running footfalls caught her attention, and instinct made her turn Nic loose and reach to her waist for a dagger that she didn't have.

Tiamat Snakekiller charged into view, both hands on the hilts of her own blades. Her light hair hung loose at her shoulders, and her *benedets* gave her a wild, deadly look. Dari recognized the barely controlled panic in the other woman's face, and knew she must care very deeply for Nic, after rescuing him and guarding him so closely, even to the point of almost giving her life for him.

"I'm trouble all around tonight," Nic said as Snakekiller reached them. He bowed to Dari, adding, "Forgive me. I had intended for us to give each other comfort until Aron returned. Now it seems I'll just cost you energy and effort, shielding my legacy."

"Come." Snakekiller didn't spare Dari a glance. Tension was evident in every tight line of her face and neck. "We don't know who's approaching, or what treachery might be afoot."

Nic acquiesced, following her away toward the infirmary, where Snakekiller would conceal and protect him until these visitors departed. For her part, Dari would maintain her own protections on Nic, for as long as she believed them to be needed.

Another figure approached at a rapid pace from the direction of the Den, and Dari recognized Stormbreaker. She saw him acknowledge his sister and nod to Nic, who waved once before disappearing with his guardian into the darkness of the road.

"You should return to safety yourself," Stormbreaker said as he drew even with Dari, but she had no intention of retreating until she understood what kind of dangers Nic might be facing. Stormbreaker didn't argue with her as he fell into step beside her. They didn't speak to each other, and Dari couldn't help noticing a tension that went beyond the stress of the moment.

Was Stormbreaker angry with her?

Not that he'd ever put his feelings into words, even if she asked.

Long minutes later, as they approached the main gate and keep, he slowed, and Dari noticed that he had pulled his robes aside to give himself easy access to his daggers and short sword. His longer blades, as always, were crossed on his back, and his hard, distant expression suggested that he would draw them on the smallest provocation.

As he tended to do, he took her arm for added safety as they crossed the moat. Below them, mocker-fish splashed and gurgled, hoping a fresh meal might tumble to them by happenstance.

"Is Nic well tonight?" Stormbreaker inquired, his voice tight.

"As well as might be expected, given the worries we all share." Dari had answered him out of habit, but she found herself staring at him, surprised by the force of his question.

Stormbreaker's next comment shocked her even more. "It's good that he could offer you ease when I could not."

"Wha—are you—do you think—" Dari almost laughed at him, at the implication that she had met Nic for some romantic purpose, but she thought better of it.

First Aron, now Stormbreaker.

Did both of them believe she was secretly having some tryst with Nic?

The idea struck her as ridiculous. Nic was her friend, her companion. Nothing more.

Yet she did share an ease with him she had never known with another person save for her twin. And she did seek his company over everyone else's—but that was because he helped her relax and he made her laugh. Besides, she had a responsibility to Nic, as she once felt a responsibility toward Aron, to see to his training and safety.

Dari would have discussed this with Stormbreaker, likely with some volume and emphasis, but they had reached the entrance court-yard, and two riders thundered through the archway.

Dari recognized the first man by the way he handled his horse, despite the fact that he had let his beard grow even longer, and that he was dressed in the breeches and cloak of a farmer, without his signature battle helm.

"Lord Cobb," Stormbreaker said as the man pulled up sharply in front of Lord Baldric, and dismounted in a single fluid motion.

The other rider was less at ease on horseback, and much taller and more muscled than his companion. His hands were gloved and his face was wrapped in silken scarves like he hailed from Dyn Altar's deserts, and for a moment Dari was reminded of Canus the Bandit. No trace of legacy issued from the second rider, but he felt familiar to Dari.

As the taller man reined his mount, that sense of familiarity dou-bled, and doubled again.

She was running toward him before she fully understood that she was moving, her heart pounding so fast she wondered if she would faint before she reached him. She released the protections she had wrapped around Nic, and concentrated only on her strides, on the wind in her face, and on the man in front of her.

Stormbreaker shouted to her, but Dari ignored him. All of Tri-une faded away from her as the rider turned in her direction, then removed the scarves from his face. Moonslight struck his high cheek-bones and arched nose, playing off his dark skin and the rich, fra-grant oil in his tightly cropped curls.

As he pulled off his gloves to reveal his large, powerful hands, Stormbreaker's calls ceased, and Lord Baldric bowed his head.

Dari reached her grandfather in two steps, and threw herself into his waiting embrace.

"He wouldn't wait," Lord Cobb was explaining to Lord Baldric. "Not another day. Not another hour. It was this, or he would have landed a contingent of Sabor in your fields and gardens to make certain he reached her."

Lord Ross's arms closed around Dari, crushing the air out of her lungs as his deep voice grumbled a greeting only she could hear.

"It's a fine thing," Lord Ross said, "when I must take my Guard and go to war, just to see my own family."

CHAPTER FIFTY-EIGHT

ARON

As dawn broke over the Ruined Keep, Aron's body ached, and his head burned like his mind might catch fire and drive him into madness along with his captor. He kept dreaming he saw a glow about Falconer, bright light, like the silvery light spilling off the goddess who had so often sought to deceive him in his visions. Sometimes he thought he saw the goddess, and during those moments, Falconer would thrash and kick in his sleep, and moan like someone was torturing him. Once Aron even imagined he saw Dari standing with the goddess, holding her arm, as if lending the terrible phantasm the strength of her Stregan *graal*.

"No," he whispered, surprised to hear the hoarse rattle of his own voice. His words sounded slurred as he said, "Leave Dari alone. Leave her alone!"

Aron closed his eyes, and when he startled awake some time later, Falconer was gone. Aron realized he was probably getting rid of the bodies of the hunters—whatever the manes hadn't consumed.

In moments, the Thorn Brother would come back, and he would haul Aron away from his home, away from Stormbreaker and Nic and Dari. Aron knew he should be leaving the Ruined Keep, making his way back to the safety of Triune, and hearing the bells, the bells ringing to announce his triumph in the trial. By early afternoon, his friends would be worried. Then the bells would toll to mourn his failure. There would be a search, and blood would be found—much of it his, if anyone had the ability to assess that.

He would be given up for dead, and be trapped in the grip of this madman, this god-impostor. How long could the man keep him drugged? How long before he had use of his *graal* again? Was Thorn capable of preventing him from communicating through the Veil forever?

Thorn has need of your strength. . . .

What did that mean?

Aron tried to struggle against his bindings, and found he had a shade more strength. Falconer's healing had reduced the misery from his wound, and his side felt better. The wine and sleeping must have restored some of his strength, because he didn't feel so close to blacking out.

From the levels of the Keep below Aron came bumping and thumping noises, along with whistling. The image of Falconer whistling as he disposed of the bodies of killers he had hired and sent to their doom made Aron gut-sick.

He tried again to move his wrists, and felt the cloth ties cut into his skin.

Do it, he told himself aloud, then in his mind, making it an order, making it a command, reaching for the force of his legacy, which he still couldn't access.

Aron imagined Dari crying for him, saw the tears in Nic's sad eyes. Stormbreaker and Zed would be more stoic, and Iko, and even Lord Baldric might grieve him. How could he let these people down, when they had invested so much time and trust in his success?

He kicked his leg, but his ankle only flopped against its ties as below him, the whistling continued.

Perhaps Falconer would climb the stairs and use his dagger to slice open Aron's throat. If the man was truly insane, what boundaries did his madness know?

Aron strained backward, smacking his head against the stone wall hard enough to make himself see bursts of white light. He blinked against the bright flares and the throbbing ache blooming behind both of his temples. At the same moment, his wounded side stabbed at him, and he choked out a few curses, directed at Falconer and Thorn and the hunters.

As his vision cleared, an image rose before him as if it were sliding up from the floor that separated Aron from the murderous Thorn Brother. He leaned back to avoid it, figuring it for some mind-trick Falconer was playing to keep him off balance and helpless.

The image coalesced into a young woman with dark hair and dark skin, wearing a sparkling silver robe. Her braids hung in thin rows, pulled to her neck at the center, and her dark eyes glittered like night stars as she studied him.

"Dari," Aron whispered, his surge of excitement helping him throw off another measure of Falconer's drugging.

She was whole and solid and real, as beautiful as any vision had ever been, yet Aron couldn't shake a sense of strangeness, of desperation and danger. His blood surged, and his instincts, dulled as they were, clamored for him to leap from the nearest window rather than deal with this creature.

Aron knew she could be a trick, a hood snake illusion, something false and treacherous, but his heart refused to accept that possibility. Dari didn't seem to know him, yet she had clearly come to check on him, maybe even rescue him.

Was that possible?

Iko had walked on the other side of the Veil, seemingly with his real and actual body. If Sabor could manage such a feat, could Stregans do it?

Dari swept toward him, almost dancing across the floor, until she was standing only inches away.

"Help me," Aron croaked, flopping against the wall and floor as he struggled to snap the bindings on his wrists and ankles. "It's Falconer. I think his mind has gone over a cliff. I think he—"

Dari put a long, graceful finger against her lips, and glanced toward the chamber door as if Falconer might hear Aron's pleas.

Aron clamped his teeth together.

Dari held out both hands, as if she might be assessing Aron. He felt the heat of her mental touch, but couldn't discern it because of the lingering effects of the bullroot. Rainbow light played off Dari's fingers, surrounding first her, then him. Warmth spread from every point on Aron's skin, driven by that light, spreading upward and outward until his fingers and toes tingled. He gulped a breath, and felt his chest move more normally. An intangible pressure on his mind eased, then re-formed as Dari leaned toward him, closer, closer, as if she might be bending down to kiss him.

Aron breathed in her rainbow light, expecting to catch a hint of her spice and apple scent, or feel the whisper-soft brush of her robes on his cheeks, her lips on his. The stabbing in his side eased, only to migrate to a spot directly between his eyes.

The sharpening pain in his head made Aron grunt. His eyes teared. He tried to pull back from the image of Dari, but her spectral hands cupped his cheeks, holding him in place as her multicolored energy swept into him and blasted through his mind.

Every nerve in Aron's body answered that jolt with painful shocks and twitches. His back arched. The bindings on his wrists and ankles tore in half as his legs and arms went rigid and extended as far as his muscles and bones would allow.

He was going to break in half.

His head would explode from his neck, and he would burn until there was nothing left of him but ash and teeth.

Stop, he tried to say, but couldn't coax his rigid lips into forming the word.

All he could do was twitch and jump and moan, and try to tear himself free of Dari's deadly grip.

A moment later, she turned him loose, then swept back to stare at him from a distance.

Aron lay on the floor of the Keep chamber, his muscles still hopping like frogs in a rainstorm. He had no control, then some, then more.

He pulled himself to a sitting position, and the remnants of the numbness and weakness left him in twitches and spurts. His mind felt newly sharp and calm, and his body fresh, as if he had slept the night through in his own bed at Triune. When he reached for the Veil, he achieved his goal immediately, and he could see Dari so clearly it made his heart ache. He focused his *graal* on her, and knew she was real. This was no false image, no deception.

This was Dari, only not at all the Dari he knew. Her image now had the haggard, spent look of a spirit about to explode into sparkles and fly toward the heavens. She sagged instead of stood, and her hands were shaking as she clasped them together.

Aron leaped to his feet and moved toward her, on both sides of the Veil. "You gave me too much of yourself. Take some back, Dari. Here." He reached for her, intending to embrace her, but she drifted away from him, toward the Keep wall.

Her eyes now looked frightened.

"Dari!" Aron grabbed for the hem of her robe, but missed.

She moved around him in a circle, never taking her eyes off his face, studying him as if she might never have the opportunity to see him again.

"What did you do to yourself?" Aron's voice rose with his distress. His pulse was normal again, but accelerating, making blood rush against his ears until he feared he might not hear her response.

Dari mouthed something to him, her eyes wide and terrified and sad.

Aron jumped toward her and tried to capture her robe again, but failed. "What? Tell me again, Dari. I didn't hear you."

The apparition made a noise that sounded almost like a sigh.

Aron put his hands behind his back so he wouldn't scare her away from him, leaned forward, and did his best to hear every word she spoke.

Kill . . . me. . . .

The words formed in his mind instead of in the stagnant air of the Keep.

Aron thought he must have heard her incorrectly. Surely she meant for him to kill Falconer when the Thorn Brother returned.

"What, Dari? Did you—"

The image of Dari lifted her hands and folded them together, as if she might be beseeching a god to grant her favor.

Kill me, she repeated.

Then her image faded through the wall of the Ruined Keep, and she was gone.

"Dari!" Aron's awareness plummeted back through the Veil. He ran to the wall and struck the stones with his fists. Then he ran his palms over the spot where she vanished, but found nothing. He could sense nothing of her at all.

For a moment, he considered leaping through the window, but turned for the door instead.

Falconer was standing in the archway.

The Thorn Brother's hands and bracelets and robes were soiled with blackish stains Aron presumed to be old blood, and his eyes were wide with surprise.

Aron's hand smacked against his waist to grab a dagger, but he had no weapons belt. Falconer must have taken it while he was unconscious.

The Thorn Brother, however, was wearing a short sword, which he drew. "I don't know how it's possible that you're standing, boy, but you won't be leaving unless it's under my supervision, with a new dose of nightshade elixir."

Aron calmed himself, drawing on session after session of practice with Dari. He let his awareness ease through the Veil, all the while keeping his actions and *graal* masked from the Thorn Brother. He wasn't adept enough at traveling over distances to reach out his mind to Triune, not while he had to concentrate on Falconer's drawn sword, but he would communicate with Dari or Nic or Stormbreaker soon enough.

"I won't be going with you," he told Falconer, holding his hands palm out to discourage the Thorn Brother from charging him with the blade.

"You don't understand what's at stake," Falconer said, turning the short sword in his grip like an experienced fighter. "You don't understand what Lady Pravda is trying to do."

"And you don't understand me," Aron countered. "I have no interest in your Lady Provost's schemes. Let me pass." His gaze dropped to Falconer's stained garments. "We don't have to bring this to more bloodshed."

Falconer emitted a low growl and circled Aron, keeping his short sword ready. "I don't want to kill you, boy. Not when fate has spared you once already. What you could mean to Thorn, to Eyrie—you have no idea."

Aron kept his awareness on both sides of the Veil, paying attention to the man's movements in the Keep chamber, and to Falconer's increasing red glow on the other side of the Veil. The man did have a strong legacy, and he was preparing to use it.

But how?

The Mab gift was broad, like that of the Stregans, but primarily it involved seeing what might be, what could be, and what would be.

Aron started to move to his left, but Falconer blocked him with a quick lunge. Aron feinted right but jumped hard to the left again—and Falconer beat him to the position, keeping him at the same distance from the Keep door.

Was he anticipating Aron's strategies?

To test his theory, Aron executed another series of potential escape moves.

Each time, Falconer stopped him easily.

"You know where I'm going," Aron said.

Falconer's smile was chilling, like the sunlight reflecting off his sharpened sword. "You can't get past me, and you have no weapon. I can see that you can't use your *graal* yet, either, so what choice do you have? Sit on the floor, boy. A drink of my nightshade elixir, and we'll be away from this place, heading for much kinder, brighter lands."

Aron didn't smile back at the Thorn Brother, though he was gratified that his shields prevented Falconer from seeing that his legacy had been restored to him. Dari would be proud.

Dari . . .

A surge of desperate worry nearly distracted Aron from his purpose, but he fought to maintain his concentration.

"Stone trains us to fight with and without weapons," he told Falconer. "We could be at this cat-mouse game for a long time."

Falconer's upper lip pulled back in a new snarl.

"Not all the predators on the Lost Path hunt at night," Aron continued, watching Falconer's blue eyes and the color of his legacy. "The longer I hold you off, the more likely we'll be eaten by something as we make our escape."

Falconer struck out with his sword, aiming for Aron's arm.

Aron sidestepped and spun to keep Falconer in front of him.

The Thorn Brother swore and jumped to block Aron's egress, once more occupying the space between Aron and the chamber door. His eyes had gone wider, and Aron thought he caught a gleam of worry.

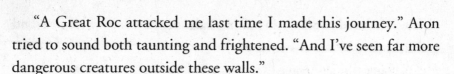

"A Great Roc attacked me last time I made this journey." Aron tried to sound both taunting and frightened. "And I've seen far more dangerous creatures outside these walls."

Falconer was definitely getting more rattled.

Aron figured the man couldn't be thinking well, given his recent actions. He didn't want to underestimate anyone with a lifetime of guild training, but something had left Falconer a shell of what he should be. Maybe it was a troubled conscience or the ravages of some illness, or some other destructive force. Aron didn't really care. He just wanted to goad Falconer into making an uncontrolled attack.

"What happened to the children you stole from Stone?" Aron increased the mockery in his voice. "Are they already dead, or did you hand them over to the Guard? I hear Lord Brailing is conscripting anyone old enough to hoist a sword."

"The children are safe," Falconer insisted. "They're on their way to Eidolon with escorts from Thorn."

The flare in his legacy let Aron know how important it was to Falconer, this belief that he was on the side of right, that he was making noble choices, for the good of others, his guild, and Eyrie.

"Who guaranteed that safety?" Aron paced back and forth, keeping Falconer off balance, "Lord Brailing? When you made alliance with that oathbreaker, you disgraced every vow you swore to uphold."

Falconer's sword trembled in his hands. "Thorn has no alliance with Brailing."

"That's a lie." Aron laughed, making sure to sound as cruel as possible. "I don't need my *graal* to tell me that. All of Eyrie knows what Thorn has become. A concubine to traitors and monsters."

Falconer lashed out with his sword and his mind, striking at Aron with a clumsy, angry thrust. At the same time, he tried to use his *graal* to shock Aron, perhaps disorient him—but Aron dropped his mental shields as he leaped back, out of range of the short sword.

He met Falconer's *graal* with his own, and he held back nothing.

Stop, he commanded, imagining Falconer freezing where he stood and dropping his short sword.

Falconer did as Aron ordered—and more.

Everything about the man came to a complete halt, from the flow of breath in his lungs, the flood of blood through his veins, the beat of his heart, the blinking of his eyes. Every motion associated with Falconer ceased to exist.

His face turned a terrible shade of red, then purple as his short sword clattered against the nearest wall. For a moment, the Thorn Brother appeared to be a piece of petrified wood, rendered in the shape of a red-robed man with thorny tattoos carved across his face.

When Falconer fell, he dropped like a dead tree, hard and fast and without any break in momentum.

Aron watched Falconer strike the stone floor, and heard the crunch of bone from the impact. He didn't have to go to Falconer and kneel beside him to know that he would find no breathing, no heartbeat, no life.

Falconer had died the moment Aron spoke with his *graal*.

Waves of cold traveled up and down Aron's spine, and he couldn't stop shaking.

He had known this was possible, killing with his mind, but he hadn't imagined it like this. No matter his fury from the night before, he hadn't intended that outcome. He had meant to disarm Falconer, to render him unable to fight. Aron had intended to take Falconer back to Triune, to explain himself to Lord Baldric.

"Too much energy," he whispered aloud, realizing his error. The force of his command had robbed Falconer of any chance to defend himself or resist the order.

If Aron could have reached into his own mind and removed his *graal*, he would have done so. He would have ripped it free of his body and thrown it from the tower window of the Ruined Keep, and let the mockers and manes feed on it.

He had killed the First High Master of Thorn. And he had done it with a single thought. A single word.

Was this murder?

Aron shook his head to try to clear his senses, but cold seemed to be claiming him inch by frozen inch.

Moments ago, all he wanted was to reach Dari, to ensure her safety and well-being. He had wanted to see his friends, go back to his home. He had wanted to hear Triune's bells ringing for him.

And now?

Aron forced himself forward.

Now he wasn't certain where he should go, or what should be done with him when he got there. As before, when he rescued Nic and Snakekiller, Aron felt his world shifting until he didn't know himself, until he no longer saw the course of his own future, even days from now, much less cycles or years.

Everything had changed for him. Again.

When he reached Falconer, he lowered himself to his knees and placed his hands on Falconer's wrists. The man's skin was already cold and hard, drained of everything that made it vital and human. Aron carefully removed Falconer's bracelets, then turned him over and felt through his robes until he located his own silver dagger, the one Falconer had removed from him the night before.

Feeling detached and less than human himself, Aron drew the dagger from Falconer's pocket, then plunged the blade into Falconer's chest. He spoke in the Language of Kings as Stormbreaker and the Stone Guild had taught him to do, summoning Falconer's spirit.

The man's cardinal *cheville* burst open, falling to dust and bits of bright red stone. An instant later, his essence burst upward, freed from its ruined flesh by the breaking of the *cheville*, the silver in the dagger, and Aron's rhythmic incantation. For a few sad seconds, the image of a powerful winged man lingered above the body.

Then all that had been Eldin Falconer lifted upward and exploded into glittering bits as it struck the Keep's ceiling. Aron knew the man's energy would keep rising, striving to reach the sky and the stars.

Aron folded Falconer's arms, closed the man's staring eyes, then withdrew his dagger and cleaned it. He fashioned himself a new belt of cloth, and used it to strap the dagger and Falconer's short sword to his waist. When he was finished, he collected Falconer's bracelets, and set out from the Ruined Keep.

His destination, at least for the moment, was Triune. It seemed the only right thing to do, to take Falconer's bracelets to Lord Baldric, and explain what had happened. The prospect of Judgment no longer frightened Aron. If that was Lord Baldric's decision, Aron would submit to it without protest. He might even submit to the killing blow rather than strike at one of his fellow guild members. It grieved him to think he had failed his trial, and failed so completely in the control of his *graal*. More than anything, though, it hurt Aron to know he would disappoint and wound the people he loved.

As he ran toward the Stone stronghold, Aron noticed the silence on the Lost Path, and knew that the truth was clinging to him like a tangible smell. It had to be obvious to anything that might choose to attack him.

Predator.

That's what he was. Like Platt. Like the Altar hunters. Aron was a killer, and even the animals knew it.

CHAPTER FIFTY-NINE

NIC

"It wasn't murder!" Lord Baldric's voice thundered through his chambers, rattling Nic's nerves.

The sight of Aron, stubbornly wearing his apprentice's tunic and breeches, sitting at the opposite end of Lord Baldric's long table beside Stormbreaker looking so utterly broken—that rattled Nic's heart. Eldin Falconer's silver bracelets, coated with remnants of blood from four Altar hunters, rested on the table in front of Aron, offering mute testimony to what Aron had suffered.

"You defended yourself," Stormbreaker said. "You defended Stone, Aron. Apprentices should contend with natural elements and the dangers of the land during their trial—never human hunters."

Dari sat on Aron's other side, and next to her was Lord Ross. Dari's grandfather was so powerfully built that he dwarfed everyone else at the table, and his smooth, dark skin gave no hint of his age or the sorrows he had suffered. He had large, dark eyes like Dari, and his hair was the same flawless coal-black as hers, though much shorter, with a dash of silver at both temples. With his dark green robes and black eyes, he was the picture of nobility, and Nic couldn't help but admire the force of his character and voice.

"I'm sorry, young man," Lord Ross said to Aron, his bass voice as commanding as his appearance. "You shouldn't have faced such an attack alone. I would have been honored to fight at your side."

"As would I," Lord Cobb agreed from across the table, pulling at his overlong brown beard. He was still dressed in the simple brown robes of a common traveler, and Nic suspected he was more comfortable in those garments than the fine silks of a dynast lord. "Gods. First Helmet Brailing's mind goes over a cliff, and he takes Bolthor Altar and the warbirds down with him. Now Thorn's leaders have followed after them—or at least Eldin Falconer did. What are we to do, Kembell?" Lord Cobb gave Lord Ross a sad look. "How are we to stop this disaster?"

Nic's stomach lurched as he thought about his mother, always fragile, never stable. Had Eyrie created a generation of lords and ladies who didn't have the constitution to lead? Were the only sane nobles in the land sitting together at this table?

"We stand with our allies." Lord Ross gestured around the table. "And we call to all who would stand with us." To Lord Cobb, he said, "The war has come to us, Westin, no matter how we've tried to keep it from our borders."

Nic grabbed the ends of the long table and did his best not to lean forward and put his head on the smooth, dark wood. He was exhausted from his emotional journey in the last day. In only hours, he had traveled from worry and agitation over Aron, to elation at being with Dari, to distress at being confined when Stone's visitors arrived, to anxiety at meeting dynast lords like Lord Cobb and Lord Ross. Real men, with real purpose and strength and confidence, the confidence a true leader needed to possess as a matter of course. The confidence Nic couldn't hope to make his own.

That anxiety had given way to joy at seeing Dari so happy to be with her family, fear for Aron all over again, despair when the mourning bells tolled, then elation when Aron came stumbling back through Triune's gates.

Lord Baldric seemed to share Nic's fatigue. The Lord Provost's color had reached peak during his pronouncement that Aron was no murderer, and now his pate had taken on a frightening pallor. "Stone remains neutral, but the war comes to us as well." Lord Baldric gazed past his guests to the window that looked out over Triune's grounds. "I have more sheltered here than guild fighters. These are people who fled the carnage, only to have it pursue them even though they thought they had reached safety within these walls."

"We won't allow the battle to reach your gates." Lord Cobb's voice was earnest and his eyes were kind, but Nic heard the note of uncertainty.

Lord Baldric's grunt confirmed that he, too, knew such a promise was futile. "And how will you stop it? Every army in Eyrie is driving toward us, intent on laying claim to our lands, our loyalty, and our resources. They'll be here within the week—two at most."

"Because of me," Aron said, and the pain in his voice was more than Nic could bear.

"It's not because of you, Aron." Nic scrubbed his palms on the table. "It's because of me."

"No one knows—" Dari began, but Nic couldn't let her finish. He forced himself to look directly into Aron's sapphire eyes as he spoke.

"This war would have had no beginning if I hadn't died. If I hadn't remained dead in the minds of the people even after I recovered." Nic couldn't quite believe what he was saying, or how much he felt it, meant it, at every level of his being. "It was a mistake— a selfish decision that ended thousands of lives, and caused more suffering than I can stand to consider. I must set it right as soon as possible, as soon as we determine the best way for me to do so."

"No one faults you for saving your own life." Aron straightened his shoulders as he rose to the task of defending Nic. "If you'd returned to the Tree City, the unsanctioned assassins would have made sure to do their task properly. You'd be moldering in some unmarked grave."

"Rectors." Nic said, shifting his gaze to Lord Baldric, then to Lord Cobb and Lord Ross. "Rectors pushed me from the castle turret. I believe the same rectors poisoned my father, my brothers, and my sister. Thorn's madness extends far beyond Eldin Falconer, unless Thorn's graduates now hire out to the highest bidder. I think the source of Thorn's dry rot lies directly at its base."

When he realized everyone at Lord Baldric's table was listening to him, Nic found he couldn't draw a full breath. He felt his cheeks flush, and his eyelids fluttered as he resisted a wave of anxiety strong enough to trigger one of his fits. His fingers skittered as he moved them along the table, and his voice deserted him.

"Thorn has already collected many children with powerful legacies," Aron said, sounding more like himself. "They've taken them in the open, and I believe they've stolen them in the night as well. Much of the child-swiping blamed on Canus the Bandit might be better laid at Thorn's gates. I don't know how they're using their captives, but they factor into Thorn's plan, and maybe into the war." He inclined his head toward Dari, and his features softened. "If you hadn't saved me, Dari, I'd be part of their schemes."

"I didn't save you." Dari looked confused. "I wanted to. So did Iko and Nic and Stormbreaker and Zed and Raaf—even Windblown spent the night pacing the halls of the Den."

Now Aron's expression of confusion matched hers. "You came to me in a vision. You helped me escape the effects of Falconer's drugged wine."

Dari shook her head. "I couldn't have mustered that kind of concentration last night. I couldn't even manage my own energy, much less lend any to you."

"It was you, Dari." Aron put his hand over hers. "My *graal* knew the image wasn't a lie. The bullroot, the paralyzing herbs—you lent me your energy to overcome it. I thought you transferred too much to me and did damage to yourself."

Dari shook her head again and withdrew from his touch. "I didn't."

"You don't have to protect me," Aron said. "No one could consider this a proper trial."

"It was a proper trial. It was—it was a terrible trial." Lord Baldric rubbed a hand across his wide face, and the emotion Nic saw was not anger or fear or anything close to it. It was grief. For his guild. For his way of life. "Lord Ross was right, Aron. No one should have faced something like that alone. I'm sorry for what you endured, and you are most certainly finished with any need to prove yourself to Stone."

Aron's shoulders sagged again, and he looked at Stormbreaker. "I didn't make it through last night on my own power. I required saving, first by a lunatic, and then by a vision. I can't wear the robes."

"You've earned them, and you'll wear them, and before you leave these grounds, you'll draw your first stone." Lord Baldric's voice broke, and his shoulders drooped as much as Aron's. To Nic, he suddenly had the appearance of an old man, overwhelmed by the sadness in his heart.

"One day when you return," Lord Baldric continued, speaking more quietly, "it'll be with your first kill behind you. You'll see that you belong here, Aron. You're a Stone of Stone, and I regret anything I might have said or done in these many cycles to make you believe otherwise."

The silence around the table was worse than any storm Nic had ever endured.

One day when you return . . .

Nic looked from Aron to Dari to Stormbreaker, then at both dynast lords. Everyone seemed weighted now, especially as Aron worked out the Lord Provost's words for himself.

"I'm . . . to leave, then?" he murmured, studying the backs of his hands.

"We're all leaving." Stormbreaker didn't bother to disguise the unhappiness in his voice, and for once, his emotions were etched across his pale, marked face. "Lord Ross and Dari and you, too, Nic. Snakekiller is readying our party for the road. Our departure must be very public, after we've made certain the countryside will be well aware of who is leaving, and that word will spread to the advancing armies."

His green eyes moved to Nic. "Everyone will need to know who we are, and where we're going, and what we intend to do. You were searching for the right way to announce yourself. I believe the opportunity is at hand. Perhaps we should have some formal ceremony for you, acknowledging your identity, and vesting you as Dyn Mab's new lord and heir."

Nic couldn't bring himself to respond. He couldn't imagine that spectacle, though he had to admit it would spread across the nearby lands with the speed of wildfire. The part about leaving, though, about taking a well-publicized traveling party full of nobles out of Triune with nothing but a few guild members and the private Guard of Lord Cobb and Lord Ross—that sounded like mass suicide. "We can't just walk out of Triune's gates and take on three marauding dynast armies." He swallowed. "Can we?"

Lord Ross's confident voice soothed Nic's nerves when he explained, "My Sabor allies will escort us out of Dyn Brailing. We'll travel for a day or two to make certain word of our direction spreads; then the Sabor will fly us directly to the heart of the combined Ross and Cobb Guard massing just above my border. It's the most safety Westin and I can offer you and Aron for now—and Dari as well, if she won't return to the Stregans."

"I won't," Dari said.

For a time, no one spoke, and Nic assumed they were giving Aron the courtesy of time to digest the blow he had just absorbed. When Aron did manage to form his next question, his voice sounded thin and exhausted, and he asked it of Lord Ross.

"Will this save Triune?"

"I don't know," came Lord Ross's honest response, and once more Nic admired the man's powerful delivery. "We suspect our party will draw off most of Stone's would-be attackers. We'll have what they seek, and they'll believe you and Nic to be vulnerable."

"Stormbreaker and Snakekiller should stay here." Nic's conviction overrode his fear of speaking his mind in such company. "Stone should spare us no escorts. Keep your people to defend your grounds and your sheltered, Lord Baldric."

Lord Baldric laughed, but it was a dry, lifeless sound. "I can command Snakekiller about as easily as I can order Stone River to cease flowing." He pointed to Stormbreaker. "He's not much better. They'll do as they see fit, Nic. Best you learn that now."

"All of Stone's High Masters can't remain here." Stormbreaker leveled his eerie green eyes on Nic and waited for Nic to understand. The implication of Stormbreaker's statement sunk deep into Nic's mind, and he saw Aron and Dari grasp it as well. By spreading their High Masters to different locations, Stone was hedging its odds that someone would survive the war to lead Triune, and rebuild the guild if their stronghold was destroyed.

"We are not an army," Lord Baldric said to Aron, who was frowning at him.

"You could be." Aron clenched his fists on the table until his knuckles brushed Eldin Falconer's tarnished bracelets.

Lord Baldric's response was surprisingly gentle. "Not and remain true to our charter, our vows, and our hearts."

"Fine. Ignore the forces of Brailing and Altar and Mab. Take your fight to the Thorn Guild." Aron's tone edged toward desperation. "Make them accountable for murdering Vagrat's lady and imprisoning her heir because the Vagrat nobles lived outside the Lady Provost's beliefs."

"Aron," Stormbreaker said. "That's far in the past."

Aron's face darkened. "What of their new crimes? The ridiculous, dangerous demands, the neglect of their guild duties, child-stealing, taking sides in a war, and the Brother only knows what else. If not Stone, then who *is* responsible for confronting the Lady Provost and ending Thorn's treachery?"

Lord Baldric glared at Aron, but Nic noted that the man no longer seemed so broken and old. His big fists clenched on the table, too, dwarfing Aron's, and for a moment, his brown eyes seemed bright with rage and determination.

Aron seemed about to say more, much more, but he left off. Still, he didn't wither beneath the Lord Provost's glowering disapproval. After a moment, he whispered, "Someone has to stop them, Lord Baldric. Someone has to stop *her*."

"We have no proof that Falconer had you attacked at Lady Pravda's command," Lord Baldric said, then held up his hand as Aron sputtered and swore.

"But Falconer *told* me—"

"The word of a dead madman will carry little weight in a dynast court," Lord Baldric continued, his voice rising over Aron's. "If we're to take on Thorn, we need much more evidence than that."

Aron seemed too furious to speak, and Nic was relieved. He thought it was pointless, trying to draw Stone more directly into the war when Lord Baldric had so often made his position clear, and when Triune would be doing well just to protect its own battlements. If Aron kept fighting, he would get nothing but wounded feelings for his efforts.

"The stone drawing is this evening, after dinner," Lord Baldric said to Aron, each word measured and tight. "Don't be late."

For some reason, the sight of the Lord Provost on edge put Nic at ease, as if this aspect of the universe had been restored to its rightful course.

Aron nodded and excused himself with Stormbreaker, who said he was taking Aron to get his robes. Dari announced she would go with them, and find her own way back to the Den. As soon as they left, Nic stood to leave Lord Baldric's chambers, but Lord Ross stopped him by holding up one large hand.

"Wait a moment, if you would, Nic." Lord Ross's face reminded Nic of a ceremonial mask, etched in place with no hint of emotion to give him a clue what this request might entail.

Nic hesitated by his chair. It was a request, not a command, but he didn't think his legs would move even if he wanted to flee. Which he did want to do.

Nic glanced at Lord Baldric and Lord Cobb, who both stated they had business elsewhere, and left quickly.

Too quickly, by Nic's assessment.

All too soon, Nic found himself alone in the Lord Provost's chambers, with possibly the most intimidating man in Eyrie.

"Sit," Lord Ross said, gesturing to Nic's chair.

Nic sat, feeling all at once like the hob-prince again, young and clumsy, and too soft for his own station in life.

Lord Ross folded hands that could probably sculpt rock without the benefit of tools, and gazed into the fire behind Nic. "Your safety will be my personal mission, I give you my oath. The Sabor have pledged their service to you as well, at my request. They will guard you as they guard the Ross bloodline, until you or I release them from that pact. That will strengthen your position, when the time comes to assert it."

Nic held on to the sides of his seat, forming argument after argument about his fitness to lead, but he spoke none of them aloud. He couldn't debate with this man as he had debated with Snakekiller, and even with Dari. In Lord Ross's presence, gazing into that stony, certain face, it seemed a fate accomplished, Nic's assumption of his dynast title, and his role as heir to Eyrie's throne.

The strangest part was, with a man like Lord Ross supporting him, Nic almost felt like he could face the task.

"Your acceptance of me and your offer is most honorable," he said, averting his gaze from Lord Ross's uncomfortable scrutiny. "And it's very kind. If my father were alive, he would give you his thanks, and his allegiance until his death."

Lord Ross's nod was regal, and his eyes were touched by sadness for Nic's many losses.

"I don't know that the rest of Eyrie will receive me so openly," Nic said, at last bringing a measure of his fear into the open.

Lord Ross allowed that with another graceful nod. "You'll have to convince the doubters. You'll find your moment to show your fortitude, Nic. All leaders do. It's a burden we all share—our trial, if you will."

We . . .

As much as he would like to, Nic couldn't see himself as similar to Lord Ross in any way. He was preparing to ask how he would know the right moment had arrived when Lord Ross cleared his throat.

Nic startled.

Lord Ross's masked expression slipped into something less formal, but no less fearsome. "Even in the very short time I have been here, it doesn't escape my attention that my granddaughter is fond of you, young man."

Nic almost startled again, then caught hold of himself. "Dari's my friend, and I hope that I'm hers, if that's what you mean."

Lord Ross raised his eyebrows. "Is that your intention, then? To be Dari's friend?"

His steady gaze pinned Nic to the chair as sharply as a well-fired arrow.

Nic's anxiety drove him to speak before he had a chance to consider his words, even for his own benefit. "No, sir. I'd like to marry Dari."

Nic closed his mouth so quickly that the pop of his teeth slamming together sounded like a powder blast in the quiet chambers.

Had he said that?

Brother help him.

Did he mean it?

But . . . he knew he did.

Thoughts of a future with Dari had been in his mind since he first opened his eyes and found her beside him in the infirmary, but he had considered them nothing but fancy. The dreams of a foolish boy, desperate for any relief from his lot in life.

But here was Dari's grandfather, speaking to him as if winning Dari's heart might be a possibility. If Lord Ross didn't draw a sword and run him through for being so forward.

Lord Ross didn't seem inclined to go for his weapons. He remained quiet for a few moments, then said, "I honor Stormbreaker and Aron, but your temperament is a much better match for Dari. I think your strength would calm her and steady her. And she told me last night—you make her laugh."

"Strength," Nic echoed, stuck on that point, and not certain he was hearing Lord Ross correctly. Still, he didn't dare contradict him.

"We could discuss the benefits of such an alliance, but my position and my dynast are secure, and yours will be, once you come forward and make known the breadth of your mind-talents." Lord Ross waved a hand, clearly dismissing these as petty concerns. "Dari's Stregan relatives will pose no objections, provided she doesn't force them into revealing themselves or where they reside. The union wouldn't be an illegal cross-mixing like that of her parents, either. Since she is a child of both bloodlines, she is allowed to choose whether to join with a Stregan or a Fae."

"I—I see." Nic felt like an idiot, but he was having difficulty trusting Lord Ross's assessment of his position in Eyrie, and imagining that Dari would ever agree to the union Lord Ross was envisioning.

"Matches made on temperament are much better than relationships born of necessity or contract." Lord Ross's expression remained contemplative, and much kinder and more approachable than it had been earlier. "At least I've found that to be the case, with respect to my own happiness. This I share with you, since your own father is deceased, and your mother—well. I suspect she hasn't been able to impart much wisdom about the business of being an adult."

Nic shifted in his seat, releasing his hold on the edges of his chair. "Do you worry that I'll pass my mother's madness to my off-spring?"

At this, Lord Ross actually smiled, if only for a moment. "If we lived by such worries in Eyrie, no one would ever marry, son. You take on risks as well. As you know, none of my heirs save for the son who fathered Dari and Kate have survived. The Wasting goes hard on my bloodline."

Nic considered this, but it didn't weigh against his feelings for Dari in the least. He was about to explain this when Lord Ross brought up another point.

"Further, Dari has no legitimate standing as my heir, because of her heritage. Her true lineage can never be revealed unless the Stregans one day come forth from hiding—but many a dynast lord has married a pigeon of his allies or enemies."

Nic got to his feet faster than he meant to, almost overbalancing and falling to the hearth behind him. When he regained his balance, he faced Lord Ross, and with all the force he could muster, he said, "Please don't call Dari a pigeon, or any other name that disrespects her."

"It's no shame, to be considered the illegitimate child of a dynast lord, even when it isn't true." Lord Ross stood, but he didn't seem to be offended, or in a hurry. "That's the assumption people will make, and you'll have to let it stand. Are you prepared to do that?"

Nic realized he had taken a fighting stance, as if he could actually strike another man—especially this man—and remain on his feet. He relaxed his arms and tried to seem more respectful himself.

Lord Ross came to stand next to him by the fire, and when he gazed down at Nic, he seemed more like a father and grandfather than a fearsome and legendary dynast lord. "Have you discussed this plan of yours with my granddaughter?"

Nic's throat went dry, but he managed to whisper, "Plan?"

Lord Ross sighed. "Have you asked Dari to be your true and honorable band-mate, until fate cleaves the *chevilles* that will bind you together?"

"I—no. I can't—I haven't." Nic folded his arms to keep his hands from shaking. "She's invested in Aron, and in Stormbreaker. She doesn't even know I—she doesn't see me that way, Lord Ross."

"I think she does." Lord Ross's dark eyes danced with life, as Dari's did when something amused her. "I think she's waiting for you to speak and put an end to her confusion."

Nic struggled to form a response, but found nothing at all in his mind. He felt obliterated, yet rebuilt, but completely uncertain about what to say or do next.

Lord Ross put his hand on Nic's shoulder, and the weight of his grip threatened to drive Nic to his knees.

"I'm taking you both to war in a matter of days, Nic. Were I you, I wouldn't wait too long."

CHAPTER SIXTY

ARON

Aron felt hot and undeserving in his new, thick gray robe.

Sweat gathered along his neck as he stood in the main chamber in the House of the Judged, a large stone room with a packed dirt floor. He was surrounded by Stone Brothers and Stone Sisters, all of whom seemed more worthy than he did. There was Stormbreaker on his left, and Snakekiller on his right, their *benedets* glowing a deep black in the ample candlelight. Windblown behind him seemed steady and comfortable, as did countless other guild members Aron couldn't even name. Gathered together like this, they formed a smooth sea of gray, down to their matching colorless *chevilles*.

He was a part of them. That much Aron felt in his blood, in his heart and bones, yet he stood separate from them in ways he couldn't name or explain. His trial had marked him, and he couldn't accept his own actions as easily as Lord Baldric and Stormbreaker. Aron had often dreamed of returning from the Ruined Keep as a vested member of the Guild. He had imagined this would finally set him at ease and fill him with the peace he so often lacked.

Instead, he felt more insignificant and unsettled than ever, a fraud amongst fellows who had better earned their station at Triune.

Lord Baldric stood in front of the crowd, and he held up a simple cloth bag that looked much older than the Lord Provost. The bag's sides were threadbare, and the runes marking the cloth had worn down to patches of darker coloration. Even the strings gathering the bag's neck were frayed, and it seemed to strain beneath the weight of the stones contained within its depths.

Aron had expected a speech and a lengthy ceremony—something to match the formality and pageantry of Judgment Day—but Lord Baldric's next words dismissed that assumption.

"Here we are again, to do our sacred duty for the land of Eyrie. Even if Eyrie abandons us or treats us poorly, we'll maintain our responsibility."

A murmur of assent rippled through the room, and Aron heard himself agreeing. His stomach twisted as he tried to accept the fact he would be leaving at sunrise, that he might never find his way back to this place, or see many of these people, his family in name and deed, again.

"Reach in, Brothers and Sisters." Lord Baldric moved to the first Stone Brother in Aron's line. "Choose quickly, and choose well."

The Stone Brother, a man Aron didn't know, thrust his hand in the bag and drew out a white pebble marked with delicate runes.

"Fate favors the just and the strong," Lord Baldric said, then waited as the Brother examined his stone, repeated the name he read quietly, then placed the stone in his pouch.

Lord Baldric moved down the line toward Aron, watching as each Brother or Sister in the front lines collected their new assignments, and repeating his benediction each time a selection was made. Stormbreaker had told Aron that each guild member had a sense for how many Judged they could hunt or fight, and they drew stones when instinct and fate compelled them, or when the number of stones in their pouch dropped below what they could manage. Stormbreaker would not be collecting the name of a new target this night. He was here only to see Aron draw his first stone.

When Aron's turn came, he wouldn't let himself hesitate. As

quickly as his peers had done, he slid his hand into the aged bag, feeling pebbles slide past his fingers. One slipped into his palm, and he closed his hand around the stone and drew it out.

"Fate favors the just and the strong," Lord Baldric said, then paused as Aron lifted his stone and studied the runes etched into the pale white surface. It took him a moment to spell out the name waiting for him in the Language of Kings, but when he did, he read it again, several times, to be certain he had not made a mistake.

With a pleased smile, Lord Baldric moved on down the line, then to the lines behind Aron, and Aron couldn't stop reading and rereading the tiny runes placed on the smooth white pebble by masons with a talent for jewel-crafting and finely detailed work.

"Hold your stone tightly," Stormbreaker murmured from beside him, ever the teacher, even if Aron was no longer his apprentice. "Feel it. Let its energy flow through every level of your essence, every aspect of your personality and existence. This is your stone, your new destiny, and the destiny of your Judged."

Many of the Judged were already in residence in nearby cells, awaiting Judgment Day tomorrow, but some were like Aron's, convicted in their absence, since they had not been captured, and they had failed to turn themselves in to Stone of their own volition. Sometime after sunrise tomorrow, when the bells rang to announce the flight of the hunted, those judged In Absence would be considered no different than any criminal who had chosen to leave Triune and take their chances with fate.

Aron read the name again, then showed the stone to Stormbreaker, since no rule prevented him from doing so.

Stormbreaker's low whistle surprised him, and when he met the man's bright green eyes, Stormbreaker was regarding him with both reverence and pride. "Fate has given you the proof your heart seeks, Aron. You have earned your place at Triune. You are one with us, and we are one with you."

Aron didn't argue with him, or even reject Stormbreaker's assertion in his mind. He was too taken aback by what he had drawn from the bag. Snakekiller leaned over and examined Aron's stone, and Aron showed it to Windblown, who had edged up behind him. The pebble was so light, yet infinitely heavy. He gazed at it so long that he memorized each line and mark, each of its hues and scratches. He didn't put it away until Lord Baldric returned to the front of the room, held up his empty bag, and pronounced, "A night of sleep, then as always, on the morrow, we do the work of Stones."

Aron lowered his pebble at last, then slipped it into the pouch tied to his belt. It was the only stone he possessed, where Stormbreaker and Snakekiller and Windblown probably had fifteen, even twenty.

Yet none of their stones bore the etched runes announcing the name of Canus the Bandit. That honor and burden was Aron's, and Aron's alone. Just the thought of it set his heart to a fast race and sent a jangle of fear through his entire body.

He had been given a fresh chance to prove his abilities, to himself if no one else. If he could complete this hunt, Aron knew he would believe that he should be wearing the robes Stormbreaker had given him.

Snakekiller put her hand on her brother's elbow as the group of gathered guild members began to disperse. "Come. Let's return to the Den. We have much planning and packing to do."

As they left the House of the Judged, she said, "Aron, I've asked Raaf to ready your talon on the morning. Tek will be going with us, if you're amenable—though Raaf and Zed will remain behind with Windblown to help in Triune's defense."

Aron glanced over at Windblown, who gave no indication of emotion about his assignment. Aron felt a twist of oddness that Windblown wouldn't be traveling with him, though his discomfort at being separated from Zed and Raaf was no surprise at all. Was he, Aron, taking Windblown's place next to Stormbreaker—or was Stone simply dividing its High Masters, as Stormbreaker had indicated earlier?

Moments later, Aron sensed Iko walking along behind them, joined so completely with the darkness that Aron couldn't even see him. This prompted Aron to ask Snakekiller a very important question. "Can Sabor fly talons?"

"Yes," she said, "though I can't say the talons enjoy it. We have some elixir that will ease Tek for her journey, and we'll mix it in her goat meat on the road, the day the Sabor take us into the skies."

Aron couldn't quite imagine his big talon sweeping through the air. Though Tek had grown to her full size with the feed and tending available at Triune, her wings had remained pitiful and tiny. They would never support her weight, even in a quick battle-leap. This charge into the heart of a war would be her only opportunity to fly, and he hoped she might be awake enough to realize that, and enjoy it if she could.

Zed and Raaf joined Aron and his companions at the door of the Den, and Raaf immediately began chattering about all he had done to prepare them for their departure. Zed whispered his question to Aron, about which stone he had drawn, then went wide-eyed when he heard the answer.

Raaf, however, was oblivious to this. Aron realized that the boy seemed to think they were heading out on some great adventure, not making themselves bait and targets for three different hostile dynast armies.

By the time they reached Dari's door, Aron's ears were as tired as his mind. He led the column, with Stormbreaker behind him, trying not to think about the first time he had come to this door, running and foolish.

And naked.

He shook his head at that humiliating memory as he knocked on Dari's door, which was slightly ajar. When she didn't answer, he pushed the door open and walked inside to call out to her—

But she was there.

Right there in front of her hearth, locked in Nic's arms, kissing him as if the world might end before morning.

Heat flashed through Aron. Anger, embarrassment, surprise—he couldn't sort the emotions fast enough. Behind him, Stormbreaker's silence seemed to expand and take on menace.

At Raaf's laughing squeal, Nic and Dari broke apart, and Dari's hand drifted to her chest as she saw the crowd at the entrance to her room.

"I—I'm sorry." She sounded breathless, then looked frustrated as her gaze moved from Aron to Stormbreaker, and back to Aron. "I was going to talk to both of you, but there hasn't been time, and it's been so sudden, these feelings. I didn't know—I mean, I—he—"

She stopped. Took a breath.

Raaf kept laughing until Zed popped him in the back of the head. A blue arm shot out from behind a nearby abutment, and Raaf got dragged out of sight, no doubt to enjoy Iko's stern supervision for a few long minutes. Someone else was laughing, and Aron thought it might be Windblown. He wished Iko would grab him, too, but knew that couldn't happen.

Snakekiller said nothing, and Stormbreaker's hostile silence stretched to fill all available space. Aron felt glad he couldn't see the man's face, and mildly surprised that he heard no thunder, either distant or near.

"Nic's asked me to be his band-mate," Dari said, and then Aron wished he could be the one to make thunder. A big, heart-crushing clap of it.

Knowing he would lose Dari and watching it happen were two

separate experiences. The joy on Dari's face tore Aron into pieces inside, yet it pleased him at the same time. It worried him, too, because of what they would face come morning.

"She's agreed." Nic sounded giddy. "I came to my senses only tonight and made my intentions known to her—or I would have discussed it with you before I acted, Aron. I would have spoken to you, too, Stormbreaker."

Aron could only nod to Nic. He couldn't hate Nic, and he still couldn't be angry with him. Though anger might have been a welcome shield against the drumming ache in his chest, in that place where his heart should be.

Nic and Dari joined hands, and Aron saw the mythical heartwood in his mind, towering above all of Eyrie, strong and endless and eternal, radiating a power that couldn't be denied. It was a beautiful thing, that tree. And the simple, complete happiness in Dari's eyes—just as beautiful, though bittersweet, because she had never looked so content in the time Aron had spent with her.

This was right.

He knew it was, and he had known it for some time now, and dealt with it as his truth-seeking legacy demanded. Yet the reality of their union was easier to accept. Aron tried to give some gesture, or at least make himself smile so they would know he was pleased for them. That he would grow accustomed to this loss, as he had the many others in his life—but how?

How could he just . . . let Dari go?

It seemed like half his life had been consumed by loving her, and he felt as naked and small as he did all those nights before, when he tumbled to the floor outside her door. This time, there was no tunic he could pull over his head to hide his emotions. He was forced to stand before his newly betrothed friends, more naked than ever, failing at every attempt to wish them well.

In the end, it was Aron's former teacher and mentor who stepped

forward to lead the way once more. Though Aron could see the lightning playing in his former guild master's eyes, Stormbreaker offered
Dari and Nic a polite bow.

"My congratulations to you both," he said in a low but well-
controlled voice. "Will you take your vows before we depart? If so,
dawn is most beautiful along Triune's east wall, and a wedding on
Judgment Day would be most opportune for our purposes."

"Yes," Snakekiller agreed as she, too, came into the chamber to
stand beside Aron. "And Stone keeps bands at the ready, though they
might not be as fine as those you would receive at a dynast castle."

"Tomorrow," Dari said, her voice so slight Aron barely heard the
word—but her excitement was unmistakable. So was Nic's. Neither
of them wished to wait, now that they had come to this decision.

"Let me speak to my grandfather and Lord Baldric," Dari said,
but Aron knew that was a formality.

This was it.

This was really it.

When he walked out of Dari's chamber tonight, the next time
he would see her, she would be a bride—a lovely, perfect bride,
pledging her life to someone else.

"Let's give them some privacy," Snakekiller said to both Aron
and Stormbreaker, and Aron realized that for all of Stormbreaker's
self-possession, he was having as much trouble walking out that
chamber door as Aron.

Snakekiller took them both by the elbow, and when Aron felt her
tug at him, he finally moved. Stormbreaker moved with him, and
moments later—moments that felt endless and as painful as straight
razors dragged across vulnerable skin—Dari's chamber door swung
shut behind them.

Outside in the hallway, Windblown waited with Zed and Raaf
and Iko, who had Raaf in a headlock, with his big blue hand over
Raaf's mouth. Blath was there as well.

"At dawn?" she asked, directing the question to Snakekiller.

"Yes," Snakekiller said, letting go of Aron and Stormbreaker. "And make sure the festivities last until after the bulk of the Judgment crowd arrives."

Zed seemed to take that as a cue, and he took Raaf from Iko's control and led the boy away, with Windblown following quietly behind. Blath and Snakekiller set off in a different direction, murmuring to each other as if they might be discussing what just happened.

Aron, Stormbreaker, and Iko stood for a time, until Iko inclined his head toward the stairwell. "With preparations for Judgment Day and now a wedding, the main kitchen will have a surplus of ale and roast tonight."

Aron didn't stop to wonder if the kitchens would serve them so late, and neither did Stormbreaker.

For once, Iko led the way instead of following, and Aron didn't mind at all.

CHAPTER SIXTY-ONE

DARI

How strange it was, to have traveled so far in body, mind, and heart that home seemed like a dream from someone else's thoughts, and the words "family" and "people" had gained enough meanings to record on a long, rolled scroll.

Dari held out her arms for Blath to drape a Sabor wedding shawl across her shoulders and forearms and tried once more to grasp that today she would take a band-mate, a partner to stand beside her for the rest of her life. The reality of it made her breath come in flickers like the small torches in the sconces of the preparation tent near Triune's east wall.

The shawl's golden lace tickled her neck, stirring up a light musk of amberwood and heather from the lotions Blath had used to enhance the natural glow of Dari's skin. Dari's hair had been pulled back and oiled into hundreds of ringlets, then braided into a pattern as intricate as the shawl. Dari felt softer and more beautiful than ever in her life, yet infinitely stronger.

Blath finished the shawl's draping, then stood back and folded her powerful blue arms. Her golden eyes appraised Dari, from the small silver diadem at her forehead with the Ross crest of the rising gryphon to the gauzy peridot gown Blath had borrowed from one of the sheltered. Dari's feet and ankles were bare save for the false *cheville* at her left ankle, as both Fae and Fury tradition demanded, and she almost dug her toes into the soft dirt as she awaited Blath's opinion.

"You look like your mother," Blath said, her usually stoic voice thick with emotion. "A woman so beautiful and kind a dynast heir gave up his own heritage just to win a kiss."

Heat suffused Dari's limbs. "You exaggerate, but I love you for your kindness."

Blath lifted her fingers and touched Dari's cheek. "Nicandro Mab would choose you over his throne, if fate demanded it of him. I believe he would choose you over life itself."

Dari closed her eyes.

Nic.

No matter how much this felt like a dream, Nic was more than real to her—and worth whatever sacrifices this union might ultimately require. If only Kate could be here with her today, standing beside her as her help-mate to witness this odd comingling of Fae traditions and Fury vows she and Nic had prepared for their joining. That would have made the day perfect.

As it was, Dari could ask for little else, so long as she kept war and battles from her mind.

Outside the tent, at the exact second predicted to mark the first moment of dawn, Triune's bells began to ring in fast, joyous bursts. So close to the castle's walls, the sound was near to deafening, and Dari felt each peal in her bones.

Blath walked solemnly to the nearest wall of the preparation tent and took down two torches. One she handed to Dari, and the other she kept for herself. Dari's fingers closed on the rough-hewn wood, and the warmth of the flames near her cheeks made her smile.

As the bells went silent, Blath said, "Those camped in the valley to attend Judgment Day will be confused by the unusual ringing— and intrigued. This was a good plan, Dari. Your wedding will be well attended." She held the tent flap aside for Dari to pass, and Dari slipped outside into the gradually lessening darkness.

Her grandfather was waiting for her, resplendent in his green ceremonial robes. The image of a golden gryphon had been stitched into the velvety cloth, and the design made his chest and arms seem twice as powerful. His smile, however, was what touched Dari at her deepest levels. Her grandfather's happiness for her claimed his entire face, and set his dark eyes to a dancing twinkle that rivaled the flames on the torch she carried. When he bowed to her, his oiled beard and ponytail rested against the gryphon like dark waves bearing the creature aloft.

With Lord Ross was Tiamat Snakekiller, dressed in the simple gray robes of Stone, austere yet somehow no less splendid than Dari's grandfather. Her *benedets* moved and swirled in the firelight, and it was difficult for Dari to grow accustomed to seeing a Stone Sister completely unarmed, and not even wearing her belt of pebbles and poisons and elixirs. "We are honored to stand Strong beside you," Snakekiller said, and bowed as deeply as Lord Ross.

"Thank you," Dari said, grateful that these two would be the ones pledging themselves to defend and support her new husband. It was unusual for a woman to stand amongst the Strong in a Fae ceremony, but Dari would challenge anyone to present a more worthy warrior and protector than Snakekiller. Nic would need her, and Lord Ross, too, Dari had no doubt. And so would she.

"They're coming," Lord Ross said, nodding in the direction of Triune's main gate and keep as a swell of voices and shouts and moving feet began to claim the morning. Soon after came the unmistakable rattle and clatter of blades and bows being surrendered and stacked in piles outside the designated ceremonial area. No one in all of Eyrie brought weapons to a wedding, and the Judgment Day crowd, even surprised by this additional festivity, would be no exception.

The sky above Stone's stronghold grew lighter, and lighter still, and the bells began to ring again, still brightly, but more slowly. Dari's heartbeat took up their rhythm, and she found she could barely swallow as she took her place behind Blath and in front of the two who would stand Strong. They walked almost in step, winding down the path that led to a small platform resting against Triune's east wall. In normal times, it was used for weddings for the sheltered, and promise ceremonies for Stone Brothers and Sisters. Sometimes traveling minstrels gave performances there, or set up shadow-puppet shows for the children. Today it would serve as a uniting point for two dynasts and two cultures, and two people who never expected their lives to take them east at dawn, to marry each other and hopefully stave off a terrible battle.

As Dari drew closer to the platform, she saw two lines of Ross Guard forming a corridor for her approach. On the opposite side, Cobb Guard comprised the corridor. As for the platform itself, the wood had been decorated with white wildflowers and dark green ivy, with light golden-brown stalks of new grain and sprouting fallow grasses, and even bright red winter berries already strung to dry for powders and wines. How very like Stone, to select practical adornments that would later be put to use. That made much more sense than silks and cloths and flowers no cow or goat would enjoy.

Lord Baldric was already waiting atop the platform in his gray robes, and beside him was Stone's rector, who held a quill and a thick parchment that would be Triune's official record of births, deaths, and marriages. The bells subsided, but Dari's heart beat even faster when she saw a torch-lit procession approaching from the other side of the platform, with Aron in the lead. As Nic's help-mate, he moved slowly, careful to allow Nic to keep up with him. Lord Cobb and Stormbreaker walked behind Nic, prepared to stand Strong for him— and catch him if need be, to get him through this journey to the platform.

I love these people, Dari thought as she climbed the steps of the platform behind Blath, scarcely able to remember a time when she considered Fae to be loathsome and dangerous, worth less than a moment of her time and consideration. *I love them all, and if they're here, they love me, too.* Fae and Fury, dynast lord and Stone Guild— such an unlikely gathering. As Blath stepped to the side and left Dari facing the man who would shortly become her husband, Dari understood completely that "family" and "people" were not always decided by birth or bloodlines, and that love and respect were perfect antidotes to the poisons of prejudice and fear.

Nic's golden hair and blue eyes seemed to glow in the light of the slowly rising sun. His ruby-red breeches and tunic bore the dragon of Mab stitched in a white so bright it would be blinding in the full light of day. Where he obtained such a garment for this wedding, Dari had no idea, but she suspected the many towers and storage buildings at Triune held secrets and surprises far greater than ceremonial dynast garb.

She smiled at Nic, and he smiled at her. The tight lines of his face told her he was in pain, that he had refused elixir, intent on joining with her with his senses completely intact, no matter how brutal that might be for him. She wanted to throw her arms around his neck and hold him, take away every hurt and bit of agony, but she knew that these things were part of Nic now. He had learned to survive suffering no living creature should be asked to bear, and that agony was part of what had shaped him into the man she chose to marry.

She quickly got lost in his eyes, in the cut of his jaw and the stooped line of his shoulders, so much so that she barely heard Lord Baldric ask the ever-swelling crowd for silence. Onlookers were still murmuring when Triune's bells rang again, long and sweet and lovely, the perfect opening to any wedding, as far as Dari was concerned.

"Today we join together to celebrate a band-mating between Dari and Nic," Lord Baldric announced, his voice almost as loud as

Stone's bells. Dari noted that he deliberately omitted both her family name and Nic's. The presence of Lord Ross, Lord Cobb, and Blath would say much, not to mention Nic's appearance, and his obviously Mab clothing. It would be too great a risk to announce Nic's identity outright, even to an unarmed group of onlookers at a Judgment Day wedding.

As the procession torches were extinguished, the onlookers cheered nonetheless. Weddings were weddings, and most people took joy from them. Dozens upon dozens of eager faces stared at the platform, awaiting the next step in the pageant, and Dari tried not to remember that these same faces would be eagerly awaiting combat in the Judgment Arena later this day.

The whistling and shouting died away, and Lord Baldric clapped his hands.

Through the crowd came Zed, carrying a wooden tray with a wooden cup and a loaf of bread. Beside him walked Iko, carrying another wooden tray, this one adorned with two crystal *chevilles*, as yet just open bars of polished rock. The dawn light caught the bright lines in the clear rock, so bright it brought tears to Dari's eyes.

Zed climbed the steps on Dari's side, while Iko carried his treasures to Nic's side of the platform.

Once more, the crowd below shouted and cheered, welcoming these obvious symbols of Fae joining. Thankfully, they were too far away to hear the private words that would be spoken, which bore little resemblance to Fae vows.

"Darielle Ross," Lord Baldric said, his voice quiet and gentle, "have you come this day of your own will and wish, to take this man as your true and honorable band-mate, until fate cleaves the *chevilles* that will bind you together?"

Dari reached forward and took Nic's hands in her own. Her heart lurched against her ribs, then seemed to grow three sizes too big for her chest. "I have," she whispered, unable to speak any louder.

"Who stands Strong for you, to take your band-mate's fate as their own, to defend him and support him, and to recognize him as your husband, and a member of your family?"

"We do," Lord Ross and Snakekiller said from behind Dari.

Dari's head swam.

Nic's smile grew broader, and she felt the pressure of his fingers as he shifted his grip to hold her hands in his.

You are half of my heart and soul, his gaze told her. *Mine now, and always.*

When Lord Baldric asked Nic about his will and wishes, he answered, "I have," in a voice much stronger than his body. Stormbreaker and Lord Cobb stood Strong for him, each offering Dari a slight bow when they spoke their vows.

Lord Baldric began to beam, and the expression was so unusual for him that Dari almost moved backward. "By rock and leaf, by stone and thorn, may your love carry you high on the most powerful wings." He reached toward Iko's tray, selected one of the two crystal bands, lifted it, and waited for the crowd's cheering to wane. "Nic, it is not within my duties or powers to band you. Dari, this right belongs to you and only you. If it is your wish to become Nic's bandmate, then place this band on his ankle if he agrees."

Hands trembling, barely breathing, Dari took the crystal band and felt its cool perfection. "I join you to me," she murmured, still unable to speak louder than the softest of breezes. "Tell me your heart. Do you agree?"

"Now and always." Nic extended his right ankle.

Doing her best not to pitch forward, Dari knelt and placed the crystal against the top of Nic's bare foot. Iko knelt with her, and took the stone from her shaking fingers. She sensed the heat and motion of energy as he used his Sabor mind-talents to shape the stone, then join the ends into a seamless, flawless whole, resting against Nic's ankle.

Dari gazed at the beautiful crystal ring, tried to breathe, tried not to cry, and failed at both. When she stood, she had to wipe the tears from her cheeks. She was grateful for the yelling and laughing and celebration from the crowd, as it gave her moments to gather her composure before Lord Baldric turned his attention to Nic.

"Dari, it is not within my duties or powers to band you. Nic, this right belongs to you and only you. If it is your wish to become Dari's band-mate, then place this band on her ankle if she agrees."

To Dari's ears, Nic's voice sounded like sweet music as he said, "I join you to me. Tell me your heart. Do you agree?"

"Now and always," Dari said, extending her right ankle. If she didn't breathe soon, she would faint, and she was certainly not the fainting kind.

Nic knelt slowly, obviously with difficulty, but without help from Aron or Lord Cobb or Stormbreaker. He pressed the crystal band into Dari's skin, and kept his hand in place over the cool, firm rock as Iko worked with its energy.

When Nic rose, Dari couldn't stop looking at her ankle, or at his.

Joined.

By the bands.

Two crystal *chevilles,* born of the same fire, forever linking them together.

She knew she was smiling as the crowd shouted its approval, but she could scarcely feel her own body as Nic took a drink from the wooden cup Zed held out to him, then offered it to her.

She took it, somehow managed not to drop it, and sipped the clear, lightly sweetened water within it. She put the cup down, ate a bite of the crusty, delicious bread, then offered Nic his bite.

He accepted, and gave her fingers a gentle kiss as she moved her hand away from his mouth.

The shouts from the crowd seemed even louder now, and Dari could feel their anticipation expanding with her own.

"I witness this joining," Lord Baldric boomed, spreading his arms. "As do we all."

"As do we all!" shouted Lord Ross, Snakekiller, Blath, Aron, Stormbreaker, Lord Cobb, and seemingly everyone in Triune.

Nic pulled Dari to him and held her close as the rector dutifully recorded their names on Triune's register, making their joining official.

Dari didn't care how official their marriage was. Nic was hers, and she was his. She pressed her face into his neck and let go her emotions. Her tears flowed, some happy, for herself and Nic, and some sad, for Kate's absence from this blissful moment.

Below the platform, onlookers were tossing hats and shoes and cloaks into the air, then scrambling to reclaim them and toss them again.

Nic allowed Dari the time she needed, then kissed her ear and whispered, "We'll find Kate, Dari." He pulled back from her and gazed at her with the bright blue eyes she had come to love, then tapped his newly banded ankle against hers. "I know it seems impossible, but we'll find her, just like we found each other. Nothing is impossible—and I'd say we're walking, talking proof of that."

CHAPTER SIXTY-TWO

DARI

The dawn banding ceremony at Triune's eastern wall was indeed the perfect method of making their presence public and dramatic enough to be discussed by every resident of Triune, not to mention the crowds that had swelled in for Judgment Day. Dozens of Sabor increased the pageantry by flying in formation above the castle walls. All morning and even throughout Judgment Day, they traveled, passing above Brailing villages and into Dyn Altar, swinging wide to make certain they passed over the edges of Dyn Cobb and Dyn Ross as well.

It was a spectacle that couldn't be ignored, and Dari knew the moment the crowd left that word had been spread all over Eyrie. People from the far reaches of Dyn Ross to the borders of Dyn Mab and beyond had to be talking about the flight of the Sabor—and they spoke not only of the gryphons in the sky, but how they heralded a strange wedding at Stone on Judgment Day, in the midst of a war.

Dari treasured the next quiet days and nights she spent with her new husband in a private cottage amongst the sheltered, anonymous, with no concerns save for attention to their meals, and to each other. Those were the most peaceful and hopeful moments she had ever known, perfect but for Kate's absence in her life, and the fact that she had those days only to give time for word of her marriage to reach hostile armies.

She loathed having to rise the morning of the fifth day, eat her breakfast quickly as Nic drank a large dose of elixir to help him with the rigors of travel, and prepare for their departure. Nic, however, remained as steady and positive as he always did, and Dari allowed his buoyant mood to sustain her.

Before the sun finished rising, Darielle Ross-Mab rode forth from Triune with her husband, who had donned the dark ruby robes befitting an heir of Dyn Mab. They traveled between Lord Cobb, Lord Ross, and their personal Guard regiments, and a small group of Stone Brothers and Sisters that included Aron, Stormbreaker, and Snakekiller. Merchants stood at the sides of the outer byway as they passed, and some released messenger passerines before the rear guard even cleared the main gate and keep. Soon, everyone from Can Rowan in Dyn Mab to Can Elder in Dyn Ross would be wondering about the quiet, newly banded young man traveling beside his bride, under the banners of Dyn Ross, Dyn Cobb, *and* Dyn Mab.

It was something, the goodfolk would be saying.

A union of Ross, Cobb, Mab, and Stone—did you see?

I heard one of the Stones used to be a Brailing—and that other boy, the one who looks like he had an accident—he must have Mab blood.

That girl, the one wearing those scandalous breeches and tunic like a man—she has to be a Ross. And she's traveling under protection from Lord Ross! What does that tell you?

"Do you sense it?" Nic asked her, edging his mount closer to hers as they traveled upward on the byway, moving slowly out of the valley that cradled Triune. His speech was slurred from the elixir. "A wedding on Judgment Day, and now this. I can almost feel the air humming with rumors and reports. We couldn't have attracted more notice if we had released a thousand flocks of passerines."

"We pretty much did that," Dari said as another few passerines streaked past them. "The whispers will fly with the speed of birds on the wing."

The thought scared her and made her proud.

The armies would know that their quarry had departed Triune, and that they were moving east at some speed, in the direction of the combined Altar and Brailing forces marching south to meet them. Mab's armies might join the fray, as scouts placed them not a day's ride from the main portion of the Altar and Brailing warriors.

As for the Thorn Guild traitors and their stolen children, or Canus the Bandit and his rogue army, Dari couldn't begin to imagine where they might be, or what they might do with this information. She turned her attention back to riding beside Nic and savoring the weight of the simple crystal band at her ankle. So long as they both lived, the new bands would keep them joined. She would always be able to find him, and he would always be able to find her.

When Nic smiled at her, Dari wondered why it had taken her any time at all to understand that he was her destiny. Had she known, as Aron had known, but just refused to acknowledge it in her heart until Nic came to her room, flushed and breathless and stammering out his feelings? At least then it had been clear to her that she belonged with him, that Nic brought her a contentment and wholeness she found with no one else, not even her family, or her lost twin. Dari wished the world could fall away from them, and she could go back to doing nothing but spending time with Nic.

"Soon," he said, as if reading her thoughts, which was something he did with enough regularity to make her wonder if he had that talent. "This war can't last forever, Dari. We'll do what we must, then locate your sister and plan the shape of our future."

"I like the sound of that," she said, imagining how it would be when she had Kate with her again, and the rest of her family. When she could reach for a new future and shape it as she wanted it to be— as she and Nic wanted it to be, and as it should be—full of love and joy and the normal trials of life instead of the madness they had both survived in these last years.

Madness that continued, even as they rode away from the Stone Guild stronghold.

They traveled at the center of a column of fighters, with Aron and Stormbreaker forming the front guard on their talons and Snakekiller and another Stone Sister taking up the rear. A dozen more Stone Brothers filled out these first ranks, talon-riders on the left and horse riders on the right. Lord Cobb and his personal guard formed a second layer of human shields. Lord Ross and his personal guard made for a third ring, completing the wall of warriors on the ground. In the air, Blath, Iko, and a silent group of Sabor more than twenty strong flew in challenge formation, letting any who saw know that those who traveled beneath them were under their protection.

These defenses might not stand up to an army, but no simple contingent or fighting group would dare to start a conflict with them. They would travel this way until they reached the open plains near the border of Dyn Brailing and Dyn Cobb; then more Sabor would meet them and transport them to the main strength of the Cobb and Ross armies, camped in the grasslands above the Scry and the Cobb-Ross border.

Dari hoped Nic could make the journey, and resolved to lend him whatever energy he would accept. From sunrise to moonrise, they had to move, or they'd never reach safety before they were attacked.

• • •

The second morning of their ride, Dari helped Nic pack their tent as Stone Brothers and Sisters and soldiers tamped out tallow rings that had been protecting their encampment. The scent of oiled smoke made Dari's eyes water, but Nic didn't seem to notice the stench.

Dari marveled that Nic was holding up despite his damaged,

twisted body. His bravery touched her, and once more, she felt blessed to have been given time with him, even in the midst of a war and a forced ride into danger they might not survive.

They mounted quickly, and moved out before the mists of morning had cleared from the byways. As the ride grew longer, Dari's thoughts shifted from Nic to Aron and Stormbreaker. They had taken her news and her decision about Nic as well as could be expected, and Dari found she didn't worry about Stormbreaker at all. Aron, however, was a constant cause for concern.

Nic nodded toward Aron. "Do you think we're the source of his tension, or is it the trial he thinks he failed—or the drawing his first stone on Canus the Bandit?"

Dari's heart grew heavy. "I don't know, Nic. The world always weighs painfully on Aron's shoulders."

Nic's frown held no jealousy or reproach. He showed only concern for Aron, which was nothing less than Dari expected, and one of the reasons she adored him. "Maybe he would talk to you."

Dari shook her head. "I think it's more likely he'd talk to you, Nic. You didn't reject him and hurt his pride."

Nic steadied himself in his saddle, and his response was quiet, but direct. "No. I only married the woman he loves."

Dari glanced at her band-mate to see if he was joking, then realized he was serious. She also realized he was right. She probably had the better chance of getting through to Aron. She maneuvered her stallion close enough to Nic to lean over and kiss his cheek, then urged her mount forward, until she drew even with Aron.

He looked down at her from his position high on Tek's back, and his smile of greeting seemed genuine enough.

"Are you well?" Dari asked, studying his face to judge his truthfulness, but when he responded, she knew there was no need.

"Do you mean am I grieving myself into illness over your

marriage? No." Aron smiled again, and when he exhaled, he sounded relieved. "I had a vision of the two of you together, that last *graal* lesson between the three of us. I wasn't sure—but, then again, I was. My mind-talent leaves me less and less room for self-delusion. If I don't tell the truth, if I don't accept it, I can't relax at all."

"A vision. That's why you pushed me away so abruptly. Why didn't you tell me?"

Aron kept his gaze forward, but his hands visibly tightened on Tek's reins. "Would you have believed me?"

The talon snorted.

"Probably not," Dari admitted. "I'm sorry for that."

Aron relaxed, as did his mount. "No apologies necessary. I assure you, I didn't want to believe it."

Dari's surprise expanded until it became something like awe. "Aron, do you have any idea how much you've grown—how much you've changed since I met you? There was a time when your anger and jealousy would have destroyed you, and possibly me as well."

"Life demands change, Dari." Aron stroked the scales just above Tek's battle ring. "Look at my runt talon. Even she has grown to her potential with the proper challenge and care."

Tek whistled from the attention, then blew a load of excretions in Stormbreaker's general direction. Stormbreaker deftly steered his bull to the right to avoid it.

Dari moved her stallion closer to Aron and Tek to ask her next question, so she wouldn't cause Aron embarrassment if one of the other Stone Brothers overheard. "Will Canus the Bandit be another one of those challenges that changes you?"

"Perhaps." Aron immediately seemed distant again. "I—I don't know."

Dari kept her mount on a steady course. "Are you afraid to face him?"

Aron's posture relaxed again, and she knew she'd asked the right question. "Yes, but I think what I fear is failing my responsibilities to Stone."

"Will you use your *graal* to survive the fight with him, if it comes to that?"

That inquiry drew an instant frown. "Not unless he attacks me in that fashion."

Dari frowned in return. "Is that wise?"

"It's honorable." Aron shifted in his saddle to look at her more directly. "That will have to be enough."

Dari didn't like the answer, even though she understood it. "You took down four Altar hunters and the Lord Provost of Thorn—and they were the ones who ambushed you. I think you can manage one bandit who won't see you coming."

Aron didn't smile at the compliment, as she had hoped he might. Instead, his brow furrowed, and he seemed to be digging through something in his mind—something painful, or very confusing. "Dari, why didn't you let me thank you for helping me during my trial? Were you afraid Stone would look poorly on my return, knowing that I had to have assistance?"

"I really didn't help you." Dari felt her own brows drawing closer together as this question arose yet again. "I never went through the Veil that night. I spent some time with Stormbreaker, then accidentally punched Nic, then went to meet my grandfather. There was nothing out of the ordinary, except my concern for you."

"You punched Nic?" Aron's shock was almost comical.

"He startled me," Dari said. "I thought I saw something at the Shrine of the Mother, and—"

She stopped herself, and considered her own words. "There was a light that night at the Shrine, Aron. Like you used to see. Nic said it was visible to him as well. We never went to explore it because my grandfather and Lord Cobb arrived."

"In the Keep, after Falconer drugged me, I thought I saw you twice." Aron steered Tek around a crevice in the road. "The first time you were standing with that false goddess creature I've told you about, and she seemed to be drawing all the color out of your *graal*. The second time, you came to heal me and free me, and you said something strange."

Dari was having difficulty keeping her hands steady on the reins of her stallion, but she trusted the horse to keep a true course. Aron's vision of her with the false goddess. The goddess draining away her energy. The light in the Shrine of the Mother. All of this seemed to add together, though she couldn't see how.

She asked Aron to wait until Nic could catch up to them, and Aron agreed.

As soon as Nic had joined them, Dari asked Aron to repeat the vision he'd had at the Keep, and Aron obliged. Nic listened to each detail, weighing them as carefully as Dari had done.

"I think we have to consider your visions anew, Aron," Dari said. "All the things you've dreamed since you arrived at Stone. You don't see the future, but you *do* see the truth, at levels the rest of us may never comprehend."

"I already have reconsidered my visions." Aron guided Tek carefully, keeping her between Dari and Nic. On all sides of them, and in the bright morning sky as well, their escorts pressed ahead, pushing the pace as much as they dared. Dust rose at the edges of the traveling party, and the air grew heavy with the scent of horse sweat and talon oil.

Aron kept his focus on the road, but Dari could tell he was also steeped in thought. "I believe that in my visions, the Brother—the illusion that looked like the Brother—that was Falconer. Falconer masqueraded as a god to see what he wished to see, learn what he wished to learn, without me or anyone else being the wiser."

"And the false goddess." Dari remembered Aron as a younger

boy, sobbing out his terrible dreams. "Do you believe that was Lady Thorn?"

"I'm certain of it." Aron's response was calm, but Dari heard the undertone of anger at how many times he had been duped.

"The light in the Shrine of the Mother would be their *graal* energy." Nic's speech was more slurred, and he seemed to be having more difficulty keeping himself steady on his horse. "I'm sure when Aron and I have projected our legacy over distance, when we've observed people from the other side of the Veil, we've left some residue that trained eyes could see."

"The Shrine would be a perfect place for that energy to be contained." Dari was beginning to share Aron's anger at how deeply and how often they had been fooled. "Most of Triune never went to the Shrine, and believers in the Mother would take visions of light as a reward for their faith."

"Who is Cayn?" Nic slouched forward in his saddle, then righted himself.

Dari stared at him, concerned. At first she took his question literally, but as she put her hand on his shoulder to help him regain his balance, she understood what Nic meant.

"The god of death in my visions." Aron adjusted the reins at the base of Tek's scaly neck. "Another illusion, no more real than Snakekiller's hood snake. If I had my guess, I'd say Cayn was Lord Brailing or Lord Altar—take your pick."

Nic gripped the pommel of his saddle with both hands. "Cayn might be a stranger. Someone we don't know."

Aron shook his head. "Cayn was familiar to me. I know the person, or I've met him. If I could just see him again—but that's probably not something I should wish for."

Dari didn't respond because she was too distracted by her sense that she should understand more, realize more. "Aron, what did I say to you in your vision at the Ruined Keep, after I helped you?"

"I'm not sure I heard you correctly, but I could have sworn you asked me to kill you." Aron frowned before she could ask him if he had gone mad. "*Kill me.* Those were your words, but I knew you must have meant Falconer, that I'd have to kill him to get out of the Ruined Keep alive and free."

Dari wrestled with the strangeness of Aron's vision, and she had ridden some distance when she realized Nic was no longer keeping pace beside Aron and Tek.

She reined her stallion hard and turned her mount, and Aron did the same with Tek. Their sudden reversal sent a ripple of concern through their escort, and with a great bunch of snorting and pawing, the procession ground to an awkward halt. Above them, the Sabor overflew, then wheeled back, and a few peeled toward the ground, shifting even as their paws struck the grasslands.

Nic was still on his horse, but he was holding the reins too tightly, seemingly frozen in his saddle.

"He's going to have a fit," Aron said, throwing Tek's reins to the nearest Stone Brother as he leaped down from his saddle. Stormbreaker was already off his bull and running.

Dari dismounted, dropping her reins to the ground and trusting her stallion's battle training. She dashed toward Nic, worry charging through her chest as she cursed herself for not keeping a closer watch on him.

Stormbreaker and Snakekiller got to Nic first, and Dari was relieved to see him wave off their concern as if he still had his full wits about him.

When Dari reached Nic, Snakekiller was calling for a supply wagon, and grumbling mightily to her brother that she knew Nic couldn't cover much ground on horseback.

"I can," he argued. "That's not it. That's not the problem. Dari. Dari, listen to me." His blue eyes glittered with a wild excitement she hadn't seen from him before, and something in his expression disturbed her even more deeply than the fear Nic was about to topple from his mount, senseless and seizing from his old injuries.

When he spoke again, his voice had a new depth and resonance. "Aron saw Kate, Dari. He saw your sister."

Dari gazed at her husband, wondering if he was about to fall into a fit after all. "What?"

"It was Kate who came to Aron at the Ruined Keep." Nic straightened himself until he no longer seemed on the edge of collapse. "And I think Aron has seen her before."

Dari's heart began a strange, uneven beating as she glanced from Nic to Aron to Stormbreaker and Snakekiller. Lord Ross and Lord Cobb were making their way between ranks of soldiers and guild fighters, leading their mounts behind them. Close behind them came Blath and Iko, still dotted with vanishing golden fur and feathers from their flight. Swords and shields rattled as they pushed their way through, and the two lords and two Sabor finally came to a halt beside Stormbreaker and Snakekiller just as Aron put his palm on Nic's knee. "I've never seen Kate," Aron said. "You're confused. I saw—"

Nic grabbed Aron's hand. "You saw Dari, asking you to kill her. What kind of sense does that make, Aron?"

"None, but—"

"*Kill me*," Nic repeated, once more studying Dari with his unnaturally bright eyes. A soft red glow seeped around his shoulders, arms, and neck, his *graal* energy coming to life as if he wanted to join with her on the other side of the Veil, so she might see what he saw, feel what he felt, and understand him. "That's the plea of someone who's trapped, someone hopeless and in so much pain she can't see any other salvation."

He spoke with such conviction that Dari felt the agony of his memories as her own. Her hand rose to her throat, and from the corner of her eye, she saw Snakekiller fold her arms and look away from Nic.

Dear Gods.

I wonder how many times he begged her for Mercy, and she refused to grant it because she knew who he was.

"I never had the courage to face death outright," Nic said, as if to vindicate Snakekiller, but he was speaking only to Dari. "Your twin sister would. Kate's begging for release—and she's been begging for it since the first time she appeared to Aron."

"But I've never seen her before." Aron moved back from Nic and opened his arms like he was pleading his case to Lord Baldric and Lord Cobb. "I can accept that the vision I had at the Ruined Keep was Kate, that it might have been Kate who helped me, but that was the only time."

"If Nic is correct, it wasn't." Stormbreaker reached for Snakekiller, but she wouldn't accept his comfort. "You reported another vision, from earlier that night, Aron." Thunder rumbled in the distance, and a flash of lightning played off Stormbreaker's free hand and bounced between the crossed hilts of his swords. "You thought you saw Dari with the false goddess, and you said the goddess was bleeding away the color of Dari's essence."

Kill me. . . .

Aron's arms drifted to his sides even as Dari's hand moved upward, until her fingers covered her mouth. It was the only way she could keep from screaming.

"The Lady Provost of Thorn has Kate," Nic said. "You haven't been able to find her because she hasn't remained in one location. Lady Pravda is traveling with her—and she's using Kate's energy to increase her own abilities." Nic's tone remained gentle, but his words beat at Dari like brutal punches. "Kate's mind-talents have allowed Lady Pravda to travel over distance and spy on Triune at will. You caught her the day you came to Stone, Aron—but you and anyone who could see Lady Pravda could have seen Kate, too. Lady Pravda would have forced to her to assume a disguise."

Aron tensed as he seemed to grasp the reality that Dari was still fighting. "Kate took the form of another god. A religious figure that I wouldn't question."

"You, or anyone else." Snakekiller's voice came out in a low growl, and she still refused to look at Nic or let her brother get a step closer to her. "Kate chose to present herself as Cayn, the god of her people, and the harbinger of death. It was the only message she could send without Lady Pravda being aware."

"*Kill me,*" Dari said, her words soft against her own palm as her heart seemed to tear in half.

Kate hadn't been trying to fool Aron into believing she was Cayn.

Kate had been doing everything she could to communicate her location to Dari, and to plead for someone to free her from such torture—even if freedom meant death.

"You can't sense her because she's drugged." Aron's face was now as red as Stormbreaker's and Snakekiller's. "When she's not being used for her energy, they're probably keeping her drunk on bullroot, and maybe something like the wine Falconer used to paralyze me."

"Where is Lady Thorn?" Lord Ross asked Lord Cobb, and if Dari had been standing next to her grandfather, she would have run from the murder in his voice. For all his wise-headed talk of sacrificing Kate to save Dari or the Stregans, now that the moment presented itself, he could no more do so than Dari could. The rage in his eyes mirrored her own as he said, "I know you have some idea, Westin. Tell me. Now."

"I wish I did know." Lord Cobb's own cheeks shaded maroon across the bridge of his nose, and his hand already gripped the hilt of his sword. "At the last sighting our scouts made, Pravda was traveling by carriage with an unmarked escort, somewhere within my borders, presumably picking up orphans."

"Carriage," Aron said as Dari's mind reeled outward, soaring through the Veil as she grabbed for some sign or vision of her twin.

"What kind of carriage?" Aron demanded. Then, "Kate really wants me to kill her?"

He sounded horrified.

Dari could no longer contain herself. She sent her awareness pelting through the Veil, across the world carved over the world.

Kill me. . . .

The words thundered through her mind like one of Stormbreaker's unnatural bursts of weather.

Kate was being drugged. Used. Drained like a wineskin whenever Lady Thorn needed more *graal* than she herself possessed. Kate's damaged mind and damaged body couldn't withstand such mistreatment. The drugs probably kept her from shifting too, which would have been fresh torture to Kate.

Dari and Kate weren't identical twins, but alike in many ways except for one. Dari felt completely comfortable in her human skin, but Kate—poor Kate! It was only in her Stregan form that Kate became whole. Feral, but complete and rational. Her mind played no tricks on her when she hunted and flew.

Dari felt warm arms taking hold of the body she had left behind.

Moments later, the calming flow of Nic's energy reached her, given freely. His image joined her on the other side of the Veil, and she grabbed the essence of his tunic and held on to keep herself from dropping to the ground, or letting her Stregan essence burst forth and consume her. The fury inside her wanted to chew through her skin and explode into Eyrie, destroying everything between her and her imprisoned twin.

The world on both sides of the Veil swam around Dari, and nothing seemed real save for Nic, right there beside her, helping her hold herself together.

Kill me. . . .

For the first time since she came to Eyrie to find her twin, Dari wondered if death might be the greatest kindness she could offer her sister now.

Then, for the briefest of moments, she felt what Kate was feeling, and she saw what Kate was seeing.

For the first time in too many cycles to count, Dari touched her twin's mind.

She shouted across the Veil as the connection settled into place, restoring a wholeness to her soul she thought she would never experience again. Kate's warmth surged toward her, through her, wrapping her in a love she had known before she knew any human voice or touch.

Dari.

Kate's whisper seemed so weak, a ribbon of thought Dari could barely grasp.

"Kate!"

The word reverberated through Dari's mind and *graal*, through the other side of the Veil, and if she could have thrown her entire essence after that thought-ribbon, she would already be flying.

But the ribbon vanished.

The warmth broke away.

Agony racked every fragment of life in Dari's body as she lost sense of her sister again. Her awareness slammed back into her body with wicked force, and she swayed and fell forward. Only Nic's support kept her on her feet.

"Kate," she wailed, unable to hold back a scream of rage, or the sobs that followed.

Kill me. . . .

Was that her thought? Her sister's?

In that moment, Dari wished she could die herself rather than go back to her maimed existence, her twinless world, no matter the wealth of love and friendship she had discovered since she left her home.

"Come back to me," Nic said as his essence began to fade away, back through the Veil. His voice struck the wall Dari was throwing up around her heart.

The wall shattered as quickly as she had constructed it.

She opened her eyes to find him waiting, worried but patient, the depth of emotion in his crystalline eyes enough to keep her from bursting into a fresh round of sobs and screaming. Gradually, she became aware of Stormbreaker and Snakekiller and Aron nearby, and her grandfather, and Lord Cobb. Soldiers and Stone Brothers and Sisters stood in silence, weapons at the ready, as if they had been prepared to invade the Veil to protect Dari and rescue her from whatever threat had presented itself. More distant still were Blath, Iko, and the rest of their Sabor contingent, landing in human form to ring the large traveling party.

"She's at Stone," Dari gasped. "Kate's with Lady Pravda, looking at the main gate and keep. I saw Lord Baldric standing with Windblown on the battlements—through Kate's eyes." She came back to herself more completely, and held tight to Nic's hand as she spoke loudly enough for everyone near her to hear. "We've made a terrible mistake. Eyrie's armies aren't following us. They're surrounding Triune."

CHAPTER SIXTY-THREE

ARON

Lord Ross embraced Dari, then returned her to Nic's tender care, and Aron saw her features shifting ever so slightly. Soft became hard, frightened became angry, and that fire she had in her eyes when he met her on his Harvest day ignited with a fury he had never seen before. Her hands twitched as Nic rubbed his palms against her arms, and he didn't attempt to hold her or restrain her in any fashion. Aron knew Nic understood that Dari was a warrior in her own right, more powerful than many of the soldiers who would draw swords to defend her at her grandfather's command.

Aron's mind shifted to the discovery of Kate's captors. He was so busy working out how he had so completely failed to understand Kate's presence in his visions, her desperate communications, that he didn't realize Lord Ross's attention had shifted to him. His skin chilled as he felt the force of the man's stare, but he held himself upright and didn't lower his head like a frightened boy.

A moment later, Nic came to stand beside him, and Dari joined them.

"My intention was to see you, Nic, and Dari safely to the heart of the Cobb and Ross armies, Aron, and to save Triune in the process." Lord Ross's voice was deeper than usual, and Aron thought he might be troubled, but he detected no uncertainty in that firm tone. "I had hoped to draw Altar, Brailing, Mab, and the Thorn Guild to us, and to reveal Nic with the might of our forces standing behind him. That would have given the soldiers pause, and offered us hope of talks, of negotiation and treaty."

Lord Ross's gaze moved to Nic, and his dark eyes seemed both sad and determined as he spoke louder, for all to hear. "The time for talking has passed. There will be no treaties in this war, only death and blood and tears. Dyn Mab and all of Eyrie will meet its fate in the valley around Triune."

Nic's assent came with a single nod. Aron knew Nic's twisted spine wouldn't allow him to stretch up from his stooped posture, yet somehow Nic seemed straighter and taller. The soldiers and Stone guild members attended to him with the same rapt attention they had paid to Lord Ross.

"We must give aid to the innocents at Triune," Nic said, red wisps of his legacy falling from his shoulders like a silken cloak of dynast colors. "We must save Kate before Lady Pravda finds a way to unleash her in the battle. I don't know how to sort through the many possible outcomes I can perceive, but I know for certain that all paths to victory depend on our reaching the valley as quickly as possible."

Dari gave an impatient snarl.

Wait, Aron told her on reflex, loading the force of *graal* into his command, just enough to hold her in her human form for a few moments.

"Yes, wait." Nic rested his hand on her wrist and seemed to be looking past her, almost into the sky. Aron wondered if the future stretched before Nic like a landscape, and he couldn't imagine finding his way through such an overwhelming image.

"If you join the battle as a Stregan, only death will come of it, Dari." Nic grimaced as he turned her loose and came back to the here and now. "Archers could bring you down, and swordsmen could hack you to bits. Fight with your sword. Fight with your *graal* if you have to, but don't shift, for the sake of us all."

Dari's muscles tightened.

For a moment, Aron thought she would argue, or even go ahead and shift if he didn't intervene. Her expression reflected the force and depth of her inner struggle, but a bit at a time, she seemed to master her urge to revert to her true nature and attack her sister's captors with teeth and claws and billowing gouts of flame.

When Nic seemed certain she was in control of herself, he addressed Lord Ross again. "Please lead us. I have the Mab name and bloodline and *graal*, but I am no warrior, and certainly no battlefield commander."

Nic didn't bow when he finished his sentence.

Thrills of surprise ran through Aron, but he could tell Lord Ross didn't take affront to this. Dari's grandfather was no longer expecting deference from Nic. It seemed, as Aron glanced around their small circle, then farther, into the wider group of fighters awaiting instructions, that no one was.

Lord Ross bowed to Nic, accepting Nic's request to retain command of the battle.

It was a quick gesture, underscored by a clap of Stormbreaker's thunder, but in that one small moment, Aron watched the future of Eyrie shift into Nic's hands.

Aron's heart hammered as he perceived this truth, a real and golden energy, sinking into Nic's body and heightening the color of his *graal*. It was as if Nic's use of his legacy in the fashion it was intended, to guide the fate of Eyrie, strengthened Aron's *graal* as well.

Lord Cobb spoke next, though his shoulders slumped forward. Aron understood that Lord Cobb wasn't afraid to fight, but that it crushed him to think of so much death. "Our armies are hours away as yet, maybe even more than a day, but they are moving. Perhaps we can hold the day until they arrive to assist us."

"I know that you and your people cannot join in this battle to defeat dynast forces," Lord Ross said to Stormbreaker, "but can you defend your stronghold? Can you help to rescue my granddaughter for that purpose?"

"We can protect our own, and fight for the weak and infirmed like Kate," Snakekiller confirmed. By the ever-increasing thunder blasts in the distance, Stormbreaker had moved beyond the ability to speak without losing control of himself.

"We can take our dispute over Thorn's conduct directly to Lady Thorn," Snakekiller continued, crossing her arms over her chest to tap the hilts of her blades. "At sword point, if necessary, if her guild protectors won't allow us access."

Her skin seemed to gleam with the desire to do just that, and shed as much cardinal red blood as possible.

"Then I place a portion of Kate's safety in Stone's hands." Lord Ross approached Stormbreaker and Snakekiller, extended his hand, and clasped theirs when they offered. "You have served Dari and Nic as true friends for these many cycles, and I believe you have the best chance of a successful frontal assault in our rescue of Dari's twin."

Lord Ross let go of his Stone allies, and his next words were for all the soldiers within hearing distance. "From our scouting information, we know we'll be dealing with contingents, not armies—but they are large in number, and fortified by Thorn Guild renegades. They'll outnumber us ten to one, but we have advantages they don't expect." His expression remained blank, but the lines of his face tightened as his eyes narrowed and his fist closed on the hilt of his sword. "Lord Baldric will be digging in, and by now Triune will be proving more a challenge than their attackers imagined. Fate willing, our battle will be fought outside the walls."

A shout went up from the soldiers, and Aron shouted, too, caught in the force of Lord Ross's address.

"Talons can move faster than horses, and they draw more attention." Lord Ross wheeled toward Aron, Stormbreaker, and Snakekiller, his black eyes almost silver-white with the drive to succeed in his quest. "The Stone Guild's talon-riders will approach from the hill near the main byway. Draw Thorn's attention, and engage what you can of the Brailing and Altar forces on your way to confront Thorn."

He turned back to the soldiers on horseback, all of whom were drawing closer to their commander, to hear their charge for themselves. "My granddaughter remains with me, and she'll take my command should I fall. Our riders will flank Triune and attack Thorn from the rear. Dari and I will have one purpose, and that's to rescue Kate. We will be a spear, moving only forward, never slowing until we reach our target."

To Aron and the Stone Guild, he said, "Fight your way through, and join us when you can. Help us if you can."

"We will," Aron said, wanting to shout all over again. Stormbreaker and Snakekiller agreed by turning toward their talons and mounting for the rough ride ahead.

Aron followed them as Lord Ross's instructions continued to ring out above the murmuring crowd. "Cobb will take the east, and shattered be any blades raised against them."

The Cobb soldiers let loose with deep, blood-pumping battle-cries.

Tek stamped as Aron steadied her and thrust his foot into the stirrup to mount. He pulled himself into the saddle as Lord Ross moved toward Blath and Iko. "Get to our army and the rest of your people. Bring as many as you can. You'll have to leave the mounts behind, but fly well, and fly hard. Fly until you fall out of the sky."

Blath's bow was deep and reverent, and as she rose, her gaze was only for Dari.

"It's the best way to help me." Dari came forward to grab Blath's hands. "It's the best way to help Kate. In doing this, you will be keeping your vows to me, and going far beyond that duty."

Blath pulled Dari's hands to her lips and kissed them. Dari hesitated for a moment, then wrapped her arms around Blath's neck. When the Sabor woman released Dari, Aron saw pain and resolve mingled across her usually unreadable face. He caught a movement below him, and looked down to find Iko gazing up at him much as Blath had gazed at Dari.

With a start, Aron realized the Sabor had come to him seeking release, just as Blath had gone to Dari for the same purpose. Iko wanted permission to leave Aron's side, to surrender his vow of protection in answer to Lord Ross's command.

"Please help Kate and Dari," Aron said, pressing one hand into his chest to staunch the quick ache in his heart. "Do whatever you have to do. I can take care of myself now."

Aron was unprepared for how much he didn't want to see Iko leave him, and for Iko's deep bow. Aron returned the bow as best he could from his seated position on Tek's back. When Iko once more stood to his full height, something in his gaze told Aron that his service to Aron had ended forever. Iko had a new charge now, to defend his dynast lord and Dyn Ross's only surviving heirs, and Aron knew Iko would give his last breath and drop of blood to see the task done.

Lord Cobb mounted his ebony stallion and donned his battle helmet, shaped in the form of a great black stallion's head. He shouted to the nearest Cobb soldier wearing a helm reflecting rank, "Zeller. Dolf Zeller! Go with the Sabor and take control of my army. Ride for Triune like you've never ridden before—as if Cayn himself were storming across the grasslands behind you!"

Aron watched as the father who had once begged Stone for Mercy for his only son leaped off his mount and charged toward the nearest blue warrior. A man from Dyn Brailing, leading Cobb's army into battle. War did make for strange situations, and strange sights.

Soldiers and Stone Brothers moved aside for Blath and Iko to pass. They ran toward Zeller and the waiting Sabor at the edges of the gathering. Moments later, the pounding of massive wings filled the air. Golden gryphons burst into the sky, screeching louder than Altar's Great Rocs as they went. The sight of them made Aron's pulse surge, as he hoped it made any enemies who could see them quake where they stood.

Lord Ross mounted in one flowing motion, and Dari leaped aboard her battle stallion Toronado, bareback as always, with nothing but a halter and lead to guide the animal. Aron waited for Nic to struggle back to his own stallion, but instead, he abandoned the horse and limped toward Aron.

When he reached Tek, Nic turned back to Lord Ross and Dari. "I'll be going with Aron."

"You will not." Dari's stallion struggled against his lead as she leaned forward, her eyes wide. "You can't hold a sword to defend yourself—it would be suicide for you to ride in the vanguard."

"Nic," Lord Cobb said, turning his mount to face Nic. "Prince Mab. It would be better for you to remain with your wife and Lord Ross and their Guard contingent. The more blades to protect you, the better."

"I'm not asking for permission or opinions in this matter." Nic spoke as calmly and forcefully as he had when he asked Lord Ross to lead them. Fresh wisps of red escaped his shoulders and neck, wreathing him in a regal light. "My place is with Aron, just as Dari's is with her grandfather."

Aron tightened his grip on Tek's reins to hold her still. He wanted to argue, too, but Nic no longer sounded like his friend and peer. Nic was speaking as a man with the full measure of the Mab *graal* guiding his actions, as a dynast heir and lord—and as Eyrie's next king.

Dari sat back, her mouth open. Shock moved to worry on her pretty face, then to outright fear.

"I'm certain," Nic told her, his tone much more gentle. "I would never leave your side if I didn't know it was necessary." He lifted his fingers and sent her a kiss on the breeze.

Lord Ross tilted his head forward, acknowledging his future king's wishes with, "Prince Mab."

Lord Cobb did the same, and the matter seemed to be settled for everyone but Dari. Her free hand drifted to her belly, as if she might be protecting herself from a blow, or holding back a powerful bunch of curses. Aron sensed her pain and uncertainty like dark ripples moving across his brow and chest, and when she looked at him, he could tell Dari wanted him to reason with Nic.

Aron's insides clenched, but he couldn't bring himself to argue with Nic, not even for Dari. The red haze around Nic grew by the moment. Now that Aron had watched the force of Nic's *graal* begin to show itself, and felt how Nic's mind-talent fueled his own, he knew he wouldn't challenge Nic. It wouldn't have been right, not for Nic or the battle or Eyrie—though Aron wasn't at all certain what would have been right for Dari.

Her look of frustration and betrayal when Aron refused to speak crushed something deep in Aron's heart. He turned his face away from her, but he heard her clearly enough when she said, "You keep him safe. Aron, you owe me that. You keep my husband alive. Promise me."

The vow rose to Aron's lips, but he didn't speak it.

Brother help him, he wanted to. He needed to promise Dari what she wanted so badly that tears almost found a way to his cheeks—but he didn't. He had already condemned Nic in such a fashion once, to stay alive when death should have claimed him. He wouldn't agree to do that again, not to Nic, or anyone.

"Aron," Dari cried, and Aron knew she thought he was refusing out of retribution or spite, or worse yet, jealousy and a wish that Nic wouldn't survive the battle. Her tone made him sick, but he had to believe she would reason through his actions at some later time, when the world was calmer and more forgiving.

"Steady," Snakekiller said, and Aron thought at first she was speaking to him.

When he raised his head, determined to survive Dari's bitter gaze, Lord Ross had the lead of Dari's stallion. Her features seemed blurry and indistinct, and Aron knew only Nic's prohibition about shifting to her Stregan form was keeping her from becoming a giant, furious dragon.

Lord Ross gently pulled Dari away with him as he went to assume the head position in his riding column, Nic stood below Aron, trembling.

"Steady," Snakekiller said again, and this time Aron realized she was comforting Nic.

Nic swayed, and used Tek's massive, scaled flank for support. His breath left him in quick whistles, and his *graal* flickered around him as Aron had seen it do before a fit, or in those frightening, dark times when Nic drifted between life and death afterward. It was gut-kicking to watch Nic racked with agony and dying, yet unable to cross over to the next life because of the damage done by Aron's first *graal* command.

Aron placed a hand on Nic's shoulder. He imagined his own energy, sapphire-blue and soothing, flowing down his arms and through his fingertips. He hoped that would be enough to chase back the energy storm threatening to cripple Nic during the battle he most needed to help fight.

At last, when they could no longer see Dari, Nic came back to himself enough to withdraw from Aron. He pulled his red *graal* energy fully into his own body, and let out a deep sigh full of regret.

Aron moved his foot from his stirrup, helped Nic gain purchase, then pulled him onto Tek's back behind him.

"Thank you," Nic said as he settled at Aron's back and wrapped his arms tight around Aron's waist. "For your help, and for not fighting me on Dari's behalf."

"I'm not sure you're welcome," Aron grumbled as he urged Tek into position behind Stormbreaker and Snakekiller. "Even if we live through this battle, Dari will probably kill both of us. And I don't think she'll be nice enough to use some painless poison."

CHAPTER SIXTY-FOUR

NIC

Nic's joints cracked with each running step Tek took.

On either side of them, bull talons bellowed as they trampled grass and saplings on their breakneck journey down the main byway. Dust clogged the air, and the stink of talon oil made it all but impossible to draw a full breath.

Nic kept his eyes squeezed shut and his face pressed into Aron's back so he wouldn't scream from the bone-wrecking pain. Sweat coated his shoulders and neck, and he shivered despite the absence of cold in the air.

They had been running for hours, but it felt like days, and he didn't know if he could stand it another moment. He had more of Snakekiller's elixir, but he didn't dare drink it for fear of dulling his senses and losing his ability to understand and decide between the visions hammering at his consciousness. Whenever he began to drift into the void of blackness he had so often known following his fits, a bit of Aron's energy would flow into him, shoring him up enough for another few miles.

Nic tried to breathe, but he couldn't fill his lungs without a new, stabbing agony. He settled for quick, short gasps, like a beast giving birth.

What do you see now? Aron asked through the link they shared, shielded from eavesdropping on the other side of the Veil by Nic's abundant *graal*. Dari had taught him the skill, but at some point in their lessons, he had simply absorbed all she knew of mind-talents, and how to use them. Learning in such a fashion was a feature of his legacy, according to her.

Nic wished he could touch Dari in similar fashion, speak to her as easily as he spoke to Aron, but he wouldn't allow himself that bit of comfort at her expense. She was fierce and strong, but now that Nic sensed two lives instead of one whenever they were joined on the other side of the Veil, he felt driven to protect his unborn child as well.

I see us dying, Nic answered Aron honestly. *Quickly, almost as soon as we enter the battle.*

Aron's frustration flowed through their link.

What if we attack from another angle, another position? Aron's mind shifted through various points on the approach to the valley. He knew the lay of the land much better than Nic, but in Nic's advanced state of awareness, using his *graal* so freely, he absorbed Aron's mental maps as quickly as he absorbed Dari's knowledge of mind-talents. He ground his teeth and screamed behind his mental barriers, overcome by details and images and the sawing of his mis-shapen bones against his flesh.

Then the information sorted itself into a complete picture, and he could answer Aron's question. *No approach offers us a better fate, and most would cost Dari, Kate, Lord Ross, and Lord Cobb their lives.*

Damnation, Nic! What good is your future-seeing graal *if it can't find an answer for us?*

Aron's surge of emotion rocked Nic backward. He clung to Aron's waist to keep his seat, and the roar in his mind almost blocked Aron's apology. Tree branches smacked Nic in his shoulder, and pebbles churned from the road by the thundering line of clawfeet stung his ankles and legs.

Find an answer. Nic gripped Aron's robes and bit his lip until he tasted blood. That *is the answer, isn't it?*

Nic closed out Aron's confused response, and focused on the images streaming through his thoughts and senses. Leaving only a portion of his attention on staying in Tek's saddle behind Aron, he let his consciousness flow through the Veil. It took little effort to rise above the byway, high enough into the sky to have room to do what Aron suggested, and even less to keep his endeavors private.

Nic imagined his visions outside of his own mind, until he could see dozens of smoky, wavering figures drifting before him. They had no real substance, these moving pictures of what might be, and each represented a possible future based on the next set of actions taken by Aron and Nic.

So many.

Too many.

The essence of Nic's head ached so badly he feared it would crack open. The relaxed confidence he had been feeling since he asked Lord Ross to lead them into battle left him like a passerine taking flight. Sparks spit through his senses, the first awakenings of a fit.

Stop it. No. I won't. I can't.

He pulled back from the images, dousing the sparks, helped by a rush of Aron's cool blue energy.

Nic pulled on that flow of soothing light more than he should, like he imagined Lady Pravda did when she drained Kate of all that made Kate who and what she was. Murder. Soul-murder.

Nic ripped himself free of his connection with Aron.

The pain in his body grew so great that it followed him through the Veil.

He was running out of strength.

He was running out of time.

Nic swore and fell to the essence of his knees. With his ghostly hands, less gnarled on this side of the Veil, he pawed through the waves of images his mind created. He pushed at them. Pulled at them. Dispersed and reshaped them.

Which one, which one . . . ?

Nic heard his mind's voice, and it sounded disturbingly thin and unbalanced, like the cries of his mother in her more troubled days.

Was this legacy what broke her mind?

He understood her insanity now, in ways he never imagined he would.

His vision flickered and dimmed, and for a moment he sensed his mother, sampled the morass of her cluttered thoughts and unhinged feelings. He recognized her instantly—and she seemed to recognize him. Her energy grabbed for his, and he didn't have the strength to push her away.

How close was she to him?

A mile?

Two?

Not far, and riding on horseback.

He hadn't thought his mother capable of going into battle, least of all mounted and armed like one of her Guardsmen.

Was this some new insanity, or some trick of the rectors seeing to her care?

Whatever it was, Nic was sinking into her mind, losing himself in her joyous greeting—as if that could ever happen, as if it could ever be real.

A burst of Aron's *graal* woke Nic's nerves and pulled him back to safety, then increased his focus on his true goal. Nic shook as the sense of his mother lessened, until he could control it, until he could force it far from his mind and heart, despite the tears rising to his eyes.

He watched Aron's blue energy weave through his own red *graal*, and stared at the images of the future through their combined strength. The flavor and style of Aron's *graal* became part of his understanding, and the mixing of truth and possibility gave Nic new purpose.

He attacked the images with a fervor, grabbing for the right one, the correct one, the one they needed and must have.

Come to me, he urged, much as he had urged Dari to return to herself when she had briefly been lost to him when she lost her connection to her twin again.

When the images wouldn't cooperate, Nic snatched at more of Aron's *graal.*

Aron gave freely of his energy, and Nic flung the force of Aron's power and his own at the rushing array.

Come to me! He shouted the words aloud, on both sides of the Veil.

The sound crushed against his ears, his awareness, until his teeth seemed to rattle in his skull. His vision darkened again, and this time, no energy came to rescue him. Nic pitched forward, tasting blood and smelling nothing, seeing nothing, into darkness, into a great, cold, black void—

With only a few streams of images.

With just two or three possibilities, instead of thousands.

Nic's body screamed for release as he grabbed at the pictures and studied them. Pain clawed at him, dragged at him, but he ignored it. He refused it. If all his limbs fell off and he bled to death as he searched, so be it. Perhaps he could get the proper images to Aron, who could carry on in his stead.

As Nic stared at the moving pictures, sorted through them, rearranged them, he let the frozen truth of the future creep over him, toe to head.

So there was a way. Maybe a few ways. A few paths, at least, where Dari and their child and even her family survived. Or where Aron triumphed in the battle, and Eyrie didn't plunge into endless bloodshed and destruction. His mother. Triune. The armies.

Dear gods and goddesses, any and all, known and unknown— how was he supposed to choose the fates of people he loved?

How could he pick between them, or select Eyrie's welfare over the warmth of smiles and faces and heartbeats he knew almost as well as his own?

None of these possibilities worked out particularly well for Nic, and all of them would require new sorts of courage he wasn't even sure he possessed.

But how—how could he?

How could anyone do this?

Nic let go of the images as he felt himself sinking down, down, back through the Veil and into the body that was even now rebelling and attempting to die without him.

He knew what came next, the fit, the long recovery—but he couldn't allow it.

Help me, he said to Aron, and Aron did, this time costing himself so much of his own essence and energy that he slumped forward on Tek. They both slid in the saddle, and Nic's fit sparked and fizzled in his mind, spreading, threatening to rise over every effort he and Aron were making.

Thunder ruptured the silence expanding through Nic's brain, and lightning forced stars into the places where sparks had been.

He sat up straight, towing Aron with him, but Aron was already regaining his balance.

Beside them on the back of his bull talon, it was Stormbreaker who sagged now.

"No!" Aron's shout broke through Nic's stupor, and the two of them thought as one as they closed their eyes and joined their *graal*, seeking to return the essence Stormbreaker had loaned them.

A massive snake exploded into Nic's awareness, blocking the energy he had released and sending it rushing back into his own body. Aron gave a cry as the same thing happened to him. As they both opened their eyes and turned to their left.

"It's rude to reject gifts," Snakekiller growled. She glared briefly at them, then returned her attention to the road. "Especially so close to our destination."

Nic could have sworn he heard a hissing sound laced through each word. It took a moment for Snakekiller's meaning to reach him— a moment, and the slowing of Aron's talon, and the talons on either side of them.

The beasts came to a halt at the top of a hill, just off the main byway, and Nic gasped at the sight spreading beneath them like some terrible dream come to reality.

"Goddess be with us," Snakekiller whispered, the hissing in her voice replaced with a flat, cold hopelessness.

Yellow sands, bare rock, and blue-gray mists framed a massive valley, Triune's valley, but the ground below was so full of soldiers Nic could scarcely make out the patches of green grass so plentiful in the grounds around the Stone stronghold. Guardsmen wearing the steel and copper colors of Dyn Altar were moving to fill barrens and outlands, showing no fear of the mockers and predators they had battled most of their lives.

Soldiers with the blues and yellows of Dyn Brailing occupied the grassy sections of the valley, lighting huge pyres of fire that would set arrows ablaze, towing battering rams and catapults into place, and heaving ladders toward the tall walls that formed Triune's main resistance. Small groups had breached the moat using boards to stretch across the mocker-filled waters, and they clustered along the bottom of the massive main gate and keep. Its twin towers rose high, high above these breakaway soldiers, who seemed to be digging.

Nic wondered if it was possible to tunnel under the castle's walls.

"Where are the sheltered?" Aron murmured, and Nic felt him shift in the saddle for a better view of the village toward the back of Triune's inner grounds. It did seem deserted, as did much of the castle, but Nic had supposed that was because of the number of Stone Brothers and Stone Sisters waiting in grim stillness along the thick battlements connecting the castle's many towers. Here and there, colored garments stood out amongst the gray robes and weapons. These fighters had to be sheltered or other allies, come to fight alongside the guild.

Still, there were nowhere near enough guild members or people to account for the castle's population. Grazing fields, paddocks, barns, woods, bridges, byways—even the House of the Judged—everything seemed to be standing open and completely deserted.

"They're withdrawing to the Ruined Keep," Stormbreaker murmured, sounding so weak Nic almost didn't recognize his voice. "Stone's last line of defense, and the last hope of those Stone protects."

Stormbreaker gestured in the direction of the Lost Path, and Nic saw that the side gates were indeed open. From what he could see through the dense mists, Stone Brothers and Sisters were lining either side of the path, shepherding apprentices and their many charges into the dangers waiting in the clouds of the Deadfall.

"The trial," he said, as much to himself as to Aron. "Every guild member knows the way, and knows the dangers of the path. Because of the trial, they know exactly what to do, and they don't fear the Deadfall like everyone else."

"And there are supplies, checked regularly and restocked," Aron said, sounding awed and chagrined. "I never understood—but, yes, all the children and infirmed will fit inside the Ruined Keep, and the guild and other able adults will defend them. The mockers and manes and predators will be like an extra army, this time in the service of Stone."

Nic held on to Aron as he stared into the valley.

He had heard that no army had ever successfully laid siege to the fortress at Triune—but what of two armies?

And if his visions of his mother and Mab's forces were true, Stone would soon be contending with three massive forces, assuming they joined in the same aim and didn't fall to fighting each other.

Nic reached out with his *graal*, careful to keep his search private, and estimated the positions of Lord Ross and Lord Cobb.

"The others are nearly in place," he told Aron and Stormbreaker and Snakekiller. Then, to Aron, he said, "Do you sense Kate?"

Aron searched the ground below with new intensity, and Nic did what he could to share his *graal* strength with his friend, wondering if this might be the last time.

"There." Aron pointed to a spot near the center of the main gate and keep. "I'll get word to Dari and Lord Ross before we start down the hill."

Nic thought he could make out a large covered carriage, and some red-robed figures surrounding it. A tiny flow of multicolored *graal* seemed to cling to the carriage. If he hadn't been looking so closely, and sharing energy with Aron, Nic wouldn't have noticed it at all. It was similar to Dari's, yet different, and Nic supposed that even identical twins might have some differences.

The carriage and its protectors were located directly in the middle of the thickest part of the army, and Nic had no doubt the fighting would be brutal—which made his next words even more difficult. "I have to go, Aron. And I need Tek."

Aron went stiff in his saddle, and didn't even turn to confront Nic's bold statement. Nic sensed Aron using his own mind-talents to assess the truth of Nic's statement, and felt his friend sag forward when he found it.

For a long few moments, Aron didn't move at all. As Nic well understood, knowing the truth and acting on it were two different struggles.

At last, wordless and wooden in his motions, Aron placed Tek's reins on the talon's neck. Snakekiller and Stormbreaker offered no argument, but Nic saw Snakekiller check the cinching on her stirrups and refasten the strap on her nearest scabbard.

"You can't go with me," he said.

"I will ride beside you," came her response, absolute and unwavering. "If I can't accompany you to your ultimate destination, I'll see you as far as I can—or as far as I'm able."

Nic weighed this as Aron slipped out of the saddle and landed nimbly on the ground. Nic slid himself forward and took Tek's reins in his own hands, and he understood that Snakekiller would be going with him.

He hadn't seen that in his visions, but he should have.

Snakekiller would never leave him unprotected, though when he reached the Mab army, she would have to turn back or seek shelter. Nic didn't have time to weigh out what this would mean, or sort it out in his visions of the future.

All he knew was that when he came face-to-face with his mother again, when he at last stared down her madness and forced her to acknowledge him and the reality of her choices and actions, he would have to do so alone.

Nic paused only to give Aron time to mount Stormbreaker's bull and secure himself behind his former guild master in the saddle.

"If I don't come back—" he began, but Aron stopped him with a loud curse.

"Don't," Aron said. "Telling me the future—I can't stand it, Nic."

"One possible future." Nic drew a breath, and took a bigger risk. "See to Dari if I don't come back. I want your word on that, Aron. And see—" Nic's voice cracked, but he forced out the rest of his words. "And see to my son. I'm counting on you."

Aron turned to gape at Nic then, and so did Stormbreaker. Some of the nearby Stone Brothers murmured amongst themselves, but Nic couldn't worry about what they might be saying or thinking. He could only stare at Aron, at the man who had forced him to live, what seemed like four or five lifetimes ago.

"I'll do it," Aron said. "I'll take care of them as best I can. I promise."

"As do I," Stormbreaker said, touching his chest to make the promise an oath.

Snakekiller gave no promises, but then, she didn't have to. Nic had no doubt that if Snakekiller survived and he did not, she would shadow Dari and his unborn child like a viper, silent and deadly to any who might approach them meaning harm.

"When you draw your blades, don't stop cutting," Nic told Aron as he turned Tek and aimed the talon north, toward the Mab army. This advice was the best he could do to stay true to the visions he had seen, without burdening Aron with knowledge of the future.

Nic urged Tek forward, with Snakekiller falling in beside him.

"If fate truly does favor the foolish," Nic said, "I'll see you again."

He and Snakekiller plunged into the woods on the far side of the byway, and behind them, the Stone Brothers let loose with a blood-stilling battle-scream. The sound rose like one voice, joined by the trumpets and bellows of the bull talons.

Tek shrilled in response, as did Snakekiller's bull. Their battle rings sprang outward, spraying oil in every direction.

Nic wiped the stinging, foul liquid from his eyes, relieved, at least, for that excuse for his tears.

CHAPTER SIXTY-FIVE

DARI

When Dari captured Aron's mental image of her sister's location, she thought she was going to explode. Her Stregan essence felt like an immutable force, tearing at her mind and insides, demanding release.

But Nic warned her.

She couldn't.

She had to stay in her human form.

Why hadn't he been the one to speak to her through the Veil?

She would have taken such strength from his mental touch. His absence and slight felt like a hot oil in her belly, but she had no time for minor pains and grievances.

Sword drawn, galloping behind her grandfather with two Ross Guard on either side of her, Dari roared with rage and frustration even as she heard Aron's battle-cry through the Veil. The sound was magnified by her surging desire to shift, but she held herself back.

Her grandfather charged forward behind his small vanguard, with less than forty soldiers comprising the force behind him.

Dari intended to count for five men, or even ten. She couldn't see her grandfather's face, but she felt his fury and determination like a moving wall that would crush anything between them and Kate.

She raised her sword as they burst from the tree cover at the edge of the valley.

The attention of the south side of the Brailing forces had been completely captured by the charging, screeching row of bull talons and Stone Brothers storming down from the main byway into the valley around Triune.

They scarcely had time to turn toward this new attack, much less position their pikes to menace mounted soldiers.

Dari's guard split wide, taking on any foot soldier who charged toward them. Toronado trampled men under his wide, sharp hooves as Dari swung at helmets and shields and blades. Anything that moved. Anything she saw.

Keep moving, her grandfather commanded, aloud and through the Veil. *If we hesitate, we die, and you will* not *be dying this day.*

Like a massive, dark plow, he and his vanguard cleared the field in front of Dari. With each severing sweep of his blade, her grandfather showed why he had long ago earned his nickname—the Sword of Elder. His arm and his tempered steel were little more than a bloody blur, and his battle-bellows terrified whoever he failed to kill on the first strike.

Dari reached for those same talents within her own soul. If they were his, then they could be hers as well. She was his granddaughter. She was his rightful heir, no matter what Eyrie might know or believe—and on the battlefield of Triune, she was determined to fell whatever beast or man the Sword of Elder might miss.

Her grandfather's legacy surrounded Dari, the full force of his Ross mind-talent, shielding her from any attack she might not expect, protecting her from any form of mental assault. Blood flecked her arms and legs and face, and the stench of sweat and fear and gore made her insides heave. Each impact sent stinging bolts from her fingers to her shoulder. Her arm ached and tingled from blow after blow. Her whole body seemed to jar half out of its saddle whenever her sword connected with another sword, or a neck, or an arm, and soon her sides heaved like Toronado's. She didn't look at the men she killed, but she felt them die, every one of them, and she didn't even know if she was sorry.

"For Kate!" she cried as she raised her sword again, again, again. Throats opened beneath the force of her slashing and driving. Men screamed. Men choked on their own life's fluids, but she spared them not even a glance. She kept Toronado close to her grandfather's stallion, even when her guards fell under the onslaught of the Brailing soldiers.

Stinging fire seemed to spread along Dari's legs as blades nicked her calves. Guardsmen clad in Brailing blues and yellows charged ever closer to her. Pikes jabbed at Toronado, and the stallion's terrible squeals of pain only doubled the force of Dari's thrusts. She blocked blows, knocked away two spiraling daggers and struck down spear after spear after spear. Her breeches soon hung in rags, and her leather boots had been sliced open.

Keep moving! came Lord Ross's repeated command, as compelling as any Aron could give, and Dari moved. Left, then right, then left again. She struck out with her sword, and with her *graal*, too, knocking back anything that drew near to her.

Throaty trumpets of talons drew closer, and even through her grandfather's protections, Dari sensed Aron's presence thundering toward her.

She didn't sense Nic's.

Was Aron shielding Nic?

Her eyes widened, and the battlefield came into sharper focus.

Ross Guard were dropping so fast she couldn't even figure how many were left.

Where was that carriage?

Had they turned astray in the madness?

They weren't going to make it!

Her chest tightened until she could barely force herself to gulp air.

The talons and Stone Brothers hurtled toward what was left of the Ross soldiers, crushing the Brailing soldiers between the two groups even as more Brailing Guard rushed in to try to surround them all. From farther ahead near the castle came the crashing boom of a battering ram striking wood, and the *smash-crash* of catapulted stones blasting into the castle walls.

Battle-cries rippled along the battlements, adding to the morass of sound and stink and movement filling Dari's senses.

A burly Brailing man with a mace waded toward her out of the blur, knocking aside Ross Guard like they were no more than twigs.

She jerked her stallion's lead to avoid him, but not in time.

The big, spiked metal hammer caught Toronado in the chest, and her faithful stallion spilled beneath her, his wild consciousness tearing free from Dari's mind and shredding a piece of her heart. Dead. He was dead before his big, beautiful body even struck the bloody ground.

Dari half jumped, half fell free of him, shouting at the loss, then screaming as her sword flew from her grip and planted itself tip first in the dirt.

She, however, never struck the ground.

Powerful hands gripped her forearms and swept her straight out of the air.

She looked up, hopeful, expecting to see Blath or Iko or another Sabor, shifting into full gryphon form and hoisting her above the battle to fly her straight to Kate.

Instead, she slammed into the oily, smelly side of a lumbering bull talon.

Scales scratched her face as for a moment she saw Aron. Felt the soothing, forceful surge of Aron's *graal*.

Then he was gone, dropping away and striking the ground beside her at a full run, short sword and dagger in hand, but quickly falling behind.

Dari scrambled for balance behind Stormbreaker, and he turned loose her arm as she grabbed his waist. Lightning blasted around her, and thunder seemed to shake the skies.

Stormbreaker. Aron.

They had been riding together?

"Where is Nic?" she shouted to Stormbreaker, but her words were lost in the roar of the battle and the endless clamor of weather from his renegade *graal*. He trembled beneath her grip, and she realized his energy was almost at full ebb. Instinct drove her to reach for his thoughts, to offer some of her own *graal* to fuel him, but he shoved her efforts away.

Yellow bolts from the sky fractured the ground near Brailing soldiers, sending them flying like children's toys. Rain broke out in patches, and wind knocked down yet more Guardsmen attempting to charge at Lord Ross. Brailing horsemen, just now joining the fray, fought with their mounts, horses hardened and trained to battle, but not to withstand thunder exploding next to their sensitive ears, or explosions of lightning ripping up the earth around their hooves.

Stormbreaker was using his legacy. He was fighting with both swords and his mind. Dari had never imagined he would do it—and never imagined how much damage he could do. Though he didn't seem to be killing anyone directly with his bursts of energy, he laid low entire sections of the Brailing force.

A rushing contingent of Brailing swordsmen stopped short of Dari, Stormbreaker, and her grandfather, seeming to be confused. They stared down at their weapons, or flung them away like they might be writhing, biting rodents. A few began to scream and run hard away from the battle. Nearby horses seemed to grow addled and run in random directions. Any fighter who came too close to Dari or her grandfather met a strange fate at the tip of a lightning bolt, or staggered as if struck by a sudden blight of dullness, forgetting to fight altogether.

Sapphire light played across the chaotic retreat of the nearest Brailing forces.

The few warriors who fought through the first blast of Aron's *graal* commands fell dead before they could raise their weapons. Three men. Five. More than that. Ranks of Brailing Guard twitched, jumped, and collapsed as if Cayn had stormed onto the battlefield to gore them all.

Dari ripped at the sides of Stormbreaker's robes, knowing what it must be costing Aron to kill in such a fashion.

The bull talon nearest to Stormbreaker snatched a horse from the ground and flung it, rider and all, into another group of horsemen.

Dari realized Snakekiller wasn't nearby, but she caught a hint of her snakelike energy—from far away, a mile or more in the distance.

Stormbreaker reined in his bull, causing Dari to pull herself closer to him, then push back as Lord Ross, swords sheathed and expression near panicked, reined his stallion next to them.

"Here!" he shouted, and Dari shoved off, leaping from Stormbreaker's talon into her grandfather's arms. He caught her and hoisted her onto the saddle in front of him, then drew one sword and pressed it into her palm. "Take the right," he told her, and she shifted to lean in that direction.

He leaned to the left and drew his other sword.

Both of them swung their blades at onrushing soldiers, slicing as they rumbled forward, his stallion wheezing and laboring beneath their combined weight.

From the corner of her eye, Dari saw Stormbreaker's big bull flap its wings, leap toward the sky as he shouted and let loose a barrage of thunder, and drop its full weight onto a clutch of archers readying arrows.

The wet, crunching smash almost made her vomit, but she kept swinging, had to keep swinging, as her grandfather clung to the waistband of her breeches to keep her in the saddle.

Flashes of red ahead of them drew her attention.

At first she thought they were charging into a group of bloodied soldiers, but then she recognized the brilliant cardinal robes of the Thorn Guild.

Dari's snarl was matched only by her grandfather's as the covered carriage Aron had shown Dari and Lord Ross in his mind-picture came clearly into view.

Kate.

Almost there.

Thorn Brothers ringed the carriage, three men deep, each wielding two barbed swords. They had no *graal* that Dari could see, no expression on their pale faces, and they didn't seem to want to move their weapons. They weren't even in tight formation, as if they assumed Dari and her grandfather would make no attempt to breach their ranks.

"Not much time," Lord Ross said as he once more pulled back on his stallion's reins and jumped from his saddle. "Find your sister."

Dari vaulted off the horse and landed beside her grandfather. Her shredded boots fell from her feet, and her breeches and tunic hung on her like unsewn strips of cloth. Blood oozed from dozens of tiny wounds, but the pain was manageable, at least for the moment. Smoke and flame and the sweet-sick stench of fresh death made her eyes water, but that cleared her vision of soot and dirt. She coughed and spit out a mouthful of battlefield dust as they stopped shy of the Thorn Guard, swords at the ready.

Behind the Thorn Guard and the carriage they protected, just across the moat, Triune's main gate and keep loomed like the valley's last sentinel. The Stone Brothers and other fighters spaced along its battlements moved only to knock away flaming arrows or hurled rocks and spears.

Dari reached out with her *graal*, slamming the entire force of her mind against the carriage before her, but she sensed nothing. Felt nothing.

"Kate!" she screamed, as if her sister could hear her above the unbelievable din of the battle unfolding around them.

The carriage door opened—but it wasn't Kate who came forth.

Stormbreaker and the remaining Stone Brothers reached them on talon-back, forming two lines of protection on either side of Dari and her grandfather. They were joined by the few surviving Ross Guardsmen as Dari stared through the ranks of Thorn Brothers.

At toddlers and very young children.

Three, then five, then ten, now fifteen or more—spilled out of the carriage. They wore red robes like fully vested members of the Thorn Guild, and each bore a thorny spiral tattoo on their right cheek—no matter how small that cheek might be. It seemed like a bad joke or some dark travesty, like these children were nothing but dolls dressed to be guild members.

"Some of them are barely out of diapers," Lord Ross rumbled, and Dari heard and shared his distress.

No wonder the Thorn Brothers weren't moving.

Who could swing those awful, spiked swords so close to a group of unarmed children?

Dari couldn't imagine cutting her way toward them. What if the children moved, or got in the way? Cutting down grown men trying to kill her was one thing—but this?

"How could Thorn carry a load of tiny children into a battle?" she asked, but even as she spoke, she tried to use her mind-talents to better understand these little ones, or see what she could do to protect them.

Once more, she found nothing, sensed nothing—not even the life essence of these children. Yet they were very much alive. None were crying. None had thumbs in their mouths, or bottles, or soothers. None had the soft, innocent look children of that age should possess.

"They're completely shielded," Lord Ross said. "Someone's blocking our ability to touch their thoughts more thoroughly than I've ever sensed before."

Dari's more powerful *graal* told her something much, much worse.

She couldn't stop staring into the bright eyes, blue and green and even golden. She might not be able to see the colors and strengths of their legacies, but their eyes spoke loudly enough.

"I think the children are the source of the shield," she told her grandfather, a sense of dread beginning to descend upon her like a Great Roc dropping from the sky. "I think the children are shielding themselves."

Her grandfather's horrified expression summed up Dari's feelings and multiplied them—but before her grandfather could respond, loud shouts filled the air.

Dari's attention shifted toward the sound.

The Guard charging toward their protectors seemed to swell in numbers. One group in the front contained Brailing's standard-bearers, and a thin soldier led them. He wore a bright silver helm studded with sapphires, and great eagle's wings jutted out from either side. The sword he carried flashed in the bright light of day, and Dari saw more jewels on the blade's massive hilt. A pale cloud of blue clung to the soldier. *Graal* energy. Weak, yet deadly against those who had no defenses.

A few Stone Brothers gave startled cries and toppled off Triune's massive battlements as the man's killing burst billowed outward. They fell into the moat, and the water churned and darkened with blood as the mocker-fish made short work of them.

Dari's heart gave a stutter, then sank as she understood what was happening.

This fresh wave of Brailing Guard hadn't been on the battlefield when they began their charge. Led by the thin, bejeweled man with the meager but effective Brailing mind-talent, these soldiers were pouring from the woods ringing the valley.

The villain was here. Already at Triune.

Lord Brailing was coming for them, leading his army behind him.

Dari staggered as new *graal* energy slammed into her with the force of a battering ram.

She tried to push back, but the energy assaulting her had no real form or color or definition. Nothing she could understand or grasp to defend herself. It felt like wind howling into her face, pressing her backward, away from her grandfather, and then away from Stormbreaker and the other protectors still trying to fight for her safety.

Stormbreaker pitched off his talon, striking the ground limp and heavy, like he might have died before he fell. Energy rushed out of him in a glittering silvery wave. Two more Stone Brothers collapsed, turning their talons loose to feed on Brailing horses and soldiers.

More cries rose from the wooded edge of the valley, but Dari couldn't think well enough to sort them out. Men wrapped in veils and scarves, wielding the big, curved blades common to the Altar Barrens, stormed into view, but some of them broke away and stumbled as the formless *graal* overtook them as well. A few more retreated, dropping their blades and hurling themselves back toward the tree cover.

Aron reached Dari's side, but fell to his knees, his short sword and dagger dropping from his open fingers. His legacy flared brilliant sapphire, then went dim and began to spout from his body like an uncontrolled geyser. His eyes closed, and he collapsed at her feet.

Dari watched all this, saw every bit of it, but couldn't cry out or even lift her sword. Her head ached as if her skull had been dissolved. Her grandfather's protective energy broke around her, and she heard his pained, enraged shout. Once more, she could see *graal* coloring—the rainbow hues of her own energy, flowing straight out of her body.

Nic!

Her mental shout rose from her heart, her soul, flying against the energy beginning to crush her thoughts into so much dust and nothingness as she fell helpless to the battlefield before the sword-wielding Thorn Brothers.

Nic, help me!

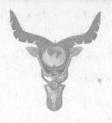

CHAPTER SIXTY-SIX

NIC

Dari's scream echoed through Nic's muscles and bones.

His teeth slammed together, his fists clenched, and he almost dropped to his knees in the midst of the halted traveling column of hundreds, maybe thousands of Mab horsemen, archers, and foot-soldiers.

In front of him, Snakekiller held a dagger to his mother's throat. Snakekiller's dark blue eyes had gone so flat Nic had no doubt she would enjoy spilling Lady Mab's blood at Nic's feet, to avenge the thousand pains he had suffered from her neglect.

How had this gone so wrong?

None of this had been in his visions.

Not the way he had used his *graal* to punch through the Mab lines. Those with no mind-talents never saw him, and those with legacy did, but knew him for who he was and fell away from him, fleeing what they thought was a ghost with the full measure of the Mab legacy.

Not the way he and Snakekiller set Tek free before soldiers could skewer her with pikes and reached his mother's personal guard on foot, or how Snakekiller's hood snake illusion sent the horses thundering away, dragging their riders with them, weapons and all. His mother had been thrown—which Nic had not foreseen, any more than he had caught a glimpse of the way his mother had drawn her silver dagger and tried to thrust it into his heart, her blue eyes wild with terror.

"Abomination," she had shrieked, taking him for a mane. "Monster!"

If Snakekiller hadn't grabbed Lady Mab, Nic might indeed be shifting into a mane.

"He's your son," Snakekiller was telling her. "Nic is not a mane or a ghost or some cruel illusion. He's your own blood, your heir."

"Dari," Nic said aloud, turning his head toward Triune's castle, where his wife and friends were now under some attack he couldn't sense or understand.

There was no way to divide his attention between his mother and Dari.

"Hold her another moment," Nic told Snakekiller, then closed his eyes and sent his mind blasting through the Veil.

The abrupt change in sights, smells, and sounds sent tremors through his physical body, and once more the sparks of a fit began to rise and flicker through his mind. Nic ignored this and struggled to move through the world carved over the world, until his awareness hovered over the madness spreading out around Triune.

A thick gray cloud of *graal* energy hovered above the battlefield, seemingly leeching the power and life out of everything beneath it. Nic could sense nothing below that cloud, and see very little beyond the cardinal red blaze of Thorn Guild robes. The color drew him like a beacon, but as he tried to drop his awareness through that strange gray fog, it repelled him like an iron shield.

His real body wavered again, but he made himself think of Dari, of the baby she didn't even know she was carrying. Of Aron and Stormbreaker, of Lord Baldric and Zed and Raaf and all the many people he had met at Triune. His *graal* surged back to him, driven by the rush of his emotion and his wish to protect those he loved. More sparks danced through his mind, and his muscles began to weaken so badly he wasn't sure he could hold his body upright.

Nic imagined his energy to be a thin red blade, and he stabbed his awareness downward at the cloud, aiming to reach the person he thought could help him the most.

Aron. But where was Aron?

Nic couldn't find him, even a hint of him.

The shield caught his energy again.

Held him.

Trapped.

Nic doubled his effort to rip his awareness free of the shield's grip, even though he didn't have the energy to support it.

How could he have left Dari—or Aron? Any of them?

What had he been thinking?

The essence of Nic's knees buckled, and he knew he was collapsing in the physical world. His thoughts twitched and jumped as the fit moved across his awareness—only to be driven back by a solid wave of silver and deep blue hues. Vagrat mind-talent, healing and strengthening. Cool, blue Brailing energy, very like Aron's but not Aron's, joined this flow—and red *graal*, Mab legacy, so blindingly ruby it made Nic blink on both sides of the Veil.

The shared energy washed into him, lifting him upward and helping him re-form his mental strength into the sharp, powerful point he needed. He spared no thought for the body he was leaving behind as he threw himself at the shield over Triune, this time bashing his way straight through to the other side.

The screams of children shattered through his consciousness, but he couldn't accept the reality of such young, tiny cries in a battle. It had to be some trick or illusion of whoever had mounted this *graal* attack.

Below him, soldiers slammed sword against sword along the walls of Triune and all through the valley. Arrows and stones flew through the air toward the castle. The Altar Guard was hammering down from the Barrens and Outlands, and Lord Cobb and his small group of Guard were charging up to meet them before they could crush what was left of the Ross Guard and the Stone Brothers on the battlefield.

Dozens upon dozens of soldiers wearing many different dynast uniforms lay dead. Still more had collapsed, many in front of the main gate and keep. *Graal* energy rose from them like colored rivers, flowing toward the covered carriage Aron had identified as Kate's location.

Dari . . .

Nic drew on all the knowledge he had absorbed from Dari, drawing yet more information from the minds and energies assisting him. He let his *graal* flow over the battlefield, lower than the menacing colorless shield, forming his own barrier and cutting off the flow of energy to that carriage.

Once more the shrieking cries of little children troubled his mind, but with another blast of determination, Nic reversed the flow even as the people he was shielding began to wake and lurch to their feet.

Nic located Dari, and in an instant he assessed her condition and used the healing energy at his disposal to reduce her pain and bring her back to nearly full strength. Lord Ross was next, and needed very little assistance to roar and grab his sword as he dragged himself up to stand beside his granddaughter. Nic went to Aron next, but reviving him was harder. More of his sapphire light had been taken from him, and Nic wasn't certain how much he had been able to return.

Children were screaming. Brother help him, they sounded so real he wanted to sob and reach out to them, hold them, cradle them, and put a halt to their misery.

Stop! Dari cried. *You're killing them. We're all killing them!*

Nic turned her loose, confident she was once more able to see to herself, especially with Lord Ross and Aron to assist her. Flickers of lightning let him know that Stormbreaker was coming back to himself—and there, near the carriage, multicolored energy, but not Dari's twin. Too different. Too strange.

This was mingled *graal*, many types, not fully differentiated, or even fully formed.

Many small wisps of consciousness.

Children?

Nic's question rippled through the Veil, along with the full force of disgust and horror he felt, followed by intense shame.

Had he just used his *graal* to crush the minds of babies?

He opened his eyes, shouting as he came back to himself. On either side, someone had hold of his arms, supporting his weight.

Snakekiller and his mother were no longer standing in front of him.

Nic automatically looked at the ground, searching for his mother's blood and body—but he saw nothing.

The billowing red clouds of his own *graal* dissipated enough for him to see the nearest Mab soldiers, standing in absolute silence, and seemingly in awe. He knew most of the higher-level fighters in Mab's army had enough legacy to see his, and to know it for what it was. That was probably all that had saved them thus far.

A few had removed their helms to look at him more closely.

"Steady," came Snakekiller's voice in one ear, and the command was so familiar that it helped him to marshal his strength and begin to find his balance again.

"Nicandro," was the whisper in the other, and Nic heard the rattle of his mother's voice, fragile but connected to his reality, at least for this one moment in time. "I know your energy. I know your essence. It's you. It could be no one else."

Snakekiller turned him loose to face his mother, and he managed to turn to her without falling. He could still feel the hot ruby energy she had lent him, part of what had kept him alive and beaten back the fit that tried to claim him as he saved Dari.

Lady Mab didn't let go of Nic's arm, and he felt her trembling grip tighten as her eyes widened. They were light steely blue, the color of a winter sky drenched in sunlight, and this day, at least, clear enough to make Nic believe she understood what was happening around her. Her pale blond ringlets were pulled tight into a bun, the stray strands held in place by her circlet with the red dragon head pendant dangling in the center of her lined forehead. From her neck to her feet she wore a fitted black leather tunic and skirt split and tied at her knees—the only proper fighting garb for a noble lady. The leather had been stitched with runes and etchings of dragons announcing the power and skill of Mab warriors. She also wore silver vambraces, though she had left her midsection unprotected to better wield the swords belted to her sides. At her waist, the bags holding the *chevilles* of her dead children and husband hung like the poisons and elixirs and stones carried by Stone.

"You fell," she said, reaching her free hand up to trail her fingers across Nic's scarred cheek even as her fingernails pressed through his tunic into the scant meat of his forearm.

"I was pushed," he said, distracted by her touch, and the warmth and tortured surprise in her voice. "I think I flew."

Lady Mab didn't challenge this. She just kept staring at him as her many commanders pushed through Mab's ample ranks, drawing in for a closer look at the young man who had just given them such a huge display of the Mab legacy.

"My son!" she cried out to them. "Nicandro Mab lives, and he returns to us this day." Then, more quietly, she added, "A grown man, tall, if scarred and crippled. You are the hob-prince no more."

"I am not," Nic said, surprised to realize that term seemed so strange to him now, "though in truth I cannot tell you what new nickname I'll earn for myself in the days to come." He wasn't certain what he was feeling, beyond increasing urgency to win his mother's allegiance and take her forces into the fight to save his wife and his friends. Was he as heart-cold as she was, to be thinking so simply, with no regard for her emotions or welfare?

Lady Mab's chilling gaze shifted to Snakekiller. "It was Stone that saved my son?"

Snakekiller's palm rested on the hilt of the dagger she had drawn in Nic's defense, now sheathed at her hip. "And hid him from the rectors who would have killed him."

At the mention of rectors, Lady Mab turned her head away from Nic and spit on the ground. When she looked back at him, madness had edged out some of the reason she had managed to capture and reflect in the cold blue depths of those eyes. "They're all dead. I had every rector in Dyn Mab put to the sword."

Nic's mouth drifted open, and he sensed Snakekiller tensing beside him. Beyond them, some of the commanders hung their heads, as if they knew what a monstrous crime this had been. They would have been helpless to stop it, short of outright rebellion against their own dynast leader—the crazed woman who was Eyrie's queen.

"All of them?" Nic whispered to his mother, growing numb inside at the thought of Temple doors ripped from their hinges, and the guilty and innocent alike slaughtered on the floors of their own churches.

His mother let go of him and folded her arms. "It had to be rectors who killed my children and my husband. Your father—your brothers and sisters! And when you fell from the tower under their care, I knew."

Nic still couldn't quite grasp her words, or believe them to be true. "But all of them? All over Dyn Mab?" He thought about Lord Brailing's Watchline massacre, and couldn't see a difference between the two deeds. "That would be hundreds."

"That many fewer traitors to nip at our flanks as we marched out to meet our enemies." His mother's eyes grew ever more narrow as she spoke. "Loyalty is a tricky thing, my son. Those who do not stand with you stand against you—which I'm sure by now you've realized."

Nic wondered if his mother had seen who he rescued when she lent him energy to stop the attack on Dari. He wanted to lift his leg and force her to stare at the second *cheville* he now wore to bind him to the granddaughter of the man his mother had hated, seemingly without reason, for most of her life. The man she had first blamed for the deaths of her family, and the dynast she had been crusading against despite attacks from other dynast armies.

"We have much to discuss later," he said. "For now I must know your intentions. When you take your forces onto the battlefield at Triune, against whom will you fight?"

Lady Mab gave him a look that said perhaps he was still slow in the mind, after all. "We will fight any who stand against us."

The commanders encircling them shifted. Armor rattled, and swords clattered. They didn't speak, but even at such a distance, Nic saw the anger on many of their faces.

"Lord Brailing and Lord Altar attacked you." Nic tried to hold himself together, but he was feeling smaller by the second, his own thoughts beginning to swim as he tried to reason with his mother's twisted perceptions and irrational plans.

How many times had he done this in his life?

And had he ever succeeded?

"Helmet Brailing is a doddering fool," his mother announced, straightening her vambraces. "Bolthor Altar would never harm me."

"Until they broke off attacks to head for Triune to capture or kill a friend of mine, their armies were ravaging Dyn Mab's country-side." Nic heard himself speaking, his words choked off by pain in his heart and his body, too. This was too much. He couldn't reach her. Why had he thought anything might be different now?

I might as well climb the nearest tower and leap off. That would do as much good as talking to her.

The thought passed through his mind more than once as she kept speaking.

"Kembell Ross is another matter. With his Sabor, he could be a threat like no other, the one dynast lord who could take the throne from us." She patted Nic's arm like he was little more than a child. "That's what you must remember."

The Sabor would never participate in treachery, even at Lord Ross's command. They were loyal allies, but not oathbreakers. Nic kept this to himself, saying only, "Lord Ross battles on the side of Stone and Cobb—and Mab as well. He has nearly given his life to see me safely this far."

"He's treacherous. Don't let him fool you, my boy." Another pat. His mother's eyes were growing distant again, as if she might be listening to warped visions instead of Nic.

Snakekiller's frown was so intense Nic could tell she wanted to try a dose of elixir on his mother, to see if the medicine might calm Lady Mab's madness enough to make her see reason.

He knew better.

His mother was about to lead a force of thousands into a war she didn't even understand how to fight, though her commanders seemed to have a fair enough grasp. Nic tried to read their faces, to make eye contact with each one and determine what they planned to do, irrespective of her orders.

If he seized his mother, or had Snakekiller take her again, would they defend her?

Nic didn't even know if he and Snakekiller could hold her if she poured the force of her insanity into the powerful *graal* that was his legacy from her.

The risk was too great.

He was certain that if Lady Mab had been a man, and if she had possessed even a measure less *graal* to allow for vulnerability, one of these commanders would have killed her by now, whether or not she had a viable heir.

How many would act against her wishes and come over to him, when Lady Mab still lived, still ruled Eyrie and wielded her will with brutality enough to slaughter hundreds of rectors in their Temples, just to weed out a handful of traitors?

"Ride with me," he said to the commanders, though his mother thought he was speaking to her. "Ride with me to save those who gave me aid—and to save Eyrie."

"Of course I will," his mother said, unaware of his dual purpose.

Of the dozens of men who could hear him, at least half gripped the hilts of their swords in silent assent.

As for the others, Nic had no idea if they meant to follow her command or his. Their eyes and faces gave no indication of their intentions, and he couldn't blame them. If he died in battle and his mother lived, she would kill them all and their families, too, if she thought they hadn't given her proper service.

She might kill them all anyway, no matter what the outcome.

"Bring my son a horse!" Lady Mab shouted, and Nic heard the movement in the ranks as a battle steed was passed forward for his use.

He turned to see the horse just as his mother pointed to Snakekiller. "As for her, this Stone Sister who put a blade to my throat—kill her."

"No!" Nic yelled, turning so quickly he lost his balance and smashed to the ground at his mother's feet. He loosed his *graal* in a fierce burst, using all he knew to shield Snakekiller and drive back anyone who meant her harm.

A burst of silver-blue light exploded around him and the advancing soldiers, deflecting his *graal* and knocking the soldiers aside like so many armored gnats.

Where Snakekiller had been, a huge hood snake reared, taller than a heartwood and thicker around its coiled midsection.

The great beast opened its fanged mouth and struck, terrifying its attackers. Many threw down weapons and backed away, hands raised.

Nic wanted to shout, to shift into some monster himself and roar beside her, taking down anyone who dared to do her harm. He had no idea if this was illusion or some secret skill Snakekiller had nurtured, telling no one of her full and deadly potential. And he didn't care.

When the big snake launched itself over the heads of the fighters who would have killed it, when those fighters lunged aside to save themselves, he did shout.

By the time Nic managed to pull himself to his feet, Snakekiller was gone, leaving a swath of bloodied soldiers on their knees in her wake.

"We'll deal with her later," Lady Mab said, oblivious to Nic's attempts to pull free the light sword he carried. She grabbed the stallion meant for him as it tried to run by her, using her legacy and the unnatural strength granted to her by insanity to stop the beast and bring it to the ready for his use.

Nic stopped struggling with his sword and snatched the reins away from her. She commandeered a horse for herself as he bit back shouts of pain and hauled himself into the stallion's saddle, intent on finding Snakekiller, then Dari and Aron. If some of the Mab commanders came with him, so be it. If they didn't, then he hoped they fell in battle right beside his mother, or what was left of the woman who once was Lady Mab.

"Ride with me!" she shrieked, to Nic, to the commanders, to all the soldiers who could hear her as her *graal* swelled above her like a deadly red cloud. "I see our future. I see it clearly and it's there, over that rise, in the valley below. Ride against Ross. Ride to Triune!"

Before Nic could react or speak against her, the great tide that was the army of Mab swept him up in a clatter of hooves and shields and swords, battle-cries ringing as they rode.

CHAPTER SIXTY-SEVEN

ARON

"Can you hold them?" Stormbreaker asked as he and Aron took down the last of the Thorn Brothers who had attacked them, sending their barbed swords flying into the moat around Triune. One of the men toppled to one of the many sets of hammered boards that had been used to breach the waters and carry attackers closer to the castle.

"Can you stop those children?" Stormbreaker shouted again, sounding more urgent as he engaged two charging Brailing soldiers, dispatching one with a cut to the throat and another with a spinning stab to the gut. He used his lightning to shield Dari and Lord Ross, who were battling beside him, as fierce as any five Stone Brothers, dealing death like assassins born to the task as Lord Cobb shouted and slammed his blade against foes on the other side of the mocker-filled waters, doing what he could to reach them.

Lord Brailing and his forces were advancing nonetheless, riding and running, moving ever closer, like a blue tide of destiny.

Above them, on Stone's battlements, Lord Baldric barked orders and bellowed commands to shove away ladders and shore up damage done by catapulted stones. Blazing arrows sailed above them like crazed, burning birds. Smoke almost blinded Aron, and he couldn't smell anything but mud and fish and the stink of molten tallow ready to spill through the castle's murder holes. His arms ached from stabbing, thrusting, slicing, and the dozen wounds he had taken across his shoulders and elbows. Yet he was supposed to concentrate. He was supposed to go through the Veil.

And attack children.

Bile surged up his throat as his shoulders struck the stone walls of Triune.

He stared at the group of children on the other side of the moat, huddled next to the overturned carriage. Sixteen or so tiny bodies were still standing, and being reassembled by four Thorn Brothers who had thrown down their weapons and refused to join the battle around them.

At first glance, they seemed to be protecting the little ones, but Aron's *graal* told him differently. They were readying the children to launch another attack. He thought about striking down the Thorn Brothers, but what would happen to those children then?

"Where is my sister?" Dari shrieked, beheading a Brailing soldier who had leaped from the nearest moat breach. The man's head rolled into the moat, where a mocker-fish shifted to human form long enough to grab it and haul it below the water's surface.

"Where is she, Aron? I can't find her. Why can't I see her?"

Aron made it through the Veil, trusting Stormbreaker's blades and weather to keep his body alive as he tried to figure a way to block the inhuman *graal* these children were bringing to bear. If they joined their energies again, Aron didn't think he could stop them. Not without Nic, if Nic was even still alive. Not without every bit of mind-talent he possessed, plus the loan of some of the strongest abilities in Eyrie.

His awareness seized on the first child, a boy, maybe five years, maybe six. Blond and blue-eyed like Nic, with the slight build of a Mab child in his formative years.

Powerful *graal*, trained, yet unformed, threatened to burst from the boy and overwhelm Aron.

Stop, Aron commanded, careful to focus on the energy, not the child's life essence.

For a moment, the boy's mind-talent faded to a dull shade of pink, but a shock of copper energy made the boy's essence twitch. He redoubled his efforts, rudimentary but effective, with a child's single-minded focus.

Aron held fast against the blast of red *graal*, already separating himself from the child's attack and searching for the source of that copper energy. Altar *graal*, but joined with other colors.

Who did that? Aron demanded, letting the question rise and flow through the Veil. *Who just struck this child's mind?*

His awareness soared over the battlefield, taking in a new rush of fighters, veiled and primitive, disorganized but crushing toward the moat as they swung curved silver blades. Aron couldn't discern who they were attacking. Everyone, it seemed, save for the children and their Thorn handlers. These new menaces seemed only to want to reach the spot where Aron's body sagged against Stone's fortress.

Stormbreaker's thunder exploded through the Veil, making some of them stumble, and Dari's Stregan *graal*, shielded in the forceful green of her grandfather's energy, pounded forward, knocking more to their backsides.

Aron tore his thoughts from the spectacle and chased after whoever was communicating with the freakish children stranded on the battlefield in front of Triune. He drove his energy toward the wisp of copper *graal* retreating into the nothingness of the void at the edge of the Veil.

Show yourself, he demanded, flinging a tendril of his own mind-talent outward with the full force of his legacy. *Show me where you are!*

A scream of rage answered him, and a figure came tumbling out of the void, as if someone had fastened it to a catapult and fired.

It landed, ghostlike and shrieking, near enough for him to make out familiar features.

The tall frame.

The wisps of blond hair. The blue eyes, cornflower but blazing with hatred.

As Aron's false goddess lifted both hands to the sides of her head, he roared and struck at her with his sapphire energy. She absorbed the blow, but staggered and dragged at the multicolored energy supporting her own.

"Stop!" Aron shouted, intent on severing Pravda Altar's connection with Kate, and stopping the evil woman's mind and heart as well. Before his bolt of *graal* reached her, she fell straight through the Veil, down, down to the woods closest to the fallen carriage below.

Her location glowed a brilliant copper and silver, ringed by a rainbow, as obvious to Aron as if someone had struck a flint to the land's largest funeral pyre. Then a gray shield of formless energy sprang over the spot, covering it and preventing him from sinking down to take hold of Thorn's Lady Provost.

Aron swore and forced his awareness back into his own body.

"She's in the woods," he called to Dari and Lord Ross, forcing his voice above the raging clatter of swords. "They're in the woods nearest the carriage—but hurry. I don't know how long before they bolt. The children have them shielded."

Beside him, Stormbreaker spun, both jagged blades moving with the speed of his lightning. Veiled bandits poked and struck at him from all sides, but with each step, he drove them back, back toward the moat, and the eager, hungry mockers waiting below the churning surface.

Dari and Lord Ross stormed forward onto the nearest moat breach, and Lord Cobb thundered toward them, chopping a path through Brailing warriors as his few remaining Guardsmen did the same on either side.

Aron turned his focus to the children, but before he could select a course of action, shadows crossed his vision. Huge shapes wheeled in the sky above Triune.

His pulse raced as he prayed this would be the Sabor, arriving with Cobb and Ross reinforcements—but this cloud of screeching motion was coming in from the wrong direction. Great wings battered the air, swooping down from the west, from the direction of the Barrens and Outlands, and Dyn Altar.

"Rocs!" Stormbreaker shouted. "Rocs carrying warbird soldiers!"

Above them, Stone Brothers took up the call on the battlements, and Lord Baldric bellowed, "Take cover! Take cover now, now, now! Where are my archers?"

Aron counted ten massive birds diving toward the battlefield, each overmastered by a thin but well-disciplined cloud of coppery *graal.* Each carried four to six Altar warriors, swords gleaming and flaming arrows ready to fire. The first bird dived behind Stone's battlements, breaching the fortress as no battering ram or ladder or tunnel had been able to do.

Aron ripped his focus from the children across the moat and attacked the *graal* controlling the Rocs.

Exhaustion swept over him as he took on that sharply focused energy and the wild impulses of the birds themselves. It felt like slamming his head into Triune's walls, and he couldn't stay on his feet as he cracked through first one copper cloud, then the next. Aron's vision blurred on both sides of the Veil. Dirt brushed against his lips as he toppled belly first to the berm, close enough to the water's edge to hear the snapping jaws of fish creatures only a few feet from his face.

He beat at the tiny but deadly mockers, feeling needle-teeth lance into his fingers as he used his mind to tear apart the soldiers' control of the Rocs. At least two birds made it through into Triune's grounds, but Aron ripped open the *graal* driving seven others, and Stone's archers brought down the eighth. The massive bird plummeted to the ground near the overturned carriage, landing in a crash of feathers and armors and swords. Some of Brailing's Guard fell beneath the bird's bulk, but not enough.

Aron heard an old man's shrill cry, and saw a thin, reedy soldier dressed in Brailing colors, wearing a sapphire-studded helm with eagle's wings, wading through the Brailing Guard unhorsed.

Distant memories stirred inside Aron's mind, and he knew the soldier for who he was.

His sapphire-crusted sword hilt raised, Lord Brailing bore down on Lord Cobb, Lord Ross, and Dari, who were just breaking free of the moat breach and starting across the main battlefield toward Kate's last-known location.

Dark, bleak hatred surged through Aron, familiar and seemingly as old as Lord Brailing himself. He tried to rise to stop the monster from robbing him of his family a second time, but the most he could do was pull his bleeding, bitten fingers into fists. He was spent, and even as Stormbreaker hauled him to his feet and shared some of his furious, storming *graal* with Aron, Aron couldn't muster the force to hurl a single command at the person who had torn his life and heart asunder.

The banditlike men Stormbreaker had been battling had turned away from him, inexplicably raising their swords to drive back the Brailing Guard who managed to make it across the moat. Above them, freed and furious, seven Great Rocs winged back into the sky away from the human tumult below. They turned their great necks and beaks on those who had sought to use them for unnatural purpose, and for a time, it rained swords and arrows and screaming Altar soldiers.

Brailing and Altar forces flooded past the fallen men, filling all available space, overrunning the remnants of Ross and Cobb protectors and beginning to surround Dari, her grandfather, and Lord Cobb.

From within Triune came screaming and the shrieks of the Rocs who made it through the defenses.

A body struck the ground beside Aron, and his knees buckled all over again as he beheld the large, twisted form of Lord Baldric. With his neck at such a terrible angle, there was no way the man could be alive, but Stormbreaker cried out and threw himself on the ground. He worked his fingers over the Lord Provost's chest as if he could force life back into his former mentor and guild master. Lightning struck in every direction, indiscriminate, felling bandits and Brailings alike, and barely missing Aron twice.

The sky darkened again, and Aron shouted a curse at the Brother in hopeless frustration. He couldn't even lift his short sword yet, and his bloody fingers didn't have the coordination to unsheathe his silver dagger.

This time, the threat poured in from the Eastern sky.

Winged creatures, so many they darkened the ground like clouds of doom.

It took Aron long moments to realize that the golden, winged beasts were gryphons, bearing soldiers clad in Ross's greens and golds, and the obsidian and ruby uniforms of Dyn Cobb.

Almost at the same moment, a massive mounted force crested the farthest hill of the valley, the hill opposite the spot where Aron and the Stone Brothers had charged into the battle.

Aron picked out the banners, and saw Mab's ruby colors, and the great red dragon's head seeming to roar from their battle flags.

In the front rode a small figure, a woman on horseback, and he could see the wild stream of red *graal* floating behind her.

The *graal* wasn't . . . normal.

It exploded in bursts and spouts, uneven and as uncontrolled as Stormbreaker's weather.

Just behind her came an essence Aron recognized as Nic.

Riding into battle.

Riding into battle with his mother.

The shock of seeing Nic on horseback with the Mab army, looking so strong and brandishing a sword, nearly drove Aron back to the ground.

For a moment, Aron thought Nic was whipping the Mab forces to a frenzy, but then he realized Nic seemed to have some other purpose.

Brother save them.

Was Nic trying to reach his mother to cut her out of her saddle?

A snake the size of two Rocs arched from the woods to strike at Lady Mab, but it overshot its target and took down Nic and his mount as well.

Aron wasn't certain he really saw that—a giant snake. A giant snake attacking Eyrie's queen and heir. It was there, then gone.

And so were Nic and his mother.

Aron fell forward, desperate to send his energy to Nic, but unable to even maintain his own body weight. He dragged himself in the direction of where Nic fell, but that was so far away, and Aron couldn't see anything but the moat and soldiers and swords and blood.

Sabor and Cobb and Ross Guard landed like saviors in every direction, but the Mab forces engaged them as fast as they took on Altar and Brailing soldiers. The gryphons screamed and roared, stamping and flinging soldiers out of their paths.

Aron rolled onto his back, gasping, fighting to control the faltering beat of his heart as gray, formless energy washed over him.

The children.

The children had caught him unaware.

Their leeching would kill him in moments.

He stared into the sky, watching the last of the pounding cloud of gryphons sailing in from the east. Maybe these would make the difference. Maybe these Sabor and soldiers could turn the tide and save Triune and Nic and Eyrie, maybe even Dari and Lord Ross and Lord Cobb, even if Aron was beyond assistance.

The energy attacking him shimmered, then shifted away. He saw the little children running, herded by their handlers, making off toward the trees with the *graal* force they had stolen.

Seconds later, an ear-splitting roar overrode the chaos on the battlefield.

Aron's pulse stilled, and he wondered if that sound would be the last he ever heard.

He didn't need to see the creature to know what it was, but it filled his vision, covering all of the empty sky before his eyes.

A scaled, long-necked beast the size of a castle tower—one he had seen before.

This dragon was stark white, and its barbed tail seemed polished and sharp. Its outstretched wings pumped once, stirring debris on the ground, which bounced and struck soldiers who had gone as still as stone monuments. Brilliant black eyes surveyed the battlefield, and the dragon's mouth opened to show its curved teeth just before it let out a blast of fire that reached from the woods to the stones of Triune's castle.

As the flames died away, only silence remained.

Aron turned his neck for glimpses of the battlefield. It seemed as though all the soldiers had stopped riding, stopped clawing and fighting, from Mab to Brailing to Cobb. Altar warbird soldiers lowered their hammers and pikes and swords. Ross Guardsmen backed away, green *graal* energy shoving outward to be taken by the children—as if it would have made a difference against a Stregan in full battle fury.

The white dragon flapped its massive, leathery wings again, rising higher above the conflagration. When it roared, Aron's muscles jittered as the animal instincts left to him tried to answer that call. It was *graal*, yet natural. Energy, but also spirit, almost tangible. The children didn't seem to be able steal it or to stop it.

Why would they?

This was Lady Pravda's ultimate weapon.

Kate. A Stregan maddened by illness, then by cycles of captivity and misuse.

In her arrogance, Thorn's Lady Provost had thought she could control such a force, but Aron suspected she had no idea what she had done.

Kate's cry was a power unto itself.

It was a summons, and a warning.

The few talons left standing on the battlefield let out terrified bugles, and charged away behind fleeing horses. Aron thought he saw Tek amongst them, riderless and frightened, still swiveling her massive head as if she was searching for him.

Go, he thought, wishing he could command her. *Save yourself.*

From the mists of the Deadfall, the sands of the Barrens, and the rocky land of the Outlands came the wails of manes and mockers and rock cats, the screams of Great Rocs still infuriated by their enslavement, the howls of wolves and jackals and other creatures Aron couldn't even identify.

A hand closed on Aron's forearm, and Stormbreaker's silvery energy dribbled into his own, giving Aron enough power to pull himself to a sitting position.

Stormbreaker was on his knees beside Aron, head sagging. "She's . . . calling them," he said, the words barely squeezing out of his throat. "The manes and mockers and predators. She's a ruler of beasts, and she's calling them . . . to kill us all."

"Kate!" came Dari's wavering cry, and Aron heard the resonance in that single syllable.

Dari, yet not Dari.

Kate's cries were rousing her Stregan instincts as well, punching through her exhaustion and the damage done by the children. In her weakened mental and physical state, what could Dari do but answer that call, and save her own life?

Nic's earlier words rushed back to Aron.

If you join the battle as a Stregan, only death will come of it. . . . Don't shift, for the sake of us all.

"Don't do it, Dari," Aron shouted, on both sides of the Veil, but his words had no *graal* force behind them—and it was too late.

A second dragon, this one also white but with black *benedet*-like swirls on its massive clawed forelegs, rose to greet its twin in the skies above Triune.

"She is lost," Stormbreaker whispered, unable to loose so much as a rumble of thunder or a drop of rain as soldiers began to shout and arrows began to fly at the Stregans. "And we are lost with her."

The two massive dragons blasted great gouts of flame toward the woods, burning the trees down around Pravda Altar and her quaking child protégés. Aron winced and Stormbreaker sobbed as the children fell. Aron hoped that the little ones felt only the briefest pain before the heat rendered them to ash beside their mistress.

Energy returned to him in small measures, then more, and more, as the pall exerted by Lady Pravda and those poor children evaporated with their life essence. A crackle of lightning let him know Stormbreaker was feeling relief as well, though the price of that relief was far too terrible to consider.

Dari and Kate turned their assault on the rogue energy of Lady Mab's *graal*. Likely no one would ever know which twin actually killed Eyrie's queen, if any human walked away from this battle to debate the issue.

Nic . . .

It was Aron's turn to sob, for he saw no flare of Mab's ruby-red energy, save for the weak issue of Mab's many soldiers, who seemed to be scattering in disarray.

Aron cried for Nic, for Dari, and for Kate, and for the children he had never even known. The twins had no understanding of what they were doing, or of the arrows tearing into their wings and flesh. When they fell—and they would, if they didn't flee—Aron didn't think he could survive the pain.

"Take what I have left," Stormbreaker begged, thrusting his *graal* energy toward Aron, intending to give his life to allow Aron enough power to do something to help Dari, or maybe Lord Cobb, who had roused his forces to battle back a surging host of mockers and rock cats and wolves. Humanlike monstrosities spit poison, striking holes in armor and Sabor fur—and Lord Ross had locked swords with Lord Brailing, their Guard scattering to get out of the way of the fierce battle.

Aron hated himself for taking Stormbreaker's energy, but he let the essence of lightning, thunder, and rain flow into his mind, his muscles, his essence. He fought his way to his feet, dragging Storm-breaker with him. They clung to each other as those tiny children might have done in their last moments.

"Let me fall, Aron," Stormbreaker said, trying to pull free of him, but Aron wouldn't turn him loose. "If you don't let me fall, you can't save her."

Aron couldn't do it. He couldn't kill Stormbreaker even to save Dari. Tears flowed down his face and through his essence—until Stormbreaker was ripped from his grasp. Aron stumbled but man-aged to draw his short sword as Stormbreaker crashed to the ground near the moat.

A tall man dressed in dark robes towered over Stormbreaker's fallen form. He had an old military sword raised in one hand, and in the other, he hoisted a great curved blade to hack Stormbreaker's head from his shoulders. The man's fingers were red and scarred, but Aron could see nothing of his face, because the man had wrapped himself like a Barrens sand-farmer.

"Bandit!" Aron cried, striking the man with a burst of his *graal* energy, and spending most of it in that instant. His hand dropped to the belt at his waist, the one holding the pebble with the runes naming his first Judged. "Canus the Bandit. If you touch him, you'll die where you stand."

CHAPTER SIXTY-EIGHT

NIC

The world made sense to Nic, but only in moments and pieces.

Visions flooded his consciousness as the spark of his *graal* tried to reignite, failed, then sparked again.

Had he suffered a fit?

But no, he was not in Snakekiller's wagon, or in his bed in the Stone infirmary. He was in a field on a hillside, lying next to his mother.

A moment later, Nic remembered more.

When he rolled over and touched his mother's burned face, he knew she was dead, but he didn't know if he was sorry.

The feral cries in the skies above him punched at his mind, but he couldn't focus on them, couldn't hold on to their meaning.

Mab soldiers ran past him, and he realized their ranks were breaking and falling into chaos.

They would be no help in this battle. Thanks to his mother's madness, the soldiers couldn't name their enemies, much less destroy them. There was something he had to do, but his *graal* seemed so sluggish he couldn't call out to Aron or Dari for help, or even put his task into words. His mind-talent reached out for anyone and anything that might help him, making contact with more beasts than people, but maybe that was all right. Maybe a beast was what he needed.

Minutes later, or maybe longer, a blast of snot covered his face, and Tek bumped him with her big, square nose.

Nic reached up and grabbed her thick neck, willing himself to his feet, and somehow forcing his twisted body onto her back. His muscles burned, and his bones popped and cracked with each movement. More than once, he screamed aloud as he settled himself into the talon's saddle.

"Get me to the main gate and keep," he told her, pulling at her one remaining rein until her head turned in the correct direction. "There's something I have to do."

Tek gave a frightened trumpet, but she stomped forward, pushing through Mab soldiers, brushing past gryphons and Guardsmen, and dodging blasts of fire from the sky.

Nic's thoughts swam back and forth, but he saw little, and made sense of even less. His mind showed him his path, Eyrie's path, and all he could do was follow it.

CHAPTER SIXTY-NINE

ARON

Fire strafed the ground near the moat, setting the water to boil and cooking corpses and mocker-fish alike.

Aron and Canus the Bandit both leaped away from the destruction, but Aron never took his eyes from his quarry.

With one hand, Aron dragged Stormbreaker away from the water's edge, enough to be certain the remaining water-bound mockers wouldn't kill him. His *graal* was nowhere near strong enough to reach out to Dari, and he didn't think he could have much impact on the battle at hand.

Flashes of silver at the far edges of the woods caught Aron's attention, and a glistening wave of energy rippled out from the trees. It took Aron a moment to understand that the wave was actually made of people, tall and light-skinned and unarmed, dressed in simple cloth instead of armor. Led by Rakel Seadaughter, the citizens of Dyn Vagrat—nearly all of them, it looked like—flowed onto the battlefield and spread out amongst the fallen, reaching to minister to wounds and suffering.

Almost at the same moment, Canus the Bandit lowered his blades. When his attention shifted to the rise on the side of the valley behind Aron, Aron figured it for a ruse.

Then he heard the shouts from the battlefield, and the change in the cries of the dragons.

Turning himself so he could see both Canus and the rise, Aron noticed what looked like a hundred golden-skinned, leather-clad people standing along the hilltop that had given him his first view of Triune, and his full understanding of the destruction the castle now faced. His senses sharpened, and his *graal* told him that none of these people were armed.

His instincts led him to focus more closely on one man, who stood slightly forward. Aron let his awareness slide through the Veil, and his enhanced sight showed him a familiar leather tunic, stitched with the ruby image of a dragon in flight.

The man seemed to sense Aron's presence, and he nodded as if in greeting.

It is, in part, for you that we are here, Aron Weylyn.

The voice was so quiet that Aron wasn't positive he heard it, but the light in the man's eyes made him more certain. *You, and your friend Nic. If Fae like you have returned to this land, perhaps we shall find our place amongst you.*

Dari and Kate let off a fresh round of screams, sounds that dug so deeply into Aron he couldn't answer the man. He could barely keep his senses as Dari's cousin Platt raised his hand, and his host of Stregan warriors charged down the hill, forms shifting with each step they took.

"Brother save us," said someone, maybe even Canus the Bandit. "They're Stregans, too. They've come to protect their own."

A talon ran past Aron, and at the same moment, a battering ram once more struck the gates of Triune.

"Tek?" Aron called, but the talon didn't slow. Her rider was wreathed in a red so ruby-rich and deep Aron knew it had to be Nic, but that made no sense to him.

With a great cracking groan, the beleaguered wood finally gave way, just in time to admit Tek and Nic, and a host of Altar warbirds behind them.

As the skies of Eyrie exploded with fire-breathing dragons, Canus the Bandit fled past Aron toward the ruined gates, as if he were chasing after Nic and Tek, or maybe the Altar soldiers.

It took Aron a moment to react, but he started running, too.

To reach Tek and Nic.

To pursue the Bandit.

To escape the fire raining down on the battlefield—he really didn't know.

Aron just ran, brandishing his short sword before him.

CHAPTER SEVENTY

DARI

Dari came back to herself on the ground, with her cousin Platt beside her, holding her hand and guiding her quickly through her transition.

Kate had landed with them, and was also fast returning to her human form.

Dari gave a cry at how thin her twin was, and how fragile she seemed, then she let go of her cousin and wrapped her sobbing twin in her arms. For long moments, Dari could do nothing but savor their connection even as she searched through the Veil for some hint of her husband and grandfather, or of Aron, or Stormbreaker.

Graal energy was still so muted from the attack of the children Thorn had stolen and trained for their own purposes. Dari wondered what had become of the poor little creatures. They were dead, surely, and if so, Dari hoped Lady Pravda had perished with them.

Stregans still in dragon-form surrounded them, an impenetrable wall of claws and teeth and fire. Beyond them, Sabor formed ranks in their gryphon forms, adding another layer of protection. No arrow or spear or pike would penetrate this wall of flesh and scales and fur.

Dari located her grandfather and joined her energy with his just in time to feel the rattling jolt of sword on bone.

Through her grandfather's eyes, Dari watched as Lord Brailing's helm flew off.

The old wretch spewed blood from between his pale lips, then fell forward as Lord Ross yanked his blade free of the man's half-severed neck.

Kate and Dari snarled together, one sound, both human and Stregan, welcoming this victory, and letting Lord Ross know they were both alive and safe.

His shout of joy rang across the battlefield, and across the Veil.

Dari felt the shifts in energy as Platt directed and controlled the Stregans with his *graal*, working with their untamed energy, never allowing them to break free and feed on friends as well as foes. He dispersed most of the manes and mockers and beasts tearing into the armies of Eyrie. Those creatures attacking Brailing and Altar forces, he left alone, except to make certain they didn't advance on the soldiers of Dyn Cobb or Dyn Ross.

Dyn Mab's soldiers were the most numerous, but seemingly the most confused. They attacked without sense or direction, both a menace and a help, and Dari couldn't understand their purpose as they plunged the battlefield back into absolute chaos.

Platt's dark eyes weren't focused on anything save for the main gate and keep of Triune. "You're with child," he said, matter-of-fact, and Dari turned Kate loose when she realized Platt was speaking to her.

Her hand moved to her belly, and Kate's hand slid across hers. Kate's dark eyes widened as they both took in the stirring of life in Dari's womb.

"A son," Kate whispered. "A son with powerful *graal*. Stregan and Mab energy joined together—just as the rectors tried to do during the mixing disasters, but failed so many times." She paused, then added, "That's good, Dari. For us, for Eyrie, I think."

Platt grunted his agreement, then pointed to the tallest point on the right tower of the main gate and keep. "Would that be the father?"

Dari's gaze whipped toward the tower, and her awareness leaped through the Veil.

Nic.

Cayn's mercy.

Her husband was perched on the tallest point of the tower's roof.

Nic! she called across the Veil, but he didn't seem to hear her. His mind was so focused on his task that he had closed out the rest of the world.

As Dari watched, clinging to Kate and crying out with all the force left in her body, Nic spread his arms and leaped off Triune's tower.

CHAPTER SEVENTY-ONE

NIC

Air blasted against Nic's face and body, tearing at his skin, his senses, his mind as he dropped toward the hard battlefield ground below.

His stomach lurched upward, just like before, like the weightless blankness nothingness that took him when he sailed off the castle turret at Can Rowan.

What happened then was clear to him now.

I reached for something and grabbed hold of the future.

I called the future to me.

And I flew.

The ground seemed closer, and closer still.

He doubled his fists.

The miracle had to happen again, before he died, before Mab's soldiers killed their countrymen and one another, before Eyrie descended into war after war, until there was nothing left but death and suffering.

If Nic didn't unite his people, no one would.

The muscles in his back tore and ripped, and Nic shouted from the fresh agony, suspended in time, but not in space.

He threw the force of his will behind his intent, and with every bit of *graal* available to him, he pulled Eyrie's future into his mind, into his essence. He let the future explode from the cells of his body, from his fingertips and toes, from his screaming mouth and disintegrating bones.

Heat rushed through him like the wind, transforming him into something beyond his own flesh.

Nic felt himself shifting, like a Sabor or a Stregan, only this shift made him more of what he was, what he was supposed to be, what all Fae were meant to be.

Brilliant ruby light bathed him.

He heard the shouts below as he almost struck the ground—then swept upward into the waiting sky.

CHAPTER SEVENTY-TWO

ARON

On the battlements of Triune, standing between the bodies of two Altar warbird soldiers he had just slain, Aron's short sword slipped from his numbed, damaged fingers. The blade clattered off the battlements to the courtyard below, coming to rest beside more dead soldiers and the bloody carcass of a Great Roc, upon which Tek was happily feasting.

He couldn't believe what he was seeing.

Nic, spreading a pair of massive wings and taking flight over the battlefield.

The wings seemed so fragile, like they might be made of gossamer and silken feathers, but they lifted him higher, higher, over soldiers who were shouting and pointing and throwing down their swords.

Sabor shifted back to human form.

So did Stregans.

In moments, it seemed all of Eyrie had focused its attention on the sky, on the first Fae with wings the land had known since the mixing disasters robbed them of their heritage and legacies.

Nic's ruby glow was so powerful Aron knew that the colors could be seen on either side of the Veil, likely even by those who had no mind-talents at all. The magnitude of that power drew Aron's senses through the Veil, and heightened his awareness of every detail of the tableau below him.

The Mab soldiers stopped fighting, dropped to one knee, and lowered their heads, placing one fist on their chest in a gesture of fealty to this, their new dynast lord and king. Cobb and Ross soldiers knelt with them, and many from Altar and Brailing as well.

With his Veil-enhanced sight, Aron picked out Bolthor Altar standing beside the body of a woman on the far hillside. The body's burned features were beyond recognition, but not the ruby dragon head pendant still clinging to her ruined forehead.

This was Lady Mab, Nic's mother, whom Aron believed had been struck down by some sort of giant snake, then finished off by Dari or Kate when they attacked the hillside in their Stregan forms.

Bolthor Altar threw his blade to the ground beside Lady Mab's body, sank down beside the dead woman, put his face in his hands, and began to cry.

On the field stretching below him, his sons were being taken into custody by Mab and Cobb and Ross commanders, and none were resisting. Lord Brailing's heirs were nowhere to be seen, and Aron figured all of them for dead.

Before his eyes, Eyrie had just changed, and changed forever, moving back to a better time, yet forward toward the future Nic was calling to them with the magnificence of his *graal* and the wondrous flapping of his wings.

Stormbreaker stirred, unable to come to consciousness until Aron lent him a bit of energy. When he opened his eyes and saw Nic floating above him, it seemed too much for the man, and he passed out cold even with Aron trying to help him stay awake.

Dari stood with her twin in a circle of Stregans, and Aron almost connected with her—but her twin caught his attention instead. Kate was gazing at him, her mind open and welcoming as he joined his essence with hers. So familiar, like Dari, but different as well.

Warm and soft, without the prickly edges he had come to associate with Dari. Without thinking about it, Aron offered Kate a portion of his energy to help keep her mind settled, and she gratefully accepted it.

I'm glad you didn't kill me, Kate said, and Aron felt very glad of that, too. More than ever, he understood Dari's drive to save Kate, and why Lord Ross and even Platt, the king of the Stregans, would take such risks to protect her even though she had periods of madness. Perhaps he could help her with those difficult times, if she wished him to do so.

Yes, he was glad to know Kate, and to see Dari safe, and to see Nic so transformed. Aron was even happy, despite all the death wrought by this terrible battle. He felt happy for everything in the universe until a moment later, when Nic's amazing red glow sparked and faltered, and a fit seized him in midair.

The storm in Nic's mind moved so fast, so forcefully that Aron and Dari could do nothing to save him as he tumbled out of the sky.

Aron felt his insides plummeting to earth with Nic even as he yelled and grabbed the edges of the battlements, almost hurling himself outward to try to catch his friend.

Nic struck the ground with such force that stones and rock sprayed in every direction, sending soldiers and Sabor to their knees, faces covered to shield their eyes.

Dari's screams echoed through Aron's agonized mind as he tore his awareness out of the Veil and hurled himself past stunned Stone Brothers and Sisters, running toward the battlement's nearest stairs. He found the steps and pounded to the ground, bursting into the courtyard only to run headlong into a wall of blue *graal* energy that hit him so hard he tumbled backward.

Aron's grief and rage drove him to rip his dagger free of its sheath before he even got to his feet to locate his attacker.

There.

In the archway of the main gate and keep, retreating onto the byway.

Canus the Bandit took a few steps, then waited for Aron, his many veils and wraps flapping in the light-afternoon breeze.

Aron hated the man almost as much as he hated the sunlight that shouldn't be, that shouldn't exist, now that Nic had fallen. Aron's gaze shifted toward the opening that led to the battlefield and his friends, but he saw only *graal* energy, sapphire blue like his own.

The meaning was clear enough.

Canus the Bandit had the Brailing mind-talent, almost as strong as Aron's, and not depleted by battle and *graal* attacks.

The man intended for their combat to happen here and now, no matter what it cost Aron or Nic or anyone else.

Aron roared at the veiled man and hurtled toward him, pursuing him onto Triune's main byway.

First strike would be the last strike if Aron had his way, even if he had to carve the bastard into pieces with nothing but one slim silver dagger.

CHAPTER SEVENTY-THREE

ARON

Canus the Bandit ran with a speed and grace Aron didn't expect, and he had to push himself to near past his limits to keep pace. They pelted past the House of the Judged and farther into Triune, heading, it seemed, for the High Masters' Den.

The castle grounds seemed unnaturally still and quiet after the clamor of the battlefield. The crunch of boots grinding into rocks seemed to echo off the distant walls. Familiar smells washed over Aron. The soil of the fields, the stink of the barns. Old smoke from the forge, and a lingering yeasty sweetness drifting down from the main kitchens.

This was home, and this man was nothing more than a marauder, an invader no better than the Brotherless Altar soldiers who lay dead in the entrance courtyard.

At the last turn in the road, Canus broke to the right, and Aron gave chase, gripping his dagger so tightly that the hilt drew blood from his palm.

His senses were clearing with each step, and his *graal* strength growing.

Somehow, he wasn't surprised when the Bandit plunged off the main byway and made his way toward the ring of stones marking the Shrine of the Mother. It seemed a fitting place for this battle, and if the Goddess truly existed outside Pravda Altar's perversion of her likeness, perhaps she would watch this fight and bless Aron's victory.

Aron sprinted around the first monolith to find Canus waiting for him a few yards away, swords sheathed but a dagger already drawn and palmed. He raised it to the ready position.

Aron hurled his dagger and struck the Bandit's hand with such force that his wrist cracked and the blade he held flew wild and broke against the nearest pillar of rock.

Canus grabbed his injured wrist, then turned it loose and let his damaged arm hang loose at his side.

"Impressive," he murmured as Aron grabbed for swords and daggers he no longer had. The only weapon he now possessed was the white pebble in the bag at his waist, the one marked with the Bandit's name.

With his good hand, Canus unsheathed his curved desert blade.

Aron's heart raced as he judged the distance of the dagger he had thrown.

Too far.

He could hurl stones from the ground, but that would last only so long before the Bandit overpowered him.

Canus raised his blade, then turned the strange sword and tossed it on the ground.

It landed at Aron's feet with a loud clatter.

He snatched it up, holding it with both fists to judge its weight and balance. He was unsure why his quarry had given him such an advantage, but he didn't take time to wonder long.

Canus drew his ancient-looking military sword, an old Guard weapon, and held it at the ready. With three of his fingers, he beckoned for Aron like a training master daring an apprentice to charge.

Aron flew at his foe, going low to miss the arc of the taller man's swing. He gave Stone's battle-cry as he slashed and missed, slashed and missed, as the Bandit stepped nimbly out of his way each time.

"That's it," Canus said, his voice hoarse and gravelly. "Let it out. I know you just lost your friend."

Aron backed off, curved blade raised at an angle to deflect any sudden charges.

Once more the Bandit readied his own sword and taunted him, curling his free fingers in a gesture that said, *Bring it to me, boy.*

What madness was this?

Aron roared at the man and charged again, his mind focused only on killing his quarry and returning to the valley outside Triune's walls. He struck at Canus with the wide end of the curved silver blade, but Canus met his swing and knocked the desert sword free of Aron's grasp.

Aron swore and grabbed his stinging wrist as he lunged out of the Bandit's range.

Sapphire *graal* energy flowed toward Aron, but he blocked the mental assault as fiercely as Canus had stopped the swing of his curved blade.

"Let me speak to you," Canus murmured. "Mind to mind. You won't accept what I have to say any other way."

Aron snarled, drawing on his own legacy. If the Bandit fought with *graal*, then so could he. He threw the force of his energy at Canus with only one thought, one command.

DIE!

Canus met Aron's *graal* command with a burst of his own sapphire energy, deflecting it but not returning it. The man stumbled from his efforts, and his sword hand trembled.

Aron threw himself toward the curved blade the Bandit had bestowed to him, then knocked from his grasp. He snatched it from the ground and spun, cutting through the Bandit's veils and robes and opening the skin at the top of the man's chest.

Righting himself and finding his balance, Aron glanced at his foe's wound. His head snapped back from the sight. The ridges of scars, terrible corded pieces of flesh, now with blood staining them an even darker red.

The Bandit's scarred hand covered his wound, his injured wrist hanging limp against the mangled flesh. "Don't," he whispered, his voice reaching Aron on both sides of the Veil. "You'll regret this."

Aron's next charge was twice as fast and fierce, so frenzied he almost didn't hear the Bandit add, "Seth always did, when he acted out of rage instead of reason."

Aron was already swinging the terrible curved blade at the Bandit's midsection, intending to disarm him or open his belly and watch him bleed out his life like wine from a sliced wineskin.

He tried to pull the blow, but he couldn't do it.

Canus the Bandit stepped back from the swing and met the curved blade with his old Guard sword.

The sword's blade shattered and the man's other wrist broke under the force of the blow. The sword hilt fell from his useless grip even as Aron shouted and threw his sword to the side. He reached for the veils covering the Bandit's face, and Canus made no attempt to stop him.

Still shouting with disbelief, Aron gripped the cloth and tore it free, but he had already seen the man's eyes.

Black eyes, bright and powerful and stern, yet also kind. Familiar eyes, so painfully real and known to his heart.

Wolf Brailing's eyes.

Aron knew his father even before he saw the tufts of brown hair clinging to the man's scarred head, or the rows of *dav'ha* marks, barely visible beneath the burn scars the veils and scarves had concealed from him.

Sobs choked Aron as his father took him into his scarred arms and held him tight against his chest. Their thoughts flowed together, and Aron saw his father battling the Brailing Guard who killed their family, only to fall beneath their many blows, and find himself barely alive and clawing his way from beneath his dead loved ones on the funeral pyre in the woods.

He burned with his father as he healed, and traveled with him mile upon mile as he searched for Aron, madness and grief driving him even harder than stubborn will and determination. He understood how his father came to see the suffering of the people in Dyn Brailing, and rise to the defense of the goodfolk even though it meant leaving off his quest for Aron for days at a time, then weeks, then cycles.

Wolf Brailing had taken the name of Canus, of the ancient wolves of Brailing, as he prowled the countryside and took down renegade Guard. He restored food and safety to those who sought his aid, then worked with ever larger groups of men in Dyn Brailing and Dyn Cobb, training them to defend farm and family from the very soldiers who had sworn to protect them.

Yes, his father had made mistakes, kills he shouldn't have made, and thefts that weren't strictly necessary for his quest—but Aron couldn't see him as a criminal. He couldn't agree with the Judgment that had put his father's stone in Aron's hands.

"You have to kill me," Wolf Brailing whispered in Aron's ear, squeezing his damaged wrists into Aron's back. "You can't let me walk away, or you'll be an oathbreaker like me."

Aron clung to his father and cried, hearing the truth, knowing it with his *graal* and rejecting it nonetheless.

"Help me hold my sword and I'll do it myself," his father said as he gently separated himself from Aron. Tears streamed across his scarred cheeks. "Just seeing you again, that's been enough. Knowing what a powerful warrior you've become, and how much good you'll do Eyrie in its time of greatest need. Hand me my blade, son, and let's have done with this."

Aron couldn't stop his own tears, and he couldn't kill his father, no matter what that meant for his father's future, or his own. There had been too much killing and death already. Aron wanted no more of it, by his own hand or anyone else's.

"I won't," he said, knowing he'd have to think quickly, or his father would find some way to spare Aron from breaking his vows to Stone.

With all the *graal* strength he had left to him, Aron struck at his father fast and hard, using a single word, limiting his command only by a mental image of the Adamantine stretching far and wide, mile after mile of dense woods, in which only an old hunter like Wolf Brailing could survive.

Flee, he commanded, watching as his sapphire *graal* struck his father like a swinging anvil, driving him backward out of the Shrine of the Mother, then sending him toward the gates of Triune at a dead run.

Aron dropped to the ground, drawing his knees to his chest.

He wanted to rip his gray robes off his shaking body and run after his father, but Wolf Brailing had a better chance of reaching the Adamantine alone. Aron doubted his father would take his own life once he left Dyn Brailing, for his death would do nothing to save Aron now.

Though Aron could keep the secret of his crime for a short time, he knew his own truth-seeking *graal* would give him no peace until he confessed to Stormbreaker, who would be the new Lord Provost of Stone as soon as the dead were counted and laid to rest.

"Oathbreaker," Aron said aloud, knowing he would be given no quarter, no mercy for sparing his Judged, even if that Judged was his own flesh and blood. The order and fairness of Stone wouldn't allow it.

Aron himself wouldn't allow it.

Oathbreaker.

That was his identity now, the full sum of it.

He forced himself to rise and walk, though he wished he could do anything else. Only the desire to see to the welfare of his friends and family of the heart kept him moving forward, back to the castle's shattered gates.

Aron left Stone's stronghold, his own ruined home, passing by groups of apprentices and the sheltered returning from the Ruined Keep and running out onto the battlefield to take stock of what had happened in Eyrie. He even brushed past Zed and Raaf, who stood with Windblown, grieving over Lord Baldric's body. Aron didn't speak to them, for he didn't want to taint them with his own crime, should they sense what he had done.

He had eyes only for the small group across the moat, clustered near the center of the battlefield, guarded by soldiers and Sabor and Stregans alike.

Aron knew he would do what he could for Dari and Kate and Nic, if somehow Nic had survived. He would thank Lord Ross and Lord Cobb and Platt, and Snakekiller, if she, too, had lived through the chaos.

Seeing them all once more was more than he deserved, but he would take this small liberty before he gave himself over to Stormbreaker's sword, and hoped for a quick and merciful blow.

CHAPTER SEVENTY-FOUR

NIC

Nic woke screaming, tasting thick elixir on his lips, far stronger than he had ever been given before. A cloudless sky stretched above him, and he remembered, and he knew he was still lying broken on the battlefield at Triune.

Dari knelt at his side, drawing back the wineskin she had emptied into his mouth to ease his suffering as he came back to consciousness. She dabbed a bit of blood from his bare chest and arms with her sleeve and tried to smile at him. Nic loved her for the attempt, even if she couldn't achieve her goal.

Behind Dari stood her thinner, frail-looking twin. Lord Ross kept his big hands on Kate's shoulders. His dark face was streaked with dirt and sweat, and his sharp eyes seemed sad beyond measure. At his side was a man Nic didn't recognize, but he knew him for a Stregan by the blinding hues of *graal* lifting from his powerful shoulders. This would be Platt, Dari's cousin, and the Stregan king. Iko and Blath formed an honor guard on either side of him, and Iko was supporting an obviously weakened and wounded Stormbreaker.

Lord Cobb and Lord Baldric were nowhere to be seen, and in his depths, Nic understood that those two heroes had fallen, and were lost to Eyrie forever. His anguish sent fresh racking pain through his back and limbs, but he couldn't move, even to escape the burning torture his body had become. Only his eyelids and mouth obeyed his commands, and not without rebellion.

"Be easy, love." Dari's fingers stroked his forehead and slipped through the edges of his matted curls, and he tried to be easy, if only for her sake.

Snakekiller's energy was oddly absent from the landscape, but Nic didn't believe Stone's viper was dead. Just gone. Hiding herself away from him, perhaps because her rage had driven her to attack his mother, and wound him by accident.

Dari's energy eased into Nic's awareness, bolstering him, but he refused to take too much. There would never be enough spare *graal* force to sustain him. He understood that, even if his beautiful wife didn't.

With the fragment of strength he allowed her to grant him, Nic focused his thoughts on Stormbreaker, and let the Stone Brother know to get word to his sister when she came out of hiding that Nic loved her, and forgave her. That he owed her too much to ever be repaid.

I will, came Stormbreaker's simple reply, as soft as a summer wind through the Veil.

Aron, Nic tried to say, with his voice and his mind, failing at both.

Aron was who he needed to see.

Aron was the only one who could help him now.

"A prince among killers," Dari whispered, her sweet scent of spice and apples soothing him for a moment as her lips pressed against his forehead. "You never belonged in this battle, did you? Come back to me. Come back to the son who hasn't had the chance to know you."

Her warm tears fell across Nic's face, and he wanted so much to grant her this gift, this boon that was far beyond his reach. He knew he'd have to face her and say his good-byes, but he couldn't do that to her or himself.

Not yet.

He accepted a bit more of her offered energy, and this time, he addressed Lord Ross.

Lords, he managed. *Ladies. Provosts. Commanders will do.*

Lord Ross's composure fractured, and the big man's lips trembled as he rubbed his eyes with his thumb and forefinger. Nic knew he understood what Nic wanted him to do, but he could scarcely face the task.

"They'll come," Dari told him as she gave him another gentle kiss on the forehead. "They all know you're Eyrie's king now, and dynasts who have no heirs or rulers present to speak for them will learn soon enough, from their surviving Guard captains and messengers."

Lord Ross turned to his nearest Guardsmen and whispered instructions.

The man straightened and bowed, then hurried off to do his lord's bidding.

Nic closed his eyes and fell into oblivion, only to jerk awake some time later, coughing down another mouthful of elixir so strong he might as well have been swallowing burning tallow oil. All the people who greeted him before were still present, along with a brawny, bearded man dressed in Cobb's obsidian and ruby robes. Nic assumed this would have to be the new Lord Cobb. An Altar warbird carrying a broken arrow in his fist as a sign of surrender had joined them, along with an old man garbed in the colors of Cobb but wearing a sash of Brailing blue. He introduced himself as Dolf Zeller, the new commander of Brailing's devastated Dynast Guard.

Beside Zeller stood a tall, thin woman with stark silver hair and bright silvery eyes. Nic felt a jolt of surprise as he realized she had to be Lady Rakel Seadaughter, Vagrat of Vagrat. Since citizens of Vagrat never took up arms in any conflict, Nic realized she must have brought her people across all of Eyrie to help with healing the wounded. Lady Vagrat had her hand on the shoulder of a scrawny boy who looked to have Vagrat heritage, bearing Thorn's cardinal red badge on his chest.

"He's a sanctioned messenger," Dari told him as she rested her palm against his forehead. "This is the best we can do, since Brailing has no heirs, and Lord Altar and his sons have been taken to the House of the Judged, as have any Thorn Brothers not dead on the fields around us."

"It's enough," Lord Ross said. "No one will challenge what you say here, Nic. Your word is our law, and all dynasts and guild leaders, or their nearest representatives, are present to accept your commands."

Nic closed his eyes for a moment to muster his strength, and accepted yet more energy from his wife, until he could raise his voice enough to be heard by all who stood near.

"Come forward," he told Lord Ross. "Kneel beside me, please."

Lord Ross did as Nic asked, crouching to the ground on the side opposite Dari.

Though Nic thought he would die yet again from the brutal stab of the movements, he used *graal* energy, his own and that which he borrowed from Dari, to move his left hand enough to lay his fingers in the blood on his chest, directly over his heart.

It was at that moment Dari seemed to realize what he was doing, and why.

She cried out and would have stopped him if Kate and Platt hadn't seized her arms and hauled her back from him. The sound of her anger and grief stabbed him deeper than any physical pain, but this he did as a king, not as a husband.

Lord Ross didn't flinch as Nic raised his bloody, trembling fingers and touched the man on both cheeks.

Every witness in the circle drew a sharp breath as they recognized the passing of power in the oldest of known ways—blooding the victor on the field of battle.

"Rule in my stead," Nic told Lord Ross. "Protect my queen and help her serve as regent for my son, until he, in turn, assumes my throne. If my bloodline doesn't live to adulthood and to sire his own legacy heirs, then it will be your heirs who guard and protect this land."

"My great-grandson will survive." Lord Ross took Nic's hands in his and held them to his massive, muscled chest as he made his oath. "On that I stake my honor and my dynast. On that I stake my *soul*."

"Stop this," Dari shouted as Lord Ross folded Nic's hands atop his broken chest and got to his feet to the deep bows of many of his watching subjects.

"I won't have it." Dari's voice was muffled by Kate's relentless embrace—then it turned louder and sharper, a new sort of screaming, fresh and angry and desperate. "No! Don't let him near my husband. You stay away!"

And Nic knew, at last, that relief had come to him.

Platt's *graal* and Kate's arms restrained Dari as the crowd parted to admit Aron Weylyn, who once was Aron Brailing, and always would be, in some distant corner of Nic's heart. Nic's dimming vision saw not the Stone Brother in his soiled and torn gray robes, but the skinny, terrified boy Aron had been when Nic first saw him through his spirit-eyes, the night of Harvest, when Nic tried to die and Aron used the full force of his burgeoning Brailing legacy to order Nic to heal himself.

Nic's body was still following that command, all these years hence, beyond his own wishes, and beyond any reason.

Just as he had done that fateful night, Aron turned loose his own *graal* and let his essence flow into Nic's. Unformed thoughts and words rushed between them. Love and pain. Victory and defeat. Damnation and redemption.

"I will never forgive you," Dari said to Aron, "Never, Aron."

Aron kept his connection to Nic as he lowered his head.

"I know," he said, but Nic didn't feel Aron's resolve weaken.

You've wanted to make amends, Nic told him. *Now is the time. You know it's the truth, just as I do.*

I don't know if I can, came Aron's sad mental whisper, but already, he was massing his *graal* energy to right the worst—and best— wrong he had ever committed.

Dari was pounding her fists against Platt and her grandfather and trying to reach Nic. Nic knew if they turned her loose, she would kill Aron, so he reached out to her with his mind, with the strength that Aron's legacy shared with him.

I love you, he told Dari, who broke down and sobbed her own love back to him, on both sides of the Veil, over and over, as if she understood he could never hear the words too many times.

I love you, Nic said again, this time gazing at her, and at Lord Ross, and Stormbreaker and Aron.

He felt the soft press of Aron's hands on his chest, then the unbelievable cool force of Aron's *graal*.

The command was simple enough, and perfect to Nic in every possible way.

Peace, Aron said, his voice as loud as a mountain's heartbeat, and as soft as a tide in a tiny pool of rain.

Sapphire light filled Nic's awareness, and for one brief and blessed moment, he felt no pain at all.

Then he was standing at the edge of a forest much grander than the Adamantine, sensing the strength of his healed body and his thick, powerful wings. The air was splendid and warm, and a fine breeze ruffled his curls and flight feathers. The scent of flowers and cedar tickled his nose, putting him at ease in this wondrous, beautiful place.

His sister Kestrel drifted out of the trees on her own golden wings, arms wide and smile broad as she called out, *Welcome, brother.*

Nic's father joined her, beckoning toward the forest. *Come, my son. Come fly with us.*

How he had missed them! And now they were here, his father, his sister—and all of his brothers, too.

Nic leaped off the ground and spiraled into the sky, leaving all the worries and agonies of his former life far behind him, and already forgotten.

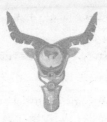

CHAPTER SEVENTY-FIVE

ARON

Aron worked quietly beside Stormbreaker in Stone's now deserted infirmary, where the new Lord Provost was placing flowers in a vase beside the bed Nic had so often occupied. Raaf was not with them, or Zed, for Aron had continued to keep himself apart from them, knowing they would understand and thank him for it someday, if only in their prayers and visions.

Too many funeral pyres had come and gone, and so many tears since Stormbreaker had taken on Stone's mantle of power, then given his blessing to a young Vagrat girl who rose to the title of Lady Provost of Thorn, once Eidolon had been purged of its oathbreakers.

Rakel Seadaughter, her daughter, and some of her people were still at Stone, assisting with repairs, healing, and the sowing of the year's crops. Darielle Ross-Mab, however, had withdrawn to her new home in Can Rowan, to the castle in the Tree City that her Stregan ancestors had once claimed as their own. For now, and until her son reached the age to rule, Lord Ross would be with her, and upon his death, Dari would assume control of the Ross Dynast. Now that the Stregans had come amongst the Fae again, no lord or lady in the re-formed Circle of Eyrie seemed inclined to challenge her rights to inherit.

For his part, Platt had returned to Stone with Kate, and the two were making ready to journey to the as-yet hidden and secret stronghold where the Stregans had rebuilt their ranks and power. Kate had recovered from her captivity, and Aron had used his mind-talents to help her find a stability of mind and thought she had never known before. Lord Dunstan, once known only as Stormbreaker, had assisted his own people and Thorn's, and rectors all over the land, in identifying the few orphans and children who needed to go with Platt and Kate for their own safety. The Stregans would train these children and protect them until Eyrie was better prepared to handle the newly resurgent and far more powerful dynast legacies, and the newer—or older—mind-talents, some forgotten even to those who kept histories about such matters.

"I'm sorry Snakekiller hasn't returned," Aron said to Stormbreaker, trying his best to find the courage to say what he knew he had to say.

Stormbreaker arranged another bunch of flowers in a vase. "I don't believe she will. It's something I sense, though it pains me to say so aloud. My sister may have moved beyond anything Stone or I might offer her."

Aron thought about the giant snake he had seen on Stone's battlefield, the creature who had struck down Lady Mab and left her vulnerable to Kate and Dari's killing fire. He hoped that wherever Snakekiller was, she understood that most people in Eyrie viewed her as a hero, even if her own guild might be forced, after trials and Judgment, to hunt her as an oathbreaker.

That would not be Aron's fate.

His heart felt so heavy he didn't know how he would make his confession to Stormbreaker, but he was determined he wouldn't put his guild through the spectacle of a trial and combat involving a Stone Brother. He would confess his crimes to his Lord Provost, who in turn would be compelled to mete out the immediate punishment prescribed by the Code of Stone.

Sten il'dur Sten.

"A stone cannot be undrawn," he whispered to himself, translating the Language of Kings, and filling in its meaning. "To let a Judged go free is Unforgivable."

Aron lowered himself to the nearest cot, and as Stormbreaker clipped flowers ever more slowly, then finally began to drop the untrimmed stems and petals on the infirmary floor, Aron described what had taken place in the Shrine of the Mother. He explained how he had found his father and why he had let him go and broken his vows to the guild he loved so dearly.

For a time, Stormbreaker stood in silence, with no hint of motion or thought, or even the weather Aron so often sensed when the man was distressed. His greener-than-green eyes gazed out of a window, seeing nothing, yet seeming to see everything too much, and all at once.

"Lord Ross and Dari are likely to pardon Wolf Brailing," he said at last, his tone too even and quiet as his fingers flexed then released near the hilts of the daggers at his waist. "His actions were born first of the madness that comes with grief, after a horrible crime perpetrated against his family by his own dynast lord. After that, he showed an abiding desire to help the goodfolk his name and bloodline bound him to serve, even though it cost him his son." Stormbreaker finally looked at Aron, at least long enough to say, "I think that your father may be the only true heir to the dynast seat at Can Rune, and the Circle will be much relieved to hand that seat to him, since the Brailing people already trust him."

This scenario had never occurred to Aron, but it felt both right and wonderful to him. His father was the only person bearing the Brailing name who fought for the goodfolk, and the people of Brailing, warriors to a one, weren't likely to forget it.

"It won't be easy to find him in the Adamantine, or to undo the force of the command I gave him," Aron said as he made himself stand, "but I think Eyrie's new Circle and the Stregans may be up to the task."

Fear wasn't part of Aron's mix of emotions as he approached Stormbreaker and knelt before him, lowering his head to expose his neck. He was able to name fatigue and sorrow and shame, but also curiosity, and even hope that he might meet Nic in the next life, or Lord Cobb—even Lord Baldric.

Aron's heart was beating, beating, and he tried to ignore the wild flow of life through his body, since it so shortly would be brought to an end. It would be messy, doing this here, but also private and less painful for the apprentices who used to be his friends. In the end, it was the right thing, and Aron knew that he at least could be proud of himself for facing the consequences of his actions.

The sharp edge of one of Stormbreaker's huge, jagged blades bit into the back of his neck, and Aron knew that the Stone Brother was measuring his stroke, so he would need to make only one swift, strong cut.

The cool steel against Aron's flesh trembled and stung him again, then retreated.

Aron closed his eyes, hoping he would feel little before oblivion claimed him.

When no killing blow sent his head rolling, Aron glanced upward to see Stormbreaker standing, sword raised, tears flowing down his pale white cheeks. His arms shook, and the new *benedet* on his chin trembled as he said, "I cannot do this."

"You must," Aron told him, preparing to use his *graal* to force the issue rather than let Stormbreaker join him as an oathbreaker. "Stone needs you. Eyrie needs you."

"And I would wager Eyrie needs you, too, Aron, Son of the Wolf."

Both Stormbreaker and Aron startled at this new voice.

Platt entered the room as quietly as any Sabor, his black boots making no sound on the polished infirmary floor. As always, he was dressed in simple stitched leathers, and he carried no weapons save for his powerful mind-talents and the dragon-form always waiting to burst free of human essence.

He raised his hand, and his *graal* froze Stormbreaker in place, making certain that Stormbreaker didn't change his mind and strike Aron's head from his neck.

"I didn't bring my people out of hiding just to save Dari and Kate, as I told you on the battlefield." Platt sounded almost angry, or at the very least, worried. "We came for Nic, and for you, too, Aron. Now Nic is lost to us, but you—this—this doesn't have to be. How can our alliance with the Fae survive if you all go about killing your best talent, and your strongest warriors?"

Aron's cheeks heated.

He couldn't believe he was feeling flattered, here on the floor of the infirmary, waiting to be beheaded.

"Stormbreaker—I mean—Lord Dunstan can't let me go, or he'll be as much a criminal as I am." He pressed his fingers against the floor to keep himself in position for his own execution. "I know it may make little sense to you, but like the trial at the Ruined Keep, Stone's strict codes of justice serve a deeper purpose."

Platt didn't seem persuaded. "Cayn spare me from Fae honor. Especially that of Stone." He let out a breath, and then his lips twitched into a smile more dangerous than five of Stormbreaker's swords.

"Perhaps I can offer another solution," Platt said.

Before Aron could argue, a burst of Stregan *graal* rendered him senseless.

The last thing he perceived was Stormbreaker's jagged blade clattering harmlessly to the stone floor between them.

• • •

"Look at it this way," Snakekiller said to Aron as they rode slowly on talon-back through the mists, as they had been doing for over a cycle now, through Dyn Ross, through Cayn's arch, past the Watchline, and into the depths of the Deadfall. "Stone has much to do beyond reading our charges and searching for us. It may be many years before Dunstan gets around to sending assassins after his sister and a run-away Stone Brother—who by the way, is also a dynast heir."

She smiled, turning the spiral *benedets* on her tanned cheeks into nothing but tiny circles. She looked so very human in her black tunic and breeches, but Aron couldn't help sensing her viper essence, which seemed ever closer to the surface of her skin the farther south they went.

"You'll be as much legend as Canus the Bandit," she said, wink-ing at him to lessen the tease. "Before he gave up his veils and turned legitimate again, I mean."

Platt, who kept pace beside them on foot, let out a soft laugh.

Aron felt outnumbered. He had since Kate had departed with the aid of some Stregans and a few Sabor, shepherding the children they would be sheltering to the Stregan stronghold. It had been just the three of them for so long after that, shrouded in the fog, that Aron wondered how he would begin to adjust to life around people again.

"You'll learn much in the City of Dragons, Aron." Platt sounded confident. "By the time Stone tracks your path—if they ever do—no assassin will be able to touch you."

Aron appreciated this promise, but he knew if Stone ever did come for him, he would meet his fate with as much honor as he could muster.

The mists around them grew a bit thinner, and Tek gave a happy whistle.

Aron didn't share his talon's optimism, because he had seen the fog dissipate before, only to re-form at double strength over the next mountain rise. He guided Tek forward beside Snakekiller and her bull, but as Platt crested the rise, he stopped and waited for them, his body tense with anticipation.

Aron almost choked up, remembering his ride to Triune, and how he had felt when Stormbreaker brought him to the lip of the valley, to view his new home below.

How could this hidden city in the mists possibly compare?

His pulse picked up, but he tried to brace himself for disappointment and acceptance. It's what he would need to face this new change, to tolerate starting his life over again once more, in a home he might not even be able to keep.

Tek carried him to Platt's side, Snakekiller right beside him, and together they stepped out of the mists on the mountainside.

"Oh," Snakekiller said. Then again, "Oh."

"It's not what I thought," Aron murmured, staring in disbelief at the sight below him.

Not a valley. Not a castle.

A wide and vast kingdom, stretching as far as he could see, north and south, east and west. A wonder of mountains and ivory lattice and heartwood towers studded with crystals. It was Adamantine wed to grasslands, and rivers and lakes, and everything in between. This was a countryside and structures made for creatures who flew and ran and rode. A dynast unto itself, hidden so far south, beyond the land of the dead.

Aron tried to breathe, and had to push his chest with his hand to succeed.

Snakekiller slipped off her talon and shifted into the great viper Aron had seen her become on the battlefield at Triune. With a hiss of rapture, she leaped from the edge of the mountain, her coils striking the ground as she made for the brilliant lands below. Her bull talon took off after her, his big clawfeet stamping rocks and grass as he ran.

"Now that," Platt said, watching Snakekiller go, "is one fine woman." He gestured to a white dragon winging toward them across the sun-drenched sky, letting off jets of flame. "Go, Aron. Fly with Kate. I'll take care of Tek, and I'll see you later at my tower, for dinner."

Aron's heart hammered as Kate drew closer, closer, reaching toward him with her mind, even as he reached back to touch the simple beauty of her thoughts. Since Aron had used his *graal* to help Kate master her thoughts and emotions, she gave off none of the carnivorous threat she or the other Stregans had in Eyrie. Even as a dragon, she seemed to retain the awareness that she was also Kate, and he was Aron, and she was happy to see him.

Thinking of Nic and how Nic's wings had opened to carry Eyrie into a new and brighter future, Aron abandoned caution and leaped off the mountain.

Kate swept under Aron and caught him, and Aron knew Nic's joy as his own.

Welcome, Kate said in his mind, and the sound seemed to stretch out for miles. *Welcome, Aron.*

As he sailed through the sky with Kate, Aron let the energy that rose from this city—no, this land—of dragons wrap him in its bright rainbow of hues and colors. Infused by such guileless, honest power, Aron understood that he had a destiny, a fate beyond Harvest and his lost family. Beyond Stone. Beyond his many mistakes and transgressions—even beyond the father so recently restored to him.

Aron's *graal* glowed within his mind and essence, bathing him in those truths.

"Take me up," he shouted to Kate. Then in his mind, *Take me all the way to the clouds.*

Kate's wings gave a mighty push, and as they rose ever higher above the haven below, Aron felt nothing but joy and freedom, nothing but his own power and Kate's, and the endless, perfect rushing of the winds.

S R VAUGHT is the author of *Stormwitch, Trigger, My Big Fat Manifesto,* and *Exposed.* She is a neuropsychologist working with adolescents. She lives with her family and many animals in Kentucky.

J B REDMOND is a lifelong fantasy fan who, because of cerebral palsy, used a tape recorder to tell this story. It was transcribed and added to by his coauthor (and mother), S R Vaught. He lives in Kentucky.